PRAISE FOR THE DCI RYAN MYSTERIES

What newspapers say

"She keeps company with the best mystery writers" – *The Times*

"LJ Ross is the queen of Kindle" – *Sunday Telegraph*

"Holy Island is a blockbuster" – *Daily Express*

"A literary phenomenon" – *Evening Chronicle*

What readers say

"I couldn't put it down. I think the full series will cause a divorce, but it will be worth it."

"I gave this book 5 stars because there's no option for 100."

"Thank you, LJ Ross, for the best two hours of my life."

"This book has more twists than a demented corkscrew."

"Another masterpiece in the series. The DCI Ryan mysteries are superb, with very realistic characters and wonderful plots. They are a joy to read!"

OTHER BOOKS BY LJ ROSS

THE DCI RYAN MYSTERIES IN ORDER:

THE ALEXANDER GREGORY THRILLERS IN ORDER:

SYCAMORE GAP

A DCI RYAN MYSTERY

SYCAMORE GAP

A DCI RYAN MYSTERY

LJ ROSS

ISBN: 978-1-912310-02-9

First published in 2015 by LJ Ross

This edition published in April 2020 by Dark Skies Publishing

Author photo by Gareth Iwan Jones

Cover layout by Stuart Bache

Cover artwork and map by Andrew Davidson

Typeset by Riverside Publishing Solutions Limited

Printed and bound by CPI Goup (UK) Limited

For my Mum and Dad, with love always

"The soul that has conceived one wickedness can nurse no good thereafter."

~ Sophocles

PROLOGUE

Tuesday, 21st June 2005—The Summer Solstice

A large sycamore tree grew in the dip of the valley. It stood proudly silhouetted against the last light of day, which burned fiery amber red in the sky beyond. The landscape around it was dramatic and old; the Roman wall cut through the hillside, over the peaks and troughs, over sharp crags and soft peat. The dimming light cast long, hazy rays over the fields and, transfixed by its beauty, Amy did not hear the quiet tread of footsteps approaching until he was almost upon her.

"Worth the visit?"

She jumped like a startled rabbit.

"Y-yes, it's lovely," she admitted, trying to slow her racing heart. "It'll be dark soon, though, won't it?"

"I know the way back," he murmured.

"I'm a little tired," she said. "I'd rather head back now."

"Why such a rush?" He reached out to tuck a strand of dark hair behind her ear. "I remember when you wanted to spend all your time with me."

She knew that what he said was true. Once, she had been so enamoured with him, so blinded by a foolish emotion she had mistaken for love that she would have done anything to be with him. Looking with fresh eyes, she struggled to recall what she had ever seen in him.

Mistaking her regard, he leaned forward suddenly as if to kiss her. Automatically, she stepped away, holding up both hands to prevent him from coming any closer.

His features contorted, turning his bright white smile into a snarl, eyes glinting in a shadowed face.

"Bitch," he growled.

Strong hands reached for her, yanking her against him. Frantically, she struggled, finally seeing the real man she had begun to suspect lay beneath the affable social exterior.

"Please," she said brokenly. "You're hurting me!"

She shook her head and began to struggle again, but he pinned her like a butterfly. Her cheek hit a solid wall of muscle beneath his all-weather coat and his arms banded around her so that she could hardly move.

"I'm sorry." She began to sob, hating herself for the weakness. "Please. Let's try to be friends."

His arms tightened painfully against her ribcage and the breath shuddered through his body as her words penetrated.

"You're all the same," he rasped, the air blowing hotly against her temple. "I gave you everything. My time. My energy. *Everything.*"

"You—you'll find someone better," she said desperately.

He laughed, the sound of it unbearably loud in the surrounding silence.

"You're mad," she whispered, and he let go of her so suddenly that she almost fell, her legs as flimsy as jelly through a combination of exhaustion and fear.

"What did you say?"

"Nothing. I didn't say anything."

There was a short, tense silence. Recognising the danger, she turned to run, but he was faster. His arm shot out to grab her wrist and pull her back. The force of the motion was so strong that her body twisted and the delicate bone in her wrist broke with an almost audible 'snap'.

She cried out in pain but instinct set in. She fought him with a strength borne from terror, scratching and kicking until she caught him full force in the stomach. He doubled over, and she took her chance. She made for the tree, her mind working quickly. Her broken wrist dangled uselessly beside her as she flew across the uneven ground and her eyes strained to find a pathway in the darkness. She heard his harsh breathing somewhere not far behind and knew that she would not be able to escape him without a fight.

Reaching the wall, she flung herself over it and crawled one-armed under the fold of the tree. Crouching beneath it, she tugged at the stones of the wall, tearing the skin along her fingers until one came free. She held it tightly in her good hand, ready to use it as a weapon.

He was close, now.

"Come out, come out, wherever you are," he called out, chuckling softly. She shivered at the sound of it, her body trembling.

She rose to her feet and plastered herself against the trunk of the tree while she watched him creep over the wall to her left, nothing more than a silent, inky shadow.

"There you are," he crooned, lunging towards her.

With everything she had left, she swung the rock towards him and heard it connect. He faltered, but her aim had been off. He was much taller, and she had missed his head by a good few inches.

She tried again, but he had her now and the stone thudded dully to the floor.

They wrestled, but he was so strong. After a brief, hard tussle, her body fell back against the ground and winded her, giving him the opportunity he needed.

"Little … bitch …" He enunciated the words in time to the sound of her head cracking against the rocky floor and finally he felt her body jitter, then go limp beneath him. The rush of warm blood from the gash on her skull ran over his fingers and he enjoyed the novelty of it, holding out his hand in wonder. There was a momentary feeling of panic and he pressed two shaking fingers to the side of her neck. The skin there was still warm, but there was no fluttering pulse.

The enormity of what he had done surged through his body, the heady feeling of power swamping him so that he needed to rest against the side of the wall to catch his breath. He watched the final descent of the sun into the horizon and felt reborn, like a caged bird finally set free.

He stood up to check that they were still alone and then considered his options. He could carry her to the lake and dump her in there, but that would be an arduous journey with her added weight. Likewise, it was too far to carry her back to his car and there was more chance of him being noticed. He supposed he could bury her somewhere, but he had not brought the tools to dig.

His eye fell on the wall where she had dislodged the stones, then back to where Amy lay motionless. He was wearing gloves, but he wondered about the rest. She did not carry a backpack, so he searched her pockets and removed any identifying articles. It might buy him some time, once her body was discovered.

If it was discovered.

A while later, he climbed the hill and surveyed the gap with its tree in the middle. The wall looked exactly as it always had: timeless and immoveable.

He turned away, melting into the darkness.

A little further over the brow of the hill, a bonfire burned tall and bright and its smoke billowed into the night sky. Around it, men and women danced, their bodies pliant and their minds intoxicated. A man wearing a long animal pelt threw his hands aloft and chanted, calling to his Master. The Circle swayed and followed his call.

One of their number was missing, a fact which had not gone unnoticed.

CHAPTER 1

Sunday, 21ˢᵗ June 2015—The Summer Solstice

It was a perfect day for walking. The morning had broken and washed the sky in technicolour; palest lemon blending into brazen orange and deep, dark ochre. Wispy clouds were scattered here and there but, for the most part, the day was clear and the air was crisp.

Colin Hart had been up well before sunrise, allowing himself time to hike the trail and to enjoy the view from the top of the fells. He had been to this special corner of the world before, but the beauty of it never aged. The landscape undulated all around him, old as time and scarred only by the presence of the long stone wall built by Hadrian.

Alone, he stood a little longer appreciating the scenery and took a sip of water from his flask before tucking it safely back into its specialist holder. He checked the laces on his top-of-the-range hiking boots. Satisfied that all was in order, he turned away from the hypnotic sun and continued to walk along the track, which ran beside Hadrian's Wall from the Roman fort of Housesteads in a westerly direction all the way into Cumbria. He knew that a lot of visitors probably walked on top of those ancient stones, unable to resist the allure, but he was someone who went by the book. What would happen if everyone flouted the rules? The stones would crumble away to nothing and there wouldn't be anything left for the next generation to enjoy. That's what would happen, he thought righteously.

He continued to meander along the worn trail, idly wondering how many centurions had stomped the ground before him. Sprigs of lavender sprouted from the gaps in the stones and clumps of heather bloomed purple, infusing the air with their scent. Tiny white flowers had risen beside the pathway and he wondered how they had found their way to this remote spot. He enjoyed the feel of his lungs labouring as he walked the inclines and felt the momentary fear of falling as he traversed the dips. Eventually, he slowed and came to rest under a large, leafy sycamore tree whose roots had grown thick and strong. He fished out a postcard with an artsy photograph taken of this very place and was content.

Colin shifted his backpack and shuffled down to rest against the wall. Under the shade of the tree, he looked out across the valley and thought about the errands he had yet to do when he returned home, mostly for his mother. He shifted uncomfortably and rubbed at the back of his neck. The stones were sharper than they looked. Unable to find comfort, he half rose, intending to move further away, when his eye caught sight of something shiny. Intrigued, he pushed his face closer to the wall and wished for more light.

His prayers were answered as the morning came to life at that very moment. Sunlight washed over the wall and he saw it fully then, the glint of silver between the cracks.

Excited now, he began to tug at the stones and then froze guiltily. He shouldn't be tampering with the wall, like this. It wasn't right.

But the silver winked at him.

All hesitation forgotten, he put his weight behind the stones until the first one began to shift and give way. Emboldened, he started on another, then another…

His hands covered in dust and chalk, he fell backwards and stared at the hole he had made in the wall and, beyond that, to what lay in its cavity. A silver bracelet, mostly dulled with age, hung loosely from the wrist of what was once a person. Now, all that remained was a pile of desiccated bones, shoved haphazardly inside the hollowed-out space. A skull stared back at him with empty eyes and a gaping jaw.

Colin scrambled away and thought about putting the stones back, pretending he had never found the body. Wouldn't it be better just to carry on with his life? He didn't like to become involved in other people's dramas, other people's problems. He sat on the dewy grass and gnawed at the inside of his lip, thinking about what to do for the best. It wasn't too late to go home, close the doors behind him, and try to forget what he had seen, was it?

No. He shook his head. He should not be a coward.

He fished around one of the inner pockets of his jacket and pulled out his mobile phone.

No signal.

Resigned and with the heavy, sick feeling in his stomach of a man whose life had just changed irrevocably, he headed back towards civilisation.

While Colin Hart trudged the lonely road back to his car, another man was taking advantage of a rare Sunday morning lie-in. Eyes still closed, Detective Chief Inspector Ryan struggled against the demonic hangover which had made itself very much at home inside his head. The nerves between his eyes throbbed and there was a distant ringing in his ears. Feebly, he grasped at the sheets and pulled himself upward.

He risked opening his eyes and everyday objects became reality. A bed. A wardrobe. Some sort of jingle-jangle wind chime which hung in front of the window that was thrown wide open to the morning breeze. His eye caught a movement and he braced. He saw a man, wild-eyed and rough around the edges staring back at him from the oval mirror above the dresser.

Why had he let Phillips talk him into the whisky? A "quick pint"—he was sure that was all he had agreed to by way of celebration.

Yesterday, Ryan had received a call from the ecstatic parents of Detective Constable Jack Lowerson to say that their son had finally emerged from his coma. Last Christmas, none of them had held out much hope that Jack would ever regain consciousness, following the attack on Holy Island which had plunged him into darkness and robbed him of six months of his life. There was now the hope that, one day, Jack would remember who had been responsible.

Ryan dragged his legs over the side of the bed and stood up.

Then, sat back down again with a thud.

"Too soon," he muttered with a heavy dose of self-pity. "Much too soon."

Before he could move again, the bedroom door swung open and brought with it the dreaded sound that had wakened him.

It was Chaka Khan on the radio this morning.

Looking like she was every woman and more, Doctor Anna Taylor stood in the doorway tapping her foot to the rhythm and regarded him with a mixture of pity and amusement. She set a tall glass of water on the dresser beside two aspirin.

"Good night?"

He let out a heartfelt sigh and stood on legs that felt as wobbly as Bambi's.

"I'm not sure that's the word I would use to describe it," he muttered. "Water. Need water."

Anna grinned. Watching him prowl around the bed like a bear with a sore head was comedy gold. This was the first time she had seen the illustrious DCI Ryan reduced to a physical wreck and she wasn't above a bit of baiting.

"I thought we might go for a long walk along the river today, after we stop by the garden centre."

He winced.

"Or, we could go shopping. I need some new shoes and handbags."

"I don't think—"

"Maybe we could offer to babysit the kids next door. It would be good practice," she continued, layering on the icing.

"Anna," his voice croaked, and he snatched up the water, gulping it down in three swallows. "The terrifying thing is that I don't know whether you're joking."

He refocused and took stock. The muscle at the side of her mouth was twitching. Dark eyes twinkled.

"Oh, you're a real comedienne."

"People tell me that all the time, but it never gets old."

He slunk towards her smelling faintly like a brewery. Even crumpled and worse for wear, it was remarkable how he managed to look so good. Thick, black hair stuck out at interesting angles and she watched him run a hand through its length. There was a layer of stubble on his jaw, which was rugged rather than unkempt. Then, there were those bright, silver-grey eyes which killed her every time.

All mine.

Smugly, she crossed her arms and tilted her chin up at him. He came to stand in front of her, swaying a bit.

"You smell like something that crawled out of a cave," she said, deadpan.

"Flattery will get you everywhere."

"I could light a fire on your breath."

"Stop, you'll make me blush." He smiled slowly now, with intent.

"You could use a shower," she sniffed.

"That's an excellent idea." He edged her backwards, towards the en-suite bathroom. "One thing you should learn about me is that I have an excellent recovery time."

"Oh, you're going to need it."

Detective Sergeant Frank Phillips was dreaming of a feisty Irish princess with long, red hair. He stormed the castle, fought off the shadowy figures surrounding it and rescued her from a fate worse than death, for which she was *very* grateful...

Just as things were becoming interesting, he was rudely awakened by a sharp spray of cold water.

Detective Inspector Denise MacKenzie stood above him and for a pleasant moment he imagined her wearing the flowing dress of his dream. Like a baby, he held his arms out to her and smiled toothily.

Denise tried hard not to laugh. There was a half-naked, middle-aged man sprawled in her bathtub. He looked like death and smelled even worse. Her fingers itched to turn on the shower spray again.

"Frank," she snapped. "What the *hell* are you doing in the bathtub?"

"Gimme a kiss."

She watched him pucker up, chuckling to himself.

"Frank Phillips, I'm warning you. I'm not a woman to be putting up with drunken layabouts."

"But, you're *Irish*," he said innocently.

Denise flicked the shower spray to the coldest setting.

Fortune decreed that the Control Room of the Northumbria Police Constabulary dispatched DCI Ryan and DS Phillips to the remote part of Hadrian's Wall known as Sycamore Gap. The discovery of unidentified human remains qualified as a police matter, unless they were classified as being 'of antiquity'. That meant that somebody with the requisite authority needed to haul their sorry arse out of bed and take a look. Since the other detectives of the Criminal Investigation Department were busy looking into the usual rounds of manslaughter and GBH following drunken brawls over the weekend, it fell upon Ryan and Phillips to disregard their allocated day off-duty and take a drive into the hills. Most likely, the remains were ancient and he could happily pass them over to an archaeologist for examination, Ryan thought.

The drive out west of the city of Newcastle-upon-Tyne was scenic. Centuries earlier, men had laid the track for a long, straight road in that direction and although it was now tarmacked, it still followed the same course. The 'Military Road' as it had come to be known took Ryan along a route parallel to Hadrian's Wall, past reservoirs and rolling green fields populated by fluffy, well-fed sheep. When he saw the brown sign marked 'Housesteads Roman Fort', he slowed for the turn.

His attention was immediately drawn by two distinct facts: first, an inordinately large number of vehicles were crammed into the visitor's car park. Roman history wasn't *that* popular at eight-thirty on a Sunday morning. Second, his sergeant seemed to be wearing fancy dress.

Slamming out of the car, he naturally gave priority to his most pressing concern.

"Phillips? What in God's name are you wearing?"

Catching sight of the new arrival, Frank raised a cup of take-away coffee in greeting. "Morning, boss."

Ryan appropriated the coffee. "You look like the back end of a bus." It was always a comfort to know that there was someone out there who felt worse than him.

Phillips scowled. "You were the one who suggested that we go and celebrate."

"Not my fault that you can't hold your liquor."

"Can't...?" Phillips was momentarily lost for words. "It wasn't me who nearly fell flat on his face, boyo."

"The pavement was uneven." Grinning, Ryan eyed the floor. "Speaking of all things ridiculous, I repeat, what have you got on your feet?"

Phillips pointed one of his toes, dainty as a ballerina.

"These? They're my old walking boots. Got a bit of a hike ahead of us and you know me—always come prepared."

"You look like you've stumbled out of the circus. Besides, we're not scaling Kilimanjaro."

"We'll see who's laughing once you've walked up that hill in your City-boy shoes."

"Uh huh." Ryan took a thorough look around him. "Did I miss something? Why the cavalry?"

"It's the body," Phillips replied. "Older than your usual DB but apparently it still looks fairly recent. Could go either way. Besides that, the skeleton's been stuffed inside the wall."

"Inside?"

"Aye, that's the long and short of it. Some bloke found the body as he was having a morning stroll."

"What? He just *happened* to burrow inside the wall right where a body had been buried?" Ryan was incredulous. "How long is the damn wall? A hundred miles?"

"Eighty-four," Phillips put in.

"Close enough. Eighty-four miles of Roman stonework and this bloke decides to tamper with that bit in particular? What's his story?"

"Ask him yourself—he's sitting in the back of that car." Phillips thrust his square, bulldog face in the direction of one of the police cars. "But he says he went for a walk and decided to stop under that big tree for a break and a Kit-Kat. He was sitting there and saw something silver shining through a gap in the stones. He had a forage and, lo and behold, he found more than he bargained for.

"He's pretty shaken up," Phillips added. "Can't stop apologising about moving the stones. Practically wants to put himself in handcuffs for it."

Ryan blew out a breath and stuck his hands in the pockets of his jacket.

"Stranger things have happened," he said. "What about the rest? I see Faulkner amongst the crowd."

"Yeah, Faulkner's ready to start whenever you are." Phillips referred to the Senior Crime Scene Investigator. "We've got a lot of bored scientists standing around him. There's a team of archaeologists and a forensic anthropologist is on her way, but she's driving down from Edinburgh, so she'll be a while yet...there's Ambrose, the entomologist." Phillips ticked them off his broad fingers and screwed up his face in concentration. "We've got a forensic dentist on hand if we need one and the pathologist is on standby."

Ryan raised an eyebrow. "A lot of fuss, don't you think? I thought we were going to have a quick look at the remains and see if they're a job for CID. No need to bring the entire department along for that, it's a total waste of resources. Who gave the okay?"

Phillips pulled a face. "There's a shedload of bureaucracy with this one. Over there," he said, making a discreet gesture in the direction of a statuesque woman dressed in sharp clothing. "She's the National Heritage archaeologist, curator or whatever they call it—the regional bigwig. The minute she got a whiff of something amiss over here she hoofed it straight down to make sure we weren't going to trample all over the place or knock down the blasted wall."

"She wants to breathe down our necks."

Phillips scratched the side of his nose. "That's the gist of it. There's a lawyer, standing next to her. They're making noises about emergency injunctions, appropriate licences. She's been onto Gregson already, which is why we've got everybody and their maiden aunt down here."

Ryan thought of his Detective Chief Superintendent, an imposing man who was as comfortable at his desk as he was in the field. There was no denying that the man could handle the politics which came with the responsibility of his job title. Arthur Gregson could be diplomatic when the situation demanded it and *this* situation was shaping up to be one of those occasions.

"Brilliant. Great." Ryan shoved his hands in the pockets of his jacket and glanced around. Housesteads Fort was one of the larger Roman sites, boasting ruins, a museum and a visitor centre. He lifted a shoulder in their direction. "What time does the site open?"

"It's open from ten until six, every day." Phillips had already checked.

"But you can still park your car, if you want to walk around the pathways?"

"Yeah." Phillips nodded. "The ruins are closed off to the public outside those times, but generally they're not strict on parking regulations. Walkers just park their cars here and follow the trails along the wall."

"Too early for any of the staff to be around when Colin drove up here, then?"

"Yep. Colin says he was the only one around for miles when he discovered the bones. Why? You're thinking he sounds off?"

Ryan shrugged.

"Force of habit," he said, and then sighed. "I thought a little trip into the country would get me out of some weekend shopping."

"Aye, well I had high hopes for the afternoon," Phillips agreed, thinking back to his pleasant dream of earlier. "But that's the job."

"Amen to that." Ryan chugged down the rest of the cold coffee. "Come on—let's get this show on the road."

CHAPTER 2

With Phillips scampering at his heels, Ryan strode across the car park and headed directly for the group of CSIs huddled in the far corner. He made it halfway before he was intercepted.

"Chief Inspector? Professor Jane Freeman." A tall woman decked out in fine cashmere extended a hand.

Innate manners had him returning the gesture.

"Professor Freeman. I understand that you've spoken with DCS Gregson?"

"That's correct. As the Chief Archaeologist for National Heritage in this region, it is my responsibility to ensure that any interference with the stones must be done under controlled conditions."

Ryan rolled back on his heels and took an inventory of the woman standing before him. She didn't look much like any archaeologist he had ever met. No dusty khakis, no leather jacket or goofy glasses. Freeman was in her early-forties, glamorous in an expensive, understated way with a bob of expertly-dyed blonde hair and smoothly made-up skin. Her manner was direct and polished, and she carried an enormous designer handbag that Mary Poppins would have been proud of.

"Right. Well, let me assure you that we will be mindful of your concerns as the investigation progresses," he said, cutting across her automatic retort. "For now, it really is imperative that we understand what we are dealing with before we make any further decisions."

"Chief Inspector, Hadrian's Wall is a UNESCO World Heritage Site. I feel obliged to tell you that I will not hesitate to instruct our solicitor to seek an injunction to prevent any disruption of the land, should we feel that your team are unable to conduct themselves accordingly."

Ryan was starting to lose patience.

"Before anybody instructs anybody to do *any damn thing*, I need to see the body first. After that, I'll be able to assess whether this is a police matter, or something for you and your friends to look over and stick in a museum. I will decide who moves what, where, when and how. Until then, frankly, you're wasting everybody's time."

Her mouth fell open slightly, in shock.

"Excuse me." He nodded briskly, before moving away. Phillips fell into stride beside him.

"Doesn't help to ruffle her feathers too much, son."

"I haven't got time for fluffing them, Frank."

Ryan would have gone through ten degrees of torture before admitting that his thin suede boots were completely impractical for dealing with the terrain. He had a hairy moment where he pitched forwards, his feet sliding on the worn ground. Pride alone saved him from an embarrassing tumble in front of his sergeant and the team of CSIs who traipsed along behind him. Thankfully, he came to a standstill when the iconic sycamore tree came into view in the dip of the valley where the wall formed a 'U' shape. He took a wide survey of the vicinity and had to appreciate the splendour of the countryside, which was a patchwork in shades of green and purple. Not a building in sight; no dwellings, or even natural shelter where someone with criminal intent might choose to hide. His eyes tracked the ground as they walked the distance from Housesteads past the ruins of a Roman 'milecastle', which looked like a miniature fort and had been built at intervals all the way along the wall, or so the placard informed him. They continued along the pathway, passing craggy outcrops and a small lake, down and down into the valley basin until he could finally walk more casually without having to concentrate on each step.

In the habit of long experience, he began to pull on white paper overalls. Beside him, Phillips followed suit and then they, along with Tom Faulkner, moved forwards to do an initial walk-through. A wide perimeter had been cordoned off with police tape and a yellow tent erected around the body, looking totally out of place. A young police constable guarded the area like a sentry. They exchanged a few words and he added their names to the log of those entering or leaving.

Faulkner led the way.

"Depends on the age of the body," he began, puffing slightly as they walked the remaining distance down the hill. "But I don't expect to find much, unless the remains are fairly recent. Trace evidence on the ground would be long gone, I should think."

Ryan agreed. Hadrian's Wall received thousands of visitors every year, each footstep damaging or displacing the minutiae that Faulkner and his team would be looking for.

They could see the discarded stones on the ground and as they drew nearer, leaving a wide berth, they could also see what had upset the hapless Colin Hart on his morning walk.

"Nothing obvious to indicate an altercation, but then, there wouldn't be," Faulkner commented, scanning the ground as he edged closer to the cavity. He drew out an expensive-looking camera and began snapping pictures from different angles with an enormous zoom lens.

"We'll do a fingertip search to make sure there's nothing of interest. Ah, now, straight away I can tell you that these aren't very recent remains. Can't see much flesh tissue; a tiny bit of leathery skin left, that's all." Faulkner snapped on his mask and crouched down to get a better view. "Pathologist will need to have a word with the forensic anthropologist to try to come up with a firm date and make a start on identifying her."

"Her?"

With gloved hands, Faulkner took out some kind of long silver tool and gently lifted one of the bones, to see the underside.

"This looks like the pelvis. I'm no medical doctor, but from experience alone? The size and shape definitely look female." He paused again, taking an initial view of the area, the cavity, and the absence of recent decay. "The hair looks long, which probably also denotes female. More likely that a female would wear a bracelet of this kind, too." He pointed to the dulled silver bangle, which hung from one of the bones.

"I thought hair carried on growing after you die," Phillips remarked.

"Common misconception." Faulkner stood up and turned to them again. "You're going to want to have the experts give you the final say-so, but I'm thinking these bones look anywhere up to fifteen years old."

"That's recent, as far as we're concerned," Phillips commented.

"Yeah, it is." Faulkner pointed towards the remains with a gloved hand. "I'll tell you something else," he added. "I'll bet whoever killed her never thought she would be found, after all this time."

"Bad luck," Ryan returned, with a tigerish smile, before turning to retrace his steps.

Once they returned to the elevated ridge upon which the fortress of Housesteads had been built, Phillips was dispatched to deal with the necessary paperwork. There were forms to be signed and protocols to be followed, before human remains could be removed from a site of historical importance. Although it was petty of him, Ryan was relieved that the responsibility of looking after the body fell into their hands. *His* hands. Being a criminal investigation, justice took precedence over antiquity.

Clearly, that didn't present any undue obstacle to the officious Professor Freeman, who was still making herself known to the police and forensic staff on site.

Mildly irritated, Ryan turned his sights on Colin Hart, who was seated in the back of one of the police hatchbacks parked nearby. He dipped his head inside.

"Mr Hart?"

He saw a man in his forties, with light brown hair ruffled by the wind and perhaps from restless fingers. Watery blue eyes greeted him from an unremarkable, only slightly lined face, smoothly shaven. Average looking sort of personality, Ryan deduced.

"Chief Inspector Ryan. Fancy a bit of fresh air?" He held the door open to the other man and watched him shuffle out of the car.

"Thanks," Colin said. "I was starting to think you'd forgotten about me."

"Sorry about that. There were a few matters to see to, first," Ryan replied easily.

They started to walk slowly, in no particular direction.

"Can I get you some water?"

"Well, I had some earlier, in my backpack." Colin turned around, as if to look for it.

"It's still there, don't worry." Ryan stopped at the edge of the car park, where the asphalt met the grass leading down towards Housesteads Fort.

"So, Colin—do you mind if I call you Colin?"

"Go ahead."

"Tell me about what happened this morning. How did you come to find the body?"

Ryan judged him to be shaken, but not so much that they needed to pussy-foot around the subject.

Colin blew out a long breath. "I was just walking. I wanted to get down to Sycamore Gap, to try to catch the sunrise." He went over his movements in a quiet, no-nonsense way.

Ryan considered. "Don't take this the wrong way, but you don't strike me as a curious sort of man. What made you start messing around with the stones?"

Colin looked guilty as sin, Ryan thought with an inward smile.

"I'm terribly, *terribly* sorry that I tampered with the wall. I really can't explain what came over me." Colin shook his head, presumably at himself. "I would never dream of doing such a thing, normally."

Ryan made a brief, dismissive gesture. "Let's try to keep this in perspective. It may be frowned upon, but I bet hundreds of people walk all over those stones every year, when they think nobody's looking. You might have got a bit carried away, but at least you've uncovered something of interest."

"It was awful," Colin said slowly. "I saw the silver and, I don't know, maybe I thought it was some sort of buried treasure. Anyway, I just had to *know*. When the stones came loose, and I looked inside—"

He swallowed back the memory of those wide, hollow eyes.

"Did the stones come away easily?"

"Well, I'd better be honest with you and admit that they were quite tightly packed. It took some elbow grease to dislodge them."

"I see." Ryan *did* see, quite clearly, how it probably happened. Colin had thought himself on the verge of an archaeological discovery, perhaps a trove of old Roman coins, and had burrowed into the wall in his haste to uncover them. Instead, to his chagrin, he had made a different kind of discovery altogether.

"You never had any inkling that there might be something hidden there, until you happened to notice the silver?"

Colin shuddered.

"No, I had no idea. It was a shock."

To say the least, Ryan thought. They came to stand a little way from the entrance to the visitor centre and through the fencing they could see the ruined fort.

"I bet you know all about the history of this place," Colin said suddenly.

"What makes you say that?"

Colin shrugged. "Your girlfriend. She's a historian, isn't she?"

Ryan took another long look at Colin Hart.

"I didn't mean—that is—you were on the news, around Christmas. All about that stuff up on Holy Island. I recognise your face."

"Good memory." Ryan opened his mouth to say something else, but was interrupted by some wild arm gestures from Phillips, who appeared to have been cornered by Professor Freeman. Shelving the thought for now, he instructed a constable to continue taking a statement from Colin Hart.

Once Colin was safely ensconced inside a police car, Ryan took an extra minute to rifle through the man's rucksack, rules and regulations be damned. His eye passed over a small rectangular post card, which bore a date stamp but no message.

The process of removing human remains from the wall cavity was long and tedious, but necessary if there was to be a successful prosecution in the future. Somewhat retrospectively, Ryan approved the resources, which included a forensic archaeological team who painstakingly exhumed the body from its resting place, layer by layer. At the same time, the police entomologist—Doctor Ambrose, a portly man who spent most of his waking hours in his cosy office at the Faculty of Biological Sciences in Newcastle—examined the bones and surrounding area for signs of insect activity. As hour after slow hour passed, Ryan watched him shuffle around the excavation site like a mole, his myopic eyes benefiting from the help of extra-strength magnifying goggles.

Ryan remembered spending an unsettling morning in the close confines of Doctor Ambrose's office, surrounded by the pickled remains of insects in jars and decomposing rats in plastic tubs. First editions of *Faune des Tombeaux* and *La Faune des Cadavres* took pride of place on the shelf beside his desk, and lurid photographs of the process of decay were framed here and there.

Weird.

He may have been an oddball, but Ambrose could help to date a body to within a two-year period, and to within days or even hours for more recent cadavers. That made him a very useful person to know.

Standing a few feet away from where Ryan and Phillips perched atop the hill overlooking Sycamore Gap, Professor Freeman guarded her nest like a mother hen. She clucked around, watching the team of archaeologists do their work, supervising the movement of every stone, the displacement of every pebble. In an act of supreme diplomacy and in deference to his superior officer's wishes, Ryan had decided to include her in the process, as an executive consultant.

Hours later, when his staff had done all they could for the day, Ryan and Phillips made their way to the next, distinctly less picturesque stop on their tour of Northumberland. The mortuary at the Royal Victoria Infirmary in Newcastle was a triumph of clinical organisation. Banks of metal drawers lined the walls of the large, whitewashed space and trolleys stood in perfect rows; some were occupied, others were vacant. Ryan nodded a greeting to a couple of morticians he recognised and skirted past the trolleys, heading for the far corner of the room. He shivered slightly, partly thanks to the specialist cooling system, which pumped icy cold air into the rooms to offset the furnaces. Through a side door, Ryan and Phillips found themselves entering a series of ante-rooms, each set up for specialist autopsies or clinical evaluations. The lemony stench of formalin mixed with formaldehyde followed them as they headed for the door marked 'Dr Jeffrey Pinter'.

The Senior Police Pathologist was an experienced man in his early-fifties. He was tall— shoulder-to-shoulder with Ryan, who stood a couple of inches over six feet— but bonier, judging by the white lab coat which hung limply from his shoulders. For all that he bore a vague resemblance to the Grim Reaper, a fact greatly enhanced by the morbidity of his workplace, Pinter was a cheerful man. He looked up from his desk with a broad smile when they slipped inside his office.

"Ryan, Phillips." He rose and extended a hand. "Good to see you both."

"You too, Jeff. Thanks for taking time out of your weekend."

"Them's the breaks, or so they say. I've been looking at the lady you sent me," Pinter said, clasping the lapels of his lab coat in a habitual gesture. "There are a few interesting things to note."

"Such as?"

"Probably best to show you. Follow me, I've put her in Examination Room B."

The bones had been laid out on a metal gurney like a jigsaw puzzle, to form a complete skeleton. Thin strands of wispy hair fell from the skull and crusted skin remained on parts of the bone. The three men stood above it, faces covered by surgical masks and hair protected by paper caps, so that only their eyes were visible.

"As you can see, there is a complete skeleton, which is remarkable," Pinter said. "I think we can assume that she was enclosed inside the wall fairly soon after she died, otherwise I would have expected to see much more interference from local wildlife. Foxes have an excellent sense of smell."

Phillips pulled a face. He had seen a few of those bodies before; men and women whose flesh had been ravaged by hungry animals. "Aye, well, that's something," he said shortly, then cleared his throat. "How do you reckon she died?"

Pinter furrowed his brow so that the cap shifted on his head like a theatrical wig.

"Here," he said, indicating a spot at the side of the skull. "You can see there has been some serious impact, judging from the fracture just above her left ear."

Phillips leaned forward and saw the crack at the side of the skull, which was now more of an empty hole following concentrated decomposition in that area.

"Someone gave her a good bash."

"You could say that," Pinter agreed, with a chuckle that grated on Ryan's nerves. "That seems to be the most obvious sign of trauma, from a blunt instrument or a hard impact with something solid, in my view. Probably suffered multiple whacks. Having said that, we can't say one hundred percent for sure that's how she died; the remains are mostly bone, as you can see, so there's no way for me to examine her internal organs for evidence of other trauma there." He sucked in a breath and carried on. "Other than the fact that her bones have separated through the expected deterioration, there is a minor break in this bone in the wrist which might have occurred around the time of death. I also note a couple of healed breakages, probably from her childhood." He pointed to the left forearm.

"I'm waiting for the histology report to come back—that should be in the next forty-eight hours, unless you need me to put a rush on it? I've taken samples from the bone and remaining tissue, though there wasn't much of that."

"Technically, this one's non-urgent. What about identity?"

"Faulkner couldn't find any identifying markers on the body or around the site; no handy bank cards or anything like that. We're looking up dental records now. In the meantime, we'll run a DNA test on the samples and compare them with the database to see if there's a match. Otherwise, it'll be a question of Missing Persons and good luck."

Ryan merely nodded. "How old is the body, do you think?"

"Well, as to that, I was going to introduce you to our new forensic anthropologist. She's the one you really need to talk to. She's been working with Doctor Ambrose and myself to come up with an accurate timescale. Shall I fetch her?"

With a spring in his step, Pinter skipped out of the room and down the corridor. In his wake, Ryan and Phillips exchanged a surprised glance and eagerly awaited the woman who seemed to have awakened a new *joie de vivre* in at least one member of the mortuary staff.

Doctor Ann Millington was a methodical woman in her late twenties. She wore her long, ash blonde hair in a tail down her back and slim designer spectacles perched on her straight nose. Where Pinter had bounced out of the examination room like a character from *Winnie the Pooh,* she entered it more sedately, a slim blue folder clutched in one hand and a mug of steaming coffee in the other. Ryan eyed the mug covetously as she set it on the desk in the corner.

"Doctor Millington?"

"My friends call me Millie," she said, offering a pale hand in greeting.

Younger than he had anticipated, Ryan thought, but she was still their go-to person for all things forensic-anthropological. That meant she had made good use of her time. He took the hand that she offered and gave it a firm shake.

"DCI Ryan, sergeant. Doctor Pinter told me that you would like to discuss what we've been able to find out so far. He'll join us in a few moments because he's had a last-minute delivery."

Ryan wasn't sure how to feel about them referring to dead people as 'deliveries'. In his world, a delivery meant a parcel or a gift of some kind. He didn't understand how they could see rotting cadavers in the same light.

He set that thought aside and moved to stand opposite her, on the other side of the trolley. "We appreciate you taking the time to come down from Edinburgh to look at this," he began. "In real terms, it's not an urgent case."

She smiled slightly. "Every case of unexplained death has a sense of urgency."

He nodded, pleased that she was of the same mind. "We're particularly interested in determining the age of the body."

"I understand. Doctor Pinter has begun DNA and toxicology sampling and is cross-referencing dental records. For the sake of completeness, I've already begun the process of analysing the remaining tissue samples for carbon-14."

The reaction from the two men seated opposite her was almost comical. Ryan adopted a carefully neutral expression in an effort to mask his total ignorance of the process of carbon-14 dating, his basic training on the subject long since forgotten. Phillips nodded wisely and adopted a fatherly expression, with the same goal in mind.

"Would you like me to run through the process?" she offered.

Relief flooded both faces as they nodded.

"Radioactive carbon, or carbon-14, naturally makes its way into the human body via the biological food chain. It decays over time at a mathematically predictable rate and, as soon as an organism dies, its body will stop taking on any new carbon.

"Now, during the 1950s and 60s, several nations, including the United Kingdom, authorised the testing of nuclear weaponry above ground. Although this stopped, the residual effect is a higher than normal level of carbon-14 in the atmosphere. Almost double the normal level, in fact. This is particularly useful in my profession and yours, because we can test a body for carbon levels. The teeth absorb carbon very easily," she added.

"So, you measure the carbon in someone's teeth and compare it with known levels of atmospheric carbon around the time the teeth would have developed. Anyone born since the fifties will have a higher level, right?"

Phillips was a quick study. He turned and met Ryan's surprised face with a shrug.

"What? I watch the Discovery Channel, sometimes."

"Sure, when you're not watching Sky Sports," Ryan muttered.

"In simple terms, yes, that's the process" Millie agreed, cutting through their byplay like a primary school teacher. "Carbon readings have been taken every year since the fifties, so we can use our equations to extrapolate a birth date for our unknown victim. The results should be available very soon and will be useful in the event that nothing turns up on dental records."

"That's appreciated."

Millington drew out a few sheets of paper from the folder she held. "Here's a copy of my preliminary report, which I've also sent to your office e-mail. Obviously, I will update it when the lab results come through, but I can already confirm the following things: the skeleton is definitely a female judging by the circular indentation in her pelvis, most likely of Western European ancestry. She would have enjoyed a comfortable socio-economic environment in her early years, including a balanced diet, since her bones are well-developed. The fact they remain largely intact rather than having crumbled would suggest a healthy specimen, of a height somewhere between five-feet-three inches and five-seven."

Ryan listened while skim-reading the neatly typed report.

"Judging from the length of the femur, the molars, the cranium…I would put her age within the range of late teens to mid-twenties."

Millie indicated the relevant areas on the skeleton lying before them, with the same detached voice cultivated by many medical and scientific professionals. From his position a good few feet away, Phillips tried not to hold it against her. He'd never had a stomach for this part of the job and already he could feel his innards objecting to the close proximity with death.

For a murder detective, it was a bit of a conundrum.

"You say there were injuries?"

"Yes." She drew out another sheet of paper showing the black outline of a skeleton, annotated with markers to denote the presence of abnormalities. "Ante-mortem injuries include a couple of healed breaks in her left forearm, probably from a childhood fall. More interesting would be the break in her left wrist, which I would judge to have been sustained around the time of death, or shortly before. There is no evidence of the bone having knitted back together, you see."

Her fingers hovered over the broken wrist, which looked more like a mass of jumbled bone matter to Ryan's untrained eye. Still, all manner of possibilities presented themselves—had their victim struggled, fallen or been forcibly restrained around the time she died?

"Mm hmm," was all he said. "What about post-mortem interval?"

Millie crossed her arms neatly.

"I've estimated the age of the remains to be approximately ten years old," she supplied. "This takes into account average temperatures in the region, the accessibility to wildlife and the general state of the body when we found it. Jeff agrees with me and Doctor Ambrose has added his thoughts. We are definitely of the view that this victim died no more than ten years ago."

"Less than we thought," Phillips murmured.

"Yeah." Ryan's voice was flat. He checked his watch. *Four-fifteen.*

"Arrange a briefing for six-thirty, Frank. I want all hands on deck."

CHAPTER 3

Phillips had done little more than make a quick detour to the gents toilet before they received a call from Jeff Pinter to say that their female victim had been identified by her dental records, which had flagged as a priority given that she was already registered as missing at the National Crime Agency's UK Missing Persons Bureau.

"Amy Llewellyn, reported missing on the evening of 21st June 2005, aged twenty-one." Ryan held out his smartphone, which displayed a departmental photograph of Amy, stored on the Missing Persons Database from the original case file, and taken on the night of her birthday. She had been lovely, he thought. Petite, with dark curly hair worn in a playful bob and laughing green eyes which smiled up at the camera. He wondered if it was the fact that her features were even; the kind of generic, symmetrical beauty, which made hers the kind of face that people found familiar.

He couldn't for the life of him think why, but she was familiar.

Naturally, her details were registered on the database, so it was possible that he recognised her image from the original police appeal back in 2005.

Except that, in 2005, he would have been in London, cutting his teeth at the Met. He had been too busy around that time to pay much attention to one of the thousands of young women who were reported missing every year. *No*, he shook his head at the image in front of him. It had to be something else.

Phillips came to stand beside him and peered at the image on the screen.

"He liked to pick 'em," he said knowingly.

Ryan looked across at his sergeant.

"You recognise her?"

Now it was Phillips' turn to look bemused.

"You're telling me that you *don't* recognise her?" He shuffled his feet, clearly discomfited. "She's one of the missing, presumed dead that we chalked up as being one of The Hacker's earlier efforts, not that he ever confessed to it. She fits the physical type and we found nude photographs of her in his house, after the arrest last year."

Ryan looked away from Phillips, back at the young girl he held in the palm of his hand.

"You really don't remember?"

Ryan shook his head slowly. "I need some air."

Phillips stood outside the service entrance to the mortuary and drummed his fingers against the material of his trousers, wishing for a cigarette. Or any product containing tobacco. Bugger it, even one of those e-cigs would do the trick, so long as it gave him something to do with his hands.

He put his fingers to work re-knotting his tie, which was a tropical explosion of miniature pineapples and bananas embroidered on a lime-green silk background. The way he saw it, just because the job involved death didn't mean that he was required to dress as an undertaker. A man needed a bit of cheer to offset the gloom.

So thinking, he risked a glance across at the man who stood a few steps apart, still and silent while hospital staff moved around them, and vehicles came and went.

Ryan hadn't said a word. Not one solitary word since he'd stalked out of the hospital fifteen minutes earlier. He'd offered Ryan coffee in a cheap plastic cup from one of the vending machines; weak and steaming hot, but still better than nothing.

For the first time in living memory, Ryan had turned it down.

"You want to get it off your chest?"

Phillips crossed his arms and turned to the man who, despite being fifteen years younger, was his professional superior. That didn't seem to matter; Ryan never pulled rank and Phillips never felt the pinch. They had a mutual respect. Hell, more than that.

They were family.

"Son," Phillips said, keeping his gravelly voice gentle, designed to soothe. "I know what's going on inside your head."

Ryan huffed out a half-laugh. "No, you don't."

"You think I can't remember?" There was a layer of anger beneath the gentle tone, an undercurrent of frustration. "I've got my memories. Every one of us took memories home with us and woke up with them in the morning. That last day—"

"Frank." Ryan held up a hand, in protest.

"That last day," Phillips persevered, "I'll take with me till I die. Seeing you there like that, dealing with all of it—and then the aftermath…" Phillips shook his head, trying to find the words. "I never told you I was proud."

Ryan looked down at his feet, eyes burning.

"I was proud that you stopped."

The breath shuddered out of his body, as memories flooded back. Ryan, covered in his sister's blood and his own, using his fists on the man who had killed her.

"I wanted to end the man who ended her."

"I know," Phillips agreed, looking out across the car park at the people coming and going. "But you didn't."

"It was you who stopped me."

Phillips shook his head. "There isn't a person alive who could have stopped you, unless you'd wanted to be stopped."

Ryan looked up again.

"Never thought of that, did you? You stopped yourself. You brought him in, even though everything inside you wanted to finish him, to take your revenge or whatever you want to call it. You did the right thing."

They were both silent for a few minutes.

"He'll rot in prison. That has to be enough."

Phillips nodded. Doctor Keir Edwards, the man known in the media as *The Hacker of the North* or *Doctor Death*, depending on the tabloid, would spend the rest of his life in HMP Frankland, the maximum-security prison for Category A criminals in the nearby city of Durham. Last summer, after a killing spree in which five young, attractive women had been found dismembered, he had taken his final victim: Natalie Finley-Ryan. He had stalked her, tortured her, and finally killed her to punish the detective who had the temerity to try to stop him.

Ryan had been too late to save his sister, and Phillips knew that would haunt him for the rest of his days.

"We don't know for sure that Amy Llewellyn is one of his tally," Phillips said reasonably.

"He had photographs of her in his private stash," Ryan retorted. "We always assumed that he had killed her."

"He never admitted to it. He was usually one for crowing loudly about the women he'd killed."

That was true, Ryan thought.

"He never explained how he came by the photographs and he never admitted to having had a relationship with her. He clammed up."

There had been a pile of photographs, Ryan remembered belatedly, found in a private album at Edwards' home. He couldn't understand how he had forgotten Amy's name, or her face, when he could recall the detail of Keir Edwards' police statements verbatim.

Indeed, Ryan made it his business to know everything there was to know about Keir Edwards; his age, his habits, how many sheets of toilet roll he used on a weekly basis in his two-by-four cell. Edwards wouldn't so much as fart without him knowing about it, for the rest of his miserable life.

Yet, he didn't know the answer to whether Edwards had killed the girl who was now reduced to little more than bone matter, lying in an impersonal room in the building behind him, being examined by men and women in white coats.

Just as his sister had been.

He closed his eyes and Natalie's face swam to the surface. His eyelids snapped open again and he groped around for something to take his mind away from the horror of remembering that day. He caught sight of Phillips bravely sampling the gelatinous muck which passed for vending machine coffee and mustered a smile.

"Come on," he said. "Time to visit Amy's family."

The Llewellyns lived in an immaculate, semi-detached house in an upmarket cul-de-sac on the outskirts of Newcastle. The gardens were tidy and the smart car on the driveway sparkled with a fresh coat of wax.

It was always the same, Ryan thought, as he followed Mrs Llewellyn into the spacious front room. Here, all was tidy too—not a speck of dust in sight. Everything was decorated in shades of cream and unimaginative prints hung above the feature fireplace and the white leather sofa. There was always a sixth sense, a premonition which all families of the missing felt when plain-clothed police officers walked the long journey towards their front door. They watched from behind half-closed curtains, unsure whether to answer the bell.

For Rose Llewellyn, the sound of that simple chime signalled an end to the interminable purgatory of hope and despair she had occupied for ten years. Not a day had gone by without her imagining that her daughter, Amy, would suddenly return to them after a terrible incident. Until the moment that Ryan rang the doorbell, Rose had filled the long hours obsessively cleaning every surface of her home. Just recently, she had taken to trimming the lawn with kitchen scissors.

Before Amy left them, Rose had been a pharmacist working in Newcastle. After she realised that Amy wasn't coming home, she'd had her first breakdown and since then hadn't been able to sustain the kind of office hours that her job demanded.

She told herself that looking after her home and family was just as important, but even thinking of the word 'family' would often reduce her to tears.

So, she cleaned. She tidied. She hoped.

Until today.

Ryan would not have thought himself well-equipped to deal with grieving relatives, but his natural reserve was perhaps the key to his success, for when Rose looked up at the tall, remote stranger, she saw empathy. Beyond that, she saw tenacity.

Ryan and Phillips waited until she had seated herself before settling themselves in a couple of easy chairs.

"Mrs Llewellyn, would you like one of us to contact your husband?"

"Steven—Steven is just outside in the garden…"

The man in question stepped through the patio doors at the other end of the room and, recognising their visitors instantly, he moved to take his wife's outstretched hand.

"You're here about Amy." It was a statement, not a question.

"Yes. I regret to inform you that we have identified a body we found early this morning to be that of your daughter, Amy. You both have our deepest sympathies."

The words might have been hackneyed, but that didn't make them any less true. Though in her heart she had *known*, Rose felt the hot tears rising and her breathing hitched in great, shuddering sobs. Steven stood beside her, his face shuttered and oddly expressionless.

Phillips felt a knot rise in his own throat and he looked away to clear his head. Every police officer hated this side of the job; it was the very worst part of it and it never got any easier with practice.

"How—how?" Rose managed.

Ryan's jaw clenched. They always wanted to know, and he never wanted to tell them.

"We believe your daughter was murdered."

Rose Llewellyn sagged against her husband, whose arm came tighter around her shoulders while he visibly kept himself in firm control. Without a word, Phillips stood to offer her a small packet of tissues from his inner breast pocket.

"What have you got so far? Tell me what has been *done*." Steven snatched the tissues up and passed them to his wife.

In their long experience, relatives tended to react to terrible news in one of two ways and it seemed that they were seeing the perfect example of each. Rose had broken down emotionally, the natural reaction of a mother who had finally been told what she had long suspected: that her child had been taken from her. It didn't matter how old that child was, the anguish was always there. Steven, on the other hand, buried his grief in anger. He looked at them both with green eyes that were bone-dry and venomous.

"We're doing all we can," Ryan answered evenly. He drew out a small card with the contact details of a Family Liaison Officer and placed it on the coffee table, remaining watchful as they dealt with the worst news of their lives.

"Have you got any suspects?"

"We are at a very early stage in our investigation," he replied. "Rest assured, we will be doing all we can to bring your daughter's killer to justice."

"Screw that!" Llewellyn burst out, his skin turning red beneath his tan. "You know as well as I do, it was Keir Edwards who killed her! That bastard killed her as sure as the Pope is Catholic. He's probably laughing himself to sleep about it while my taxes pay for his cushy little cell. Now, do your pissing job and get the evidence to prove it!"

Rose lifted a hand in a mute appeal for him to stop, but he was on a roll.

"That goes especially for *you*," he hissed, jabbing a finger towards Ryan. "I thought that after what happened to your sister, you would have understood how it feels."

Mid-tirade, Llewellyn's eye fell on the single picture of his daughter, which stood proudly in a silver frame on the coffee table. The fight drained out of him, to be replaced with a dull, numbing pain.

"It's always the way, isn't it?" He pinned them with a merciless stare. "You coppers look after your own, but when it comes to anybody else, you don't give a shit."

Phillips opened his mouth to deny the accusation, feeling the burn of what was wholly untrue. Ryan gave an almost imperceptible shake of his head to shut down any angry replies that were brewing. For, despite what Steven Llewellyn thought, he did understand. He understood the pain of loss, and that first-hand knowledge strengthened his resolve. Right now, Llewellyn needed to let out his rage, his impotent fury at what could not be changed.

Ryan had been there himself.

When neither detective gave him any response besides silent compassion, Llewellyn looked down at his wife. He hadn't been able to change what happened to Amy and he hadn't been able to stop Rose's gradual decline. She was painfully thin and frail, and he knew that, once again, she was forgetting to eat. She was also trying to hide the fact that she was struggling to go beyond the edge of the garden and he could tell that agoraphobia was beginning to gain a hold on her. She had been obsessive for years now—about cleaning in particular. Since Amy, she hadn't felt able to trust anyone aside from him.

Now, he was once again being forced to accept a position on the periphery, unable to be a main player, even in the search for his daughter's killer. He had failed as a father and as a husband.

"I understand," he said finally, rubbing his wife's cold fingers.

"You have the means to be very helpful to our investigation," Ryan reminded him, seeing the dejection. "It would help us enormously to know as much as possible about Amy—her life before she went missing, her habits and so on."

Steven scrubbed his palms across his face and belatedly remembered that he had forgotten to wash his hands since weeding the garden. His cheeks were probably tracked with mud.

"I need to clear my head, first, if you don't mind," he muttered. "I'll make a pot of tea, then I'll answer all your questions."

"Thanks."

"What did you make of them?"

Phillips asked the question as he slipped into the passenger seat of Ryan's car, admiring the leather as it moulded itself lovingly to his rear end.

Ryan sat behind the wheel and considered the question.

"We were never going to get anything useful from Rose Llewellyn, at least not today," he began. "She'll need a day or so to come to terms with the worst of the shock, before she'll start to remember the answers to some of the questions we might have. In the meantime, we can look over her old statements from 2005."

"Aye, that's a plan," Phillips agreed.

"As for the husband, he seemed a bit more of a cold fish, until his outburst."

"Uh huh," Phillips said, looking pointedly at his SIO. "Men dealing with emotional trauma by repressing their feelings. Remind you of anyone?"

"Not even remotely." He had to smile. "But, on that basis, you make a fair point."

"Only one picture of Amy that I could see, and they've turned her room into a spare bedroom. Bit weird, isn't it? Families usually keep their rooms the same, hoping they'll be coming home and all that."

"Hmm."

There was a short silence, during which time Ryan drummed his fingers against the wheel and rolled his shoulders. Phillips began a silent countdown.

Five…four…three…two…

"Run a background check on both of them and re-interview them tomorrow or Tuesday. Recall the original case files and cross-check with the findings there."

"Already done, boss."

Ryan slanted Phillips a look. His sergeant was looking particularly smug.

"If you're angling for a pay rise, you can kiss my hairy arse."

"If it would get me a pay rise, I'd consider it."

CHAPTER 4

The commander of the Northumbria Police Constabulary's CID division had been expecting Ryan's visit. Detective Chief Superintendent Arthur Gregson was in his late-fifties, though his face held few lines, most of which had been dug in the early years when he had walked the beat. Nowadays, his skin was weathered by the sun, from weekends spent tending to his extensive garden or from the twice-yearly holiday to the South of France, which his wife insisted was 'good for his constitution'. He owed his trim physique to regular tennis sessions with friends at his club and the beers that followed were offset by the militant diet his wife imposed on them both.

Low cholesterol, he thought with a sneer.

While he briefly considered the possibility of sneaking a kebab on his way home, he linked his broad fingers together loosely atop his desk. When the expected knock came at the door, he was ready.

"Come!" he barked.

Ryan entered and moved to stand before him, like a soldier to his captain.

"Take a seat, Ryan."

"Thank you, sir." He settled his long body into one of the uncomfortable olive-green chairs arranged opposite Gregson's desk. He noted that his commander was dressed in casual clothes, which was something of a first, before remembering that it was a Sunday.

"You've come to talk to me about the body found inside Hadrian's Wall."

"Yes, sir. I understand that you have already spoken with Professor Freeman—"

"And you want to know why I didn't consult you before ordering half of the force to attend the site?"

Ryan's jaw snapped shut.

"Call it a blessing, call it a curse," Gregson said, shrugging his wide shoulders. "Part of my job is to keep the public happy. Last thing any of us needs is this Professor kicking up a fuss, calling in the local media to complain about the department."

"Empty threats."

"Of course they were," Gregson agreed, with a flick of his wrist. "Still, you pick your battles."

Ryan nodded.

"I trust you've been able to get a handle on things?"

"I believe so. You've seen my summary," he said, referring to the e-mail he had sent earlier in the day. "The forensic archaeological team have spent all day excavating the site. The remains were transferred to the pathologist at the RVI, who has been working with an anthropologist to produce a report. I have their preliminary observations already and should know more within the next forty-eight hours. The ground operation was overseen by Faulkner and his team of CSIs."

"That's fast work," Gregson commented mildly.

Ryan paused, glancing away then back again. He knew that there was a question somewhere in that statement.

"Sir, following your lead, I felt it best to expedite the excavation in order to avoid any undue delay or further loss of evidence. Despite the fact that we found no identifying items on or around the victim's body, we have nonetheless been able to identify her very quickly."

Gregson's face broke into what could loosely be described as a smile.

"That's good, very good indeed. Who is she?"

"Her name is Amy Llewellyn, sir. Next of kin have been informed."

"That should make life fairly simple," Gregson said, with satisfaction. "Hopefully, Faulkner will uncover some useful evidence from the site and you'll have your man in no time."

"We may already have him."

"Is that so? This is one for the record books."

"It's Edwards, sir."

"Impossible," Gregson replied without inflection. "You're looking at a ten-year-old body. This girl died years before Edwards became active."

"That we know of," Ryan put in quietly. "Edwards had in his possession nude photographs of Amy Llewellyn. It would be a safe assumption that she is one of his victims."

There was short silence, punctuated only by the sounds of the world outside, everyday comings and goings. A pigeon cooed on the window ledge.

"What do you propose to do?"

Ryan had already considered this; he had weighed up the pros and cons, thought about the different angles.

"I have a team briefing scheduled for six-thirty. Faulkner's CSIs might have made some progress by then, or within the next forty-eight hours at the latest. In the meantime, Phillips and I will look into the victim's cold case file from 2005 and start to build up a picture. After then, should the evidence support my theory, I plan to conduct an interview with Edwards."

Gregson's eyebrows shot up into his hairline.

"You only have a photograph to support your suspicion, which Edwards denied taking. In contrast to his extremely vocal confessions to the murders of five women, he denies killing this girl. Put bluntly, Ryan, unless you can come up with something forensic to support your theory, it's going to look like a vendetta." Gregson didn't hold his punches. "Look," he said, spreading his hands, palms up. "The events of last year were traumatic, they affected you on a personal level—understandably so."

"Yes, sir." *What more could he say?*

"It's one thing to return to the job, to investigate other deaths ..." Gregson thought of the events on Holy Island and tried to search for the right words. "It would be healthier, surely, to put the past behind you?"

"If there is another victim, or indeed victims plural, our investigation into Keir Edwards remains unfinished."

Ryan baulked at the thought of more lives lost, of more waste to be found, more families to ruin.

"Another detective can handle it. Phillips could run this investigation, easily."

He could, Ryan agreed, thinking of his sergeant with fondness. The man was a terrier, experienced and capable, with a nose for the business.

Still.

"This is my case."

Gregson sat back in his chair and considered, weighing up his own options.

"I want you to attend regular counselling sessions."

"Not necessary—"

Gregson overrode the immediate denial. "You won't fob me off this time, Ryan. You got away with it once, so don't push your luck. It is for *me* to decide what is necessary, if you insist upon remaining the Senior Investigating Officer in this investigation. Now," he said, fishing around in his drawer for a business card, "here's the number for the departmental psychiatrist, in case you've managed to mislay it."

Gregson smiled triumphantly.

"I expect you to make an appointment by the end of the day, failing which an appointment will be made for you. Non-attendance will signify to me that you no longer wish to be part of this investigation. Do we understand one another?"

Ryan's jaw ached from the effort of restraining himself.

"Perfectly." Recognising dismissal, Ryan rose from his cramped position and prepared to leave.

"Oh, one last thing."

"Sir?"

"I hear that young Jack Lowerson has finally come out of his coma?"

Ryan managed to work up a weak smile. "Yes, just yesterday. His family are overjoyed, as are his team."

"Wonderful news," Gregson agreed. "Has he been able to remember anything?"

"Unfortunately, not." *So far.*

"Ah, that's a pity," Gregson was sympathetic, his tone aggrieved.

"One day, that might change."

"Perhaps he may wish to put the past behind him, even if you would rather not."

"We'll see," was all Ryan said.

Gregson watched the door click shut again and took a moment to contemplate some of the memorabilia on the shelves and the walls of his office, which told of thirty years' service. There were pictures of him shaking hands with the Police Commissioner and the Mayor of London;

snapshots of garden parties spent with minor royalty and local hoi polloi. He had seen his department go through many changes—in policy, management and staffing. The inevitable edicts that a new government handed down every few years did little to change the workforce; he saw to that. He knew the best way to run his staff and no political upstarts would tell him otherwise.

Above all, there was an order to his life—a careful balance, which he was unwilling to change.

He thought of Ryan and began to feel uneasy.

It took a confident man to recall several tired and irritable members of CID, depriving them of their well-earned Sunday roast dinners and sofa time with their families.

Ryan was, fortunately, such a man.

After his meeting with Gregson, he headed straight to the large conference room at the other end of the hall and tacked up a sign, which read, 'OPERATION HADRIAN'. He spent another fifteen minutes pinning salient images to the large board at the front of the room, scrawling a long black line along the length of it to signify Amy Llewellyn's timeline. He knew that there were computer programs that could do all of this for him, and he would use them as well. Still, seeing those images enlarged on the wall and creating a mental picture of the work they had done that day could not be bettered in terms of visual impact. When Phillips finally trudged into the room, heavy-footed and flustered after his latest dealings with a certain detective, Ryan was prepared.

Ryan waited until Phillips had settled himself into one of the faded orange scoop-back plastic chairs before he asked the pertinent question.

"Everything alright?"

Phillips crossed his arms over his bulky chest.

"Well you might ask," he muttered. "I knew that woman would be trouble—I *told* you that woman would be trouble." He jabbed a finger towards Ryan in accusation.

"You're going to have to be more specific. Which woman? What trouble? If you need me to speak to Professor Freeman—"

"MacKenzie!" Phillips blurted out. "Who else would I be talking about? Who *else* could manage to make a man feel guilty, just for doing his job?"

"Ah—"

"I rang to let her know there was a briefing at six-thirty." Phillips paused briefly to glance behind him before continuing. You could never be too careful. "Next thing I know, she turns up just as I'm dealing with that archaeologist—Freeman—in the foyer downstairs. Then, she tells me I was flirting with her. *Me!*"

He jerked his thumb into his chest to punctuate the statement.

"You were flirting with Professor Freeman?" Ryan asked mildly.

"Don't you start!" Phillips huffed. "Can't even go about my business without someone or other sticking the knife in."

"Aw," Ryan cooed.

"Freeman only turned up to drop off her report," Phillips continued, waving the report in front of him to prove it. "She said she wanted to hand it over and thank me personally for treating the site with respect."

"You cad!" Ryan grinned widely. "Breaking hearts, left, right and centre."

"Can I help it, if I have superior people skills?"

"If those skills include superior buffoonery, then…" Ryan trailed off, thinking that Phillips had seen enough mockery for the present.

They turned their attention to Amy Llewellyn, whose smiling face crowned the top of the murder board.

"Why her?"

"Why anybody?" Ryan countered.

If she had been younger, from a less secure background, homeless or with a history of alcohol or substance abuse, Ryan might have thought Amy was a random choice. Young, vulnerable men and women often ended up on the streets, in one form or another. Some wanted to escape, others had no choice. Nameless, faceless, with no family to care whether they went missing or not.

The perfect hunting ground for a certain breed of killer.

But Amy?

"Nice girl, nice home, nice family. What happened?" Phillips voiced the same thoughts.

"Keir Edwards is what happened."

"We don't know—"

"Yeah, yeah—I've heard the party line."

Phillips refolded his arms mutinously. "Just trying to keep things on a level playing field, guv. Last thing we want to do is barge into HMP Frankland, guns blazing at Edwards, only to uncover some other bit of evidence pointing to the bloke in the cell next door."

Ryan agreed with him, but it did little to dilute the sense of driving urgency, which he felt whenever anybody mentioned the man's name.

While he ruminated on it, the rest of the team began to file into the room. The first things they saw were the large, colour photographs of Amy Llewellyn. One clearly showed her in life, the other showed her in death. Ryan waited until they had settled themselves, after all the handshaking and backslapping they seemed to need before they concentrated on finding a killer. With admirable poise, he watched DI Denise MacKenzie stalk to the front and take a seat, leaving a pointed gap between herself and Phillips. Ryan wondered how opposites so often attracted. There, on the one hand, was his sergeant: gruff, canny and loyal as a basset hound, but he was no oil painting. There, on the other, was MacKenzie: feisty and smart with a striking mane of golden red hair and a quick brain beneath it.

Ah, l'amour.

Briefly, he thought of his own Anna. She was probably sitting in her little study, immersed in some old book or another. He loved to find her like that, her elegant neck bent over an inscrutable text while she toyed with the ends of her dark hair.

The sooner he got on with the briefing, the sooner he could go home to her.

"Alright, settle down."

Chairs scraped, conversations died.

"Welcome to the first briefing of 'Operation Hadrian'. Another original name from The Powers That Be," he added. "Thanks to all of you who worked at the scene today and to those of you who have abandoned your day off to join us. Your commitment is much appreciated."

He tapped a knuckle on the board behind him.

"For those of you who need to catch up, here's a potted summary. Our witness, Colin Hart, found what we now know to be the remains of Amy Llewellyn, inside a hollowed-out cavity in the stretch of Hadrian's Wall known as 'Sycamore Gap'. Early this morning, around five-thirty, he was out walking along that stretch. He parked his car at Housesteads, walked west towards that spot to catch the sunrise, and natural curiosity got the better of him.

"He reported his find to the Control Room, who referred the incident directly to Gregson before dispatching Phillips and myself to the scene. The Chief felt it was necessary to call out the infantry on this one, given the potential media intrusion alongside the active presence of interested parties."

"That's one way of putting it," MacKenzie sniped, with a deadly sideways look at Phillips.

Ryan decided to let the interruption pass.

"*Professor Freeman* is the senior archaeologist for National Heritage in this region. She has been vocal in her objection to any undue interference with the site. Regardless, we were able to confirm that the remains fall under our remit. Faulkner," he said, eying the senior CSI who had discarded his customary overalls in favour of navy cords and a matching blue jumper. It made him seem less like a scientist and more of an ordinary man; not somebody who picked over the scenes of violent crime on a daily basis. "Special thanks to you and your team for such sympathetic handling of the excavation site, particularly under that level of scrutiny."

The CSI mumbled something and adjusted his glasses. He was not a man who enjoyed attention.

Ryan turned back to the board and tacked up a large copy of the diagram the anthropologist had given him earlier that day, which showed the presence of injuries on Amy Llewellyn's skeleton.

"Phillips and I paid a visit to the pathologist this afternoon. He and the forensic anthropologist agree that, aside from childhood injuries, there are two main things to note. The first is the presence of a fairly large skull fracture running along the squamosal suture, which divides the left temporal and parietal lobes," he read from the report, then tapped a finger behind his left ear to illustrate. "The second is a break in her left wrist, which happened on or around the time she died."

He turned back to the room and stuck his hands in the back pockets of his jeans.

"They're running further tests on the body, to see what else comes up, but in the meantime it's looking like there was some kind of violent struggle, resulting in massive head trauma."

There were a few sympathetic murmurs around the room.

"Tom? What can you add to the forensic side of things?"

Faulkner fiddled with his notes before answering. He never enjoyed public speaking, even when the crowd was small and consisted solely of colleagues and friends.

"As predicted, we've found very little in the way of trace evidence. Due to the age of the body, as you can imagine, any prints or drag marks are long gone. We deconstructed the grassed area in a radius around the wall cavity to see if any items might be found underneath the first couple of layers of grass and soil. We're analysing the soil to see if there's a DNA match so that we can locate the site where she was killed."

"What about inside the wall cavity?"

"There were no identifying markers on the body, other than a silver bracelet and the remains of the clothing she was wearing at the time she died. The clothes have deteriorated to the extent that we can only presume they were made from an organic fabric, cotton probably. We're running the tests for prints and DNA—the lab boys are looking into it now—but it'll be another twenty-four hours before we'll have something more definitive."

Ryan nodded his thanks. "That's good, fast work. Let's look into the origins of that bracelet—Phillips, check the file or call her family to see if they reported any articles of jewellery missing. Maybe check with her old university housemate, too. It would be good to know if any of them recognise it or could tell us who gave it to Amy. Failing that, let's look at the jewellery shops. In the meantime, I've got another spanner to throw into the works."

That recaptured the attention of the room.

"Amy Llewellyn is already known to the department," he said, keeping his voice carefully neutral. "She went missing on 21st June 2005 and it was reported the following day. Phillips will be going over her case file, but the basics are these: Amy was a medical student in her third year at Newcastle University, from a solid family background. She left the house she shared with another girl, without telling anyone where she was going, or who she was going to meet. Her mobile phone was never recovered. There were no financial leads, no family connection to give us cause for concern. She was twenty-one."

"There was no physical evidence and no witnesses, so the investigation went cold," Phillips added. "Amy just, sort of, 'poofed' into thin air."

"*Poofed?* Is that a technical term?" MacKenzie drawled.

"It is now," he replied haughtily. "Anyhow, the original team initially put her disappearance down to suicide, on account of the fact she hadn't been herself before she died."

"We now have something that the original investigative team *didn't* have, and that's a body. They don't call them 'silent witnesses' for nothing," Ryan put in. "But that's only the half of it. Amy was also known to us because her photograph was found amongst a collection recovered from Keir Edwards' home, after his arrest last year."

Instantly, an awkward silence descended on the room, which Ryan almost found funny. He could see the doubt in their minds and read the questions on their faces. Was he able to look at this dispassionately? Could he separate his own feelings on The Hacker, from the facts of this case?

He hoped so.

"You're looking at Edwards? He confessed to five murders," MacKenzie said, breaking the uneasy silence. "He was quite chatty about his exploits in general. Wouldn't he have owned up to it, if he had killed her?"

"Aye, it's worth remembering that he's always been full of himself," Phillips agreed. "Nothing he loves more than bragging about what a loony he is."

MacKenzie's lips broke into a smile, against her better judgement.

"It doesn't seem like his style, to hide her away all these years, rather than displaying her for everyone to see his handiwork."

Ryan had thought of that. "I agree that it isn't his usual style, but we've known others who changed their MO to avoid capture." He leaned back against the desk at the front of the room and reached for his cup of lukewarm coffee. "It's also relevant that Amy died back in 2005. Ten years can make a big difference to a budding serial killer. Who's to say that she wasn't one of his earlier efforts? Back then he was a young doctor, working in the hospital where she was a student. Their paths would have crossed—obviously *did* cross, for him to have such an intimate photograph."

"Edwards dismembered his victims…" Phillips spoke without thinking and wished he could claw back the words. As if his SIO could ever forget how Edwards preferred to kill, having been an unwilling witness to it, first hand. "Ah, that is, I mean to say that Amy Llewellyn died in a different way to his other victims."

Ryan deliberately blocked the image of Natalie and looked into the bottom of his cup while he did.

When he looked up again, his eyes were a flat, stormy grey.

"Full marks," he said. "The style is, as you say, completely different. But we're still left with the simple fact that he had a picture of her in his house. We don't know enough about what lies in his past. He might have been killing for years before he had his summer spree last year."

The prospect of that was terrifying.

"We cover every eventuality and we follow all leads. That's why I've asked Freeman to oversee a wider survey of the surrounding area at Sycamore Gap."

"You reckon there might be more out there?" Phillips asked.

"It's possible."

"What do you need?" The quiet words spoken by Faulkner signified to Ryan that he had his full co-operation and that of his team of CSIs. There might be hard times to come, but they would do their jobs. He was stupidly grateful, and it made his voice gruff when he answered.

"Professor Freeman's team of archaeologists will start the geophysical prospecting first thing tomorrow," Ryan began, holding up a finger to stem the inevitable question from Phillips. "Never mind what that means. As far as we're concerned, it will answer the question of whether there are any other missing women lying out there in the wall, or around it. I've instructed her to cover a radius of half a mile, in both directions, from the excavation site."

"How long will that take?"

"We're looking at weeks, with a full team of archaeologists on board, working full pelt."

"Expensive," MacKenzie commented.

"Necessary," he countered.

"Another question," MacKenzie said, holding up a slender finger topped with bright red polish. "I was under the impression that this *professor* was the leading lady of all things old and decrepit."

Ryan stuck his tongue in his cheek to stop the chuckle. Phillips rolled his eyes.

"What's your question?"

"Well, that being the case, how come nobody noticed that the wall had been tampered with?"

Damn good question, Ryan thought. "Well, it's quite a long wall to keep track of," he said fairly. "But you're right. Unfortunately, thanks to the efforts of our amateur archaeologist Colin, we aren't able to see what the stones looked like in situ before he loosened them."

"In her report, Freeman says that there wasn't any cement residue on the stones, or anything like that," Phillips chimed in, leafing through the papers. "She seems to think that some of the inner stones were removed to create space for the body and the outer stones returned to their exact former positions so that nobody would notice the difference. She's adamant that they would have noticed any obvious changes on that part of the wall considering its popularity with hikers and tourists."

"Maybe she doesn't want to admit that somebody cocked up," MacKenzie retorted.

"Now, now, children," Ryan said lightly. "That's interesting, because it suggests that whoever we are looking for was organised. He killed her up there and was then able to remove and replace the stones so that they weren't noticeably different. I have to assume that he managed all of this under the cover of darkness, or near darkness, to avoid being seen."

"Even in the early hours, the place isn't overrun with visitors."

"Right. Let's widen that slightly to darkness, twilight or early hours of the morning."

"He also has an eye for detail," Faulkner put in. "To remember the exact placement of the stones. Either that, or he knew that spot really well."

Ryan nodded. All of the precision and planning reminded him of Edwards.

"So," he said, as he leaned back against the edge of his desk and crossed his ankles, "the excavation work will continue. Faulkner, I want you and your team on standby to work on any other sites that crop up."

He turned to MacKenzie. "Denise, I need you to oversee the archaeological work from tomorrow."

MacKenzie's eyes heated. "I'd rather not—"

"It's not a question of what you would *rather*." Ryan overrode the objection, his voice like granite. "Whatever personal view you take, I need you to get past it and stay professional. Understood?"

"Yes, sir."

"I need your diplomacy on this one." Ryan softened, marginally. "I want someone I can trust not to let Freeman run amok and, right at this moment, I can think of nobody better than you."

Considerably more cheerful at the prospect of handling the oversight of Freeman and her team of boffins, MacKenzie smiled broadly.

"Leave it to me."

"Phillips," he said, turning to his sergeant, "I want you to look into Amy's file, alongside like crimes."

"We looked into them fully, last year," Phillips was bound to say.

"Then look again, with fresh eyes."

"Aye, I'll make a start."

When the team began to file out, Ryan gestured Phillips to one side.

"While you're at it, I want you to put the wheels in motion to set up an interview with Edwards. Keep it under your hat."

Phillips grunted.

"You're a man of few words, Frank. I've always liked that about you."

CHAPTER 5

It was after nine by the time Ryan finally let himself into Anna's cottage. It was conveniently located in the centre of Durham, not too far from the history faculty where she lectured and only a short drive from Newcastle-upon-Tyne. The place was barely large enough to house one person, never mind two. Quaint, it may be, but practical, it was not.

Wary of the low wooden beams as he entered the tiny living room, he ducked his head at the appropriate times and slung his jacket over the back of the sofa as he passed through. The jacket still smelled faintly of lemons and he would have to remember to have it dry-cleaned.

Then, with a small sigh, he immediately went back to retrieve it because he knew that sloppy housekeeping was one of Anna's major irritations in life. Apparently, he was being house-trained. Strange, how the prospect didn't bother him as much as he might have imagined.

"Anna?"

He made another pitstop in the miniscule galley kitchen, which looked like a stall in a Turkish bazaar; colourful copper pots hung from hooks on the ceiling and green plants flourished on the window ledges. Ornamental bric-a-brac serving plates adorned the antique shelves on the only wall not fitted with kitchen units, and the scent of some kind of roasted meat filled the air. He nabbed an apple in the meantime and expanded his search to the first floor.

He found her in the smallest bedroom, which she had converted into a well-equipped study. Top-of-the-range technology met old-world charm in her little sanctuary and he thought, as he often did, about whether he would ever be able to entice her away from her hobbit hole into his more spacious penthouse apartment on Newcastle's bustling quayside.

He paused in the doorway and tried to picture her there with all her books and the trinkets she seemed to like to collect from her travels. Somehow, it didn't fit.

Sensing him, she spun around in her desk chair and smiled. "You've had a long day," she said simply, scrutinising his tired face.

He couldn't have explained why the acknowledgement moved him. It was there in her eyes: warmth, compassion and an understanding that he needed his work, as she needed hers.

"Yeah, things got complicated."

He leaned his tall frame awkwardly against the architrave and Anna smiled. The house was much too small for him. Watching him stalk around it was like watching a large panther scaling the perimeter of its cage. Yet, his home had no *character*. On the occasions she had visited the large, airy apartment in a prime spot overlooking the River Tyne, she had admired it in much the same way she would view an expensive show home. Very nice, but not for her.

Besides, the place held unhappy memories. She wondered how he could ever stand to be in the apartment where his sister had died. Her ghost was everywhere.

She wondered what they were going to do about it, but filed the thought away for now.

"Hungry?"

"Depends what's on offer," he said, favouring her with one of those show-stopping smiles he reserved only for her.

"Roast beef, for starters," she replied primly, saving her work with a brief click of the mouse before rising to meet his kiss. Slow, melting, but with just a thread of discord.

"Something on your mind?"

He tugged playfully at the long tail of dark hair she'd bundled at the back of her head and rubbed a small speck of blue biro from the tip of her ear. Lord only knew how it got there.

"Read me like a book, don't you?" he murmured.

She just smiled.

"Dinner," he said, taking her hand. "I need to spend thirty minutes being normal. Then we can talk about murder."

They worked their way through the roast beef and half a bottle of a fairly decent Malbec. Ryan took an extra few minutes to clear their plates and set the dishwasher humming before he joined her in the sitting room. Nina Simone was turned down low on the stereo and he found that, for once, there was some music they could agree on.

He settled beside her on the sofa and took her hand, rubbing his thumb across the softness of her palm.

"A body was found inside Hadrian's Wall," he began.

As he had anticipated, she could barely contain her excitement. She turned to him with shining brown eyes.

"Inside the wall? I was under the impression they had scanned it years ago. It was strictly forbidden, in Roman times, to bury the dead around built-up areas. But, if you've found a body, perhaps I'm wrong …" Her brow furrowed.

"No," he said, squeezing her fingers. "I don't mean that we found the body of an old Roman soldier in there. The remains are female and roughly ten years old."

"Oh."

"Yes, quite." He blew out a breath. "She was only twenty-one when she died. And she died badly."

"I'm sorry," Anna said quietly. "Do you know who she was?"

"Yes. Her name was Amy Llewellyn."

Ryan knew that he could speak of such things to Anna. She had seen, close up, the ravages of a murder investigation only six months earlier. She had been an unacknowledged member of his team while she had grieved for the loss of her sister—and had been hunted herself. She was a survivor.

"It's better that she was found. It's better for her family to have the answers."

Ryan exchanged another look with her, which she read correctly.

"What else haven't you told me?"

He rubbed a tired hand over the back of his neck, then looked at her again. His eyes were a turbulent grey, like the North Sea. She remembered being frightened of those waters as a child, because they often appeared peaceful but were also unpredictable.

"She was on the database of missing persons, although since last year we've been pretty certain that she would be found dead, if she was found at all," he said frankly. "A photograph of her was amongst Edwards' possessions, recovered after his arrest."

Anna recognised the tone that had crept into Ryan's voice and knew instantly who he was referring to.

"The man who killed your sister?"

"Exactly."

They sat quietly, letting the music flow and comfort them both.

"It might not be," she said hopefully. "He could have had a relationship with her, but nothing more."

"That's what Phillips said. I'm more realistic."

She sighed. It was no use trying to debate the subject when she wasn't in possession of all the facts and, besides, she hadn't been there to witness the damage up close, as he had been.

"You'll want to continue running the investigation," was all she said.

"It's a question of whether Gregson will allow it," Ryan corrected. "He's lassoed me into seeing the departmental psychiatrist as some sort of box-ticking exercise, but that's because he doesn't really think that Edwards will own up to it, or that we'll find enough evidence to pin him with it. If Gregson really thought this case would lead us back along that route, he wouldn't be letting me anywhere near it."

"Bias? Protocol?"

"Yeah, all of that," he said, taking a sip of his wine. "Looks bad, from whichever angle."

"But?" She waited.

"I *know* the man," Ryan said, his voice suddenly hard. "He's England's answer to Ted Bundy. Edwards is charming, educated and intelligent. He exploited all three of those traits, not just to lure his victims but to mask what lies beneath. Because, underneath the well-dressed doctor, there was a rampant psychopath, a seething, wretched, animalistic mass that briefly passed for human."

Anna could say nothing. Her throat was too tight.

"Do you know what's funny?"

Again, she said nothing. The question was rhetorical, in any case.

"At first glance, you could have lined the two of us up and you would struggle to find the differences between him and me. We're both from the south of England. We both attended highly academic schools and played rugby. We went to red brick universities, for God's sake."

Ryan looked away, his spine ramrod straight.

"I've seen the press pictures of Keir Edwards," she said, calmly. "I know that he's tall and dark, like you—and he might have come from a similar background. But that's where the similarity ends. I couldn't say whether he had charisma, but I suppose he cultivated some sort of specious charm so that he could draw people into his web. You don't play people like that, Ryan. If anything, you can be an offhand, miserable sort of git when you want to be."

It took him a moment, but then he couldn't suppress the laugh that welled up. Leave it to Anna to keep his feet firmly on the ground. He turned to her with a wicked grin.

"Are you trying to say that I'm…impolite?"

Now she laughed.

"Let's just say that you don't suffer fools gladly," she qualified. "Besides, I think I would have recognised by now if you were a raging nutter."

"True," he mused. "Very true. But they *do* exist. We know that better than most."

She had to agree with him there.

"If you manage to keep hold of this investigation, it might be … difficult."

He had thought of that. "Anna, if you want me to pass this over, I will."

She looked down at their joined hands and smiled. "I know that you would, but I *also* know that it would eat away at you, having to watch from the sidelines."

He said nothing. She was right, after all.

"I just want us both to be prepared for what might come," she added. "It's always painful to rake up the past, and you have to be careful not to let it influence your decisions in the present."

He turned and kissed her, very gently. "I love you."

"Ditto."

There was another long pause while the playlist switched to Dusty Springfield.

"Here's a question," Anna said. "Why hide the body in the wall, at that particular spot? It's quite memorable, isn't it? Do you think her killer attached some sort of meaning to it?"

Ryan crushed her against him for an unexpected kiss before releasing her again.

"What was that for?"

"You'd have made a good detective."

News travels fast in certain circles. The man replaced his telephone receiver and the room fell silent. With an economy of movement, he re-crossed his legs and reached for the crystal tumbler on the antique side table beside him. Floor lights cast shadows here and there; large, leafy plants accented the space and tasteful landscapes adorned the magnolia walls. Each item had been chosen and positioned with care and an eye for the aesthetic.

He liked beautiful things.

As the alcohol warmed his tongue and shot through his oesophagus down to his belly, he allowed himself to open the door to memories. He could admit to a certain measure of unease when he had first heard about the discovery, but that had passed quickly enough. Now, he settled back against the cognac-coloured leather and consciously relaxed his body and mind, enjoying the remembrance. Excitement surged through his loins, as he thought of that first time.

The first time was always the sweetest.

All these years, he had basked in the knowledge that Amy would, forever, be his. Only *he* had known her final resting place—only *he* had known the exquisite, omnipotent pleasure of having taken her life.

Now that she had been found, another man would be credited with her death. He should be thankful that nobody even suspected his involvement. He should be grateful that he could continue, happily enjoying his life's work without fear of exposure.

Yet his fingers trembled on the heavy glass at his side with growing rage.

Edwards *dared* to try to take what was rightfully his? *Again?*

He could not allow that to happen.

After night had fallen on the longest day of the year, those from the island and from the mainland met on consecrated ground beneath a star-studded sky. The High Priest cast his sword high above his head and called to the Master, while his circle of followers fell on bended knee to celebrate the summer solstice.

The High Priest watched them dispassionately, understanding that not all of them truly believed. Yet all of them appreciated the rewards of loyalty, which they had each earned in one way or another.

He recognised Jane Freeman, naked but for the long black cloak and animal mask which covered her face and half of her bright blonde hair. She had been an early convert, all those years ago, when another High Priest had presided over their circle. Hers had been a necessary conversion, following her accidental discovery of things that were not for the public domain. He had to respect her obstinacy in making her demands; he might have done the same himself.

But there could be only *one* High Priest, a position he presently occupied and intended to continue occupying for many years to come. He would brook no opposition to his authority and there would be no mutiny.

He had made examples of others before and would not hesitate to do so again.

After the small crowd scattered back to their cars, three remained, dressed once again in their ordinary clothes.

"Why are you allowing him to remain in charge of the investigation?" The High Priest snapped out the question which was in the forefront of his mind, causing him the most unease.

Gregson spread his hands in supplication. "If I give him enough rope, he'll hang himself. He believes there's a connection between Amy Llewellyn and Edwards."

"You've said this before." They thought back to winter on Holy Island, when Ryan's competency to conduct the investigation into three murders had been in doubt. They thought he would fold then, but instead their former High Priest now slumbered in a maximum-security psychiatric ward as penance for his conceit.

"This time, I think it's inevitable." Gregson was quick to reassure him. "He will ask to interview Edwards, I'll make a show of trying to stop him, but he'll go and be faced again with the man he's desperate to kill."

"I suppose that we do have the resources to manage the situation ..." The High Priest considered the men and women in various guises around the county. "He'll be running like a hamster on a wheel."

"The only conclusions he will draw are the ones we want him to draw," Gregson said with a confidence he didn't entirely feel.

"Make sure that he does," came the quiet reply. "I will also take certain measures to ensure that he is distracted."

The third member of the group listened to the conversation with interest.

"He might make for a useful addition to our circle," she mused.

The High Priest turned on her. "Whom we choose to take into our fold is exclusively *my* decision to make."

Freeman smiled a wide, cat-like smile. How the man had succumbed to the power of his position, she thought. It wouldn't be long, now, before she could contest it.

"Of course," she said meekly. "I merely thought that his personality might be suited to it."

Gregson snorted derisively.

"I hear that Lowerson is awake." The High Priest moved onto the next pressing matter. "That gives me sleepless nights, Arthur."

"He has no memory of what happened."

"How can you be sure?"

"I've had eyes and ears on him, ever since he went into hospital. He hasn't so much as breathed a word of anything which might give us cause for concern."

"Yet."

Gregson sighed. He could sense the direction that the conversation was taking. "What do you want me to do?"

There was a rustle from somewhere in the grass and the three fell silent, their ears straining for any further sound to indicate the presence of a fourth person.

"We cannot afford any slip-ups, not so soon after the events on Holy Island." The High Priest considered the possibilities. "In which case, it's better to be safe than sorry."

Gregson felt some measure of sadness when he thought of the young detective constable who lay in a hospital bed miles away. Still, who was he to argue with the wishes of his Master?

"It can only be done when the timing is right," he said. "Too many accidents or missing persons will draw unwanted attention. Ryan isn't a fool—he may already suspect something amiss in the department. But, as soon as an opportune moment arises, I'll see to it."

Their resolution made, they bade each other farewell and turned their minds to the future.

Claire Burns had missed the last sodding bus. Her feet were aching in the four-inch heels, which were a necessary part of her uniform as an American-style waitress at the new All-American Diner in Newcastle. Even on a Sunday night, there had been a busy crowd. Maybe because it was summer, she thought. People never realised how late it was getting until they suddenly looked up from their root floats or alcohol-laced milkshakes. The Diner was the latest venture from a group of dubious entrepreneurs who had colonised Newcastle with rebranded and refreshed bars and clubs which could take people seamlessly from day through to night.

She hated it.

Claire wanted to be a nurse. She had planned for it, studied hard at school, and spent hours as a volunteer in respite and nursing homes from the age of fifteen, in the hope of securing a place on the Nursing degree course at Newcastle University. You needed a degree, these days, not just a diploma. The diploma might have been affordable, but now that she needed to do the full degree, even with a student loan she just couldn't manage it. Not when her family needed all the help they could get, after her dad had been made redundant. They had been forced to move away to the Isle of Man to stay with her grandparents, to take whatever work they could find. Still, she was determined not to give up. For the past three years, she had deferred her place on the course to earn money the best way she could, squirreling away as much as possible.

That was how she found herself waitressing six days a week and most nights too. She rented a room in one of the old Victorian terraces in the part of Newcastle known as Jesmond. It was popular with students because of its close proximity to the centre of town and the university, as well as the nightlife. She liked being amongst them—it reminded her of what she was working towards.

Tonight, she was struggling to keep that goal in mind. The warmth of the day had given way to a cold breeze as the sun dipped in the sky and she was exhausted after nine hours on her feet. Her skin felt sweaty from the hot air in the kitchen, her dark hair was greasy, and her muscles protested with every step she took.

Missing the bus wasn't a disaster, she told herself—but it wasn't ideal. The Metro closed early on a Sunday evening and she couldn't justify the expense of a taxi when the walk home would only take fifteen minutes, so she might as well suck it up and carry on. Maybe she should have accepted a lift, but…well, she didn't want to face the inevitable attention from her boss.

So, she had two choices: either take a circuitous route home, along well-lit roads, or take a short-cut skirting around the edge of the Town Moor, the large area of common parkland which lay in the centre of the city.

She warred with herself and wished that she had remembered to bring flat shoes.

She was so tired.

The moor beckoned.

CHAPTER 6

Monday, 22nd June 2015

"I don't believe this."

Ryan stood with his feet planted slightly apart and his arms folded while he stared at the television screen.

"Problem?" Anna listened while she collected her house keys and scooped up her leather satchel, a half-eaten slice of toast clamped between her lips as she hurried around the house.

"Look," he said, still staring at the television, which cheerfully blared out the local morning news. Anna stopped beside him and watched a journalist interview an attractive blonde woman standing outside the visitor centre at Housesteads Fort. It didn't take much to figure out what had happened.

Anna studied the woman on the screen. "That's Jane Freeman."

"You know her?"

"The world of academic history is a small one."

"What do you think of her?"

It was a big mental leap for him, Anna knew, to seek help from another person. For, in Ryan's mind at least, to ask for help was to make himself vulnerable.

She cocked her head while she watched Freeman schmooze with the journalist.

"I knew Jane when she was finishing her doctorate in Durham. She was older than the average—and I don't say that to be snide—simply that I think she did her first degree in something fairly scientific elsewhere, then followed it up with archaeology at Durham. I only knew her for a couple of terms, while she was tutoring."

"What did she teach?"

"Let me see…" Anna thought back, to nearly ten years ago. "I would have been eighteen or nineteen, in the first year of my degree. Methodologies!" she remembered suddenly. "She taught a class called 'Methods', which gave you an overview of several approaches to looking at historical texts. She taught the class to first year undergraduates while she studied towards her doctorate."

She glanced across and saw that a fixed, glazed expression was beginning to form on Ryan's strong face.

"Anyway," she said, gesturing with the toast, "I remember her being competent, but I have to say that physically, she looked very different ten years ago."

"Oh yeah?"

"She was very…well, I guess you would say she was quite mousy back then. Not really somebody that you would pick out of a crowd."

One dark eyebrow flicked up as Ryan digested that snippet of information. Professor Freeman had definitely undergone some sort of overhaul in the intervening years, if her current image was anything to go by. Now, the world would see a polished, sleek woman with an expert dye job and good bones.

"I wonder what prompted the makeover," he murmured.

Anna shrugged and finished the last of her toast. "Could be nothing more than the simple fact that she fancied a change. On the other hand, she was always submitting papers, constantly researching and looking for the next opportunity to progress in her field. She was a competent teacher, but I don't think her heart was ever really in it. She struck me as quietly determined and very ambitious."

"Had her goals in mind and went for them in her own quiet way until she decided to go for the 'big reveal'?"

Anna laughed.

"Yes, something like that. She's done well for herself, to rise so high in a relatively short timescale." Anna reflected briefly on her own career path and found herself content with exactly where she was.

"Have you had any other dealings with her?"

"No, not really. She crossed over to archaeology quickly, so I had very little interaction with her after that. I know that to the layman 'history' is 'history', but there *are* different fields of study." She struggled to think back, with half an eye on the time. She was now running very late. "Look, why don't you leave it with me? I'll have a think and see if I can remember anything else about her."

"Thanks," he said, and pulled her in for a farewell kiss, then watched her run out of the front door.

Looking back at the screen, he pinched the bridge of his nose with thumb and forefinger as he watched the end of the interview.

"Naturally, the police have deferred to our team of experts to assist them in the excavation of the site where the body of Amy Llewellyn was found."

Nicely done, he acknowledged. Professor Freeman had managed to make his team of experienced detectives sound like a bunch of amateurs whilst simultaneously claiming oversight of the excavation, thereby solidifying her own sterling reputation.

He had learned a few interesting titbits about the good professor this morning, he thought, and the most important was the fact that she was an operator.

"Our hearts go out to her family. Of course, it is significant that she was found inside this ancient wall, which has been the stuff of myth and legend for thousands of years. Who knows what other secrets may be revealed, in time?"

Ryan could feel his temper rising, inch by inch. He had made it very clear that any media communication would be handled by his department. As the Senior Investigating Officer, it was for him to decide what information should be divulged to the general public and he was never in favour of the kind of sensationalist commentary that Professor Freeman seemed happy to dole out to the press.

He felt his mobile phone vibrating inside his trouser pocket and placed odds on it being either Phillips or Gregson. He glanced at the screen.

Phillips.

He slipped the phone back inside his pocket. Frank would be calling to break the good news to him—ha ha—but since he already knew about the Professor's busy-work that morning, that chat could wait until he was back in the office.

He turned to face another day.

Ryan's stride through the corridors of CID Headquarters slowed only briefly to pour some indifferent coffee into a mug emblazoned with a picture of himself and Phillips, their heads superimposed onto the bodies of Batman and Robin.

It had been a novelty Christmas present.

He carried it with him along the long, familiar corridors with their industrial-beige walls, cheap linoleum floors and faint scent of bleach, into the open-plan Incident Room that housed his team. They had done their best to cheer up the ugly décor of the conference space; there were dying ferns on the windowsills and framed photographs of family on a few of the desks. In a surprising move, he had softened the starkness of his own desk by the addition of a small, silver-framed portrait of Anna and him, taken on a trip to his parents' home on the south coast. It had been a perfect day, balmy sunlight shimmering over the harbour in St Ives and his mother—ever the paparazzo—had caught their laughter as they stood looking out to sea. The memory of it softened the day job and he found himself glancing at the little frame whenever the relentlessness of murder, or rape, or some other violence threatened to engulf him.

As he muscled his way through the double swing doors, he assessed the people already sitting at their desks, which were scattered in a rough semicircle facing the large board at the front.

MacKenzie was absent, which was no surprise. She would be up at Sycamore Gap, giving the Professor a few choice words regarding her little performance on the breakfast news, then supervising further excavation with hawk-eyed concentration. He had favoured the Professor with a few expletives of his own, over the telephone on his way into the office. He wasn't entirely convinced that his authority was accepted, which was a mild irritation. It wasn't that he needed the ego boost; he needed to be sure that each and every member of his team were on the same page. Judging from the news report, Freeman must have contacted the reporters as soon as the police staff had packed up yesterday, and that kind of underhand manoeuvre didn't sit well with him. It added to the burden of their investigation, knowing that he would need to keep her on a short leash.

Phillips was tapping away on his desk computer with two forefingers. Slow but methodical, that was Frank. Sensing that he was under observation, he looked up, ventured a cheerful 'Morning!' and raised his own coffee cup in salute. Frank's choice of tie—a garish blue speckled with large red ladybirds—led Ryan safely to presume that he had managed to patch things up with MacKenzie since the previous day's mishap.

"Take it you caught the news?" Phillips bellowed across the room, uncaring of conversations carrying on around him.

Ryan grunted and took a swallow of his coffee.

"Pain in the arse," Phillips added, for good measure.

"That's putting it mildly. I doubt the victim's family will take kindly to their daughter's remains being used as a promotional tool for National Heritage."

"Aye, it's bad taste. What do you plan to do about it?"

Ryan opened his mouth to answer and then heard his desk phone begin to shrill. He weaved his way through the other desks and grabbed the receiver.

"Ryan."

"It's MacKenzie," Denise began, her lyrical accent sounding down through the wires. "I think you'll want to head up here. There's been a major development."

Ryan frowned and his eyes swung up to the clock on the wall above the door.

Eight-forty. The excavation team were due to continue prospecting from eight-thirty. What could have happened in a mere ten minutes?

"There's another body." Denise answered his unspoken question without preamble.

"Where?"

"In the wall cavity."

Ryan automatically brought the image of the wall cavity back into his mind. It had been fully excavated, the day before.

"You mean, further along?"

"No, I mean we've found another body inside the *same* cavity," MacKenzie reiterated. "And this one is as fresh as they come."

"Secure the scene, contact Pinter and Faulkner. No—I repeat—*no* leaks to the press. No access, no interviews—I want it locked down. Tell Freeman to halt excavation work because this one takes priority for the moment. I'm leaving now."

Ryan replaced the receiver slowly, his mind working overtime. Overnight, once the ground team had packed up their gear, person or persons unknown had snuck up there to make another deposit, taking advantage of the momentary lack of police presence. Was it a case of opportunism? Had somebody decided to broadcast their own foray into crime, taking advantage of the expected media interest?

Whoever it was, they moved fast.

There was one thing Ryan was forced to admit: there was no way Keir Edwards could have decamped from his snug home in the confines of HMP Frankland to kill and deposit a body, in the space of a few hours. Still, it bore his theatrical style, so Ryan took an extra couple of minutes to put a call through to his contact at the prison.

All prisoners were present and accounted for, including Edwards.

Face thunderous, he gestured to Phillips, who had been listening to the telephone exchange with interest.

"Another drive into the country, then?"

"Yeah. Bring your boots and cancel any lunch plans."

Less than an hour later, MacKenzie had taken a thorough approach to securing the scene. After making short work of dispatching Professor Freeman, she had ensured that the area remained cordoned off and had issued strict instructions that there should be no access to the press. That didn't stop local journalists swarming around the entrance to Housesteads Fort, clamouring for a soundbite in time for the lunchtime news—nor the intrepid few who had taken a circuitous route to Sycamore Gap from the other direction. That was dedication to their trade, Ryan supposed.

Luckily, police constables manned the entry points, armed with logbooks and serious faces. It was enough to deter even the most hardened hacks—for the time being. As Ryan donned his polypropylene overalls, he could see Faulkner and his team of CSIs were ready to make a start with Jeff Pinter, the pathologist, in tow. Yesterday had been all about searching for clues to the past, with most of the police contingent feeling the silent frustration of having to rely on the expertise of archaeological specialists who weren't regular members of their team. In other words, they were outsiders, to be distrusted until they proved themselves trustworthy. However, today was a chance for Faulkner to shine. With conditions overnight having been dry and clear, if there was anything to find, he would find it.

With a distinct sense of déjà vu, they made the familiar journey from Housesteads Fort towards Sycamore Gap. It was another fine morning: cottony white clouds moved slowly across the blue skies overhead, pushed along by gentle winds. Only the rustle of their overalls broke the peaceful hush as they made ready to inspect the wall.

As before, they descended into the valley. Almost immediately, the scent of death, which had been noticeably absent the day before, assaulted their nostrils. Only mild, but definitely there. Ryan felt an uncomfortable clutch in the pit of his stomach.

Moving closer, being careful to leave a few metres between themselves and the wall cavity, they rounded the corner. A few early-hatched maggots had begun to feast on what had formerly been a woman with long dark hair, but now was mere body parts stuffed inside a makeshift tomb. Ryan forced himself to observe and to look upon the waste with dispassion.

God, it was hard.

Like a series of shuttered photographs, which his mind would later recall as nightmares, he took in the scene. The body parts were all an ashen, waxy shade of pale grey, which—together with the fact that there was little blood to be seen around the wall cavity—indicated that she had bled out elsewhere before being transported. Experience told him that the millions of bacteria that lived on inside the body long after it had died had begun the process of putrefaction. This caused the scent of methane and sulphide that carried faintly on the air.

Looking beyond the decay, he noticed that the dissection lines were clean and precise.

If he had been a religious man, Ryan might have said a prayer. Instead, he made a silent promise to find the person responsible. He was inclined to think it was a more productive outlet for his grief, for that was what he felt.

The sound of Faulkner's suit rustling as he moved around taking photographs of the area brought him out of his reverie.

"Initial thoughts?"

Tom blew out a long breath and took another survey, though he too had committed much of it to memory.

"Might be able to pick up something, but the ground was dry last night. No juicy mud for us to capture a boot print, if that's what you're thinking. Jeff should have a lot more to work with on the body since the tissues are still there," he said, looking across at the pathologist, who was crouched near the cavity, mask covering his face, hairnet protecting his hair. "There's no clothing on this one and zero in the way of personal possessions, which is disappointing. On the upside, there's white tape strapped around the body, which we might be able to trace. We'll do a fingertip search for anything else."

Ryan could see what he meant. There were no obvious tracks on the ground, and no blood spill to indicate a kill site.

"Might be something on the skin," Faulkner continued, sounding tired. His body seemed to hunch inside its white suit. "We'll look for chemicals, fibres, DNA. The usual."

"I'll leave you to it." Ryan was about to turn away, but placed a hand on Faulkner's shoulder before he left, the only thing he could think of to express solidarity, because it got to you sometimes. "Call me if you find anything."

Faulkner nodded and snapped his mask back into place.

Ryan left the CSIs to their work and re-joined Phillips at the top of the hill.

"How bad is it?"

"How long is a piece of string?" Ryan muttered, shrugging out of the overalls before dropping them into a sealed container. They would be inspected for trace evidence later. "It's bad enough. Looks like another young, dark-haired female, but this time the body has been dismembered."

Phillips pursed his lips in distaste.

"It's hard to believe she was still a person eight or nine hours ago."

"You reckon that's the timescale?"

Ryan ran a hand through his mop of black hair. "Rough estimate. Pinter will be able to give us a better idea. For that matter, give it a couple more hours and Ambrose would have a field day down there."

Phillips took his meaning straight away. Doctor Ambrose was an insect man and he held off scratching the phantom itching, which began whenever he thought of the forensic entomologist.

"Thought it'd be a bit early for maggots and all that," he muttered.

"It was warm last night ..." Ryan trailed off and looked away. Some things didn't require further explanation.

"If it weren't for that professor, blabbing about it all on the morning news—"

"No." Ryan shook his head decisively. "This girl was killed overnight, *before* the discovery of Amy's body was made public."

Phillips tugged at his ear while he tried to make sense of it all. "Word spreads, boss. You know that. Got more leaks in the department than a drippy tap."

Ryan had to admit it was an unhappy truth. Members of CID ended up having a few pints after work and blabbing about their exploits of the day to all and sundry. He had always shunned the local booze hole, on the basis that his presence might make others in his team feel uncomfortable. It was hard to relax with your boss hanging around, even after you'd clocked off.

He remembered one occasion when Gregson had invited him along to one of his wife's drinks soirees. The event could only be described as a *soiree*; it far exceeded the classification of 'informal gathering', taking into account the five-star catering, professional cocktail waiters and uniformed serving staff. For Ryan's part, his background had provided him with extensive training in the business of *soirees,* but it didn't necessarily follow that he enjoyed them. When he entertained—*if* he ever entertained friends—he was more of a barbeque and plastic cup sort of man.

It saved time on the washing up, for one thing.

In any event, the evening had been nothing more than a gigantic bore, from start to finish. As soon as it was polite to do so, he had extricated himself and caught a taxi home.

Rousing himself from his recollection, he was amazed to find that his disdain for the Gregsons' invitation had apparently conjured up the man himself, for the Chief was at that very moment battling his way through the pack of journalists at the car park barrier.

"It was only a matter of time," Phillips thought aloud, unconsciously straightening his tie.

Gregson cut a debonair figure as he promenaded across the car park, his dress suit spotless and his steel grey hair brushed back from a strong face, which bore a pleasingly grim expression for the benefit of any photographers who happened to be observing his progress.

"Boys," he greeted them with his usual baritone. "I hear there's been another one. I want a progress report."

"Pinter and Faulkner are working over the scene. They'll transport the body back to the mortuary shortly."

"Female?"

"That's correct, sir. Twenty-something, mixed race, dark-haired. She was found dismembered."

Gregson harrumphed. He was the only person Ryan had ever known to make a noise that could be described as such.

"Who was first on the scene?"

"That was MacKenzie. She was here early, to oversee the work of the archaeologists."

"Yes, Professor Freeman tells me she was dismissed from the scene in a very high-handed manner."

"Yes, sir," Ryan replied easily, without a hint of apology.

"Freeman seems to think she has a right to be here."

"She can think what she likes," Ryan countered. "CID have been granted oversight because this is a double-murder investigation, not an archaeological dig. Her presence here yesterday was much appreciated, but there are other forensic archaeologists we can use if she finds my management style clashes with her own."

"Playing hard ball?"

"It's the only way."

Gregson's eyes narrowed a fraction at Ryan's newfound defiance and he wondered whether it might be time to burn the man's ego a fraction. Phillips cleared his throat and looked between them.

"Perhaps we should give those vultures something, so that they'll back off a bit and let us get on?"

At Phillips' well-timed intervention, they all turned to look across at the group of reporters who waited with mounting impatience for a press statement.

"I'd rather we took control of PR. So far, you've allowed Freeman to run rings around the department," Gregson said, pointedly. "Why don't you do the honours?"

Ryan recognised the challenge for what it was: a test to see if he could deflect the inevitable questions surrounding Amy's connection with The Hacker. When her image had been discovered among his possessions last year, they had done their best to keep her name out of the limelight, but as Phillips had rightly observed, there were always departmental leaks. Any journalist with half a nose would have recognised her name and sniffed out the connection.

Ryan turned on his heel and made for the crowd of media affiliates. When his intent became clear, they parted like the Red Sea, giving him centre stage while they fired up their cameras and microphones.

"Good lad," Phillips muttered, under his breath.

"Thank you for taking the trouble to come all the way out here into the wilderness, I'm sure out of concern for the memory of a young girl whose life has been sadly cut short," Ryan began smoothly, with a liberal sprinkling of sarcasm.

"Can you confirm a second body has been found, only hours after the first?"

Several more voices shouted out the same question and he waited for their calls to die down before answering. He had received his public relations training alongside all the other senior police officers, but he needed no training to project an air of authority. That came naturally.

"Yes, I can confirm that a second body was discovered early this morning. Until she has been identified and her next of kin have been informed, that will be all I have to say on the subject."

He ignored the inevitable follow-up questions.

"It was reported on the morning news that the body of a girl who has been identified as Amy Llewellyn was found at Sycamore Gap yesterday. Her family have been informed and we offer them our sincere and heartfelt condolences. Northumbria CID will use all means available to bring her killer to justice."

"How did she die?"

Ryan sighed inwardly. Would they never learn?

"I am not going to divulge the specific details of an ongoing investigation. To do so might prejudice the task we have ahead."

"Amy Llewellyn went missing in 2005. How has it taken so long to find her?"

"Her disappearance was widely reported at the time," Ryan said. "There was an extensive police appeal and a thorough forensic investigation. Unfortunately, the trail went cold, as is the case with many unfortunate people on an annual basis—"

"But you knew who her killer was!" A persistent young reporter made sure that his voice carried. "Amy was named as one of The Hacker's unclaimed victims, only last year. Do you deny it?"

Fatalistically, Ryan accepted that he was not going to be offered a reprieve. It was therefore better to face the question head-on.

"Last year, there was some circumstantial evidence linking Amy Llewellyn to Keir Edwards but not enough to charge him, or anyone else for that matter. At this stage, we are concentrating our efforts on gathering the forensic evidence which may, in time, confirm or deny any connection."

"Was Amy murdered in the same way as your sister? Is it wise to continue running the investigation given your personal interest?"

Ryan's face betrayed no emotion whatsoever. To all the world, he appeared unmoved by the question, but from her office at Durham University where she watched the interview later that day, Anna knew that he buried his pain somewhere deep in the alcoves of his mind. He erected an emotional barrier around himself, one she suspected he renewed each morning, to ward off the demons he still fought at night.

"I will not be discussing any specifics. To do so would be highly improper and, speaking on the question of *propriety*, I should remind you that this is an open investigation. We are following all available leads, which calls for a Senior Investigating Officer with experience. You are all aware of my track record in the field, so I won't bother to list the cases I have closed during my years of service."

He cast his eyes over his audience, then trained his gaze directly into the television camera which had been set up squarely in front of him.

"What I will say is that, after what happened to Natalie Finlay-Ryan"—he could manage to get the words out, just so long as he didn't say, *my sister*—"there is no-one better qualified to hunt the person who has deprived another family of a daughter, or of a sister. I won't make Amy's family any promises, except these: I will follow every line of enquiry. I will knock on every door and shine a light on every shadow. I will do everything within my power to find whoever is responsible. If fortune finds that they are already serving time for another offence, then I can promise that there will be no barrier to further prosecution, because I understand that their loss is just as important. That's all."

Ryan stepped away and didn't bother to look back. That was enough wind-bagging for now.

Another man tuned in to watch the interview when it was broadcast on the local news later that morning. He admired the seemingly effortless way that Ryan managed to bury his feelings beneath a professional exterior, projecting an air of strong dependability.

Bravo! he thought, with a touch of malice.

They would see how long his emotional reserves lasted, before the end.

He listened intently to the answers Ryan gave when the question of Amy's connection to The Hacker came up and he found himself very, very dissatisfied.

In point of fact, he was furious.

How long would it take him to catch up? He knew that the police were slow, but he had given Ryan credit for being endowed with some small measure of intellect. Clearly, he had been over-generous in his assessment of the man.

For who could fail to see that only a person of the finest, most acute intelligence could have kept Amy's death hidden from the world for so long?

Oh, how he wanted to tell him how it happened. He wanted to tell the story in all its magnificent detail, to savour it and have Ryan look upon him with amazement. In his heart, he knew that Ryan was just like him. Beneath that controlled exterior, there was an animal longing to break free and do what man was designed to do.

To kill. To exert his power. It was survival of the fittest and a punishment to those who were not worthy of mating with men such as himself.

It had taken him a while to understand his purpose and to appreciate fully why he had been born—but that night ten years ago had given him the answers he craved. Since then, life had been one long dance.

Ryan's words replayed themselves over and over in his mind. Despite their kinship, he was severely disappointed in the Chief Inspector. He seemed prepared to credit Amy's murder to a man who had been *caught*, of all things.

He would never have been so careless.

CHAPTER 7

"Claire Burns, aged twenty-two," MacKenzie began, without preamble. "We saw her straight away, as soon as we made it down the hill at around eight-thirty this morning."

A large colour photograph of Claire Burns, taken from her driving licence, had been tacked up on the wall to the right of Amy Llewellyn. Casting his eye around the room, Ryan could see the men and women of CID committing her face to memory. They had convened in the Incident Room for a lunchtime briefing and Ryan even had the foresight to order in some sandwiches from the nearby deli, which his team attacked with gusto.

Clearly, he was turning soft.

"Whoever put her inside the wall cavity wasn't fussed about returning the stones back to where he found them, because they were dumped on the ground beside it. We could speculate that whoever did this *wanted* her body to be found, because she's been open to the elements for most of the night," MacKenzie continued.

"I bet Professor Freeman wasn't happy," Ryan said mildly.

"No indeed," MacKenzie replied, only just managing to rein in her glee. "She was doing her ends about the damage to the wall. I took the trouble to remind her that the damage inflicted on the *person* found *inside* the wall was a more pressing concern."

Ryan flashed a grin.

"Anyhow, after I rang you, the area was cordoned off and I contacted Doctor Pinter to examine the remains. Faulkner's team arrived around the same time, at nine-fifteen. You and Phillips arrived shortly after then."

"Out of interest, when did the press hounds turn up?"

MacKenzie consulted the logbook entries from that morning.

"Early. The first one arrived just after eight, before we'd even discovered Claire's body."

Ryan's brow furrowed. "Name?"

MacKenzie consulted the log again. "Ophelia de Lacy-Brown, from the local news."

"Are you kidding me with that name?"

Denise laughed. "I thought the same myself, sir. I hope it's a professional pseudonym."

"If it isn't, her parents should be reported," Phillips mumbled as he bit off a chunk of ham and pease pudding stottie.

"Have a word with her, MacKenzie. I want to know who tipped her off to get up there so early. The press already had their interview with Freeman last night, so why the urgency this morning? As far as they knew, we would be picking over the scene from yesterday, which is old news."

MacKenzie nodded and made a note. Watching them, Phillips felt an odd twinge of envy at the easy manner of exchange that his SIO enjoyed with Denise. In fact, with any woman between the ages of sixteen and sixty. If Ryan weren't such a decent bloke, he'd be minded to hate him for it.

"Claire was identified quickly, as well," Ryan continued. "She wasn't reported as missing until her landlady called in this morning, by which stage we'd already found her."

"The body matched the description from the landlady," MacKenzie said, nodding. "After then, it was an easy job."

"What's the word from Pinter?" The pathologist had spent the morning compiling a report on Claire Burns' remains.

"He hasn't completed the post-mortem yet, but he's sent through some observations. Other than the dismemberment, there's no obvious head trauma or other major impact, as there was with Amy," MacKenzie supplied.

Phillips replaced the flapjack he had just unwrapped. His appetite had vanished as quickly as it had come.

"Do you have any idea what sort of timescale we're looking at?"

"Taking into account ambient temperatures overnight, the condition of the body, and early stages of decomposition, he seems to think that she had been dead between eight and ten hours when she was found."

Ryan took a pen and drew a long line beneath Claire's image. He added the time she had been found and the time they thought she had died.

"Here's what we know about Claire," he said, flipping the pen from hand to hand, feet planted firmly on the thin brown carpet.

"She was an attractive girl," he noted, taking in the sleek dark hair, simply cut and pulled away from a face that was a perfect oval with smooth, caramel-toned skin and big, dark eyes. "Aside from the colour of her skin, she conforms to the same physical type as Amy, and Edwards' previous victims, for that matter."

"Next of kin?" This, from one of the constables.

"Her family moved to the Isle of Man while Claire decided to stay here. I notified her mother and father earlier." Ryan thought briefly of that difficult telephone call. "They're travelling over later today. She had some friends at the bar where she worked. We'll be speaking to them by close of play today."

"D'you reckon it's a copycat?"

"The style doesn't ring any bells with Amy's murder, except the similarities in physical type and the fact that her body was dumped in the same place. At this stage, it could easily have been some crackpot looking to make a name for himself."

Ryan thought of all the men and women who answered public appeals for information, claiming to be murderers and rapists. Often, they were sad, unwell individuals who

110

lived mundane lives. Their claims to a morbid kind of fame only hindered police investigations, wasting hours of police time. It was possible that one of them had taken their opportunity to bask in the limelight, turning fantasy into reality and picking on an unsuspecting young girl as their vessel. Had one of them tipped off the local press, to ensure the story was covered? It was worth looking into.

"Have you heard anything from Faulkner?" Phillips asked.

Ryan swallowed a bite of steak pasty and washed it down with a gulp of something fizzy and sugary before answering. He never claimed to have highbrow culinary tastes.

"He's still up at Sycamore Gap, working around the site. It'll be tomorrow at the earliest before he's able to tell us anything solid, but the basic summary is that Claire was found nude, her body cut up, no identifying features on or around her. No obvious kill site where he might have expected to find major blood spill, but they're expanding the search."

Phillips dabbed at his chin with a napkin.

"Unless it was part of this guy's 'plan', or whatever the hell you want to call it, I don't see the point in dismembering Claire's body, if she was going to head up there with him anyway."

There was a short silence while they thought it over.

"He might just enjoy it," MacKenzie said. "There's no telling what some of these wackos like to do in their spare time."

Ryan was usually the first and last to agree that it was often a waste of time trying to apply logic to the machinations of an illogical mind but, sometimes, there was a practical reason behind their actions.

"Could be for transport," he offered. "With Amy, it's fairly certain that she walked out to Sycamore Gap on her own steam and was killed there, where she was interred still in one piece. In the case of Claire Burns, we don't know yet whether she walked the distance herself, or whether she was killed elsewhere and required transporting afterwards. Much easier to transport a body in pieces than as one dead weight."

Phillips had always admired Ryan's unique skill for putting himself into the mindset of a killer, but sometimes the image was so vivid that it worried him. It was good to keep a healthy distance from the kind of mind they were seeking to find.

Ryan appointed a reader-receiver from a selection of keen young detective constables who had begun filtering into the room. They would sieve through all the paperwork that was already piling up and try to order it. He felt absurdly guilty choosing someone to fill the shoes usually worn by DC Jack Lowerson, but it couldn't be helped. He made a mental note to stop by the hospital on his way home.

"MacKenzie, I'm delegating the legwork on Claire Burns to you," he began simply. Denise sat up straighter in her seat and professional pride bloomed. Knowing that Ryan would trust her to run the investigative work into their most recent victim was a huge compliment coming from a man whose perfectionism was a bit of an urban legend around CID.

"Let's start looking at the CCTV footage. Claire was taken on her way home from work—she must have been. That means our perpetrator needed some kind of transport to get her from there to Sycamore Gap, stopping off somewhere to make the kill. There are a bunch of ANPR cameras in a ring around the city. He would have to be a lucky bugger to miss going through one of them, so let's start getting the footage."

MacKenzie made a quick note. "What sort of timescale should I ask for?"

Ryan paused to consider. "The place where she works closes at ten-thirty on a Sunday. Factor in some clearing up and you're looking at her leaving work any time after eleven."

He started to say something else, then considered the geography of the city. "He will have headed out west, most likely, because it's the most direct route. Going along the A69 would be quicker, so check the footage there first. On the other hand, if he took the B6318 his journey would have been more scenic, it would have taken longer, but there are fewer cameras."

MacKenzie sighed.

"Let's hope he didn't put that much thought into his route."

Ryan said nothing. They all knew that a person who was able to kill and transport a body with the kind of attention to detail that they had seen, would be the same kind of person to consider CCTV cameras.

"Bollocks."

The room turned to Phillips, whose statement captured what they were all thinking.

Ryan moved back to the board and gestured towards the picture of Amy Llewellyn. "Let's catch up on our progress with Amy. I don't want any of us losing sight of the fact that both girls are equally important and should be treated as such." He could not forget Rose Llewellyn's misery the previous day. She deserved some answers. "Claire's body will demand much of the forensic effort, given how recently she died, but in all else I want to see a strong effort on both lines of enquiry."

There were nods of agreement around the room.

Phillips had taken over the bulk of the work digging into Amy Llewellyn's background and cold case file, alongside looking into the missing persons reports relating to any similar women who had gone missing over the past few years. Ryan concentrated his attention on the forensic evidence found on Amy's person.

"I didn't know that you could do a tox report on a set of bones?" Phillips was always the curious one in the class.

"The technicians look at the hair. It's one of the few parts of the body that remains stable, even after a long period of time. It can also tell us a lot of interesting things about her diet and what was swimming around in her system, because it grows at a rate of around one centimetre per month, so we can compare her system, month-on-month."

"So, you can see if she was drinking or doing drugs or whatever?"

"Yep," Ryan agreed, picking up the printed copy of Doctor Pinter's summary. "In this case, Amy lived a healthy life with a balanced diet and, judging from the older portion of her hair, there were no unusual chemical substances. However, more recent growth indicated a different chemical balance. Poor diet alongside an altered chemical composition for approximately three to five months prior to her death, Pinter says."

Ryan considered the new information and thought of the statements taken from the Llewellyn family around the time Amy went missing.

"Her family said that she became withdrawn and that this seriously affected her health and disposition. There was some suggestion of mental health issues."

"You mean she was a bit down in the dumps?" Phillips asked.

"Thank you, Frank, for distilling an entire field of psychological disorder into one handy catchphrase," Ryan drawled.

"Always happy to help. When you say there was a 'different chemical balance', what do you mean by that? In layman's terms," Phillips emphasized.

"Pinter seems to think we're looking at artificially increased levels of phthalates. That says to me that she was on some kind of SSRI-based antidepressant."

"What the hell is a fart-late?" Phillips could feel a headache coming on.

"A 'phthalate' is a group of chemicals which are produced when certain drugs metabolise in the body. Usually, they find it when someone has ingested one of a group of antidepressant drugs known as 'selective serotonin reuptake inhibitors.'"

"You could have said that in the first place," Phillips grumbled. "But I guess the point here is that if she was on antidepressants, that's consistent with what her family said about her being unhappy. Only thing is, there's nothing about it in the medical history we've got from her doctor."

Interesting, Ryan thought.

"Phillips, see if you can double check those records from her GP to make sure that there wasn't an administrative oversight. Failing that, see if there's a record of her picking up a prescription at any of the local pharmacies. There probably won't be anything, given the length of time, but it's worth a shot."

"Her mother's a pharmacist," Phillips offered. "But she categorically denies dishing out any drugs to her daughter. The records at the pharmacy where she used to work support her story."

"Amy might have been depressed, but that isn't how she died." MacKenzie brought the discussion neatly back around and Ryan nodded his approval.

"Pinter confirms that Amy would almost certainly have died following one or more hard blows to the side of her skull. We're looking at a hard, blunt object—or impact with something flat and solid."

"She didn't just fall and crack her head on something?" Phillips popped a stick of nicotine gum in his mouth.

"Sometimes happens," Ryan agreed. "But that goes against Pinter's opinion that she suffered multiple blows."

"Poor lass," Phillips said gruffly. MacKenzie walked her fingers across the space between them and squeezed his hand. Catching it, Ryan raised a single black eyebrow and she snatched her fingers back again.

"Faulkner has come up trumps," Ryan said, picking up another printed report and re-reading it while he paced the room. "His technicians were able to extract several samples of skin cells which had imprinted on the underside of Amy's bracelet. While it remained attached to her wrist, it was largely preserved while the body decomposed around it."

"I'm surprised there was anything to extract at all," Phillips said.

"Low copy number DNA profiling," Ryan explained. "They can pick up even the tiniest samples. In this case, just a few skin cells."

"Bet her killer never thought of that," Phillips said.

"I can only hope he's quaking in his murderous boots," Ryan replied, without looking up.

"Faulkner has found a total of three separate DNA samples on the bracelet and on Amy's clothing fibres. One of these samples is a match to Amy Llewellyn's own DNA."

"What about the other two?"

"There are a further two male samples. No matches found on the database."

Ryan was disappointed at the outcome, because it seemed the evidence was not in support of it being Keir Edwards' handiwork. His DNA was very firmly on record, yet there was no match with the samples found on Amy Llewellyn. It wasn't *absolutely* conclusive, but it certainly didn't support his working theory. He wasn't in the habit of swallowing humble pie and it slid down his throat with difficulty.

"That's still great work, despite the fact we couldn't find further matches on the system. 'Every contact leaves a trace', or so they say."

"Any idea where the bracelet came from?" MacKenzie asked.

"I showed a picture of it to Amy's family," Phillips said. "They don't recognise it."

"So, that's something to look at. Once Faulkner has finished with it, I want you to find out where it came from. Does the father check out?"

Phillips nodded. "I'll get around to talking to him again, but so far, both parents are clean. They had dinner, then stayed in the house all night when Amy went missing."

"Blood runs thicker than water," Ryan commented, thinking that family members often corroborated each other's alibis.

"It does," Phillips agreed, "but we've got no hard evidence against either of them."

"Yet," Ryan snapped. Now, they had Amy to help them find out the clues to her death and, so thinking, he turned back to Faulkner's report.

"Faulkner's still examining the fibres, so we'll have to wait for the results." He let the papers fall back onto his desk and rolled his shoulders. Time was marching on and he could feel his team starting to get restless.

"We interviewed the victim's family this morning and the bottom line is that Amy was a clean-living girl, with a medical career ahead of her. At the time she went missing, her family were solid, too. Since then, her mother has suffered from recurrent anxiety and depression, which is understandable given the circumstances. Her father seems to have coped pretty well, all told."

"The mother—Rose Llewellyn—didn't have depression before Amy went missing?"

Ryan met MacKenzie's sharp gaze and understood where her mind had wandered.

"That's good thinking, but there's no suggestion that Rose Llewellyn suffered from depression or was prescribed any SSRI-based medication before Amy went missing."

MacKenzie shrugged.

"Phillips has been looking into like crimes. Bring us up to speed, Frank."

Phillips tore off a scrap of paper and wrapped his gum in it before speaking. "Right. Aside from the number tallied up by The Hacker last year, there are a few cases which might be worth a second glance." Phillips shuffled in his chair to ease the numbness in his rear, which was beginning to react to the hard plastic seat cover. "I had a gander at Missing Persons since 2005—locally, that is. Happens that I found a few other women who've gone missing since then."

"That's hardly surprising, Frank," Ryan felt obliged to point out.

Phillips waved away the comment with one broad hand. "Give us a minute! I was going to say, all these women who went missing are the same *type*. They were all early-twenties, slight build, dark-haired. What's more, they all went missing around June." He wiggled his brows and thumbed through his notepad to find the list he had made. "Here we are: June 20th 2006, June 21st 2008, June 21st 2009, June 18th 2011 and then June 21st 2012."

"Well," Ryan said, clapping his hands together, to wake them all up. "Call me crazy, but I think there's a pattern in there somewhere."

"You're darn tootin' there is," Phillips agreed.

"We're looking at one- or two-year gaps, if we work on the basis that these crimes are connected. Phillips, can I rely on you to carry on looking into the cold files and report back to us?"

"On it like a car bonnet, boss."

Ryan flashed a grin. He could feel renewed energy building in the room.

"Hasn't anybody noticed something else which is a bit … peculiar?" MacKenzie rose from her chair and picked up a bright marker pen, then circled the dates.

"They're all on or around 21st June."

Phillips leaned back in his chair and looked heavenward. Ryan felt his stomach plummet to the floor. The young reader-receiver asked the obvious question.

"I don't get it. Why's that date so special?"

Ryan remembered having asked the same question six months earlier, on the windy grounds of an island priory. "It's the summer solstice," he said quietly. "Neo-pagans and several other religions, including Christianity, consider the date an important one."

"Aye," Phillips said, turning to the detective constable. "But what you *really* need to know is that those loonies we caged up on Holy Island thought that the solstice was important. Now, we're wondering if there isn't somebody else out there thinking the same thing."

"Or if it's somebody else at all," Ryan muttered.

CHAPTER 8

The list of more important things that he could be doing was long and varied, Ryan thought. For starters, he could be investigating two murders, which—unless he was very much mistaken—was about to turn into an investigation of several older murders, too. When he had, with rigid calm, tried to explain this to his superior officer less than thirty minutes ago, his remonstrations had been met with a bland look and a force as strong as iron.

"We made a deal, Ryan. An appointment has been made for you. If you choose not to keep it, you will be removed from this investigation."

With almost anybody else, Ryan might have been tempted to call his bluff and blow off the appointment with the departmental psychiatrist and to hell with the consequences. But one look at Gregson's face told him that the man was serious.

That was why, instead of interviewing potential suspects, he found himself sitting awkwardly in the waiting room of the serviced office building where Doctor Patrick Donovan worked. He had been here many times before, mainly to attend what they liked to call 'psychological supervision', which all officers in his line of work were required to submit to from time to time, particularly following a difficult case. Over the years, he had seen more than his fair share. Those sessions had never bothered him greatly. They consisted of a sixty-minute chat with someone who had, much to Ryan's surprise, turned out to be a very amiable person. Patrick "Paddy" Donovan was a man very comfortable in his own slightly-sagging skin. Hair which had once been as black as Ryan's was now peppered with grey as he edged closer to fifty and there was a definite paunch beneath the linen shirt he wore, but in general he was a man unfazed by the passing years.

No, Ryan mused, he had no personal grievance with Paddy Donovan—but he did have a problem with what he represented. Voluntarily-arranged, promptly-attended sessions which came part-and-parcel with his job had morphed into strictly enforced appointments recommended by the occupational therapist attached to the Northumbria Police Constabulary. Following his sister's death, he had not been left to grieve in private. The press had hounded him, hungry for a glimpse of the detective who had failed to stop the man who killed his sister. Then, pressure had come to bear from The Powers That Be, who felt that it would be in everybody's best interests if he attended some sessions with Doctor Donovan.

You know, just to get a few things off his chest.

He could understand that the department wanted to cover its own arse. The last thing they wanted was a prominent murder detective suing them for post-traumatic stress disorder or something equally predictable.

Not that he ever would have. He considered Natalie's death to be his fault and his alone. He may not have wielded the knife, but he had allowed a dangerous man to keep killing.

There was nobody who could convince him otherwise, though they had tried.

Ryan leaned forward to rest his forearms on his knees and looked at the beige carpet. It was the same colour as the carpet tiles in the Incident Room, but managed to look a whole lot more plush. That was what a career in private practice gave you, he surmised—healthy-looking potted palm trees, a fancy coffee machine, subscription magazines on a glass coffee table, and thick-pile carpet.

Presently, the door to Paddy's office swung open and the man himself appeared in the doorway, his healthy bulk filling most of it. With a gentle arm, he ushered a young man through the door who had the mottled skin of someone who had recently been crying.

"Keep in mind what we discussed today. Drive safely and I'll see you at the same time next week."

He watched the man leave and sighed deeply before turning to his next patient with a smile that lit up his entire face.

"Maxwell!"

Ryan winced as he rose from his chair. Only a small handful of people knew his full name, Maxwell Charles Finley-Ryan, let alone called him that.

"Ryan. Just Ryan."

The other man boomed out a laugh and held both hands up. "Honest mistake!"

But his eyes twinkled with humour. If it was intended to be an icebreaker, it worked, because Ryan found himself smiling too.

He followed Paddy into his office, which was really more of a cosy sitting room. Deeply-cushioned chairs were arranged in a circular setting with a small table in the middle holding a box of tissues and a jug of water. A large window on one wall gave the room a feeling of light and space. There were built-in shelves along the length of another wall, stuffed full of books of diverse genres spanning AA Milne to Jung. For a clinical space, it was far from clinical.

Ryan took one of the offered chairs and he almost declined the water, but his system was pumped with too much caffeine and it would do him good to flush it out a bit.

"So," Paddy said, as he sat down heavily, "you don't want to be here."

Ryan just stared. Should he think of something polite to say? Honesty was usually best.

"No, I don't."

"Don't worry about my feelings, will you?" Paddy chuckled, folding his arms across his middle. "Why don't you tell me why Arthur Gregson thinks you *should* be here?"

Ryan deliberately avoided looking at his watch. "It's the investigation I'm working on," he said. "It bears some connection to the events of last year. Coming to see you is a condition of my continuing to work on it."

"So, you feel that Gregson's condition is motivated from a desire to make sure that the department is seen to be following procedure, should you make any mistakes?"

"I rarely make mistakes," Ryan said quietly. It wasn't an arrogant assertion, just a simple fact.

"We all make mistakes," Paddy replied. "It's part of being human."

"Let me rephrase, then," Ryan said, crossing one long leg over the other. "I rarely make mistakes which could bring the department under fire."

"I don't think anybody is questioning your dedication to the force."

"Aren't they? The fact I've been corralled into coming here tells a different story."

"You see this appointment as a mark of distrust in your abilities, or as a mark of disloyalty?"

Ryan lifted a shoulder.

"Could it be that Gregson simply wishes you to take advantage of the outlet, as an acknowledgement of the serious impact that your work has on your wellbeing? He cares about his staff."

Ryan let the air hiss out between his teeth. "Look, whatever the motivation, I'm here now. What the hell do you want me to talk about?"

Paddy sighed inwardly. As a person, Ryan was intriguing. He had seen him numerous times, over the years, yet he was such a hard nut to crack.

"At the risk of sounding like a cliché, it's more a question of what *you* would like to talk about."

"The weather?"

Paddy let out another booming laugh. "You're a slippery one," he said. "Let's start with something simple. How are things with Anna?"

Paddy had spoken with Ryan after the events on Holy Island last Christmas and had found a man disturbed by the things he had seen, but also a man rejuvenated. He wondered if it wasn't due in part to his attachment to the woman he had met along the way.

At the mention of her name, Ryan's shoulders relaxed.

"Things are ... really great, actually."

Somehow, the words seemed inadequate, but he wasn't in the habit of waxing lyrical about personal relationships. That was why they called them *personal*.

"She seems like a very lovely woman," Paddy agreed.

"One day, I'm sure the bubble will burst."

Paddy raised a bushy eyebrow. "What makes you say that? She's seen some of the good, the bad and the ugly, hasn't she?"

Ryan thought back to their first meeting, on Holy Island. He had been in the early stages of a fast-paced investigation and out to prove himself. He had been prickly, at best, and downright rude, at worst.

"Yeah, I guess she's seen some of the ugly."

"Well, then."

"She hasn't run for the hills."

Paddy nodded sagely. "So, all is ticking along nicely on that score. How about Phillips? Haven't seen that old hound dog in a while."

Ryan knew that Paddy had a lot in common with Frank Phillips. They were both burly, dedicated men who had made a good life for themselves from modest beginnings. Aside from that, they both enjoyed Irish whiskey and a game of chess or a round of karaoke, depending on their mood.

"Solid as a rock, as always," Ryan answered without a second thought. "He's enjoying a blossoming relationship with Denise."

"MacKenzie?" Paddy's eyebrows shot up. "Well, blow me down."

Ryan grinned. "He's done well, there."

"I'll say," Paddy agreed. Denise MacKenzie was a fine catch, whichever way you looked at it. "It seems that love is in the air."

"Yeah, seems like." There was a long pause, which Paddy did not interrupt. He knew the value of silence in drawing people out.

At length, Ryan spoke again.

"I don't know how to say this…" Ryan searched for the right words. "When you're in my business, there's a lot of the darker side of life. If you're not going over dead bodies, you're at the morgue, speaking to the victim's family, or you're talking to victims of rape, or assault, or some other kind of violence. Like I say, there's a lot of *dark* in that."

"There is," Paddy prompted.

"I worry that … without meaning to, some of that will spill over into the personal side of my life. I don't want to spoil what I have with Anna, but I don't know how to stop it."

Paddy nodded, understanding his concern.

"Let me make an observation. Anna knew this about you, when she met you. You were thrown together in highly unique circumstances and, rather than pulling you apart, it brought you together."

"Yeah, but what if that is all it was? The circumstances—a need for comfort?"

"Is that how you feel about her?"

"No." The response was immediate. "But I've worked around murder long enough to know the difference. Anna hasn't."

"You worry that you're a flash in the pan, for her?"

Ryan said nothing, but his silence spoke volumes.

"I think that, perhaps, the underlying issue here is not Anna's feelings—though I can't speak for her. Perhaps the issue is your own inability to *trust*. It would be natural to develop a certain defence mechanism, after all you have been through."

"I trust her."

"On one level, perhaps."

Ryan ran a restless hand through his hair. Damn the man for shining a light on what he would rather lay buried. "I'll talk to her."

Paddy smiled broadly. "How are you feeling about the investigation, so far?"

"How much do you know about it?"

"Only what I've heard from Gregson. The body of a young woman was found up at Sycamore Gap and you're leaning towards murder. I heard today that a second body was found this morning. Does the investigation bear some similarity to The Hacker's crimes?"

"If it does, then *my* crime was in pointing out that similarity. The moment I breathe the words 'Keir' and 'Edwards' in the same sentence, people automatically think I've gone off my chump."

Paddy roared with laughter.

"That's one I haven't heard before," he said. "Don't you think that this is all a matter of perception? From where you're sitting, you find a young girl who is known to have had some link with Keir Edwards, an association which is highly personal and a source of great pain to you, for obvious reasons. From where Gregson sits, he respects your professional opinion and therefore doesn't rule out the possibility of the connection with Edwards being relevant. But, he also has to think of your wellbeing. He wants you to remain clear-headed."

"I'm always clear-headed."

Paddy simply eyed him over the rim of his glass.

Ryan swore under his breath. "Alright, I get it. He wants to make sure I'm not confusing things that happened before with what's happening now."

"Wouldn't you agree with him?"

"Yeah, except, so far, I'm accomplishing that all on my own."

"Good," Paddy said. "I'm glad to hear it. Ryan, I don't expect you to turn up at my office ranting and raving. It's not your style. I want you to think of this room as a sounding board; an opportunity to get things off your chest and to clear out the clutter so that you go forward with a fresh outlook."

"Makes sense," Ryan had to admit. He glanced around the room while he searched his mind, considering if there was anything else he wanted to say. "To be honest, things are starting to pile up."

"How so?"

"Every time I look at the body of Amy Llewellyn, I see Edwards' fingerprints all over it. But then, I look at the rest and none of it fits. I can't understand it."

"It's hard, sometimes, to admit when we're wrong."

Ryan frowned. "It's not that. When I'm wrong, I move on to the next point. Push forward. But this is different—he had her photo in his house; she was a medical student and the timing fits when he was doing his rounds at the RVI."

"You're saying that it puts him in the vicinity? Surely, that's circumstantial."

"I know that it is. He was questioned repeatedly about those photographs last year and his story never changed—he says that they aren't his and he has no idea how they got there. There's not a cat in hell's chance of me being able to interview Keir Edwards about the same thing, without something more."

"You would want to interview him yourself?" Paddy was surprised.

"It's my case."

"Is that all?"

An unreadable look passed across Ryan's face.

"No, it's not all."

Ryan made it to the hospital in time to catch the last ten minutes of afternoon visiting hours. It was a refreshing change to walk along the plastic-coated floor of an ordinary ward, rather than the intensive care unit. Instead of the incessant 'beep' of monitors, Jack Lowerson's new ward carried the sound of quiet laughter. Here, there was positivity.

He headed to the bed at the end, where the curtains weren't drawn, signalling that it was alright to approach.

"Jack."

Lowerson didn't look unwell, Ryan thought, aside from being a bit thinner. In the six months that he had been in the hospital, the skull fracture had mended following emergency surgery. His wavy brown hair had grown back, hiding the scar that lay beneath it. His cheekbone and nose had both been broken and, after some impressive plastic surgery, the only evidence that his face had been smashed could be seen in the slight dent which leaned his nose a little to the left. Looking closely, his face was ever so slightly asymmetrical, but it was better than the alternative.

"Ryan!" The man pushed himself up into a sitting position and rested against the pillows at his back.

Almost immediately, a young nurse bustled over and plumped those pillows. With a parting smile, she bustled off again.

Ryan raised a single black eyebrow. "You might be onto a winner, there, mate."

"I wish. She's breaking my heart."

It was fantastic to be able to sit here bantering with the lad, Ryan thought. It was a miracle that Jack was alive at all, that he suffered no permanent brain damage…

Don't dwell on it.

"You're looking well."

"Thanks, every day I feel better and better."

Ryan nodded.

"Look, ah—"

"Ryan, I—"

They spoke in unison. Jack gestured for him to speak first.

"Lowerson…Jack. I never got a chance to apologise."

"There's no need—"

"There's every need," Ryan said firmly. "You're one of mine. I let you down."

Jack shook his head and looked down at his hands against the crisp white sheet.

"You told me to bring them in for questioning. I went beyond that—way beyond that. I entered a suspect's premises without any support. It was basic training and I ignored it."

Ryan swallowed. That much was true, but it was a bloody hard way to learn his lesson.

"You didn't deserve this."

"No, I didn't. But that's not your fault."

Ryan rubbed clammy hands over his jean-clad legs.

"Look, I just wanted to say that we're all glad you're back in the land of the living."

"Me too." Jack cleared his throat. "I appreciate you coming down here. My mum was telling me that you and Phillips visited every Saturday afternoon, while I was out of it."

Ryan gave a quick, short nod. "It was the least we could do."

"It means a lot." Jack looked away, embarrassed to find that tears were brimming. Ryan saw them and gave the man a moment to compose himself before changing topic.

"Thing is, Jack, you can't loll about here for the rest of your life flirting with Nurse Nancy over there. We've got work to do."

Lowerson smiled. "I caught the news," he said, pointing a finger at the old-fashioned TV fixed to the wall in the corner of the room.

Ryan lowered his voice and leaned forward so that only Jack could hear. "We found another one," he murmured. "Same wall cavity, but this one's brand new."

Lowerson's eyes turned dark and serious. "You're thinking it might be a copycat?"

"Could be."

"They worked fast," Lowerson muttered. "Someone looking to cash in on the media hype?"

"They killed her before any of the news channels had even picked up the first murder."

Jack frowned. "If not that…you think it's the same guy, returning to the scene of the crime?"

Ryan smiled slowly. There was no lasting damage to Lowerson's brain. "We're waiting for the autopsy to come back. Faulkner's running his samples. But…there's a possible connection with Keir Edwards."

Lowerson searched Ryan's face for any sign of distress, but he saw only resolve.

"If it turns out to be someone else, then it's a long time to wait to kill again."

"My thoughts exactly," Ryan agreed. "That's why I asked Phillips to look into like crimes. We've found several other missing girls who fit the physical type."

"Whichever way the cookie crumbles, it looks like we've got another serial on our hands," Lowerson mused, with a hint of excitement.

Ryan rolled his eyes. Attempted murder and grievous bodily harm couldn't dim Jack Lowerson's enthusiasm for detection. "You're a morbid bastard," he joked.

"Yeah, great, isn't it? There's only so much *Murder, She Wrote* that one person can stomach before needing the real thing."

With an eye on the time and the growing tiredness on Lowerson's face, Ryan rose from the mint-green wingback visitor's chair.

"Any idea how much longer until they let you out?"

Jack shrugged. "Another few days, maybe. They're running brain scans, to double check there's nothing amiss. They're a bit concerned about the amnesia."

"You still don't remember what happened?"

A shadow passed across Jack's face. "No," he said, shaking his head. "The last thing I remember is seeing the greenhouse in Ingles' garden on Holy Island, thinking 'Morning Glory!' and then the lights went out."

"It might come back to you when you least expect it."

Jack's fingers became restless, tugging at the sheet, folding and re-folding it as he struggled. "I have nightmares," he said. "But when I wake up, I can't remember what they were."

Ryan put a reassuring hand on the man's shoulder. "Get some rest. We need you back on the team."

———

Jack watched his SIO leave and almost called him back. The sound rose up in his throat, desperate to find voice.

But these walls had ears, and they heard everything—just as he had done while he had lain on the ground bleeding and seemingly unconscious. The pain had eventually numbed his mind and darkness had fallen, but not before he had heard a voice he recognised.

Fear was like a heavy blanket and he slumped back against the pillows, tears pooling in his eyes.

So long as he couldn't remember, he was safe.

CHAPTER 9

Colin Hart leaned carefully over his mother and began the process of unwinding the puss-soaked bandages which covered the sores on her ankles and calves. She wasn't very lucid today; in fact, she was fast asleep and snoring, which was probably for the best. Her bed was her world, now. When it had become clear that she was getting less mobile than before, even with the mobility scooter that was now sitting rusting on the driveway, she had gradually taken to spending more time atop the grand four-poster bed she had demanded that he buy for her.

He didn't mind, really. Only the best, for the woman who had given up everything for him. Scrimped and saved to send him to a good school, to take care of him when his no-good father had left them. He had lost count of the times he had been reminded of his good fortune in having Geraldine Hart for a mother.

He tried to ignore the foul smell of the infected bedsores as the bandages eventually came off. He always wore gloves these days, partly to prevent further infection and partly because he just didn't want the oozing fluid to come into contact with his hands.

He washed them regularly, just in case, with strong surgical soap.

He took out a ball of fresh gauze dressing and began the process of re-bandaging. Not too tight, not too loose, otherwise she would complain. He tried not to notice the sallow, sagging flesh of her skin, or the way the folds wobbled as he manipulated her leg. He tried not to be repulsed by it, but his hands trembled slightly at the effort.

Process complete, he left her sleeping in the musty bedroom, which always carried an unpleasant odour because she refused to allow the windows to be opened. He headed instead for the sitting room he had adapted into his personal library-cum-office. It was a haven in comparison to the chintzy-covered room he had left behind. The walls were plain, the furnishings neutral. Everything was easy on the eye and, consequently, on the mind.

He needed to clock in a few hours' work, which he was able to do remotely from home. That was the beauty of working as an online stockbroker and he was glad he had made the conscious decision to change profession. It allowed him to be at home to care for his mother, which was only right and proper.

His fingers hesitated over the keyboard of his desktop computer while he warred with himself, but with a guilty look at the carriage clock on the mantelpiece, he bypassed the office systems and logged on to his favourite chat room instead.

Here, the women loved him. He was no longer plain, middle-aged Colin who lived at home with his ailing mother. Online, he was dashing, he was *wanted*.

Online, he was another man entirely.

DI MacKenzie tugged her emerald-green peacoat around her as she stepped out of her car into the windy afternoon. The sky was bright, but there was a bite in the air to remind her that whilst it may have been summer, it was still a northern summer.

"Miss Crompton?"

The door to a large, Victorian villa on the edge of a smart area of the city known as Jesmond opened to reveal a woman in her early thirties, dressed in a floaty, multi-coloured kaftan. Her hair was bundled on top of her head and had been left to fall in messy blonde ringlets around an angular, expressive face.

"Hello," she said simply, resting her hip against the doorframe.

"Hello," MacKenzie replied, drawing out her warrant card. "I'm Detective Inspector Denise MacKenzie. We spoke on the phone?"

"Yep, I remember. Come on in." She held the door open and led the way along a smart passageway covered in framed poster prints ranging from Che Guevara to the Beatles. "Sorry about the mess."

It wasn't so much messy as cluttered, MacKenzie thought. Patterned and cluttered.

A smoky-grey cat wound around her legs and blinked at her with bright yellow eyes.

"It's bloody awful," Mathilda Crompton said, plopping herself down on one of the easy chairs arranged in a large, open-plan sitting room. She tucked her legs up and the cat immediately joined her, curling itself over her toes like a furry hot water bottle. "I can't believe it."

"It is sad news," MacKenzie agreed. "I know that the CSI team have already visited you to take prints and swabs. Thank you for your co-operation with that," she added politely.

"I hope that they find something. I don't mean some sort of bloody knife in my knicker drawer," she tacked on with a nervous laugh. "I just mean—well, I hope there's something to point you in the direction of her killer."

"You could help by telling us about Claire."

Mathilda nodded and stroked the cat methodically as she spoke. "Claire is…I mean, she *was* quiet, but then, since I'm so loud most of the time, it worked pretty well. She rented the room upstairs. She's been my tenant for three years now and I think we'd become good friends."

"You think?"

"I know," Mathilda corrected. "I only hesitate because Claire isn't…*wasn't* the demonstrative type, you know?"

MacKenzie nodded. "Did she see much of her family?"

"No, not really. They're over on the Isle of Man and I think Claire was trying to save as much money as she could. Her mum would come across now and then. Last time was in February."

"What about friends?"

"Um, well, like I say, she could be a bit introverted. I think she found it hard to connect with people and realistically she worked *all the time*. I mean, seriously, that girl never took a day off."

"Never?"

"Nope, not that I remember. Never seemed to get sick, either. I used to try and badger her to have some time to herself, take life a bit easier, you know? But she really needed the money." Mathilda looked down at the cat, her wide mouth turning sad. "I never put the rent up and, confidentially, I didn't charge her much for utilities. I didn't have the heart."

"That was very decent."

Mathilda brushed it off with a sweep of her arm and the sleeve of her floral top billowed. "She wanted to be a nurse and she would have made a good one." Her voice wobbled as the reality of it all began to kick in. "I was happy to help where I could."

MacKenzie paused for a moment to give Mathilda a chance to collect herself. It wouldn't help for her to break down; it would take so much longer to find out the things they needed to know. "When did you last see her?"

Mathilda paused to think. "It would have been Sunday morning. I was heading over to see my parents for the day and I stayed for lunch. I think she had an afternoon shift from around lunchtime."

"No calls or texts after then?"

"No, nothing, I'm afraid."

"When did you first begin to worry that something was wrong?"

"I got home from my parents' after eight. She was due to get home around half past eleven and I always sort of listen out for her, you know? She kept to a routine, so when it got to midnight and I hadn't heard her come in, I started to worry."

"What did you do?" MacKenzie already knew that Mathilda had reported Claire as missing in the early hours that morning, scarcely before they had found her body underneath the sycamore tree.

"Well, I came downstairs and sort of hung around waiting. I felt a bit ridiculous, you know?" Mathilda lifted her shoulders and let them fall again, stroking the cat's ears with gentle fingers. "Like I say, it got to midnight and I tried her mobile a few times, but it went straight to voicemail."

Interesting, MacKenzie thought. That meant that the phone had still been active; just switched off. She made a note to trace the mobile phone registered to Claire and hoped they might get lucky and track its location.

"I tried ringing the place she works—it's the All-American Diner, near the station in town," she added helpfully. "Nobody was answering, and I guess they'd packed up for the evening. So in the end I just called the local police station."

"You didn't think that she had gone home with somebody, perhaps? Or was just running late?"

Mathilda shook her head vehemently. "You had to know her, to understand how *organised* her life was. She never did anything spontaneous, never deviated from schedule. That was just Claire. That's how I knew that something was wrong."

MacKenzie switched tack. "Did she seem unhappy or upset about anything?"

"No. She seemed fine, if a bit tired."

"How about friends? You say she didn't have many?"

"None that I saw—she was quite a loner. Only me, I suppose."

"How about any boyfriends or girlfriends?"

"I asked Claire once if she swung in that direction…" Mathilda smiled. "Sadly for me, she didn't. On the other hand, there weren't any male admirers who came a-calling, either."

"Could she have been seeing someone at work?"

"Not likely," Mathilda scoffed. "She couldn't stand the bloke who owns the place where she worked, and the other ones were all a bit young."

"Okay," Denise said. "You were saying she didn't like the owner?"

"Nope. She said he had tried it on a few times—she'd said 'no' but he didn't give up easily. I think she was starting to feel uncomfortable."

"I see." MacKenzie made a mental note to check out the owner of the Diner.

"Did she ever mention feeling seriously threatened?"

"No, I can't say that she did. As far as I know, she just kept pushing him back." MacKenzie opened her mouth to ask the next question but Mathilda continued, "I can tell you who definitely *did* make her feel uncomfortable. That pervy old git who lives at number 32."

MacKenzie's ears sharpened and she took out her biro, preparing to write down a name.

"Who might that be?"

"His name's Colin. Colin Hart."

Phillips found Steven Llewellyn on the golf course, which was a surprising choice for a man who had received the news of his daughter's murder not twenty-four hours earlier. He seemed to be enjoying the perks of early retirement, if his tanned face and big-ticket golfing gear was anything to go by.

They were of a similar age, Phillips judged, but he had to admit that the other man seemed to be faring a little better than himself at this present moment. He felt like a duck out of water in his conservative grey suit and comfortable Hush Puppies. His tie might have added a little colour, but nothing in comparison with the unrepentant display of pastel shades that Steven Llewellyn was modelling. Where Llewellyn looked trim and tidy in the clinging sportswear, Phillips was already feeling fatigued after a second round of sandwiches over lunch.

He puffed over to where Llewellyn was teeing up the next shot and waited until he had taken it.

"Mr Llewellyn?"

Steven ran an assessing eye over DS Phillips and clearly had no memory of having met him the previous day. It made Phillips feel like a glorified monkey in a suit and it set his teeth on edge.

"Oh God, you're not from the bailiffs, are you? I spoke to you arseholes last week. I *told* you, I'll be in a position to pay off the last of it very soon. There's no need to come all the way down here to try to intimidate me."

Pride and confusion warred for a moment. It was flattering to think that he looked sufficiently 'hard' to be considered intimidating—those hours in the boxing ring as a teenager were clearly still paying off—but he didn't much like the idea of being likened to a debt-collector.

Phillips drew out his warrant card. "DS Frank Phillips," he explained, watching recognition pass briefly across the other man's face, followed swiftly by a shuttered, wary expression. "I'm here to talk about Amy."

Llewellyn sagged against his posh golf stick. "Oh, you're here about Amy. I don't know what more I can tell you."

"I appreciate that it can be frustrating having to keep going over the same things again, but it's really very useful for us to develop as clear a picture, as possible." Phillips made sure that his voice transmitted just the right amount of deference. He had seen Llewellyn's temper the previous day and had no desire to stoke the embers of it.

"Could you tell me about the last time that you saw Amy alive?"

"Look, I've given a number of statements about it."

"Humour me," Phillips replied dogmatically.

Llewellyn sighed. "The last time I saw my daughter was about two months before she went missing. She came over to the house for dinner, we ate, we discussed university and then she left."

"Two months seems like a long time, given that she lived in the same city," Phillips commented.

"She led a busy life at university." Llewellyn's eyes skirted away, and Phillips knew that he was avoiding the truth.

"Sir, it would really help us to know as much as possible about her comings and goings, if we're going to find out who killed her."

"I've told you all I know," Llewellyn insisted. "She had been unhappy at university. She came around to the house, moping about it, or about some bloke or another. I told her to buck her ideas up and that I wasn't throwing money down the drain. She didn't like it—she stormed off and we never saw her again. I know that Rose always blamed me for that."

There was more truth in that, Phillips thought, but still not all of it.

"You say there might have been a man in Amy's life? You didn't mention that in any of your statements ten years ago."

"I was upset! We were all upset. It's perfectly possible that I forgot to mention it."

Possible, Phillips agreed, but not *probable*, since Llewellyn had given six statements in total, none of which mentioned the existence of a man in Amy's life. It had been a major stumbling block in building a case against Keir Edwards, having no supportive statements from family or friends to corroborate a relationship between the two of them. Without a confession, or any forensic evidence, all they had was a photograph. Now, her father seemed to have changed his tune and it made the skin on the back of Phillips' neck itch.

"Do you know his name?"

"Obviously, after the photograph of Amy was found, I realise that it must have been Edwards that she was worrying about."

"Did she name him, specifically?"

Llewellyn seemed to struggle with himself.

"No…I can't say that she ever told us his name." It obviously pained him to tell the truth.

"Did she tell you anything about this man?"

"She said that he was a bit older. I can tell you, that didn't sit well with us. She didn't go into any details; we didn't have that kind of relationship."

"Did this discussion happen at your last meeting with Amy?"

"She told us about there being somebody earlier than that; maybe around the February before she went missing in June. I seem to remember her mooning about going on some Valentine's date with Prince Charming. When I saw her in April, that was the last time…" Llewellyn swallowed a knot in his throat and battled through the memory. "She said she was planning to end things. Not before time, we thought. She hadn't been herself for a while."

"Why didn't you tell the police about this, back in 2005?"

"I honestly didn't remember all of it until sometime after. When the photograph emerged, I didn't like to think of what she had been doing with that … *that man*."

Llewellyn looked as if he wanted to spit out the foul flavour in his mouth and Phillips could understand that. No father wanted to dwell on the facts surrounding his own daughter's death, particularly where sex was involved.

"Do you know when Amy's remains will be released?"

"I would think in the next few days," Phillips replied. "But the departmental liaison will be in touch with you about arrangements."

"Thank you," Llewellyn murmured. "It's time we gave her a proper burial."

Phillips left him to his golf, and his memories.

When MacKenzie stepped out onto the street again after her discussion with Claire Burns' landlady, she took out her mobile phone and dialled Ryan's number. It was bad luck that, at that precise moment, he was in an elevator heading down to the deep storage unit housed in the basement of CID Headquarters. The unit was surrounded by concrete, which was a barrier to mobile phone reception. Stumped, MacKenzie then punched in the number for Phillips, which also carried a vacant dial tone while he stomped the long journey back across the golf course after his discussion with Amy Llewellyn's father. Naturally, there had been no golf buggies available for a hardworking officer of the law.

There were others she could call, MacKenzie thought while she chewed her bottom lip, but did she really need them? She would only be conducting a follow-up interview, she reasoned.

Decisively, she walked across the street and headed for the large semi-detached house bearing an ornamental placard with the number '32'. With only a slight frisson of unease, she rang the doorbell and heard it chime loudly on the other side of the thick oak door.

She heard footsteps followed by a slight pause while she was scrutinised through the peephole. There was a further pause, before the locks were opened and the door swung open.

Colin was the epitome of an average man. His brown hair was combed into a classic, conservative style, with no gel in sight. He wore a plain cotton shirt, tucked into straight-leg, mid-wash jeans, which looked like they had been pressed to form a sharp crease at the front.

"Can I help you?" He took a full appraisal, from the top of her red head, to the tips of her boots.

Denise smiled in what she hoped was an unthreatening way. "Mr Hart?" She even hammed up her accent, relying on its natural charm to soften him up. "My name is Detective Inspector Denise MacKenzie. I was hoping I could ask you a few follow-up questions regarding the body you found the other morning?"

She drew out her warrant card, which he examined.

"I'm not really sure what else I can tell you," he began, hesitantly. "But feel free to come in, anyway. I'm afraid I must ask you to be quiet; my mother is asleep in her room upstairs."

"Of course."

She passed through the hallway with its highly-polished floorboards and lingering scent of lavender, which she guessed came from the excessive number of dried flower arrangements which topped every available surface. She thought briefly of a funeral parlour.

"Can I offer you some tea?"

"No, thank you—I've just had some," MacKenzie lied easily and took a seat on one of the sofas he indicated. Glancing around, she saw a large room decorated in varying shades of cream and white. Shelves were stacked with books, arranged in what appeared to be militant alphabetical order. There were no trinkets or ornaments, no dust catchers of any kind. Her eye fell on several large textbooks of criminology and an extensive collection of small paperback books detailing the lives of famous criminals. She told herself not to draw conclusions from it—after all, she had several of the same books on her shelves at home.

On the other hand, she was a police detective. It was her business to investigate murder and she had completed a Masters degree in Criminology. As far as she knew, Colin Hart worked in finance and, before that, in research. She had done her homework.

Colin noticed the direction of her stare and fiddled with the cuff of his shirt.

"I find it so fascinating, don't you? That's probably a stupid question," he carried on inanely. "Of course, you do—you're a detective."

MacKenzie gave him another empty smile, which didn't quite reach her eyes. "The reality of murder can be very different from the reports you read in those books," she murmured.

"Oh, I'm sure," he agreed eagerly, perching on the sofa beside her. Ordinary social graces would have led most people to take the chair on the other side of the coffee table, leaving a healthy gap between them. As it was, MacKenzie was now seated uncomfortably close to him, almost able to count the freckles on his nose.

She made a conscious effort to appear unaffected. "I'm sure your experience yesterday morning was quite sobering," she said conversationally.

"Mmm." He drummed his fingers against his thighs. "I, ah, I don't need a solicitor or anything, do I?"

MacKenzie adopted a surprised expression. "You are always entitled to have one present, but I'm not conducting an interview with you under caution, Mr Hart. I'm merely here to ask some follow-up questions."

She should have consulted his statement, before barging in gung-ho, she thought with a sinking heart. Her mistake was becoming more and more obvious.

"That's all right, then," Colin said, leaning even further towards her.

MacKenzie's spine was now painfully straight and the inclination to lean away from him was palpable. She cleared her throat. "How did you feel, when you found the body?"

Colin looked momentarily confused. "I suppose I felt intrigued. It was really quite a spectacle," he answered. "More than I imagined it would be."

Denise frowned. "When you say, 'more than you imagined', what do you mean by that?"

"Oh, you know, when you read about true crime, you think it's going to be a real fright," he said. "But it was only an initial shock, the kind you might feel with someone jumping out at you and shouting 'boo!'"

He smiled, displaying yellowish teeth with a pronounced overbite. She sensed that he had enjoyed something spicy for lunch.

"I see. Do you know a woman called Claire Burns?"

Colin's facial expression remained neutral, but his eyelids flickered. His fingers began to fiddle with the cuff of his shirt, tugging at the tiny threads until one of them began to run.

"Yes, I believe I do. She's one of my neighbours."

MacKenzie shifted in her seat so that she angled away from him. "Not quite a neighbour," she commented lightly. "She lives a bit further down your street, on the other side of the road."

"It's a friendly neighbourhood," Colin said defensively.

"I understand that you are quite *friendly* with Claire," MacKenzie returned, watching his face closely.

"I try to be," he said carefully, but his fingers stopped picking at his shirt and began tap-tap-tapping against the material of his jeans instead.

"Would you like to have had a relationship with Ms Burns?"

Colin picked up on the nuance immediately. "What do you mean, 'had'?"

"I'd be grateful if you would answer the question," MacKenzie persisted.

"Claire is a lovely woman. I might have asked her once or twice to dinner, which she politely declined."

"I see. Can you tell me when you last saw Ms Burns?"

Colin's colour was up, sweat pearling on his top lip. "I would like to know why you're asking me about Claire. I thought you were here to ask about the other morning?"

"Claire Burns was found dead this morning."

Colin froze, the muscles of his face contorting into something grotesque. MacKenzie took that as her cue to leave. Every fibre of her being was screaming for her to go, and now she obeyed.

She rose quickly from her chair and Colin followed her.

"You're absolutely right, Mr Hart. I've taken up enough of your valuable time and I'm expected back at the office," she said, glancing at her watch for effect. "Thank you once again for being so helpful."

She turned quickly and exited without a backward glance. Only when she had returned to her car and locked the doors did she realise that her hands were shaking.

After MacKenzie's departure, Colin watched her walk quickly over to her bright red Fiesta parked a little way down the street.

Why had she asked him about Claire?

He didn't like it. He didn't like it at all. What was more, he knew that his mother wouldn't like it, either. He must make sure that the police never had any reason to visit him again, he thought quickly, turning towards his computer.

He began to delete the files.

"Colin!" His mother's whining voice wafted down the stairs and his jaw clenched tightly against the hot fury, which sprang so easily to the surface.

"Colin, where are you? I'm hungry. Did you hear me? I said *I'm hungry*, Colin!"

His fingers poised above the keyboard, he warred with himself. He could ignore her for a few more minutes, just long enough to finish the job, but years of conditioning had him pushing away from the desk again.

"Coming, mother."

CHAPTER 10

The All-American Diner occupied a popular spot on Newcastle's 'Golden Mile' of bars and clubs, which ran like an artery through the heart of the city. When DI MacKenzie and DS Phillips walked through the silver double doors, it was like being assaulted by noise and colour. Young women in pink candy-striper uniforms and men dressed like Danny Zucko served dinner and drinks to people lounging in wide booths decorated in a bright, cherry red. In one corner, there was a full-sized pink Cadillac and a giant jukebox pumping out classic tunes while couples boogied on the flashing dance floor.

"It's still Monday, isn't it?" Phillips asked. The place was bustling, and it was hard to believe this was just an after-work crowd.

"Last time I checked," MacKenzie muttered.

Bravely, they stepped across the threshold and made directly for the long aluminium bar on the far side. Sliding onto a couple of red bar stools, Phillips tried to signal one of the Brylcreemed waiters.

After a few minutes passed without any success, MacKenzie stepped in. With a flick of her hair, she craned her neck forward, stuck an arm out, and was gratified to find that one of the serving staff hurried over. Apparently, she still had it.

Phillips pursed his lips and decided to say nothing about gender stereotyping.

"What can I get you, pet?" The waiter flashed a bright white grin, which stood out against his perma-tanned skin.

"We're from CID." MacKenzie flashed her warrant card discreetly. "We'd like to talk to you about Claire Burns."

The young man shook his head in confusion. "Claire hasn't turned up for work today. Jimmy's going mad about it," he added.

"Who's Jimmy?"

"He's the owner."

Phillips leaned across and grabbed a handful of salted peanuts from a dish on the bar in front of him.

"Listen," the waiter carried on. "Is something up with Claire?"

"When was the last time you saw her?" MacKenzie decided it was best to be vague, for now.

"Um, it would have been last night, closing time. Has something happened to her?"

"You could say that." Phillips wiped his fingers on a white paper napkin. "I'm sorry to tell you that Claire was found dead this morning. It would be helpful if you would answer some questions for us."

The waiter, who turned out to be Barry Denham, aged twenty, paled beneath his tan.

"You're—you're joking?" His eyes watered. "You must have made a mistake. Claire always took the bus home and she never got in any trouble. She wasn't like that."

"Tell us about her usual routine," MacKenzie said, taking advantage of a brief lull at the bar.

"She worked as many shifts as she could. She's usually here more than she would be at home." He ran a hand over his slick hair and tapped it absently into place as he thought. "She wasn't into all of this, though." He gestured widely to encompass the Diner. "She was a quiet person."

They both nodded.

"Some of us go out for drinks or a dance after work, but she isn't—I mean, that is, she *wasn't* interested."

"She kept herself to herself?"

"Yeah, sort of. She was friendly, like. I think she just had her heart set on being a nurse."

"Pretty girl," Phillips commented idly, his laidback attitude giving the impression that he wasn't beadily watching and listening to every answer the man gave him. Over eighty per cent of killers were known to their victims, after all.

"Aye, she is…was." Sadness washed over the young waiter with the ridiculous quiff.

"What was her shift like yesterday?"

"She was on from about two p.m. until eleven. It took a while clearing up after closing, but I think she gave us a wave goodbye at around eleven-thirty, maybe quarter-to-twelve at the latest."

"How do you know?"

"She was making a bit of a song and dance about the fact she might miss her bus home," he replied. "She always got the same bus after a late shift, from the corner outside, at half past eleven."

"Nobody went with her?"

"Nah, although Jimmy headed out around the same time, so I assumed he gave her a lift or made sure she got on the bus." He looked like he was about to say more, but he fell silent.

"Thanks," MacKenzie said. "One of our PCs will be in touch to take a statement from you tomorrow. Can you point us in Jimmy's direction?"

"His office is through there." He indicated a silver door marked 'PRIVATE'. As they turned to leave, he spoke up again. "If—if I wanted to send some flowers ... who ... can you tell me where to send them?"

"We'll let you know."

Phillips and MacKenzie slid off their stools and, with a peremptory knock, walked through the door in question. Behind it, there was a short corridor and a heavily-muscled man rose from where he had been sitting reading a smutty tabloid newspaper. He wore a dark suit that didn't sit comfortably across his shoulders, and the skin across his face bore the unmistakeable puffy and spotted signs of long-term alcohol abuse.

"Can I help you?"

"We're looking for Jimmy."

"He's busy. Who're you?"

The question was abrupt, and Phillips noticed that the man—clearly some sort of bodyguard—kept one hand in his trouser pocket. He was surprised there was only one such person to protect the likes of Jimmy "The Manc" Moffa, but perhaps his reputation was enough to ward off potential threats.

Jimmy Moffa was one of three brothers who operated a known crime syndicate in and around Newcastle. After one bad deal too many, Moffa Senior had received a swift knife to the belly, in lieu of payment for services rendered. His boys had taken over the family business and moved from Manchester to set up shop in a new city. Jimmy was the youngest, charged with running several of the brothers' legitimate enterprises. Phillips understood now why the restaurant that had previously occupied the space here had suddenly gone out of business. He may have been the youngest of the Moffa brothers, but Jimmy had packed a lot into his thirty years on Earth, certainly enough for people to run in the opposite direction. From fraud to arson, assault to GBH, Jimmy had been there. That didn't count his juvenile history—or the family interests in gambling, prostitution and, of course, drugs.

However, he had never been tried for any of those crimes. Evidence mysteriously disappeared, and witnesses went missing or developed a sudden case of amnesia.

"We need to speak to him about one of his waitresses, Claire Burns. Could you please ask him if he has ten minutes to spare?"

Denise was giving a master class in authority tempered with charm. The bodyguard assessed her with bloodshot eyes, glanced at the warrant card she held out, and then spoke quietly into a mouthpiece on the lapel of his blazer.

"Mr Moffa can give you ten minutes," he said, then knocked and opened the door behind him.

The inner sanctum was lavishly decorated in shades of grey, black and silver, in a minimalist style. White leather armchairs were arranged in a seating area around a glossy black coffee table. There were wide photographic prints on the wall of various scenes around the UK in dramatic black-and-white. The floor at their feet was a similar glossy black tile.

Easy to clean, MacKenzie thought.

An enormous desk dominated the room, behind which sat the man himself. He was still young, but his pale blue eyes told of the things he had seen and gave an edginess to his appearance. He was dressed in clothes which he thought made him look like a successful businessman, inspired by his sixties idols, the Krays—a crisp white shirt, skinny black tie and a fat Omega watch weighed down one of his wrists. His hair was shaven, which drew attention to the sharp bones of his face and did little to detract from the general sense of danger one was inclined to feel in his presence.

That was just how he liked it.

He stood and gestured graciously to the armchairs opposite.

"Please, take a seat. I understand you're from CID?" He let his eyes roam freely over MacKenzie and he thought that there was something to be said for an older woman.

MacKenzie perched on the edge of one of the spotless leather chairs and Phillips remained standing at her shoulder.

"We would like to ask you some questions about one of your waiting staff, Claire Burns."

Jimmy leaned back in his chair, very much at ease.

"Claire? Well, this is a surprise. I wouldn't have thought she'd be the type to get herself mixed up in anything," he said, the words laced with a Midlands accent he hadn't quite lost.

"Claire Burns was found dead, early this morning."

MacKenzie and Phillips both watched the man closely for a reaction, but all they saw was a hint of genuine surprise. No remorse, no particular sadness. But then, this surely wouldn't have been the first time he'd had similar conversations with the police.

"I'm sorry to hear that. We'll be sure to send some flowers to her mother."

He probably has a running account with the local florist, Phillips thought.

"We understand that you may have been the last person to see Claire, after she finished her shift here last night," MacKenzie continued.

He shrugged one shoulder and picked up a thick gold fountain pen, rolling it back and forth between thumb and forefinger as he spoke.

"I said 'goodnight' to her at about half past eleven. I offered her a lift home, but she was happy to wait for the bus."

"Was that all? She headed for the bus stop while you went home yourself?"

"That's all." His voice grew firmer, brooking no argument.

"Did you happen to notice anyone else at the bus stop?"

"It's the centre of town, so of course there were one or two other people about."

"We noticed a CCTV camera outside the main entrance to the building. Would you be willing to give us a copy of the recording?"

He licked his bottom lip before answering. "Anything to help our officers in blue."

By the time MacKenzie and Phillips took their leave, they were both feeling highly claustrophobic. Stepping out onto the pavement, they breathed the free air again.

"Gives me the creeps," MacKenzie said, after a moment.

"Me an' all, love," Phillips muttered, thinking of those eyes that had watched her with an unwavering stare.

"I'm surprised he didn't shout for a solicitor the minute we stepped into his office," MacKenzie said, frowning. "And I nearly swallowed my tongue when he agreed to give us the CCTV footage."

"Maybe he doesn't think he has anything to hide."

MacKenzie snorted inelegantly. "His closet must be so full of skeletons rattling, it's a wonder he sleeps at night."

"He probably sleeps like a baby," Phillips replied. "And that's the tragedy of it."

"Oswald was King of Northumbria from 634 until he died at the hands of the pagan Mercian army at the Battle of Maserfield in 642," Anna said. "The account given by the historian, Bede, suggests that he was a saintly king, following his widespread efforts to bring Christianity to Northumberland."

She tapped a button on her laptop and the screen behind her flipped to the next slide.

"Oswald's remains were interred alongside those of St. Cuthbert, with whom he has been associated posthumously, but it is worth bearing in mind that the two did not know each other in life. Cuthbert became Bishop of Lindisfarne forty years after Oswald's death."

Ryan slipped into the back of the lecture theatre at the History Faculty in Durham. Tonight, Anna was delivering a late lecture to a group of postgraduate historians and it looked like he had caught the tail end of it. He leaned back against the wall, his lean frame barely visible in the darkened theatre.

Yet, she sensed him. He saw her pause for a moment and scan the room until she found him. He mouthed "hello", even though she wouldn't be able to see it from where she stood.

Anna smiled and felt suddenly self-conscious. It was curious how he still managed to have that effect on her. Thankfully, it was nearly the end of her lecture.

"Cuthbert's shrine here in Durham was a major pilgrimage centre, until it was despoiled during the reign of Henry VIII as part of his dissolution of the monasteries. Your essay topic for this week will be as follows: 'To what extent do you agree that Oswald's victory at Heavenfield defined his reign?' Answers under three thousand words, please, due by Friday. That's all."

The lights in the theatre came up and there was a collective stretch and yawn before people gathered up their belongings. Ryan waited while a few stragglers took the opportunity to ask a question before he jogged down the steps to the front of the theatre.

"Hello," she said happily. "This is a surprise."

He took her by surprise again when, without so much as a pause, he plucked her off the ground. She wound herself around him, hoping that none of her students would wander back in to find their instructor locking lips with today's answer to Neolithic man.

"What was that for?" she asked once he let her feet reach the floor again. Not that she was complaining.

"I felt like it."

"Well, Mr Spontaneous, let's head home. You wanna carry my books?"

He liked this, Ryan thought. He liked the giddy, youthful feeling she gave him whenever he was with her. Whoever heard of DCI Ryan holding hands? Next thing, he'd be asking her to prom.

"How was your day?" she asked.

They walked along the river as twilight fell, casting purple-blue shadows over the water. Above them, the cathedral loomed, dominating the city with its towering silhouette and, beside it, the castle rested like a younger sibling. Anna could tell him all about the history of those buildings and, despite himself, he would be interested because of the way she brought the inanimate to life.

But not tonight.

"It was long…" He began by stating the obvious, then rattled through the events of the day as they strolled along the riverside, allowing the charm of the scenery to offset the unpalatable subject matter.

"Gregson worked fast, didn't he?"

Ryan watched a family of ducks paddle along the gentle water beside them. Once again, she had isolated the part of his day that had bothered him the most.

"Yes, but it could've been worse; Donovan is a decent guy."

Anna didn't know how to prod him for further information if he didn't want to share it, so they scuffed along the riverbank a few more paces.

"Did you find the meeting…useful?"

Without speaking, Ryan slung an arm around her shoulders so that he could hold her close, while he let it out.

"The upshot is, Doctor Donovan thinks I'm overreacting about the referral. I should see it as Gregson taking good care of his staff, rather than any kind of doubt about my abilities."

"Do you agree?"

"It makes sense, I get that on a logical level. But it's *here*," he said, tapping two fingers on his chest, somewhere near his heart. "That's the problem."

Anna felt the warmth of him through the thin jacket he wore and smelled the scent of him that was both familiar and edgy at the same time. She had fallen for a complicated man.

"Try to see it as something designed to help you, until your heart catches up with your head. You said yourself, you like the psychiatrist."

"Have you two been exchanging notes? He told me to see him as a useful outlet."

"Well, why not? If nothing else, you can let some of the frustration out."

"Yeah." He thought of what else had emerged during the session and wondered whether to broach the subject.

They were almost home; he could see the little row of cottages set on the hillside overlooking the river.

Tomorrow. He would talk to her tomorrow. It wasn't urgent, after all.

———

Ryan could feel the shirt clinging to his back as he slammed out of the car. The day had dragged on, hour after painful hour and there was no end in sight. He was still out there, somewhere in the night, and his lust for blood had not been sated.

The river shimmered to his right, like a black snake. His eyes were blurry with fatigue and stress, his heart heavy with a deep sense of failure.

There would be another one, tonight. He knew it.

"Try to get some sleep, son," Frank was saying, from the driver's side of the car.

He mumbled something unintelligible and scuffed his way to the entrance of his building. It was a modern complex on the Quayside and in the daylight hours his apartment had unspoilt views of the river. A quaint market popped up on Sundays and the air smelled of frying onions and rich fudge as traders sold their wares from colourful stalls.

Now, the streets were quiet. The hour was well past midnight and only a handful of lights flickered in the windows around him. Squinting up to the top floor, he saw that one of them was his own.

Natalie must have waited up for him.

He thought of his sister: bright and beautiful with a mane of long black hair and eyes the same shade of silvery grey as his own, inherited from their mother. He didn't expect Natalie to look after him; in fact, he wished she wasn't there to fuss over him when he dragged his tired body through the front door. All he wanted was bed and oblivion.

The first thing he noticed when he stepped off the elevator was that the front door to his apartment was ajar.

The security in the building was top-of-the-line—had Natalie left the door unlocked? He frowned, his brows drawing together into a dark, angry line.

At a time like this, when women in Newcastle were fearful to walk home, to travel without a car, or to be alone in the house knowing that there was a homicidal maniac killing women just like them, she had no right to be so reckless.

He pushed open the door, ready to give her a lecture on home safety, and then froze in the doorway. His stomach flipped and fear hit him like a fist to the face.

With slow steps, Ryan moved forward, the blood rushing in his ears as he crouched beside the small white tray, which had been placed directly inside the hallway. On it, three human fingers, bloodied and greying, had been arranged into a makeshift teepee. A cream card bore the message, 'Catch me if you can!' in neat lettering.

Ryan wanted to throw up, to give in to the sickness that rolled in waves through his shattered body, but instead he reverted to training. His eyes scanned the room, searching the corners and crevices for anybody hidden there, but he found nothing. His hands fumbled in his pockets until he found his phone and he pressed the speed-dial for Phillips.

"Pick up. For God's sake, pick up."

But the man was driving.

Ryan put a call through to the control room, requesting backup. The ETA was eight minutes.

Eyes wide and unblinking, he moved from room to room, heading in the direction of his bedroom and the firearm lying hidden in a box on the top shelf of his wardrobe.

He didn't make it that far.

When he pushed open the door to the spare bedroom, he saw that his sister was seated so that she would immediately be seen. The central lights blazed overhead, illuminating the sickly pallor of her skin. She lay slumped and motionless, her body tied into place with long bands of surgical tape. He didn't know if she was still alive.

Tiredness forgotten, he surged forwards, intending to check her pulse and to release her from the ties. Panic and love swamped him in equal measure, overtaking self-preservation. The man who watched him judged it the perfect moment to strike.

He lunged from behind and Ryan turned too late, seeing the flash of movement as the man plunged the sharp point of a pressure syringe into the side of Ryan's neck.

Almost immediately, he fell to his knees and into the oblivion he had wished for earlier.

Ryan opened his eyes some time later to a blistering headache. His pupils were like pinpricks against his pale face. He was seated in one of the armchairs in the living area of his apartment and, remarkably, his arms and legs had not been tied.

Across the room, he saw the monster hovering beside his sister, and he made to leap from the chair. It soon became apparent why no binding had been necessary; the drugs swimming around his brain prevented his body from responding to his frantic order that he *move! Just move, damn it!*

Doctor Keir Edwards glanced behind, to where Ryan now lay crumpled on the floor, struggling to drag himself upwards.

"Sedative," he offered conversationally. "It's obviously doing its job."

The bastard was right, Ryan thought. He hadn't been able to feel a thing, yet he lay on the floor like a beached whale, unable to move his legs at all. But his arms still worked. With silent, subtle movements, he reached for the pocket of his jeans, feeling around for his mobile phone.

It wasn't there.

Of course, it wasn't there.

With hate-filled eyes, he looked across to the dining table and could see the contents of his pockets gracing the top.

"What do you want?" Ryan ground out, beginning to feel the effects of the blood loss.

"I want this ridiculous game of cat and mouse to end," Edwards replied. "It's been fun, I'll admit. Don't think I haven't enjoyed knowing that you were always a few steps behind me, plodding along in your interminable way, but I want to regain my freedom. A bird needs its wings to be able to fly freely."

He smiled genially.

"Get out."

"Tut, tut. After all the time you've spent hunting me, I would have thought you'd be rather more welcoming.

If I hadn't invited myself over, who knows when you might eventually have found me?"

"Oh, excuse me," Ryan gritted between panting breaths as he continued his painstaking journey across the carpet. "*Welcome.*"

"That's better."

Edwards strolled across to one of the dining chairs and dragged it towards Natalie. He seated himself beside her, crossing one elegant, suit-clad leg over the other.

"Get *away* from her!"

Ryan tried to heave himself upwards and cried out in frustration when his body would not cooperate.

"Calm yourself," Edwards snapped, trailing a finger over Natalie's unconscious cheek. "She should be coming around anytime now, so we'll have a nice little chat, the three of us."

"Not her," Ryan said, fisting his hands. "Please. Not her."

Edwards raised an eyebrow.

"I bet that hurt your pride, just a little. The mighty DCI Ryan reduced to begging...on his *knees.*"

"I'll beg, if that's what you want. I'm begging you now. Don't kill her."

Edwards sighed dramatically. "You don't understand, do you? You must have known that I would be following your movements, just as closely as you followed mine. By having her here, you placed her in front of me like an offering. A challenge to the brave. You must have *known* I would not be able to resist her."

Edwards trailed another finger over Natalie's bare thigh, clad only in short pyjamas that she had obviously worn for bed.

"She's a real beauty, this one."

Ryan felt bile rise in his throat.

"Take me, instead."

"Oh, I will."

Edwards turned to give Natalie a couple of sharp slaps. Her head lolled around her shoulders as she struggled to the surface again. He drew out a long, surgical knife and flicked the end of it, preparing himself for the next stage.

"*No!*"

Ryan dragged himself across the carpet and Edwards watched with the open-eyed stare of someone viewing a strange oddity.

"Save your energy," he said. "You may need it."

"My team are on their way," Ryan shouted at him, but wondered where the hell they could be. It had been more than eight minutes, surely.

Edwards smiled, pleased with himself.

"I rang them again and explained there had been a false alarm," he said. "We really do sound very alike, you and I— and you had given your passcode in such a helpful way earlier."

Ryan felt hope drain from him.

Natalie's large grey eyes flickered open, her long lashes sweeping upwards until her gaze locked onto Edwards'. Confusion and terror played across her features and she looked away, meeting Ryan's desperate face across the room.

In that moment, Ryan knew. He read the acceptance, the dreadful knowledge of what was to come.

"*No!*" Frantically, he dragged himself forward again, like a dead weight.

"Say 'Goodbye', now," Edwards rasped.

The blood pounded in Ryan's ears and a scream broke free as he watched the man tug Natalie's long hair back, exposing the slim column of her throat. The silver knife swept a graceful line across it and a river of red gushed forth, fanning a warm arc over Ryan's upturned face.

Ryan jerked upright in bed with a shout, his fists bunched in the duvet and the pillow soaked in a mixture of sweat and tears.

Anna sat beside him, fully awake, with a look of extreme concern on her face. She held his forearms firmly, to steady him.

"Ryan? I've been trying to wake you. It was a nightmare—a bad one, by the sound of it." Her voice was soft and mellow, barely above a whisper. She had turned on the small lamp beside the bed, so that he would not wake up in darkness.

Ryan said nothing straight away, but rubbed a shaking hand over his face. He looked across at the bedside clock.

Three-fifteen.

Hours left of the night and he was awake, without any desire to return to the world he had just left.

Anna rubbed a hand in soothing circles over his back and up to the tight cords of muscle in his neck.

"Ssh," she soothed, drawing his brittle body towards her, offering what comfort she could.

He allowed himself to be enfolded and drank deeply of her warmth, inhaling her scent, clutching her soft body to him.

"What can I do?"

"Nothing. There's nothing anybody can do."

Those disconsolate words concerned her more than anything else. A long time later, when he fell into a light, fitful sleep at her breast, she lay awake and worried.

CHAPTER 11

Northumberland was an overcast grey the following morning. Thick blocks of cloud sat heavily in the sky and seemed to accentuate the cheap grey-tinged exterior of CID Headquarters. The building was an anachronism sandwiched between more classic structures, having been built during the 1960s which had, in Ryan's view, been a bad era for architecture.

He glanced at his watch as he headed for the stairwell.

Seven-fifteen.

After a disturbed night, he had eventually woken up for good just after five. To jumpstart his system, he'd left Anna to sleep peacefully while he grabbed his muddied trainers and went for a long, muscle-warming run around the empty streets of Durham. There was an eerie beauty to the place, which reminded him of fantasy elven cities in *The Lord of the Rings*. It had stateliness; grandeur blended with classic town planning which spoke of untold wealth in days gone by.

While his feet pounded the cobbled streets, things had begun to order themselves in his mind.

That was why he was here, in the chilly Incident Room, long before his contractual hours formally began. Hell, who was counting anymore? It took however long it took, until the job was done.

Alone, he spent fifteen silent minutes staring at the murder board, sipping intermittently from a takeaway coffee he'd purchased from the little van parked along the street. It was owned by a man who worked as an estate agent from nine till five, and then sold tea, coffee and steak pies outside those hours.

Possibilities ran through his mind, twisting this way and that, until the lines of enquiry presented themselves.

He took another hour and a half to re-read all the relevant paperwork that had been generated so far. Telephone enquiries, witness statements, forensic and archaeological reports.

"Morning, guv."

He could have predicted that Phillips would be the first to step over the threshold. As always, his eye was drawn to his sergeant's colourful ensemble and he noticed that today's tie of choice was a sporty little number: bright green, covered with tiny black-and-white footballs.

Ryan pointed to the large takeaway cup sitting atop Phillips' desk. Caffeine was one of life's basic needs, after all.

"You're a lifesaver," Phillips said, making a grab for the cup and gulping down some of the murky brown liquid, which had been sweetened according to his preference.

"Rough night?"

"You're telling me. That woman is an animal."

Ryan held off a shudder. Much as he liked his sergeant and DI MacKenzie, much as he was happy for them, he didn't want to know any details. *Especially* not any details.

Uncaring, Phillips ploughed on. "I'm telling you, she's just got so much *energy*. If I wasn't half the man I am"— Frank adopted what he thought was a manly stance—"I would be worried for my health."

"Frank, for pity's sake …" Would it be childish to stick his fingers in his ears?

"I loved my wife, God rest her soul." Phillips tapped a hand to his heart as he thought of his first wife who had died years earlier. "But this is a whole new kettle of fish."

"I get the picture," Ryan drawled. "You're a Studly Stud from Studsville. You're the Man of the Moment. You're Mister Lover-Lover. Anything else?"

Phillips pursed his lips, thought about it, and then shook his head. "That covers it."

"Thank God. Now, do you mind if we get down to business?"

Phillips plopped down in his desk chair and flipped open his notepad.

"I spent some time last night going over what we know about Amy Llewellyn," he began.

"Was that before, or after?" Ryan queried, then waved a hand. "Forget I asked."

"Before. I managed to speak to Amy's old housemate on the phone, which is the only way we're likely to get hold of her, since she's now living in Australia. She remembers things pretty well," Phillips continued. "They went to school together and they were both studying medicine at Newcastle—same year, same course."

"She should have some decent observations, then?"

"In terms of Amy's movements, there isn't much that she could add. Amy went missing on Friday 21st June 2005, when this housemate was at her boyfriend's house. The last time she saw Amy was on the Friday morning, when they both had a lecture at the university. As far as she knows, Amy was planning to have a quiet night at home."

"What else?"

"She agrees that Amy wasn't herself for a good while before she disappeared. She thinks that she perked up a bit, just before she went missing, but she still reckons Amy wasn't just down in the dumps, she was keeping secrets."

Ryan's focus sharpened. "What kind of secrets?"

Phillips glugged down more coffee before answering. "She reckons there was a man involved, somehow, which tallies with what her father told me yesterday. One night around the Christmas before she disappeared, Amy came home late and looked like she'd been crying. Apparently said she didn't want to talk about it and clammed up, which was unusual because Amy was usually the 'open' sort."

"The housemate didn't mention any names?"

"She thinks he was a bit older, but she never met him and can't remember his name. She thought he might have been married and that's why Amy didn't want to talk about it."

"Recent events concerning Keir Edwards didn't jog any memories for her?"

"Nope, she'd never heard of Edwards until she saw it all reported on the BBC World News last year and never associated him with Amy."

"Damn."

"Yeah," Phillips agreed, scratching his chin. "She reckons it could have been this bloke to set her off along the wrong track, then Amy turned private and apparently their friendship was on the rocks."

"She said that?"

"Yeah…" Phillips flicked his finger against the notes of his conversation with Amy's housemate, from the night before. "She says that living with Amy had become difficult. She was withdrawn, a bit selfish, a bit of a slob. She was thinking about moving out and leaving her to it."

"Doesn't sound like the same 'Amy', does it?" Ryan commented, considering the girl staring back at him from a picture on the wall.

"Tends to happen when people are depressed though, doesn't it?" Phillips said knowledgeably and then tried to think of something to change the subject. It wasn't so long ago that Ryan had gone through a rough patch.

Thankfully, he was saved by the timely interruption of Ryan's mobile phone, which pealed out the tinny theme tune from *Indiana Jones*.

Phillips regarded Ryan with an indulgent look.

"Not one word," Ryan warned him, before hitting the green button on his touchscreen.

After a few moments, he returned the phone to his pocket, all humour gone.

"We need to take a trip to the mortuary. That was Pinter—apparently he's finished Claire Burns' autopsy and there's something we should see."

"Do we have to?" There was nothing Phillips hated more.

"He said it was for our eyes only."

"Oh, goody."

The Bee Gees soared over the chilly air of the mortuary at the Royal Victoria Infirmary, their falsetto lyrics encouraging the listener to shake the white suit out of mothballs and give in to the fever of the night. Phillips had some fond memories of such a suit, and the corresponding platform heels he had worn on many fun nights out on the Tuxedo Princess, the boat-cum-nightclub that had laid anchor on the River Tyne, many moons ago.

He sighed, thinking of the good old days. There was none of that now. It was all American-style diners straight off the set of *Pulp Fiction*.

They found Jeff Pinter in his laboratory scrubs, his hair and face masked to protect the body of Claire Burns from further contamination. Ryan and Phillips kept a respectful distance, with Phillips in particular keeping his eyeline a good few inches above where the body rested on a metal gurney, covered by a long white sheet.

"Hello!" Pinter greeted them in his usual jovial manner. "You're in luck—I've just finished the post-mortem."

"What can you tell us?"

"Quite a lot," Pinter began. "As I mentioned before, Claire Burns suffered no head wounds, as Amy Llewellyn did. Instead, I found a small puncture site in the tissue of her neck. Toxicology indicates that she was injected with a large dosage of Lorazepam."

"What's that, when it's at home?" Phillips asked.

Ryan could have told him. It was precisely what the medics had found swimming around his system when they'd peeled him off the floor of his apartment, with Natalie dead beside him.

Stop it, he told himself. *Stop it.*

"Lorazepam is part of a group of benzodiazepines, which in high doses can induce sleep and certainly a sedative effect at the very least."

"Ideal to immobilise a victim, then?"

"Yes, exactly."

"How accessible?"

Pinter shrugged.

"You would need a prescription, usually, but I would be lying if I said that hospital pharmacies didn't suffer from their fair share of drugs theft."

"Anything else in her blood?"

"We were able to isolate the presence of above-average levels of adrenaline, but aside from that, nothing out of the ordinary."

So far, the modus operandi was in keeping with Keir Edwards and they all knew it.

"What about the amputation sites?"

"I know what you're wondering," Pinter said excitedly. "You want to know if the wounds are consistent with those inflicted by The Hacker, in his heyday."

"And are they?"

"They are," Pinter confirmed. "In fact, we can draw further conclusions from Claire's body, since we have more of it to look at. You remember that with his previous victims, we could see that the bones had been separated cleanly, beneath the major joints, which is a manner consistent with the approach taken by a surgical professional."

"I remember."

"Well, it's the same here—only more so. Not only has her body been dissected beneath the major joints, even the nerves have been cut high up. The myoplastic flaps—"

"Jeff, speak English, for God's sake," Phillips muttered.

An unkind expression seemed to pass over Pinter's face for a moment and then it was replaced by his usual cheery expression.

"The *incisions* have been made from the anterior ... from the *front* and the back of each juncture, working around the limb in a circular fashion. Again, in keeping with a professional standard of amputation."

"Was she alive, during this?"

"Um, well." Pinter blew out a breath. "For some of it, we can say that the blood was still circulating around her body. There is some clotting around both knees, which would suggest that she was alive during that process. There's clotting around the elbows, also. For all other sites, there is no evidence to suggest circulation."

Compassion laced Phillips next question. "How did she die, in the end?"

"Major cardiac arrest," Pinter replied, without inflection. "Her system would have been severely weakened owing to the blood loss, added to which there was a cocktail of sedative and adrenaline running through her veins which would have messed about with her heart rate. Factoring in medical shock…you've got a recipe for disaster."

"This is all very interesting," Ryan said, "But you gave me the impression over the telephone that it was vitally important that we rush down here."

"Wait till you see the killer's pièce de résistance."

With a flourish, Pinter whisked the white sheet away.

Ryan and Phillips looked upon the remains of Claire Burns with a combination of recognition and disbelief. It was a sad, sorry end to a life that had only really just begun, Ryan thought. He grieved for them, for the dead that he championed. It may not have shown on his face, which was hard as marble, but his heart and his soul went out to her family. Yet that wasn't what sent a shiver across his shoulder blades. Now that her body had been pieced back together, they could clearly see that the front of her torso had been marked with deep, slashing cuts to form the shape of an inverted pentagram. It was something they had seen before.

Ryan raised his eyes to the pathologist. "This goes no further than this room," he told Pinter. "I want a list of everyone who has worked on Claire's body."

Jeff nodded and then drew the sheet back over Claire's serene face.

Outside, Ryan turned to Phillips. "Frank, give me a cigarette."

"What? You know fine well that I gave up those tar-infested killing sticks. Besides, you don't smoke."

Ryan simply held out a hand.

With a grumble, Phillips reached inside the breast pocket of his blazer and drew out the single cigarette he kept there, as a daily test of his willpower.

Ryan bummed a light from a passer-by outside the hospital entrance and inhaled the smoke as his mind tried to process the latest development.

"We have no way of knowing whether there were once similar markings on Amy's body," he said after the first few puffs.

"Her body was too far gone," Phillips agreed.

"So what the hell is going on? First of all, Pinter tells us that the dissection was done in the same way as Edwards—

in fact, the style was so similar as to be nearly identical. That suggests a copycat, or at least someone wanting to keep Edwards on the radar. Then, there's the markings, and that doesn't point to Edwards at all."

Phillips tugged at his ear while he thought. "You're right there, lad. There was no ritual stuff in any of his previous victims, more just a certain *method* of killing, which isn't the same thing. I don't see Edwards dancing around naked calling to the Forces of Darkness."

"Neither do I," Ryan was forced to agree. "He might be bat shit crazy but, as far as I know, he never believed he could conjure up Hell's fury by howling around a campfire."

"What if there's more of them?"

Ryan thought of the men and women who had been uncovered as belonging to a 'Circle' on Holy Island. People who had created their own subversive moral code, to justify the killing of innocent human beings.

"We can't rule it out," Ryan replied. "We still don't have all the answers. We still haven't found Mike and Jennifer Ingles, for one thing."

He referred to the vicar and his wife, who had disappeared from Holy Island without a trace. There was still an active All Ports Warning and a warrant outstanding for their arrest. None of those who had been apprehended seemed to have any idea of their whereabouts and they all denied any knowledge of the attack on DC Jack Lowerson.

It could be that one or two bad apples had fallen through the cracks in their investigation.

"It feels like somebody's playing with us." He crushed the remainder of the cigarette beneath the heel of his boot and turned back to Phillips, who was looking at him with an odd expression on his mole-like face. "What?"

"There's something else to factor in here. With Claire's murder, you've got shades of The Hacker and shades of Holy Island, not to mention physically similar types of victim. What do they all have in common?"

Ryan had guessed the answer, but he let Phillips do the talking.

"You, lad. The common denominator is *you*."

Ryan nodded once, just a quick jerk of his head. "I want Anna to be kept under observation at all times." He started to reach for his phone, but Phillips put a hand on his arm to stay the action.

"She won't like it, if you don't speak to her first."

Ryan nearly snarled. "She'll have to deal with it," he said, shrugging Phillips off. "You said yourself, we're looking at victims who are young, dark-haired women, just like Anna. Whoever it is seems to be fixated on two of my previous cases. It's obvious where they might look next."

"It's guesswork—"

"Common sense," Ryan argued, then turned his back to put the call through.

Anna couldn't pinpoint exactly when the prickle began. It started as a tingle along her spine; a shiver of sensory understanding, which told her that something in her immediate surroundings was not as it should be. Yet, when she looked around her, along the busy streets of Durham where shoppers and students mingled with young families and office-workers, she told herself she was imagining things. There were no hidden faces in the crowd, no madmen dressed in animal masks with murderous intent.

Yet, there it was again. That *tingle*.

It was a sorry state of affairs when she could no longer trust her own instinct to guide her, but Anna admitted to herself that six months had not been long enough to dispel the memories of that fateful day on the island. At first, the flashbacks had come frequently, replaying the horror over and over until she was almost desensitized. Gradually, they had abated, but Ryan was not the only one who still suffered from broken sleep. Her treacherous mind enjoyed nothing more than reminding her of how close she had come to death and it made her distrustful of her own psyche.

She looked again into the crowd, searching the faces of those men and women for a clue of some kind.

There was nothing.

Shaking herself, she continued her brisk walk along the High Street, back towards the university. If her steps were a little quicker than usual, she put it down to the sudden chill in the air. Passers-by brushed against her as she zigzagged through the crowd and the contact made her tense. Coat tails were like fingers, clutching at her arms. Panic was rising and she fought for composure, mentally counting her footsteps as they slapped against the pavement until the walls of the university came into view once more.

She broke free of the mass and ran the rest of the way, back into the safety of those hallowed walls, which rang with the gentle din of student chatter.

Outside, a man watched her flee the High Street, admiring the ripple of dark hair swaying from side to side as she ran with long, limber strides. He replaced the camera inside its leather holder and slung it over one shoulder, just another tourist snapping pictures of the city.

He considered following her. Desire was palpable; he could feel his body urging him onwards, to claim his prize. He started to shake, the force of it pumping through his veins, but the urge abated sharply when he noticed two men walk in the direction Anna had taken. Both wore dark suits hanging badly over rounded shoulders and scratched loafers, the ubiquitous signal that they were police. He congratulated himself on a cautious, careful approach. That's what made him the best, he thought, enjoying the sensation of having made yet another narrow escape. With some regret, he told himself to be patient and turned back along the High Street with a whistle.

Besides, it wouldn't be long now.

CHAPTER 12

"It has to be someone with inside knowledge."

Ryan's bald statement was met with a satisfactory level of awed hush around the Incident Room, as his team reconvened. He was plagued with doubt regarding his decision to have his girlfriend put under police observation, but told himself that it surely fell under the heading of 'police matter' rather than 'relationship issue'. He was also perturbed by the immediate urge to discuss the matter with Doctor Donovan. Never before had he required anybody else's input on how he chose to conduct his life, and the intrusion into his daily thought processes was one more irritant to bear.

He got up to pace around and burn off some restless energy.

"You think he's with the police?"

MacKenzie's question was a loaded one. The thought of him being one of their own number was almost inconceivable. Yet Ryan remembered reading somewhere that the greatest number of functional psychopaths could be found in those professions where the individual could feel in control of others. That included the police, top-tier business and medicine. How anybody could abuse such a position of trust was a question for others to ask. CID was left with the consequences and there was little time to worry about whether the perpetrators committed their crimes by reason of nature or nurture.

Ryan looked around the room and saw the stony faces. He read correctly the instant defence of their colleagues and understood how that unquestioning loyalty developed. It came from shared experiences, often unimaginable to the general public. He thought of his relationship with Phillips and tried to conceive of his sergeant stalking through the streets of Newcastle or luring young women to their deaths. At that moment, Phillips looked up from where he had been trying, without success, to replace a tiny pin in his sunglasses with stubby fingers that were not designed for such an intricate task.

Ryan simply couldn't imagine it.

But that was sentimentality. The facts spoke for themselves and every man and woman under his command must be made to understand that personal feelings had no place in his Incident Room. If he told them often enough, perhaps the message would eventually filter through to his brain too.

"I'm saying that whoever we are looking for had access to information which has not been made public.

That doesn't necessarily make him police, but he's getting his information from someone inside or he was part of it in some other way."

"Information leaks—" MacKenzie started to say.

"Consider this," Ryan interjected, pointing a finger at nobody in particular. "How did our killer know where to dump Claire Burns on Sunday night, when the facts surrounding the discovery of Amy Llewellyn's body had not been made public?"

"Professor Freeman gave an interview—"

Ryan shook his head. "I spoke with the film crew, as well as Freeman. The interview was pre-recorded but not aired until the breakfast news the following day—on Monday. The film crew check out, every last one of them."

"I spoke to that journalist with the silly name—Ophelia Whatsherface." MacKenzie rolled her eyes. "She said she had to 'protect her sources' or some rubbish and said that we could come to her with an appropriate warrant, otherwise she wouldn't be saying shit."

"Helpful, as always," Ryan observed caustically. "So, I repeat, how did the bastard know?"

"Somebody blabbed," Phillips said, roundly.

"Obviously," Ryan replied. "The question is who—and why? Was it a case of two colleagues discussing the incident, one of whom is suspect? Or was it a case of somebody overhearing something they shouldn't?"

"Impossible to know," MacKenzie said.

"At this stage," Ryan agreed. "But a pattern has emerged, which we can use to help us."

He opened his mouth to give them the details, but was interrupted by Phillips.

"It's all to do with muggins, over there." Frank shook his thumb in Ryan's direction. "It's looking like we've got someone with a big old crush on the Chief Inspector. He's wanting a bit of attention."

Ryan opened his mouth again, but had to admit that Phillips had hit the nail on the head. Whoever it was clearly craved attention, perhaps *demanded* it, from the world in general and him in particular.

"Amy Llewellyn connects to Keir Edwards, who connects to me. Claire Burns' death mirrored Edwards' style, once again connecting to me and, for good measure, her wounds mirrored the victims on Holy Island, which also connects to me."

The light dawned on them all. He could see it, spreading through the room.

"Remember that the ritual markings on the Holy Island victims were also not made public, which is something else he has managed to find out and use to draw attention to himself. It's as if he's saying, 'I'm better than The Hacker and the Holy Island killers.'"

"Copycatting them to show off, you mean?"

Ryan nodded.

"I think I may know someone who fits the bill," MacKenzie said quietly, and all eyes turned to her. "Late yesterday afternoon, I spoke with Claire Burns' friend and landlady, Mathilda. She told me that Claire was being harassed by a man who lives on the same street. A man going by the name of Colin Hart."

Ryan's brows drew together, a slash of black against his face. "The same Colin—?"

"Same guy," MacKenzie confirmed, remembering his breath against her face. She held off a shiver. "Sir, being unable to contact you or Phillips at the time, I took the opportunity to ask him some follow-up questions given the new information. Colin Hart was known to Claire Burns and I have a witness statement from Mathilda Compton, confirming that he had repeatedly pestered Claire."

"Colin Hart happens to find our first victim, then, also by chance, happens to live on the same street as the second?"

"I thought it was too great a coincidence, sir."

"I agree with you. Go on."

MacKenzie felt foolish, all of a sudden. How could she express the fear she had felt in Colin's home, in professional terms?

On the other side of the fence, Ryan watched MacKenzie closely. As a trained observer, two things immediately struck him as unusual. The first was that Phillips' hand rested protectively over MacKenzie's in a public display of affection, which was *not* usual, despite their relationship. In working hours, they stuck to professional boundaries, though he couldn't vouch for what happened in the copier room during lunchtimes. The second thing he noticed was that MacKenzie was pale and, rather than meeting his gaze directly, her eyes were trained on the carpet.

She was spooked.

"Mac?"

She jumped a bit in her chair, which was also a first. Of them all, MacKenzie was usually an unshakeable force to be reckoned with.

"Sorry," she muttered, drawing herself together. "I identified myself and entered his home at around four o'clock yesterday afternoon. He was not cautioned, sir."

Ryan said nothing. If she expected a reprimand, she would be waiting a long time.

"You know the legalities." Ryan eased a hip onto the edge of his desk. "Cautions are not always necessary when making initial enquiries."

"Thank you, sir." Gratitude made her tone more formal than she intended.

"Tell us why you think a caution might have been needed."

"Right enough," she murmured, dragging herself back to the point. "We already know that Colin Hart is now his mother's main carer and he has access to her medical supplies. Prior to changing profession, he was employed by the university from 1998 to 2007 in a research capacity."

"Which faculty would that be?"

"Biomedical Sciences."

"Puts him in range of Amy Llewellyn as well as Claire Burns," Ryan observed.

"Upon entering his residence, I could see that he keeps an extensive collection of literature on true crime and criminal behaviour, which he confirmed was an interest of his."

"Access to medical knowledge, potentially unhealthy interest in criminal behaviour, you think?"

"That was my impression, sir, but that's all it was. An impression."

Ryan thought back to his own impression of Colin Hart and remembered how he had claimed an interest in Ryan following the events of Holy Island. He also remembered how the man had mentioned Anna by name.

Unhealthy.

Criminal prosecutions could not be built upon impressions alone. They needed facts and evidence.

"What did he have to say about Claire Burns?"

"He appeared very angry when I brought up the subject of Claire. Given that her next of kin have been informed, I felt it was appropriate to inform him of her death and to gauge his reaction. He appeared neither surprised nor shocked by the news, but he was adamant that he had been on friendly terms with her."

"You were uncomfortable in his presence?"

"It's ridiculous, I know, but—"

Ryan held up a hand to stem the flow of excuses. "Bring him in for questioning."

"We don't have any forensic link," Phillips threw in.

"He's a known person in Claire Burns' life. Tell him we want to ask him about his relationship with her."

"I'll make a start." MacKenzie stepped out of the room to put the wheels in motion and, in her temporary absence, Ryan called a ten-minute coffee break.

By mutual assent, Ryan and Phillips convened by the murder board.

"Do I need to be concerned?"

Phillips sighed. "MacKenzie's not been herself," he had to admit. "It was a long day, yesterday. First, finding the body in the morning, then handling Colin Hart. We stopped into Claire's workplace before we packed in for the night and the owner's Jimmy Moffa. He's not exactly Mr Nice."

Ryan ran a thoughtful hand through his hair, ruffling it further out of style.

"It's not like her to be agitated, even taking all that into account. I've seen her handle bigger fish and not break a sweat."

Phillips knew it too. "She just needs a good night's sleep and some of my tender loving care," he said, trying to keep things light. "She's a good police officer."

Ryan slapped a hand on Phillips back and shook his head.

"She's the best."

Colin was polishing off an omelette when the knock came at the door.

"Colin?" His mother's voice shrilled. "Who's that at the front door? Tell them to go away!"

"I'll take care of it, Mother," he called out.

His heart jumped when he looked through the peephole and saw who his visitors were, but settled down again when he remembered that he had taken all necessary steps to protect himself.

"I'm just popping out for a couple of hours, Mother. You have everything you need."

"*What*? Colin!" She began to whine, long snivelling tears rolling down her puffy cheeks as she thumped the bedsheets in frustration. She could never 'pop out' on a whim and the knowledge of it made her even angrier.

With a brief glance around him, happy that everything was in order, Colin opened the door to where two detective constables stood solemnly on his doorstep.

"Colin Hart?"

"Yes."

"We would be grateful if you would agree to accompany us to the station to answer some questions in connection with the murders of Amy Llewellyn and Claire Burns," one of them said.

The words washed over him. He found his eyes drawn to the slightly greying collar of the man's shirt. He noticed that the other one had dirty, over-long fingernails.

"Am I being arrested?"

"No, sir, not at this time. We would like you to attend an interview, where you will be asked some questions under caution."

"I'm entitled to a solicitor, aren't I?" he asked. "I'll call one now."

They nodded silently, and he felt their eyes watching him as he made the short trip across the hallway to the telephone. He had memorised the number for the best firm of solicitors in the city, so he dialled it without needing to look up the digits. Overhead, he heard the thump of his mother's stick; one she never used for walking anymore, only to attract attention.

"*Colin?*" Her voice had reduced to a long, keening sound, which he ignored. After another moment's hesitation, he turned his back to the doorway and placed a second call. He spoke quickly into the receiver and then replaced the handset.

"I'm ready," he said.

With the wheels in motion for an interview with Colin Hart, Ryan left MacKenzie to chase up the CCTV footage relating to Claire Burns' abduction. It would give them some ammunition in the interview, if they could ask Colin why he had been captured on camera speeding out into the night in the direction of Hadrian's Wall. While MacKenzie did what she could to find a face or a car they recognised, he and Phillips made their way across town to a jewellery store, which stocked silver bangles in the same design worn by Amy Llewellyn.

Traffic was heavy with commuters eager to get across town and, in the momentary standstill, Ryan turned to Phillips.

"Any progress on Amy Llewellyn?"

Phillips fiddled with the air con while he arranged his thoughts.

"I spoke to those people who claimed they saw Amy on the night she went missing. Most of them couldn't even remember what they told the police back in 2005, let alone corroborate it."

"Helpful."

"Yeah, really helpful." Phillips shaded his eyes from the sun and watched Ryan draw out a pair of aviators. "There was one bloke who sounded solid, though. He's a taxi driver and he says he saw a woman matching Amy's description walking around the edge of the Moor, in the direction of the cut, which takes you through Jesmond."

"I know it," Ryan said, edging the car forward.

"Anyhow, when I spoke to him on the phone, he remembered her straight away. He saw the original television appeal for Amy back in 2005 and rang the Crimestoppers helpline. He says he remembered her because it was the evening, around ten, and she was walking alone. He was clocking off for the night, but he put his light back on just in case she needed a lift anywhere. He called out to her, which is how he got a good look at her face."

"How did he describe her?"

"Young, early-twenties, dark, petite, good-looking."

"Drunk, disorientated?" Ryan flicked the indicator to turn left.

"No, none of that. He says she looked smartly dressed—"

"In what?"

"Beige mac, jeans, some sort of flowery scarf."

"Okay." Ryan nodded. It helped to build a picture.

"He thought she looked like a smart young woman and he was a bit concerned about her walking alone at that time of night, in that part of town."

Ryan understood the man's concern. It wasn't a dangerous area, but it *was* quiet and any individual walking alone would need to be on their guard. It was a matter of good sense, especially in the dark, where street lighting was intermittent.

"Any CCTV footage to corroborate his sighting?"

"None." Phillips shook his head. "There was a camera, but it was broken. A lot of them were at the time. Council cuts," he added.

Or perhaps the camera had been sabotaged? There was no point getting angry about it, Ryan reasoned to himself. These were the facts of life.

"Right, so if we trust this sighting, we have her on the edge of the Town Moor at around ten, heading in the direction of Jesmond. She was sighted at a bus stop near her house after nine—what did she do in between times?"

"No idea," Phillips said succinctly. "But at least we know that she headed west, from her house towards Jesmond."

Ryan's mouth flattened. "And we all know who used to live in Jesmond—before he came down in the world, that is."

"Aye, we do."

Keir Edwards' former home stood on one of those upmarket, tree-lined streets.

"Although, we also know somebody else who resides in the same part of town," Ryan added after a pause. "Colin Hart."

Phillips tugged at his lower lip. "Those other missing women—at least three of them were reported missing or last seen on that corner of the Moor, n'all," he said glumly.

Circles, Ryan thought. Things always came around in circles.

The owner of Goldfingers was, unsurprisingly, a fan of the James Bond franchise. The shop interior was decked out like a Christmas tree, with trays of diamonds sparkling under well-placed spotlights and autographed portraits of Sean Connery and Roger Moore gracing the wall space. To cap it all off, Shirley Bassey's voice boomed out from hidden speakers.

Remarkably, the shop managed to avoid being gaudy and was instead enjoying the patronage of several customers who seemed to appreciate the kitsch style of the place.

Ryan's eye fell on a young couple poring over a tray of diamond solitaire rings and he felt a ripple somewhere in his belly. He imagined, just for a moment, standing in the same position with Anna and then immediately retreated from the thought, more out of habit than fear. He gave it a full minute, re-assessed himself, and concluded that the thought of marriage had not terrified him half as much as it should have.

Interesting.

Phillips, with a brilliant lack of complication, headed directly for the ring selection and bent over the glass case.

"I'd peg Denise as a fan of emeralds," he began conversationally. "They would match her eyes. But you can't beat a diamond…"

Ryan shifted his feet, amazed to find himself overheated in the air-conditioned room.

"You, ah, you're thinking along those lines, then?"

Phillips didn't bother to look up but smiled to himself. Times like these, he remembered he had fifteen years on his SIO.

"Why not? I'd have to be a bloody fool not to realise that I'm punching well above my weight with MacKenzie," Phillips replied, unguardedly, then cleared his throat. "Not to say that I couldn't punch a fair weight, you understand."

"Naturally."

"Aye, well. Had a fair few rounds in my time…"

"Of boxing?" Ryan asked sweetly.

Phillips looked up from the sparkles to bestow a withering look. "Less of the cheek. Point is, why wait? Life's too short."

"What about…making sure they're…you know, the right person?" Ryan couldn't remember feeling more awkward in his life. Where the hell was the manager? He looked around the shop expansively, trying to find someone who looked remotely like they were in charge.

Phillips stood up straight and fixed him with a fatherly look.

"Son, when it's right, you just *know*."

Ryan sent up a prayer of thanks to whichever god was listening, as their conversation was interrupted by a glamorous-looking woman in her early sixties. She modelled a heavy pair of ruby and diamond earrings that matched the bright red dress she wore with panache. Her smile was wide and genuine.

"Hello! Are you looking for anything in particular?"

"No—"

"Yes—"

She looked between both men and gave them an understanding smile.

"I think I have something which may suit you," she said delicately. "Some couples prefer a less traditional, more *masculine* engagement ring. Over here, we have a lovely selection of white and rose gold, which can be engraved…"

Ryan and Phillips exchanged a look and then grinned.

"You'd be lucky," Ryan mouthed across to Phillips, then got back down to business.

"Thank you," he said, stilling the woman's progress across the room. "Actually, we're not here to make a purchase. We'd like to ask you some questions regarding a particular item of jewellery you stocked in 2005 and, I believe, still have in stock."

He took out his warrant card and made the introductions. To her credit, the woman—who turned out to be Penny Sutherland and the co-owner of the shop— didn't bat an eyelid.

"Of course," she nodded. "Please, follow me."

They were seated in the back office, which boasted more shiny things, including a brand-new coffee machine.

Catching the direction of Ryan's gaze, Penny set the machine whirring.

"How can I help you both?"

Phillips drew out a picture of Amy Llewellyn's bracelet, since cleaned up so that the design could be more clearly identified. It was a silver bangle, fashioned into the shape of a coiled snake.

Penny recognised it straight away. "Yes, we sell quite a few of these. They're quite popular at the moment—it's all festival chic these days."

Ryan didn't stop to worry about what counted as 'festival chic'. "You stocked these in 2005? Could you tell us when you started to stock this particular bangle?"

"Oh yes," she said, without hesitation. "We've stocked that design ever since we opened the shop in 1992."

"How can you be so sure? Don't you need to check your records?"

Penny simply smiled. "I'm positive, because my son makes that particular model. It's part of his range. He's a silversmith."

"Would you—or he—have a record of how many units have been sold, and to whom?"

"Now, that's a bit trickier," she said, with regret. "Like I say, that range of jewellery has always sold very well, which means there are quite a few sales to go through. It would help to know a date range, to narrow it down a bit?"

"We were hoping that you could tell us the 'when' part," Phillips put in. "But how about we start with 2004-05, and go from there?"

Ryan nodded. They would work on the assumption that the bracelet had been a gift from Amy's unknown lover and hope for the best.

"You're lucky," Penny said, tapping at the keyboard in front of her until she found the correct spreadsheet. "If you'd asked me for records from the nineties, they would be long gone. It wasn't until 2000 that we really moved everything across onto the computer."

She made a clacking noise with her teeth, while she searched the digital files.

"Another thing in your favour is that we offer a guarantee on that range, so we take down a customer's details in case they need to use it."

The computer pinged. "Here we are! From 2004-5, we sold sixty-eight of those bracelets."

"Names?"

"Ah, well." She linked her hands together and adopted a resigned expression, ready to impart bad news. "It isn't that I don't want to help you, but the thing is, I can't just hand out names and addresses of customers willy-nilly. Data protection, I think they call it."

Ryan knew it well. They stumbled into that particular piece of legislation at least once during every active investigation.

"We're investigating the murders of two young women."

Penny heaved her ample chest theatrically. "Believe me, I want to tell you everything you need to know, but I've got enough years behind me to know better. If you could only narrow it down a bit?"

Ryan paused to consider.

"How about this: can you tell me how many of those purchases were made in cash, versus card?"

"I can!" She beamed at him again and turned back to the spreadsheet.

"That's certainly narrowed it down," she said after a moment. "During that timescale, only nineteen bracelets were paid for in cash, ten of which were bought by the same person."

"Ten?"

She nodded.

"How many of them preferred not to give a name or address for warranty purposes?"

"Well, now, I'm sure that most people …" She trailed off, a frown crinkling her face into a myriad of fine lines. "Well, look at that! There *was* one customer who didn't give a name and paid in cash. In fact, he's the one who bought ten bracelets in bulk."

She turned back to them and her face remained troubled. "I remember exactly who he was."

"You just said that he didn't leave a name—"

"I know," she nodded, her earrings glinting against her ears. "I remember him because he's quite famous now and what with him making such a large purchase…He used to come in here regularly, to buy himself cuff-links and things like that. He liked his finery. He was...well, I suppose I should be honest and say that he was a good-looking young man. Quite memorable."

"Who?"

"It was that man—the one they called The Hacker. It gives me the shivers to think that we used to see him all the time."

Silently, Ryan took out his phone and brought up a picture of Edwards.

"Is this the man you remember? Ten years is a long time."

"Yes." She nodded. "He's older in that picture, but I recognised him on the news last year. I'm positive that's him."

Penny watched them exit the shop with a puckered brow. She really had liked the young man and even his gnarly sergeant. If she'd been a few years younger...well, if wishes were horses, beggars would ride, she thought sadly.

Smiling over at one of the shop attendants, she closed her office door behind her and rummaged around in the bottom drawer of her desk, until she found the little pay-as-you-go mobile she kept there for emergencies.

She made a short phone call and then considered her duty discharged.

Outside, Ryan turned to Phillips.

"Did you speak to HMP Frankland?"

"Aye, they've agreed to make a room available whenever we need it."

"Put a call through, Frank. I want us there inside the hour, but I want everything by the book. He can call his solicitor, do a country jig, whatever the hell he wants—but by six o'clock I want this dirty laundry to be aired."

"There isn't a cat in hell's chance of Gregson letting you run the interview," Phillips said, matter-of-factly.

"Which is why *you're* going to run it and I'm going to observe."

Phillips didn't relish the prospect.

"We've got Colin Hart sitting back at the station, ready to go."

"He can wait. He's attending voluntarily, because we don't have enough to charge him. If we speak to Edwards, we might find something more."

Phillips nodded. "You still need to run this past Gregson."

Ryan found himself more reticent than usual to report to his superior and put it down to the sensitive subject matter.

"Gregson knows this was my intention from the start. Besides, I'm going to be in the observation area. Edwards doesn't even need to know I'm there."

Phillips looked up at Ryan with a dubious expression. It wasn't so much a case of following protocols, as avoiding further heartache. Coming face to face with the man who had killed your sibling, even with a reinforced glass panel between you, was seldom a smart move.

CHAPTER 13

Her Majesty's Prison Frankland was another architectural triumph, set on the outskirts of the city of Durham. The plain red-brick buildings which housed an interesting mix of standard and high-risk Category A male prisoners certainly fulfilled its *raison d'être*, being at once depressing to look at and well-fortified.

"Charming place," Phillips muttered from his hunched position in the passenger seat of Ryan's car. To say that he had misgivings about being here at all was an understatement.

"It's not meant to be a holiday camp," Ryan returned.

Phillips pursed his lips.

The car slid along the driveway, past an enormous sign reading, 'H.M. PRISON FRANKLAND.' As if there could be any doubt that the boxy buildings with their flat, metal-topped roofs and strategically-placed cameras could constitute anything other than a place of detention.

Drawing on a core of pure will, Ryan managed to suppress his personal feelings as they passed through the various levels of prison security. A couple of the prison guards recognised him and wondered, but none of them questioned his right to be there. Phillips risked another glance across at him.

"Does it bother you, knowing how close he is?"

They stood outside one of the many steel gates, waiting for the buzz and the metal clank which precipitated its opening.

"I prefer to keep my enemies close."

Phillips tried to choose his words with care. "There's such a thing as being *too* close, mate. What does Anna think about it?"

"She understands."

That wasn't quite true, Ryan admitted. She had listened to his explanation of where Edwards had been incarcerated, had continued to listen as he detailed how it would not be a problem for him, in the future, staying at her home in Durham. But she hadn't said that she understood, or that she thought it was a good idea, for him to be within such a short radius. The fact of Edwards' presence was a constant reminder of what had happened.

"Look, Frank. I don't need you chewing my ear off about this. Not now. Focus on why we're here."

Phillips drew his chin up, telling Ryan more clearly than words that he was offended. Well, that was tough luck. They had more important things to think about than hurt feelings.

The barrier creaked open and they stepped over the threshold into the Westgate Unit of the prison, an area reserved for those prisoners requiring more secure detainment or segregation. Ryan cast his eye around the foyer and his lip curled slightly at what he saw. This area was almost brand new and sparkling clean. He knew that there was a library, a faith room and access to TV, video games—all manner of hobbies, crafts and classes. The men here could enjoy an hour of Pilates, if the mood struck them and they needed to find their inner Zen.

He concentrated on emptying his mind, slowing his breathing. Before the events of last year, he had maintained a balanced opinion of the criminal justice system. It was easy to do that when you didn't know any of the victims, or their families, personally. It was easy to talk about restorative justice and the value of rehabilitation when the damage and destruction had never hit too close to home. He had been an active proponent of giving prisoners useful occupations during their incarceration and was a staunch supporter of psychological programmes designed to alter negative behaviour in the hopes of reducing rates of recidivism.

That was before.

Lying there, injured, holding the body of his sister as the lifeblood emptied from her and seeped onto his hands, something had broken inside him. He recognised that it had been the tiny core of idealism, which had survived his day job. Now, there was a hollow little space where it should have been, occupied every day with a mixture of cynicism and bitterness. That little space would have been swallowed whole by resentment and loathing, were it not for Anna's calm, positive influence in his life.

"Boss?"

Phillips interrupted the introspection and Ryan turned his attention to the guard who motioned them towards a private conference room, equipped with cameras and an audio recording system. The table in the middle of the room was constructed from a heavy metal, fixed in place by strong bolts to the floor.

"I'll fetch him," the guard said.

The air felt thick and heavy as they paced around the small boxy space. Or, rather, as Ryan paced and Phillips sat with every sign of comfort and ease with himself in one of the newer plastic chairs. He took his time retrieving a notepad and file of relevant paperwork, licking the tip of his thumb every so often as he flicked through the pages.

Eventually, he gave up the pretence and sighed.

"You know what we need to cover?" Ryan asked.

Phillips held back another sigh. They had been through their planned line of questioning several times during the car journey to the prison.

"Course I do."

"Good. Good." Ryan was gibbering, and he knew it.

"You'd better head on back now," Phillips said quietly. They had already agreed that Ryan would remain in the observation room. There was a long panel of thick, one-way mirrored glass separating the two rooms, which had been modelled on the standard interview suite at any police station in the land.

He didn't like it, Phillips thought, as he watched his SIO stalk out of the room, but it was for the best.

As the minutes ticked by, he could almost feel Ryan's eyes boring through the glass and sweat beaded across his forehead under the glare of the overhead light. He reached for the inner pocket of his blazer to feel the emergency cigarette stashed there and then remembered that Ryan had smoked it earlier. He patted the material nonetheless and told himself that he could smoke an entire pack at the end of the day as a reward once this ordeal was over.

The door clicked open and two guards escorted Edwards through the door. They would remain in the room at all times, and were fully kitted out in stab vests and protective gear. Phillips didn't bother to stand up or to utter any kind of greeting. He followed Edwards' progress across the room and tried to assess the man.

Superficially, he looked very much the same. He was still tall and athletic. He wore his dark hair in a shorter, military style rather than the foppish, windswept waves he had favoured before his incarceration. His handsome face was sharper, somehow, the bones showing more than before. He had kept himself in shape, Phillips noted, but that was hardly a surprise. There were gym facilities and he was a raging narcissist. Of course he would keep himself in peak physical fitness.

The eyes were the same: dark, stony pits, which stared unblinkingly from two holes in his face.

In no particular rush, he settled himself comfortably in the chair opposite Phillips and linked his fingers together. The guards clipped his handcuffs onto the steel hooks atop the table to prevent undue movement, which Edwards tolerated with seeming equanimity. Given his history, there could be no predicting what Edwards might try to do, given the chance.

All the while, his gaze trained somewhere over Phillips' right shoulder, looking directly at the one-way mirror behind him.

Sneaky bastard, Phillips thought.

Once the preliminaries had been attended to, Edwards turned his attention to Phillips.

"Well, this is an unexpected pleasure," he drawled. His eyes bored into the burly sergeant sitting opposite him. "Have you missed me?"

Phillips let the words fly over his head.

"I am here in connection with an investigation into the murders of Amy Llewellyn and Claire Burns. You do not have to say anything. But it may harm your defence if you do not mention when questioned something which you later rely on in court. Anything you do say may be given in evidence. Do you understand?"

Edwards laughed. "I seem to have heard it somewhere before."

"Do you understand?"

"Naturally. I haven't been struck by idiocy during my time here."

"Good. You are entitled to have a lawyer present."

"Hardly seems necessary, does it?" Without moving his hands, Edwards seemed to gesture to the space around him.

"Are you waiving that right?"

"Go on, then. Let's live dangerously." He bared even, white teeth.

"Let the record show that Mr Edwards is waiving his right to legal representation." Phillips wanted it all tied up in a nice, neat bow. He took a sip of water while he considered where to start, but was interrupted.

"I have a condition," Edwards continued silkily. "I'll waive my rights, but I won't be speaking to you. I think that a man of my stature deserves someone a little higher up the ranks."

Phillips listened with a sinking stomach. "Who did you have in mind?" He knew that the question was totally superfluous.

Edwards smiled again, enjoying himself. "You do like to draw it out, don't you?" His face fell into hard lines, and he leaned forward menacingly. "I'll speak to Ryan, or nobody. Your choice."

He leaned back in his chair and glared beyond Phillips to the mirrored wall, with an unspoken challenge.

Phillips said nothing but knew with certainty that Edwards meant what he said. The man had nothing to lose. They needed information and he would happily clam up for all eternity without a second thought.

He called a fifteen-minute break.

Ryan was waiting outside when Phillips exited the interview room.

"Let me talk to the bastard," he said through gritted teeth. "I'll be only too happy."

Phillips put a heavy hand on Ryan's chest.

"Use your head, son. You're giving him what he wants."

A muscle ticked in Ryan's jaw and it took willpower to drag his eyes from the doorway and the man who sat waiting, like a spider.

"You think I can't handle him?"

Phillips began to walk away, in the direction of the foyer and the seating area reserved for visitors. He kept a hand on Ryan's back, urging him forwards.

"You need to keep a clear head," Phillips said, with absolute calm. It was the same sort of voice he had once heard Robert Redford using in *The Horse Whisperer*, when he had tamed an unruly horse.

It seemed to work.

Ryan stuck his hands in the pockets of his jeans and closed his eyes for a moment while he consciously emptied his mind. Slowly, he let air in and out of his lungs, smelled the scent of industrial floor cleaner and something that reminded him of school dinners. Jacket potatoes and beans, or shepherd's pie, cooked in bulk.

When he spoke again, his voice was cool and remote. "Thanks, Frank. I needed that."

"Don't mention it." Phillips shrugged. "What do you want to do about it?"

"There's no way he'll talk otherwise."

"You sure?"

"Come on. You know him as well as I do."

"Aye, I do." Phillips scratched the top of his wiry thatch of hair then let his hand fall. "We could play it so that you're in the room, but I still ask the questions?"

"We could try it, but I'm betting he'd clam up all the same. He wants to taunt me, you see. He's bored, in here." Ryan looked around the wide, beige-coloured space. "Bored, angry and frustrated that he can't maraud around the city killing more women."

"It's not a good idea to let him use you as his punch bag. He won't hold back," Phillips added. "He'll twist the knife, no doubt about it."

"No doubt at all," Ryan agreed. He thought of his sister and how lovely she had been. He thought of his parents' devastation. He remembered watching as Edwards had killed her, while he had lain injured and immobile on the floor. Pain ricocheted through his body, singing through his nerves and along the scar marring his left arm, from shoulder to elbow. Then, he thought of Rose Llewellyn, sunken and small in her home prison, surrounded by the memories of her daughter. He recalled the broken conversation with Claire Burns' father and how he had begged Ryan to find justice for his child.

It was never easy to face one's demons, even when they looked human. But he reminded himself that, if he had done it once, he could do it again. This time, for other families—other brothers, mothers and fathers.

He turned back and squared his shoulders.

"I'm ready."

Keir Edwards' eyes lit up an unnatural, glossy black against his pale face when Ryan entered the room.

"I'm honoured," he began, his cultured voice trembling slightly. Ryan judged that to be excitement, rather than nerves.

"DCI Ryan and DS Phillips re-entering interview under caution with Keir Edwards at HM Prison Frankland. Prison guards Fran Foster and Daniel Cramer both present. Time is 18:04." Ryan's voice rang out clearly for the tape and not once did he acknowledge that Edwards had spoken.

"Mr Edwards, do you require any reminder of your rights and obligations under caution?"

"So formal," Edwards mused. "We know each other well, you and I."

"Let the record show that Mr Edwards understands his rights and obligations."

Edwards' eyes continued to roam Ryan's face. He envied his lightly-tanned skin, which spoke of days spent outdoors in the early summer sunshine.

"I think you mean, *Doctor* Edwards," he said.

Ryan raised an uninterested eyebrow.

"Last time I checked, you had been struck off the medical register," he replied without a pause. "Deciding to torture and kill people goes against the Hippocratic Oath, you know."

Edwards' mouth twisted into a smile. "Developed some teeth, have you? Must make you feel strong, knowing that I'm chained." He rattled his wrists against the metal cuffs and then leaned forward suddenly. "But you and I both know you'd be cowering like a whipped dog if I weren't."

Ryan felt the spittle spray from Edwards' mouth, and with slow movements he retrieved a tissue from his jacket pocket to wipe it from his chin.

"We would like to ask you some questions relating to Amy Llewellyn," he said.

Edwards continued to stare.

"When did you first meet Amy?"

"I've never heard of her," Edwards lied.

Ryan fished inside the file and found a copy of the image taken from Edwards' own possessions, last year.

"Do you recognise this picture?"

Edwards tilted his head to one side and ran his gaze over the image of Amy, naked and bound against the bedposts of the bed in his old home.

"I couldn't say."

Ryan slapped the file closed and rose from his chair.

"There's nothing for us here," he said to Phillips, once again ignoring Edwards. "He's obviously useless. I told you we're looking for someone with *precision*. He doesn't fit."

"You think I don't know that you're baiting me?" Edwards said, with a hint of irritation.

"Aye, you're right. It was a long-shot, anyway," Phillips agreed and then stood up himself.

"Sit *down*!" Edwards rapped out, eliciting a long stare from Ryan.

"Your manners seem to have rapidly declined, since you've been living in a cell," Ryan said. "You're long past calling the shots, here, Edwards."

"You want to know about Amy?" Edwards murmured. "I bet you do. I bet you'd love to know about all the girls in those photographs. Only one way to find out, because all roads end here."

"Did you kill her?"

There was a long pause.

"No, but I wanted to."

It sounded like an honest answer, Phillips thought, but who could tell with this animal?

"Why didn't you?"

"Missed opportunity," Edwards snapped.

"How did you know her?"

Edwards shrugged. "She was a student at the university. I was on clinical rounds in the hospital at that time. She was in one of my student groups."

Ryan nodded. It was only what he had imagined.

"You wanted her?"

"Oh, certainly," Edwards mused, thinking back. He could picture Amy clearly, as he could picture the fantasies he had only begun to play out. "She was quite memorable."

"How did this picture come to be taken—and when?"

"Tit-for-tat, Ryan. Why don't you tell me how you've been, all these months? I hear you've found yourself a lady," he rasped. "I hear she's quite a looker. But then, I *did* tell you that we're similar, you and I—more so than you would like to admit."

Ryan said nothing, but fear gripped him. He didn't want any trace of Edwards' filth to taint Anna; he didn't want her name mentioned here at all.

"It doesn't work like that, Edwards. The privilege of free movement, you see. I get to ask the questions and then I get to leave. You get to answer them, or not answer them, but then you have to stay here. That's it."

"Spoilsport." Edwards tutted. "Well, if you don't want to chat, I'll keep the conversation flowing. For instance, I hear your new lady-love is very much to my taste," he continued, tracing his tongue along his upper lip. "We like our dark-haired beauties, don't we?"

Beneath the table, Ryan's hands clenched into fists.

"I did see a picture of her, in the local news," Edwards added. "Very nice indeed. I spent a delicious few hours imagining how she would feel. *Anna*," he let the name roll off his tongue. "I don't believe I've ever had an 'Anna' before."

"Aye, and never will," Phillips butted in. "Why don't you tell us about the women you *did* have. You met Amy at the university? When was this?"

Edwards stretched his shoulders. "I met her in September of 2004. It took me a few weeks before I could convince her to become better acquainted, if you take my meaning."

"You began a relationship?"

"Now, inspector, you're not the only one capable of keeping up a pretence, at least for a while. Yes, I took her out, I fed her, and I banged her."

The casual cruelty lacing his stark words was hard to ignore, but Ryan and Phillips did their best.

"And then?"

"She didn't like it. Clever girl, really," He let out a soft chuckle. "Some of them sense what's coming."

They weren't human, not to this man, Ryan realised. They were objects, slabs of meat to be used and disposed of at his whim. Still, the admission tallied with the information Phillips had found in Amy Llewellyn's medical history, such as it was. A few weeks before her death, she had attended the GP at the Student's Union, suffering from injuries ordinarily associated with violent sex. He imagined her family would have no idea. The doctor had prescribed creams and painkillers.

"Did you see her again?"

"Of course." Edwards answered the question with a trace of boredom. "I saw her once or twice, around the hospital."

"Then, you killed her?" Ryan finished flatly. "You've confessed to the murders of five women, already, so what's with the sudden shyness? Might as well claim your conquests."

Edwards grinned like a cat. "You know me so well, Ryan, it's really quite flattering that you've taken an interest.

I would happily *claim* her, as you so eloquently put it, but sadly, as I said earlier, she was the one who got away."

"You're saying you didn't kill her?" Ryan was bemused. He could not imagine this man investing time in a project and then walking away.

"I thought I had just made that clear. Are you disappointed? Would you like to have listened to the way I might have killed her, like I killed your sister?"

Ryan's chest contracted and for a moment he couldn't breathe. There was a roar in his ears as the blood pumped through his veins and his fingernails dug little semi-circles into the palms of his hands.

"We're the same, you and I," Edwards whispered. "Deep down, you felt it, I know you did. You felt the incredible rush of power as you watched me, then you felt it again as you had your hands around my throat. How long are you going to deny your true self?"

Ryan could feel his resolve beginning to break, with every word spoken, but at precisely the right time, Phillips stepped into the breach.

"Aye, so if you didn't kill Amy Llewellyn, someone else beat you to it? Must have made you angry, after all that preparation."

Edwards said nothing, but the muscle at the side of his eye ticked.

"But then, you didn't have the balls at that stage, did you? Wasn't until years later that you plucked up the nerve," Phillips carried on, conversationally.

"You haven't got the slightest comprehension of what I'm capable of," Edwards ground out.

Phillips affected a yawn and looked across at Ryan, whose vision was beginning to clear.

"What time is it?" He looked up at the clock on the wall, not expecting an answer. "Okay, so if you didn't kill her, did you find out who did?"

"If I knew who had taken her from me, he would no longer be alive."

There was something about the way he uttered the threat that didn't ring true, and it caught Ryan's attention. It was too smooth; it lacked realism.

"You know," Ryan said quietly, meeting Edwards' eyes. "If you're angry at the coup, why not give him up?"

Edwards sighed and leaned forward. Ryan held off moving backwards.

"There is an *order*, in all things," he said. "Did it never occur to you that it was *I* who gave *her* up? Nobody takes something from me that I am not happy to give."

"Why would you do that, if you wanted her?"

"Respect," Edwards snapped out.

Phillips snorted a laugh at the thought of a serial murderer claiming to understand the concept of 'respect'.

"Respect? For whom?" Ryan remained focussed.

Edwards leaned back in his chair and the restraints clanked against the table.

"There's the million-dollar question!" He smiled broadly, enjoying the game.

"Are you aware that somebody has stolen your MO?" Ryan threw the question at him and waited to see the response. A shadow of annoyance spread across Edwards' face, followed by forbearance.

"Imitation is the sincerest form of flattery," he replied.

Edwards fixed his stare on Ryan and thought briefly about how he might end him, given the chance.

Then, he spoke again.

"I enjoyed your interview," he said, eyes racing over the man who, physically at least, could almost have been mistaken for his brother. "How you do enjoy playing the strong policeman."

Ryan waited for more and was not disappointed.

"I must say that you wear your heart on your sleeve. If I were you, I might consider talking to someone. I can't tell you how much *lighter* I feel, nowadays. The talking therapies here are very good," he said mockingly.

"Thinking of my welfare?" Ryan bit out. "Don't bother. You see, the great thing is, if things get a little much, I can take a walk. Go for a run. Feel the fresh air on my face. I can eat whenever I want, take a crap whenever I feel like it. How does it feel, Edwards, not to be able to do any of those things? To be forced to jump to somebody else's tune?"

Edwards stared into the grey eyes of his captor and let hate run through him.

"Shall I tell you, Ryan, about all the delicious memories that sustain me? I can promise, you won't like it."

Phillips intervened, always right on time. He slapped a picture on the table in front of them and slowly, Edwards looked down.

"Did you give this bracelet to Amy?"

"No, I did not."

"The shopkeeper remembers you buying the bracelet, Edwards. In fact, she remembers you buying ten of them."

Edwards' face remained impassive.

"Then it's the shopkeeper's word against mine, isn't it?"

"No offence, I'm sure, but your credibility isn't all it could be," Phillips said.

"Ouch," Edwards replied and then raised an index finger towards the photograph. "Interesting design, though, don't you think?"

Ryan took another look at the bracelet and saw nothing new.

"The serpent," Edwards supplied, with rare indulgence.

One of the symbols of Satan, Ryan thought. It wasn't Edwards' style, to dish out symbols to his victims, because to do so would presume a belief system of some kind. Keir Edwards believed in nothing but himself.

The question remained: did he purchase the bracelets and, if so, why would he now lie about it?

"We're not here for a cosy chat. You say you didn't kill Amy, you say you didn't give her the bracelet and didn't buy any—though we've got a witness who says you did."

"Well done," Edwards said with condescension. "You've grasped the situation admirably."

"Tell me, then, what is your relationship with Colin Hart?"

Edwards flashed a grin. "Now, finally, we're getting somewhere." He made to cross his legs, before remembering that his ankles were also restrained, to the thick metal rings drilled into the floor. Anger washed over him again.

"Everybody needs a guide, somebody who can help to nurture one's talents."

"You've communicated with Colin Hart? You're claiming to be his mentor?"

"I believe I might have answered a letter or two. I'm sure you will be asking for copies from the guards—they keep all of them, you know. They're probably hoping to sell them online."

Phillips stopped himself from making any obvious comments to the effect that they wouldn't get much for the ramblings of a murderous psychotic, because the sad truth was that there would be people out there willing to pay good money for letters written by Keir Edwards. It continued to fuel the man's ego, knowing that there was a fan base in the wider world outside his cell.

"Did you instruct Colin Hart to kill?" Ryan stared into the face of a murderer and thought that it was curious that they, too, could be loyal to their own.

Edwards said nothing, meeting Ryan's stare with frank contempt. He would tell them nothing more.

"What do you want?"

"What do I *want*?" Edwards laughed then, a harsh sound in the confined space. "I want your head on a plate in front of me, Ryan. I want to watch your eyes die. But, since present circumstances prevent it, I'll settle for wounding you instead."

"You'll never catch me unguarded again," Ryan replied. "For the rest of your life, you'll know it was me who put you where you are."

"And, for the rest of *your* life, you'll know it was me who *let* you."

"You believe that?" Ryan stood up now, the interview over. "You got sloppy, Edwards. You lost your edge. Maybe you never had it. The man we're looking for at least has the brains to remain undetected—for now."

Edwards watched as Ryan and Phillips stood up, preparing to leave. He burned to rise up from his chair and fight.

Instead, he fell back upon the only weapon he had left.

"It eats you up, doesn't it, Ryan, not knowing? How many others? How many did you miss?" He chuckled quietly, entranced by his own reflection in the one-way glass opposite. He looked up and into the reflected image of Ryan, as he stood beside the door behind him.

"You wonder 'how' and 'why', brooding about it until you can't sleep and you can't eat, but the answers lie inside you—you have only to look into a mirror. *The mind is its own place*, Ryan, *and it can make a Heav'n of hell, a hell of Heav'n.*"

Ryan dragged his gaze away from Edwards and burst out of the room.

CHAPTER 14

"There's nothing in these letters but a bunch of navel-gazing," Phillips complained.

Ryan looked up from his inspection of the prison records to meet Frank's baffled face. They were seated in a small conference room, which had been designed to allow inmates to converse with their legal representatives. "There may not be anything obvious," he replied. "Some of his responses could be hidden—or coded."

Phillips looked down at a copy of a letter from Edwards to Colin Hart, dated less than a month after he had been incarcerated.

"Dear Colin,

Many thanks indeed for your kind letter and sincere apologies for the delay in responding to you. I regret that the procedures in place within these walls prevent me from replying to you as soon as I might wish.

I confess myself immensely moved by your desire to understand my evolution and, for the sake of posterity alone, will do my best to enlighten you.

Where to begin? In the way of David Copperfield? I was born, I grew up…but really, the details of my unremarkable childhood aren't important. I have no family, none that share my blood.

All my life has been spent masked, my true nature hidden beneath the clothes and personality, which I wore as a cloak every morning and took off each night. How can I describe to you, my friend, the mounting pressure and the growing need, which built each day and demanded release?

If only there had been another to understand, to really empathise with the extraordinary mind I was born into…

Perhaps, now, I have found that friend.

With very best wishes,
Doctor K. Edwards"

He flicked back to the original letter written by Colin Hart and tried to understand what led a man to idolise a killer.

"Dear Mr Edwards,

I trust that this letter finds you well, or as well as can be, given the circumstances.

I hope that you will not think me too presumptuous in writing to you, as a stranger. I have always harboured a keen interest in understanding man's progression from the social norm towards that which is not readily accepted, and I wondered if you would be willing to discuss your own evolution?

I look forward to hearing from you, in due course.

Yours faithfully,
Colin Hart"

"He calls it 'evolution' or 'progression,'" Phillips muttered. "Huh?"

"Colin Hart. He writes to ask Edwards about what he calls his 'progression' towards killing. That's not normal, is it?"

Ryan picked up on the nuance immediately. "Ordinary people would consider his actions to be a descent, or a degenerative failure of some kind. Not many would consider killing to be an evolution or a progression."

"Colin does," Phillips said.

While Phillips continued to leaf through the letters in search of anything meaningful, Ryan cast his eye over the detailed record of all post delivered from, or to, Keir Edwards. There was a separate record of all internet usage, which would take a lot longer to go through, alongside a record of all calls made or received using the prison telephones.

Of course, that didn't account for any unregistered mobile phone that Edwards may have laid his hands upon. Ryan wasn't naïve enough to think that contraband didn't find its way into the wrong hands, particularly when those hands belonged to someone as manipulative as Edwards.

Ryan traced a fingertip down the list of entries, noting the many letters described as 'fan mail', and told himself not to feel disgust, or shock. After all the things he had seen in his thirty-five years, there ought to be nothing that could shock him.

Inexplicably, women wrote to Edwards on a regular basis.

Ryan continued running through the list, until he found what he was looking for.

"There!"

Phillips looked across.

"Outgoing mail, dated 1st June. One postcard image of Sycamore Gap, taken on Midsummer's Night. Recipient was Colin Hart. No written content."

"He sent a blank postcard?"

"Colin had it on him," Ryan said. "He had the postcard there, in his rucksack, when he found Amy Llewellyn."

Phillips whooshed out a breath. "Midsummer's Day— that sometimes falls on the solstice. They can be the same thing."

Ryan swore.

"Edwards sent him there. Why else send a blank postcard? It was a map, telling Colin to get himself up to Sycamore Gap on the solstice."

"Sly bastard," Phillips breathed.

"Call MacKenzie. Tell her we're on our way back to the station. Any word from Faulkner on forensics?"

"Still nothing." Phillips shook his head. "You want me to chase him again? We can't hold Colin much longer without charging him."

Ryan knew it.

"Try to light a fire up his arse. He should have Colin's prints and swabs by now—tell him to hurry up and compare them with the DNA on Amy's bracelet, for a start, then compare it with anything found on Claire. We're more likely to find something on her."

"All over it."

Arthur Gregson slid his mobile phone into the breast pocket of his blazer and watched Ryan pulling into the staff car park from his vantage point on the fourth floor of CID Headquarters. The day had been fine, but as afternoon slid into evening there had been light rainfall, leaving a glimmering sheen of moisture on the ground, which glinted in the last of the day's sunshine. Ryan unfolded his tall frame from a snazzy little grey convertible and tucked a large folder under one arm as he strode purposefully in the direction of the main entrance. Without pausing in his tracks, his head shifted upwards and met Gregson's gaze. No smiles were exchanged, no raised arms or waved hands.

That was not, of itself, too concerning. Ryan had always been a reserved sort of man, prone to bouts of antisocial behaviour and self-imposed seclusion. Yet, in recent times, he seemed to have softened. He had cultivated a kind of easy camaraderie with his colleagues, which Gregson was not privy to.

Perhaps, Gregson thought, social exclusion was one of the downsides of superior rank. On the other hand, it could signify something much more concerning: that Ryan knew, or had begun to suspect, that the carefully constructed world around him was built upon a foundation of sand.

He thought of the tense conversation he had just held and reminded himself to dispose of the cheap 'pay-as-you-go' mobile phone, which was burning a hole in his pocket. There could be no slip-ups, not now. There was too much at stake, the least of which was his job title. In certain circles, punishment was swift, brutal, and didn't make allowances for rank.

Within two minutes of entering the police station, Ryan was informed that Colin Hart had been allowed to return home. His solicitor, a well-heeled young woman from a premier legal firm in the city, had made several loud declarations about the shoddy treatment of her client and had stalked out of the building with Colin meekly in tow. Armed with new information following their visit to HMP Frankland, Ryan and Phillips walked in the direction of Faulkner's office to seek further ammunition to bring Colin Hart back in, this time under arrest. They found his staff, heads bent diligently over microscopes, but no Faulkner.

"Damn. Is he out on a call? If so, why are the rest of his team still here?" Ryan isolated a shifty-looking young lad sitting across the room who was studiously avoiding looking across at either of them.

"You!"

His eyes snapped up.

"Where's Faulkner?"

"I-I-I...He's out, sir."

"I-I-I want to know where," Ryan parodied, a bit unkindly.

"I don't know, sir."

He looked as if he was telling the truth, and the rest of the crowd looked equally devoid of useful information.

Or so he thought.

"Sir?"

A homely-looking woman edged forwards.

"I was hoping to speak to Tom about this," she confessed, feeling guilty and disloyal. "But he hasn't been back in the office for a few hours and I...well, I really think we've hit on something important."

"Go on."

"It's to do with Amy Llewellyn's bracelet, sir. We cross-checked the DNA swab Colin Hart gave us earlier and we've found that it matches one of the unidentified LCN DNA samples found on the bracelet. It's a tiny sample, a few skin cells only, but ..."

"Exactly. But." To avoid kicking any living or inanimate objects, he stared unseeingly at a nondescript landscape print of the Northumbrian coastline, which hung inside a plain wooden frame on the back wall of the room.

He should have been told the moment the results had come in. They'd let Colin Hart walk free because they didn't have enough to hold him but, ironically, the forensic evidence had been sitting in a petri dish upstairs. When he looked back from the picture on the wall, the CSI woman was practically quaking in her rubber-soled shoes. He flashed her a smile, in sympathy.

"That was excellent work. You did the right thing, letting me know."

Her skin turned a slow shade of red. She might have been a mother of three, two of them sons, but that didn't mean she had lost her appreciation for a man who looked like the chief inspector. She was only human, after all.

"Thank you," she said. "We'll keep working on the rest."

Ryan turned back to Phillips.

"Should be enough for an arrest and a search warrant. Get on it, will you?"

"I'll have a chat with the magistrate." Phillips executed a funny little dance, in anticipation.

"What the hell was that?"

"You've never seen *Singin' in the Rain?*" Phillips asked, in a shocked tone.

"Sure, I've seen it," Ryan replied. "Only I don't remember Gene Kelly doing anything like that."

"Well, you've either got it, or you ain't."

Ryan couldn't help but grin.

Geraldine Hart could hardly breathe, a state of affairs arising from a combination of stale atmosphere and the simple fact that her heart struggled to pump the oxygen around her body. Her chest heaved and shuddered as her lungs tried to open and draw the air into her morbidly obese body.

All the while, she watched daytime television from the relative comfort of her orthopaedic mattress. Beside her rested an empty tray, which formerly held all manner of edible goodies, but now only the wrappers remained. She was very aware that her incontinence pad needed changing; in fact, it had for quite some time now and the smell was beginning to bother even her unfussed nose. Colin had been out for ages. The ornate clock on the mantel, sandwiched between two porcelain figurines, told her that he had been gone for nearly four hours, and it was now approaching eight o'clock.

Past dinnertime, she thought pitiably.

Just then, her well-trained ear picked out the sound of the front door opening and then shutting quietly downstairs.

She stabbed at the volume button on the television remote to turn down the sound and opened her mouth to yell.

"Colin! It's about time you got home. I've been waiting for hours!"

There was no answering reply.

"*Colin?* Did you hear me?"

Geraldine heard the creak of footsteps on the carpeted stairway and turned to reprimand her son. When the door swung open, she began her tirade.

Almost immediately, she was silenced.

A short time later, the door swung shut again and there came the sound of retreating footsteps treading quickly down the stairs.

Colin bade his solicitor farewell and thanked her for the lift home. He didn't notice the unmarked police car parked a little further down the street, which Ryan had ordered as a precaution. He stood for a long while on the short gravel driveway leading up to the wide front door of the house, which had been his home for the past forty-four years. It was a prison; a gilded cage from which he seemed destined never to escape. He looked up to the first-floor bay window with its frilly lace blinds and knew that the author of his present tragedy slept there, a mountain of sallow flesh and wasted life.

He forced himself to put one reluctant foot in front of the other and let himself into the house, closing the door behind him with a quiet click.

He thought he heard his mother calling out his name, her jarring monotone scraping the edge of his nerves. He put his hands to his ears, to drown out the sound.

"Ssh," he muttered. "Shut up. Just shut up."

He could hear nothing when he took his hands away again and he walked to the foot of the hallway stairs, head bowed. A headache throbbed in his temples and the ache spread through his neck and the base of his skull. Memories of being in the police car and at the station surrounded by police staff played on his mind, interspersed with flashing images of Claire. He sucked in his lips to stop the weak tears, which wanted to flow as he remembered the times he had spied on her, late at night. Or the times he had followed her to the bus stop, claiming that he was catching the same bus, despite the obvious fact that he owned a car. The memories culminated in the last time he had seen her, on Sunday evening. He had finally plucked up the courage to go into town, to visit her at the Diner.

He had worn what he thought of as his trendiest gear— new jeans and a matching denim shirt. He had heard somewhere that denim-on-denim was in fashion. He had even styled his hair, being careful to smooth over the bald patch at the top of his head.

She hadn't been happy to see him.

"Colin, why are you here?"

"I came to see you, Claire. I had to see you."

"Colin, I've told you so many times before. I just don't like you that way."

"I only want to be your friend."

"I don't think that's a good idea. Why don't you go home? You can see I'm trying to work."

A heavyset bouncer had materialised from nowhere and taken a firm grip of his arm.

"*Think it's about time you slung yer hook, isn't it, mate?*" he'd jeered. "*I'd better not find you lurking around here, again. Now, bugger off!*"

The humiliation had been complete when he had been shunted out onto the street, rejected by Claire, rejected by her world.

Colin had snivelled, the tears rolling down his cheeks in salty tracks while he'd wished to be stronger, smarter, better lookin ...anything that would make him worthy of Claire's affection. Then, he had dried those tears on the sleeve of his new denim shirt and had pulled himself upright. He had friends; strong, powerful friends and women who loved him, albeit online.

Perhaps, it was *she* who was not worthy of *him*.

Back in the present, Colin rapped his forehead against the hard wood of the newel post to try to dispel the images.

He thought he heard his mother calling out again and his teeth dug painfully into the tender flesh of his tongue to prevent an angry retort from escaping. His hand shook as it gripped the bannister and he made the slow journey upstairs. The headache was turning into a migraine, he thought distractedly. His eyes were blurry, and his ears were buzzing. Still, he finished the journey to his mother's room and pushed the door open.

Soon after, he pulled the door smartly shut behind him again. He rushed downstairs, wild-eyed, without direction or purpose.

"M-mother ..." he began, chattering to himself in the quiet house. He turned towards the front door and then back again, towards the kitchen. He didn't know what he was looking for; perhaps to get her a glass of water, or something tempting to eat so that she would wake up again, but both were forgotten when he saw the contents of his fridge.

"No. No!" He pointed at the small glass vials, which stood in a proud line on the top shelf, backing away and slamming the fridge door shut again.

Confused, panicked, he ran into the sitting room and headed for the desk. Before he got there, he nearly tripped over the large, navy rucksack that was strewn on the floor, its contents spilling onto the cream carpet.

He bent down to look more closely and picked up a heap of women's clothes. When his fingers brushed the cheap pink satin skirt worn by waitresses at the All-American Diner, he fell backwards onto the floor.

"Claire?" He saw her image in his mind, wearing the skirt on the day she had died. "I didn't. No. No, I didn't. I couldn't..."

But he remembered the hate he had felt after she had rejected him. He thought of his most secret, forbidden fantasies and the encouraging words of the man who had understood them.

CHAPTER 15

MacKenzie stayed long after everyone else had packed up for the day, poring over the grainy CCTV footage which had, miraculously, been delivered by a spotty-faced youth on behalf of the owner of the All-American Diner.

Her optimism that Jimmy Moffa had turned a corner in his life was short-lived, once it became clear that the footage had been tampered with. Befitting the high-spec camera system circling the Diner, it began with crystal-clear images of Claire Burns clearing tables and mopping floors after her shift had ended. It showed her retrieving her small handbag from the staff locker room, before she waved a friendly 'goodbye' to her colleagues. She couldn't have known that it would be the last time.

The footage showed Claire opening the main doors to leave, then it skipped and jumped, the image blurring so badly that no figures could be seen. After a time-lapse of around three minutes, the exterior camera showed an empty street outside, where Jimmy stood smoking a cigarette while his driver waited from the comfort of a white Porsche Cayenne.

MacKenzie would send the footage to the techies to see if they could do anything to clear it up, but all that would take time. As things stood, the only thing that it could confirm was that Claire Burns left the All-American Diner at 11:33pm.

Disappointed, MacKenzie moved onto the communications she had received from the tech department about ANPR footage. There was a snarky e-mail from one of the IT managers, telling her in no uncertain terms that there was no way he could provide her with the footage she needed before the end of the week.

In other words, she had precisely nothing in the way of visual evidence, no leads about potential vehicles, and certainly nothing they could use to incriminate Colin Hart.

Ever the realist, she decided that it was no use crying over spilt milk, so she collected her things and turned off her computer for the night. The hallways were quiet, empty of the usual bustle of swift footsteps and echoed sounds of industrious typing or police banter. The overhead lighting had reverted to night-mode, so instead of shining a garish banana yellow, they shone a murky grey-white light.

MacKenzie locked the Incident Room behind her and made quickly for the elevator, before remembering that it too had been shut down for the evening.

That left the stairwell.

She recognised the signs of heightened stress in her own body and put it down to the cumulative effects of a disturbing few days. It was always unpleasant to find a fresh body, and her experience with Colin Hart had only compounded her distress, regardless of training and experience. So, when faced with the prospect of a dark, empty flight of stairs as her only means of getting out of CID Headquarters, she was understandably hesitant. It was classic Hitchcock, after all.

"Come on, Denise," she muttered, giving herself a firm mental shake.

She took the stairs quickly, the heels of her smart boots clicking on the concrete as she went. She counted off each passing floor, unable to shake the sense of danger and the illogical feeling that she was not alone. The sound of her footsteps echoed loudly and masked other sounds, but beneath the din she thought she heard a voice. Immediately, she froze, like a startled deer. While her eyes darted between the path she had already taken and the stairs she had yet to follow, her ears strained to hear the sound again. The silence was deafening.

She could have sworn she smelled lavender.

Clenching her teeth against the shaking which was working its way through her body, she gripped the handrail and forced herself to finish the journey. Her leather saddlebag smacked heavily against her hip as she raced down the stairs. Finally, when her feet hit the ground floor, she gave in to the impulse to run along the wide corridor leading to the car park exit, her bag flapping behind her. She fumbled with the door but, eventually, it opened. She burst outside into the cool night air and cast her eyes across the darkened tarmac to where her car stood, illuminated by one of the large spotlights lining the staff car park. As her stomach jittered, she asked herself why she had stubbornly refused Phillips' offer of a lift home, or his offer to stay with her while she went over the footage.

Pride.

Her experience with Colin Hart had shaken her up more than she realised. After a strong cup of sugary tea in the staff canteen, embarrassment had crept in. She cringed at how she had practically run away, displaying what she considered a weak attitude towards her job. Once the dust had settled, she had been keen to prove, mostly to herself, that she was back to normal.

That was why she had pushed Phillips away, telling him to pack up and go home. She had even refused his offer of dinner, made by his own fair hands. He was, amazingly, an excellent cook. She had regretted her decision the moment he left the Incident Room, but she regretted it even more now.

She peeled herself away from the wall at her back and prepared to make a run for it, and to hell with what anybody thought.

But, in horrified slow motion, she spun around as the door behind her opened again and a figure emerged, his face shadowed.

Fear clutched at her throat. A half-strangled sound escaped her, and she stumbled backwards, her feet trying desperately to catch up with the voice inside her head, which commanded her to move, to act *now*.

"Denise?" Jeff Pinter stepped out of the doorway and shrugged into his long overcoat. "Everything alright?"

"J-Jeff?"

Denise stayed where she was, one hand braced against the side of the wall for support, adrenaline pumping through her system, still primed for flight.

"That's my name, don't wear it out!" He chuckled at his own weak joke.

"What are you doing here?" Embarrassment made her voice sharp and Jeff held up his hands in appeal.

"Whoa there, calm down. I thought I might catch Ryan, since he usually works late, but apparently I've missed him."

Denise didn't back down.

"You could have called him. What do you need to speak to him about, anyway?"

Jeff frowned, his face concerned. "I was going to offer to go over the old reports I compiled on Edwards' victims, to make sure there weren't any oversights," he replied easily. "Are you okay? You look as if you've seen a ghost."

MacKenzie's heartrate had slowed and her breathing had steadied sufficiently for her to pull herself upright. She delayed answering Pinter's question, giving herself a few seconds to regain her composure by straightening her jacket and hitching her bag a bit higher on her shoulder.

"I'm fine, Jeff. You startled me, that's all."

He clucked his tongue sympathetically. "Sorry about that," he said, drawing on a thin pair of gloves. "But, you know, a lady shouldn't be out so late at night, all by herself."

MacKenzie's teeth snapped together. Her natural instinct was to respond in kind with some sort of caustic remark to the effect that it was equally dangerous for men as for women, but she was used to Pinter's old-school approach to life. Besides, she *had* felt frightened. Another thing to add to her rapidly growing list of things to feel mortified about today.

"Well, it's high time I went home. Goodnight, Jeff."

"Why don't I walk you to your car?"

It was a kind offer, MacKenzie thought. Why, then, did it sound threatening?

"No, really, Jeff. I'll be fine on my own. See you around."

"Don't be silly, it's no trouble," he persisted, picking up his leather briefcase as if to join her.

Denise started to panic, and she scrambled around her jumbled mind for another excuse to put him off. At that moment, she caught another movement out of the corner of her eye and she could have cried with relief.

Phillips ambled across the car park from the direction of what was affectionately known in CID as the 'Pie Van'. Some of the flaky pastry had crumbled onto the collar of his coat and there was a small gravy stain at the knot of his tie, which told tales of his misadventures. Spotting Denise by the side door, he raised a hand in greeting and squinted to see who stood beside her in the shadows.

"Pinter?"

"Evening, Frank," came the breezy reply.

Phillips noticed instantly that MacKenzie was not looking herself. If he didn't know better, he'd have said that she was terrified. In a subtle move, he slid an arm around her waist and felt her lean against him for support.

One of the things he loved most about Denise MacKenzie was her fierce, sometimes prickly, independence. Earlier, when she had kicked him out of the Incident Room, he had allowed her to believe that he had taken her at her word, right until he reached the elevator and thought better of it. He had taken a turn around the block and ended up at the Pie Van, where he had stalled for a further twenty minutes munching happily before shaking himself off and heading back to CID. Throughout that time, MacKenzie's car had remained within his line of sight.

Now, he was pleased he had risked her wrath and stayed nearby. Whether it was the strain of the day or the present company, he couldn't be sure, but something was clearly upsetting her.

And whatever upset Denise, upset him.

"Something I can help you with, Jeff?"

"Nothing that can't wait until another day."

With a friendly nod, Phillips led MacKenzie away. Behind them, Pinter stood and watched their progress, deep in thought. After a few minutes, he slowly unpeeled his gloves and tucked them back inside the pocket of his coat.

Anna came home after another late lecture to find Ryan engrossed in paperwork. Miles Davis was a welcome intrusion into his silent task, providing a balm to his strung-out nerves. His dark head was bent over a large file of papers and he had changed into well-worn jeans and a loose t-shirt. An empty glass of water stood on the nearby coffee table.

Anna knew that he was spending more and more of his nights with her and less in the impersonal environment of his own apartment. She had wondered, at first, whether she would find it hard to adapt to the added presence of another person. Instead, she found herself missing him in those times when he was away from her, a sure sign that he had slotted seamlessly into her life.

"Ryan?"

His eyes lifted to seek her out and he smiled, unfolding himself from the cramped position he had occupied for over two hours. He stood up, stretching out his muscles as he did, before leaning in for her kiss.

"How was your day?" he murmured, running a gentle hand over her shiny hair.

Anna thought of the endless essays she had marked, the hours spent cooped up in the library. Her body prickled as it replayed the quiver of unease she had experienced, walking down the High Street earlier that day, but she decided not to mention it. The last thing he needed right now was to listen to her melodramatic ideas about imaginary stalkers.

"Busy," she answered instead. Her eyes were stinging, and her vision was slightly fuzzy from the strain. He noticed the action and frowned.

"You forgot your glasses, again."

"Don't fuss," she said, but was touched that he would care. "Have you eaten?"

"I thought I would wait for you."

She looked closely at him. The pallor of his skin and the drawn, anxious face spoke of more than mere tiredness.

"What happened?"

He shook his head, hardly knowing where to begin.

"Edwards happened."

Self-consciously, he let go of her. He didn't want to discuss the man's name in her presence, but if he had to, it felt better not to talk about him and touch her at the same time. He didn't want her to connect to Edwards, even conversationally.

"You went to see him, didn't you?" Anna took a seat on the edge of the coffee table, because it was closest.

Ryan nodded and prowled around the small living space. "It was rough, but the day's been shitty from the get-go," he said. "Beginning with Pinter finding ritual markings on the body of Claire Burns."

Anna stared at him and felt apprehension spreading through her chest. She took a long, deep breath.

"Markings? Are they the same as—?"

"Yes. An inverted pentagram—slashed into the torso around the time the girl died. We didn't see it properly until she was, quite literally, pieced back together."

Anna looked away from his silvery-grey eyes, somewhere into the distance. The most recent victim had apparently suffered the same cruelty as her own sister, six months earlier. What did it mean? Had the Circle returned, to take another victim?

"I thought it was finished," she whispered. "I thought all that was over and done with."

Ryan took the seat beside her and held both of her hands in his. They felt cold.

"We don't know for sure yet that there's any connection to the Circle," he tried to reassure her. "In fact, it's more likely to be someone with an unhealthy obsession over the cases that I've worked on in the past."

Anna searched his face.

"You mean someone's copying the style of previous murders? Why?"

"Anna, if I could tell you why people did some of the crazy shit they do, it would make my job a hell of a lot easier." He sighed, but laid it out for her. "We're looking at someone—a guy called Colin—who's been writing to Edwards in prison, chatting like old friends. It's looking like Edwards sent Colin up to Sycamore Gap on Sunday morning, knowing there would be something to find up there. I'm betting Edwards killed Amy—maybe she was his first effort—and he hid her. He directed Colin up there because, for reasons best known to himself, he was happy for her to be found. Either that, or Colin already knew Amy was lying hidden under the stones and he was returning to the scene of his crime. We don't know, yet. As for Claire Burns, she lived on the same street as Colin Hart and we have a witness who says he was harassing her."

"You think Colin might have taken some inspiration from Edwards, in killing Claire?"

"Very possible."

"Whereas, you're thinking that Edwards killed Amy Llewellyn all those years ago and just never admitted it?"

Ryan looked at Anna for a long moment. She had summarised the situation commendably, but for all that it made sense, there were gaps that needed plugging.

"I wish it were that simple. I can't tell you how much I'd like to wrap it all up in a pretty bow like that and take it to the Crown Prosecution Service."

"What's missing?"

Ryan leaned back in his chair, staring at the ceiling as he worked through the loopholes in his mind.

"On one side of the scales, Edwards has admitted that he had a relationship with Amy Llewellyn and we have a statement from a shopkeeper which confirms that he bought the same bracelet found on Amy's body—in fact, he bought *ten* of them. On the other side of the scales, no bracelets were found on any of his other victims, so why buy in bulk? Besides which, he claims he didn't kill Amy, although he wanted to. He says he gave Amy up, voluntarily, to some unknown person."

"He *knows* who killed her?" Anna was horrified.

"So he claims," Ryan said conversationally. "But let's not get carried away. It could still have been him. He's had time to settle into his surroundings and to find that prison is not to his taste. He doesn't want another prosecution to add to his existing sentence, so perhaps he's regretting the fact that she has been found after all these years and he's trying to divert suspicion from himself."

"He's in prison for life," Anna said.

"Yes." Ryan nodded. "But he's likely thinking that he can somehow reduce his tariff on grounds of 'good behaviour'. This is a man who thinks that ordinary rules don't apply to him. He believes that he will be able to circumvent the system."

"He's dreaming."

"And then some," Ryan agreed, with a short, mirthless laugh. "But if we *do* believe him when he says that he gave Amy up, foregoing the opportunity to kill her, then that would explain why none of his DNA was found on her body, or on the bracelet. The trace samples are so small that, if he had touched it, even once, there would be a chance of something being found. Yet, it wasn't. We've got three samples on the bracelet: one belonging to Amy, another one belonging to an unidentified male, and a final sample which was confirmed as a match to Colin Hart, just this evening."

"It matched? Then, surely, that confirms he killed her?"

"No." Ryan shook his head. "It adds weight, but the downside to Low Copy Number DNA testing is that, with the samples being so small, it could have come from Colin coughing over the bones when he found them. He might have touched the bracelet when he found it on Sunday, which is almost certainly what he would argue in court. We've got some added weight, but it's not an airtight case."

Anna felt his frustration keenly. "What are you going to do?"

"The only thing I know for certain is that our killer wants attention. He wanted Amy to be found, or at least he wants to be *credited* for her murder. Claire's murder told us a lot about his psychology; he managed to copy Edwards' MO, firstly using a pressure syringe to sedate her, then using adrenaline and antibiotic to keep her alive while he dissected her, until she died from massive cardiac arrest. That was Edwards' style. But, to cap it all off, our perp has also managed to copy the ritual style we found at Holy Island, by slashing the torso. Not forgetting that all of these girls went missing or died around June 21st, which is the summer solstice."

Anna listened intently, imagining the kind of twisted mind that could conceive of so much pain.

"It's like he's giving you the finger."

Unexpectedly, Ryan laughed. "Got it in one."

"How will you handle it?" Anna saw the visible signs of strain and wondered what else had been said while Ryan had been cooped up in a room with Keir Edwards.

Ryan shrugged it off. "Same way I always do," he replied. "First thing tomorrow, we're bringing Colin back in for questioning, this time under arrest on suspicion of murder. In the meantime, he can enjoy his last night playing Scrabble with Mother Hart, who probably has no idea what a naughty boy her son has been."

While Ryan listened to mellow jazz music with Anna, another man allowed himself to enjoy some peace and solitude, after a punishingly long day. Finally, he could retreat to his own corner of the world, away from the daily stresses of his everyday life, away from other people. He could sit and ruminate.

He thought of the police and the visits they had paid, but tried to put that out of his mind. It was nothing he couldn't handle. He glanced towards the ceiling, with its ornate plasterwork and centrepiece chandelier, and felt his blood boil. Deliberately, he looked away again and tried to clear his mind, to empty it of all the inconsequential things which usually clogged it. Were it not for the prosaic events that filled his days, he would be able to spend more time on the work he really loved. Instead of living the empty, false shell he inhabited each day, he could be the man he really wished to be.

He could flourish.

He looked across at a tall, mahogany cabinet, the key for which he always kept on his person. With a sly smile, he fished around the waistband of his trousers and found the little hidden pocket, which he had sewn there himself. He drew out a small brass key.

Anticipation coursed through his body as he unlocked the cabinet. Before viewing its contents, he closed the door to the room and locked it. He pulled on two pairs of thin gloves. He was a careful, meticulous man. He opened the polished doors to reveal several file stackers, filled with different coloured plastic wallets.

His hand hovered over the files, deliberating.

Eventually, he selected a red wallet and retreated to his chair with it clutched to his breast. There, in the quiet room, he re-lived the delicious memory of it all. He re-read the neat, intricate notes he had made before and after, allowing the sensation of killing to flow through his veins. Reverently, he ran his fingertips over the single photograph he had allowed himself to take, which captured beautifully the fear and confusion of his last victim.

Much later, after he had sated himself, he closed the file again and returned it to its rightful place in his cabinet, which was ordered alphabetically. Every now and again, he needed to remember, to relive those magical moments and feel powerful again. Usually, he could survive on those memories for long periods of time before he needed to kill again.

Just lately, though, the memories hadn't been enough. He had re-opened Pandora's box and was unable to close it. Only a few days would pass before he needed to look inside the cabinet again. He recognised that it was time to choose his next project, because if he waited much longer, he would be unable to execute with the finesse for which he was known.

He had standards to uphold.

Besides, there was just one bracelet left to gift to one lucky recipient, whom he had already selected. She was not his usual type; perhaps she was a little older and worldlier than he would have wished, but she was connected to Ryan. It would make his triumph all the sweeter, and surely then the chief inspector could not deny his supremacy.

CHAPTER 16

Wednesday, 24ᵗʰ June 2015

"He's done a bunk."

"What's that?" Ryan wedged his mobile phone between his ear and his shoulder as he shrugged into a pale blue summer shirt. Phillips' beleaguered voice boomed out of the headset and Anna raised a finely arched eyebrow from her position on the other side of the bedroom.

"Colin Hart. He's not at his house."

"That hardly signals that he's 'done a bunk'. He could be at the supermarket, for all we know."

"Not likely, guv."

"Frank, we've had eyes on him all through the night. If he left his house, somebody would have seen him."

"Nope." Phillips shook his head at the other end of the line, in a manner reminiscent of the bulldog used to advertise a popular brand of insurance. "The DCs tailed him all the way home after he left the station last night and they've been on shift ever since. They never saw him leave his house, but when they knocked on the door to bring him back in for questioning less than ten minutes ago, there was nobody there."

"Okay, let me see if I've grasped this." Ryan could feel a headache coming on. "Despite being under constant surveillance, our main suspect in the murder of at least one woman has vanished. Are you having me on?"

"Wish I was."

"Damn."

"Shit and bollocks," Phillips added.

Ryan flipped the last button on his shirt and made a grab for his boots.

"Have the DCs entered the premises?"

"Yes, guv. They had the appropriate warrants, I saw to that."

"Right. I'll meet you there."

The detective constables assigned to the surveillance team for Colin Hart looked sheepish when Ryan and Phillips found them hovering on the driveway of Number 32.

"You," Ryan said, waving a hand in the direction of the nearest one. "Report."

"Sir. Having received the message from DS Phillips that we had a 'go', we exited our vehicle and approached the property. The suspect, Colin Hart, entered the house at around eight-fifteen last night, after being dropped off by his solicitor. He stood outside the property for several minutes before entering, but since then we've had no sight of him."

"Other exits?" Ryan asked.

"None, sir. The garden to the rear is inaccessible except through the house itself, and is walled off from the neighbours."

"At what time did you gain entry?"

"We received DS Phillips' message approximately thirty minutes ago, at eight-fifteen. We acted upon it immediately, intending to bring the suspect into police custody. We knocked at the door and identified ourselves several times. Believing the suspect to be inside the house and ignoring us, we forewarned the suspect that we had the appropriate warrant to enter his property and DC Fowler retrieved the battering ram from the boot of the car to force entry if necessary."

Ryan flicked a glance towards the front door, which remained intact, then back to the reporting constable.

"No, sir," he answered the unspoken question. "There was no need to force the door. We tried the handle and found it was unlocked."

"Then?"

"We conducted a search of the property and found it to be in a state of disarray, at least downstairs. There is one awkward issue, sir, which is that the suspect's mother"—he consulted his notebook to find her name—"a Mrs Geraldine Hart, appears to be asleep in one of the bedrooms upstairs.

We tried to be quiet, so as not to wake her …" He trailed off, clearly unsure of himself.

Ryan and Phillips exchanged a look.

"We'll be careful not to wake Sleeping Beauty." Ryan couldn't help the sarcasm. "Meantime, I want an All Ports Warning out on her blue-eyed boy. We've got the local lads watching out for a man who matches his description in the vicinity. Is that his car?" He eyed the blue Honda sitting on the driveway.

"That car's the only one registered to his name," Phillips chimed in.

"So he's unlikely to have transport, unless he's hired something. No pick-ups, no deliveries?"

"No sir, no visitors at all to the property during our surveillance."

"So he's likely on foot. See if you can get the traffic helicopter involved—we can cover a wider area that way. Make a start on tracing his mobile phone."

"Shall I contact Gregson?"

Ryan should have been in regular contact with his Chief Superintendent.

"He can wait," he said shortly, and then turned towards the house. They pulled on plastic shoe coverings, nitrile gloves and wished they had full body overalls to complete the ensemble.

As they stepped into the grand old house, there was a thick scent of lavender permeating the air, just as MacKenzie had described. It clung to the nostrils and brought to mind funeral parlours or nursing homes, depending upon one's degree of optimism. The hallway was clean and tidy and, beyond it, they glimpsed the reception rooms and the kitchen. They bypassed those and made directly for the stairs because it seemed obvious to both men that, in order to have slept through that level of commotion, Geraldine Hart would have to be souped up on sleeping pills, or dead.

Upon closer inspection, it turned out that she was dead.

"Did they come in on the banana boat, or what?" Phillips shook his head in disbelief at the younger generation of detectives coming up through the ranks. How they could have mistaken the state of Geraldine Hart's body as being anything other than dead as a doorknob was beyond him.

"First thing on Monday, they're on a refresher training course," Ryan muttered.

The room stank. There was no other word for it. The heady mixture of food matter gone off and fruit-flavoured medication was nothing in comparison with the scent of raw sewage, which pervaded the atmosphere. Geraldine's body had evacuated itself either before or after she died; that much was clear from the sticky brown mess on the bedclothes beneath where she lay.

The television was turned down low and the theme tune to some facile morning show invaded the room. Ryan wished he could have touched the volume control, to silence the jingle, but training held him steadfastly in his place by the door.

"Just when you think you've seen it all—"

"You realise you haven't. Not by a long shot," Ryan finished Phillips' sentence.

"Don't know how she could let herself get into that state," Phillips said, but with a trace of pity rather than judgement. He was a fair man.

Ryan said nothing. He knew from his background checks into the lives of Colin Hart and his mother that she suffered from a number of illnesses, all of which were attributable to her being drastically overweight. Diabetes, osteoporosis, high blood pressure, to name a few. Apparently, she'd had a stroke a few years back.

"We don't know enough about her medical background," Ryan said simply.

They continued to take in the scene, staying away from the body, as much in self-preservation as not to contaminate any evidence.

"No obvious signs," Phillips remarked eventually.

"No trauma that I can see," Ryan agreed.

"I'll contact Pinter," Phillips said, but made no move to retrieve his phone.

Ryan waited a beat, considering. "It looks as though Colin's our man, doesn't it?"

"Well, if he hasn't offed his own mother, I'll be a monkey's uncle," Phillips said roundly.

Ryan's lips twitched.

"I'll get onto Pinter." Phillips turned away to call in the pathologist.

Ryan spent another minute or two with the body of Geraldine Hart, conducting his own version of a private memorial service, which he afforded each of his victims regardless of the way they looked, or how they had behaved in life. It didn't matter. He wasn't any deity, to be pronouncing judgment on the lives of others. He certainly wasn't infallible, which was another good reason not to be pointing the finger. Having said that, he thought as he dipped down to the floor to look under the bed, the manner in which people lived could be relevant to the way they died.

In this case, it would appear from the discarded syringe on the far underside of the bed that Geraldine Hart's medical condition meant that her body had likely succumbed to massive heart failure after the administration of a strong dose of chemicals. He would leave it to the experts to confirm.

Ryan stood up again, his body unfolding like a concertina. It was time to see what else was lurking inside the walls of the Hart household.

Pinter arrived promptly, as Ryan and Phillips met in the hallway downstairs, preparing to do a walk-through of the scene with the CSIs.

"Morning!" Pinter was, as usual, unrelentingly cheerful.

"Jeff."

Ryan's sharp ear detected an odd note to Phillips' voice. It was remarkable, really, how much could be conveyed in one word.

"I guess there's no time for idle chit-chat. Our girl's up here, is she?" Pinter didn't wait for confirmation and he practically skipped up the stairs before turning along the landing in the direction of Geraldine Hart's bedroom.

Phillips' beady brown eyes watched his progress until he was out of earshot, then he unravelled a stick of nicotine gum and shoved it in his mouth with a little more gusto than was necessary.

"What's eating you? Apart from nicotine withdrawal," Ryan asked.

"I was just asking myself, 'Frank, how could that pathologist have known where to find Geraldine Hart's body?' " Phillips replied. "Considering that I never breathed a word of it on the phone twenty minutes ago."

Ryan folded his arms across his chest and rocked back onto the balls of his feet.

"You trying to tell me something, Frank? You know how I enjoy our little tête-à-têtes, but I'm currently pressed for time."

"Last night," Phillips said, his voice lowered a fraction. "He was hanging around the cop shop after hours. Said he was looking for you."

"He hasn't mentioned anything."

"Uh huh." Phillips nodded. "Well, he told MacKenzie that's why he was lurking around CID after ten o'clock. He scared the bloody life out of her."

Ryan tried to be reasonable. "He could have popped in on his way home," he offered. "Thinking he'd find me there.

But, yes, I'll agree that it's not usual behaviour from him. He usually prefers that we come to him."

"It's not like MacKenzie to be melodramatic," Phillips continued.

"Agreed. Do you think there's anything in it?"

Phillips shifted uncomfortably. "I know that everything points to Colin—maybe a bit of it concerns Edwards, but …" Phillips rolled his shoulders and shifted uncomfortably. "It's been playing on my mind, what you said yesterday, about it being somebody with inside knowledge."

"Colin had inside knowledge, if Edwards told him the location," Ryan replied.

"I know, that makes sense, but…"

"Spit it out, Frank."

"Pinter's been based at the RVI for over fifteen years; he would surely have come across Amy Llewellyn in one of his teaching groups. He would know how to dissect with the kind of precision we saw on Claire's body."

"That's a big call, Frank."

Phillips nodded. "I don't even like thinking it," he said. "I've got nothing to suggest Pinter is connected in any way, other than the fact he happens to work at the hospital. It's hard to imagine someone you've worked beside for years, turning out to be a killer. Still, I'm thinking about it."

Ryan remained silent. He didn't need to tell Phillips that longevity did not prevent a man from killing. Murderers had family, friends, work colleagues; all the trappings they needed to make themselves appear 'normal'. Besides, he had his own niggling sense of unease whenever he thought of Jeff Pinter and his excitement over Claire Burns' body.

"I can't get it out of my mind, the way MacKenzie looked last night." Phillips's face drooped into concerned lines, the skin falling into comfortable grooves as he spoke. "To tell you the truth, I'm worried."

Ryan hadn't heard this from Phillips before. Denise MacKenzie was a strong, self-sufficient woman and an experienced detective. She could handle herself. Yet, if Frank was worried, there must be some basis for it.

"I—ah—I've been seeing Donovan," Ryan began clumsily. "I've actually found the couple of times I've seen him to be … I guess they've been useful. Just to clear out some headspace," he qualified swiftly. "I don't want you, or more importantly, MacKenzie, to think that I'm pressing her to go running to a psychiatrist after one or two bad days at work but, on the other hand, it could be a boost."

Unlike Ryan, who could be stubborn at the best of times, Phillips was far more broad-minded. He chewed reflectively and gave the suggestion serious thought. "Paddy Donovan knows Denise," Phillips said. "He's a decent bloke, he might be able to clear a few things up for her." It was a source of sadness that he hadn't been able to offer her that kind of emotional balm himself, but he could handle the knock-back if it meant that Denise got the help she needed.

"I'll suggest it," he concluded. "No idea how she'll react, but it's worth a shot."

Ryan opened his mouth to say more, but was distracted by the sight of Faulkner and his small team of CSIs arriving at the house.

He made a thorough assessment of Tom Faulkner. He looked exhausted, which was highly unusual for a man of his character. Faulkner wasn't the kind to work hard, play hard— only the *work hard* part of that adage applied to him. He didn't look hung-over; he looked wrung-out. Ryan watched as Faulkner tugged on his white overalls and gave a couple of brief instructions to his team before he ducked into the hallway.

He met Ryan's direct stare with a sort of dull recognition.

There was a protracted silence, until Ryan snapped. "Well? Are you going to stand there like an ostrich, or are you going to explain to me why I wasn't informed *immediately* after you matched Colin Hart's DNA to one of the unidentifieds on Amy's bracelet? By the time I found out, we'd let him go without charge because we had nothing to hold him. Now, he's flown the coop and we've got another dead body on our hands."

"Boss—" Phillips started to interrupt, but snapped his jaw shut at a single, deadly look from his SIO. He pursed his lips and wondered if he should make himself scarce before the situation turned nuclear.

"Sometimes, there's more to life than just blood, guts and human waste," Faulkner replied with simmering anger.

"Is that so? Well, my mistake. I was under the impression that you were employed by the Northumbria Police

Constabulary to perform a service. I understand now that it's more of an *ad hoc* thing, where you get to pick and choose when you help us to investigate serious crimes." Ryan's voice dripped with sarcasm.

"I have never, in over fifteen years, let this department down."

"Why the bloody hell are you starting now, then?" Ryan exploded, his grey eyes cutting into Faulkner like shards of ice.

"I am entitled to my privacy, just as much as you are," came the controlled response.

Ryan gave Faulkner another long look and tried a different tack.

"Tom," he said, softening his voice as much as humanly possible. "Is there anything I need to know? Are you in some kind of difficulty?"

"There's nothing you need to know."

Ryan's patience had limits. "That's where you're wrong. I need to know that I have the full co-operation of my team. I need to know that you're on board with this. As it is, I'm going to have a hell of a job explaining the situation to Gregson."

"Then don't bother." Faulkner shrugged. "I'll tender my resignation, if that will solve the problem for you."

He turned on his heel and made to leave, just like that.

Ryan and Phillips gawked at one another in shock for a full five seconds before Ryan galvanised himself.

"Now, you just wait a sodding minute, Faulkner!" Every member of staff within range looked up at the sound of

Ryan losing his temper. It was unheard of. Ryan's anger was cold, and sometimes he got frazzled, but he never lost control. Ever.

This was worth the price of a ticket.

Ryan stormed out of the house after Faulkner, who was unzipping his overalls on the driveway outside.

"I don't know what the hell you're playing at, but the joke's over. If you're in the middle of a mid-life crisis, you're going to have to shelve the histrionics because we've got more important things to think about. Such as lives already lost and lives which *could* be lost if we don't catch this fruitcake."

Faulkner pushed his spectacles higher on his nose, nonplussed. "I've given my working life to this department, along with a pretty big chunk of my personal life. I've lost a wife because she couldn't handle the hours I put into this job, or the memories I take home. I think I've given enough."

Ryan's anger started to dissolve. He could see from Faulkner's face that he was serious. "Tom, listen to me. I know how you feel—"

"Sure, you do," Faulkner said, dully.

"You know I do." Ryan rammed the point home. "It's no fun, the work we do. It's bloody hard, most of the time. Every man and woman you see here takes it home with them at the end of the day." He cast his eyes around at the spectators, who busied themselves in work as soon as he looked up. Usually, it would have brought a smile to his lips.

"The forensic work you do is usually what helps us to find them, in the end." He referred to the perpetrators of all the violence they saw on a daily basis. "Without you and your team, we would be a bunch of suits following hunches and hearsay. If I don't say it enough, then I'm sorry. But, you're valued, Tom. By your colleagues, by the victims and their families—and by me."

Faulkner looked taken aback. He swallowed and looked down at the ground, searching for his voice. "Thank you for that," he said brokenly.

"Whatever's on your mind, you can tell me. Surely, you know that by now."

Faulkner listened to Ryan and was tempted, oh so tempted, to tell him. Yet, he couldn't seem to find the words.

Instead, he re-zipped his overalls. "Let's just get back to work."

Ryan knew that was as good as he could hope for right now. It wasn't a resolution, not by a long stretch, but it would have to do.

CHAPTER 17

Ryan gave instructions for immediate checks into Colin Hart's bank and credit card usage, methods of transportation, and phone records—both landline and mobile—in addition to the foot patrol which was already underway. The techies were poring over Colin's computer and any other electronics in the house. MacKenzie had oversight of the Incident Room, in case there were any incoming developments, while she continued to dig deeper into the life of Claire Burns.

Ryan and Phillips remained at Number 32, awaiting initial observations from the pathologist and the CSIs.

Agonising minutes slipped by as they stood on the gravel driveway, both men imagining where a desperate man with Colin's personality might choose to hide himself, until Jeff Pinter's rangy form emerged from the front door, stepping out into the overcast day once more.

"Seems pretty cut and dried, to me," he said, shrugging out of his overalls as he spoke. "Looks like Geraldine was injected with a massive dose of Lorazepam and my bet would be cardiac arrest following that, although I can't say for sure until I've completed a post-mortem."

"You're sure she was injected, though? Did she inject herself?"

"Yes, I'm sure she was injected. Her usual medicinal injections were given to the side of her hip, judging by the old puncture sites there, whereas this injection was administered to the side of her neck, almost directly into her carotid artery, which would have given maximum impact. As for whether she injected herself, I can't rule that out from my end. It's impossible to tell without checking the syringe for prints—it's perfectly possible that she could have. That'll be a question to ask Faulkner."

"How long has she been dead?"

Pinter puffed out his cheeks, then let the air wheeze out through his teeth in a manner that made Phillips' fists clench.

"You're looking at anywhere up to fifteen hours. She's definitely on the turn."

Phillips' nose wrinkled at the description. The poor woman wasn't a piece of fruit gone bad. She had been a person.

Ryan seemed more capable of ignoring the pathologist's flippancy. "So we're looking at any time after 6pm yesterday," he said, pushing back some of the dark hair which blew into his eyes. "That puts Colin within the timeframe, considering he returned to the house around 8pm."

"Thirteen hours would certainly still be a realistic timeframe," Pinter agreed.

"Anything else we need to know?"

Pinter scratched one bony finger against the side of his ear. "Nothing that isn't immediately obvious to a layperson." He gestured with the same bony hand, with the complacent manner of an expert in his field. "She was clearly massively overweight, with all of the health problems associated with that. You can see the cocktail of medications labelled to her in the fridge downstairs, including vials of Lorazepam."

Ryan nodded thoughtfully. Claire Burns was also drugged with a large quantity of Lorazepam, which had been injected into the side of her neck before she was abducted. "Phillips, we need to check the quantities prescribed by Geraldine Hart's doctor. In fact, let's take a look at her medical notes, if we can."

"Already on it." Phillips nodded, making a short, scribbled note on the miniature notepad with its worn leather cover. "Might get lucky and find some of her medical info in the house, so we don't have to get a separate warrant."

At that moment, one of the technical support staff jogged out of the front door, making a beeline for Ryan.

"Jasmine? What have you got for me?"

"A bit of a goldmine," she said, with a touch of excitement mingled with nerves. She didn't have too much interaction with DCI Ryan but, when she did, she wished she wasn't wearing baggy overalls.

"Oh?"

"We started with his computer, sir, thinking that would be the most securely protected device and might take longer to crack. Actually, it had barely any safeguards and the password was pretty basic—it was 'CLAIRE'."

Ryan exchanged a look with Phillips. "What did you find?"

"Well, it's clear that the suspect has tried to delete some of the files, but unfortunately he didn't make it past emptying the desktop 'trash'. No effort had been made to delete the files permanently, which is pretty amateurish, considering their content, sir."

"What are we talking about, here?"

"A lot of images," she replied. "There are some historic files on one or two women who aren't either of our recent victims and we've already confirmed they are both still alive and well. Then, there's a massive file dedicated solely to Claire Burns."

"Nudity? BDSM?"

"No, sir—these images are opportunistic in nature. Photographs taken of Claire out and about, some of her while she was in her own home, at work, on the street. I would say that the victim was not aware of her picture having been taken."

"Standard," Phillips said. It wasn't the first time they had dealt with a stalker, or a sexual predator. "When was the last image taken?"

"Most recent was Sunday night," Jasmine replied, causing both men to wake up and lean forward. "Just a shot of her at work, in her uniform. It looks like an image taken from his smartphone, transferred onto the computer afterwards."

"Does it record a time?"

"Yes, sir. The original image was taken at 9:17pm on Sunday evening, then uploaded onto his home computer at 6:32am the following morning."

"Unfortunately for Colin, the electronic file doesn't rule out the possibility of him being up at Sycamore Gap with Claire's dismembered body."

"Yes, thank you, Frank." Ryan noticed that the technician was turning a bit pasty at the thought of dismemberment. That was why she was an electronics technician and not a CSI.

"Anything else you've found?" Ryan pinned her with a stare, forcing her eyes to focus on him rather than thinking about body parts.

Jasmine collected herself. "Yes, sir. There may not have been any sexualised content in the files he holds on real women, but we found a mountain of sexual content in separate files saved directly from the web."

"What kind?"

Jasmine blushed. "Just—ah—normal stuff sir, nothing too kinky. No extreme violence like we've seen with some others."

It didn't fit, Ryan thought. Usually, where a man or woman had committed extreme violence, there was wider evidence of their fondness for it.

"There's quite an online history of him logging onto three sex chatrooms in particular," Jasmine said, listing their names. "And he goes by the same username in each one."

"What's that?"

"DoctorKeir79."

"He's not exactly the subtlest man in the world, is he?" Phillips muttered.

"It ties in with his obsession," Ryan said, turning back to Jasmine. "What was his activity like under that username?"

Jasmine looked away, embarrassed to talk about some of the content she had seen, even though it was her job to trawl through it.

"Well, um, he seems to write confidently about how, um, masterful he is in the bedroom. There was a lot about how he'd like to dominate the women he spoke to."

"All right, Jasmine. Forward the transcripts through to us and we'll take a closer look."

Relief crossed the technician's face. As she headed back into the house to continue her search and help with the transfer of Colin's computer back to CID Headquarters, she paused and turned back, clearly worried.

"There was one other thing, sir. We found another folder, all about you."

Ryan was silent for a long moment, then he offered the girl a smile that didn't quite reach his eyes.

"Thanks for letting me know. Just forward the content to my office desktop and I'll take a look at it."

Phillips opened his mouth to say something, but Ryan had already taken out his phone to make a call.

"Steve? Yeah, this is Ryan. How's your subject today?"

"Hasn't moved from the house, sir, since you left this morning."

"Nobody in or out?"

"Not yet, sir."

"Okay, thanks. Keep a sharp look-out and let me know if there are any developments."

Ryan let the phone fall into the back pocket of his jeans before he turned to face the inevitable criticism from his sergeant.

Phillips regarded him steadily.

"Look, I don't need any more nagging from you," Ryan said sharply.

"Aye, that's because you already know what I'm going to say."

"That I should tell Anna that she's under observation. I know. I agree with you, on one level. On another more important level, I have to think about her safety. If I tell her she's being watched, she'll kick off—exactly like she did the last time. This way, she can carry on as usual, but I get peace of mind."

"She knows Colin is AWOL."

"Yes, I've told her that much. She knows to be on her guard, just like every other woman in Newcastle and Durham. The only difference is, she has more protection than most."

Faulkner looked done-in by the time he emerged from Number 32. Before heading across to where Ryan and

Phillips stood huddled, deep in discussion, he took a few gulps of water and wished that it was something stronger.

Eagle-eyed, Ryan watched Faulkner's progress across the gravel driveway.

"What have you found?"

There would be no pleasantries, no building up to the incisive questions which needed to be asked. Faulkner understood that.

"Only one set of prints on the syringe, or 'murder weapon' as I'm minded to call it, and they're not Geraldine Hart's. Can't check remotely with the database, so I'll have to cross-check when we get back to CID, but I'll venture to say the prints will belong to Colin Hart since there are matching prints all over the house."

"Looking less like suicide by the minute," Phillips observed.

"Indeed," Tom agreed, shaking his mop of mid-brown hair out of its protective cap. He enjoyed the feel of the cool air, washing away some of what he had just seen.

"On the understanding that you're looking for any indication that Colin's house had been a kill site for Claire Burns before transportation, I have to tell you that we've gone through each room with UV. There's no large-scale blood spatter—or any blood spatter at all."

"Would you be able to pick it up, if he'd cleaned the place thoroughly?" Phillips asked.

"Yes, chemical cleaning seldom removes all traces. It soaks into the fibres."

Ryan moved onto the next point of information. "So, you're telling me there's no obvious kill site. What about his car?"

Faulkner shook his head. "Still going over it, so I can't say for certain, but I can tell you there's no large blood loss anywhere around it. The interior is clean, but not *freshly* cleaned, which I would have expected to be the case if he'd recently transported a body."

"Prints?"

"Of course," Faulkner affirmed. "The car is covered with the same two sets of prints as the house, but also a third set of older prints which look different. I'll need to check the database, because they don't match anything we've got for any of the victims."

"That's interesting," Ryan said.

"That's not all," Faulkner said. "The remnants of medical tape we found on Claire's body matched a common brand of surgical tape known as 'Micropore'. It's widely available—"

"I know it," Ryan interrupted him. It was the same brand favoured by Keir Edwards to restrain his victims.

"Well, it's looking like Colin used the same brand to hold his mother's bandages in place. There's a stock of it in the house and the bin is full of discarded medical waste, including bandages and tape. We'll check the samples to make sure none of the DNA matches our victims, but my working theory would be they all belong to Geraldine Hart."

"Okay, he had access to a supply of medical tape of the same kind found on Claire Burns, but that must be balanced against the fact that anybody could buy the same kind of tape from a local pharmacy. Is that it?"

"In one."

"Okay," Ryan said again. He watched a grey squirrel run up the bark of the large tree and was reminded of another leafy tree, miles away from here.

"We've confiscated any potential weapons we could find, which comes down to a few kitchen knives and a pair of scissors, and we'll test those in depth, but if you were hoping we'd find a bloodied surgical knife, I'm sorry to tell you that we've come up nil."

"Understood. There must be quite a lot left to go over, so let me know if anything else crops up."

Behind locked doors, Colin sat huddled in the corner of the room, in a borrowed shirt that was a size too large for him and the same trousers he had worn the day before.

Clutched to his chest was a carrier bag containing Claire Burns' uniform.

"I didn't kill her. I couldn't have killed her."

His teeth still chattered, and his wan blue eyes were haunted as they stared fixedly at the wall ahead.

"I—maybe I did kill her. I don't know." He started to cry—big, blubbering tears which rocked his body.

Against the bare wall, his mind conjured up wild dreams, crazed imaginings where Claire still lived; where his mother was thirty years younger, still the vibrant, younger woman she had been before she had allowed life to get on top of her.

"Mother will be worrying about me," he whispered, but he could not dispel the sight of her lying on the bedclothes, her eyes unblinking and beginning to film with white.

His mind retreated, to a place where reality could not touch him. In that safe cocoon, he was no longer Colin; he felt immortal.

He looked down at the postcard he held in his hand and knew where he belonged.

CHAPTER 18

Anna looked up from her computer screen at the sound of a knock at the front door. Wednesday was her day off from teaching, a time when she preferred to work from her home office undertaking research for her next paper.

She skipped down the narrow flight of stairs in her cottage and opened the door to a friend, not minding the fact that her hair was piled into a messy knot, or that she had a half-gnawed red biro tucked into it.

"Mark!"

Doctor Mark Bowers, her former history mentor and the man she considered a surrogate father stood on the doorstep with an enigmatic smile. He was tall, in his early-fifties and possessed of a year-round tan, which came from working outdoors wherever possible.

"Got some time for a weary traveller?"

Anna grinned. "Come in, come in!" She ushered him inside, happy to receive a visitor. Usually, she relished the opportunity to enjoy a few quiet hours to herself, never needing to fill the silence with background noise, but after her experience the day before, the empty house had suddenly seemed *too* empty. Now, she turned off the radio, happy to have real company instead.

She made tea for them both and they settled in the living room.

"How have you been?"

Mark considered the question as he sipped his tea. Trust a northerner to drink hot fluid even on a warm day. The sun beamed gentle rays through the window behind him, casting his face in shadow, for which he was grateful. There had been too many sleepless nights of late.

"It's been a busy time, with lots of change," he replied.

Since the events of last Christmas, he'd had his work cut out for him as manager of the National Heritage Visitor Centre on Holy Island. There had been an influx of tourists, some of whom visited the island not for its historic credentials, but in ghoulish curiosity to see where a cult circle had operated.

"How is everyone coping?" Anna referred to the families of the victims and those who had survived. It shamed her, but for her own sanity she had avoided going back to the island. Everyone needed time to heal and she, very much like DC Lowerson, had no desire to rush back and remember things she would rather forget.

"It's a tight-knit community," Mark said. "People come together when the chips are down."

There was a pause.

"We've missed you, Anna," he admonished. "I thought you might have stopped by to see us."

She sighed. "I know, and I'm sorry. I just couldn't face going back up there, not after everything that happened."

"That's all in the past," he said, with a flick of his wrist.

"Is it? Sometimes I think I'll never forget the sight of him above me, knife poised—"

"Don't dwell on it," Mark interjected. "He was out of control; a madman. Thankfully, he was stopped before it was too late."

"If Ryan hadn't made it back in time…"

Mark cast his eye around the room with its warm tones and scattered frames of Anna and Ryan in various settings. How neatly the man had slotted into her life, Mark thought. Yet he, who had known her since she was a child, still remained on the outside, forever looking in.

"How about life at the university?" He diverted the conversation neatly away from Ryan's heroics.

"Oh, never a dull moment," Anna replied gaily, but there were shadows around her eyes. Her long-limbed body had always been slim, but it was looking especially slender in the casual summer shorts and loose t-shirt she wore. He tried not to notice the length of her legs or the smooth curve of her cheek as she turned to rest her cup on a side table.

"I'm glad you visited," she began and, fool that he was, he felt a flush of happiness at the sentiment. "I've been meaning to pick your brain about something."

Of course, he thought.

"How can I help?"

"Do you remember Jane Freeman?"

Mark took his time finishing his tea, replacing the cup and saucer with care. "Yes, of course. She was one of my PhD students, whilst I was still working at the university. I believe she was appointed one of the senior archaeologists for National Heritage in the region, with particular oversight of Hadrian's Wall territory. Why do you ask?"

"Oh, no special reason—curiosity, mainly. Ryan has had some dealings with her, recently, as part of an investigation he's been working on."

"Ah, yes," Mark said knowingly. He, too, had seen the interview Ryan had given. "Those girls found inside the wall?"

"Yes, that's it."

"Jane was rather *ambitious* for my taste," Mark continued, crossing one chino-clad leg comfortably over the other. "She always managed to convey the impression that she would sell her own grandmother if she thought she could get ahead."

"Yes, I'm afraid I had the same impression," Anna agreed, grudgingly. One of the things her mother had always taught her was that, if she didn't have anything kind to say, it was better to say nothing at all. Sadly, experience had taught Anna that she was much more human than that, and much less forgiving.

"I take it she's been flapping around the site, making life difficult?" Mark smiled, the tiny crows-feet beside his eyes crinkling with shared understanding.

"I think so." Anna nodded. "Then again, Ryan always seems so capable of handling himself and other people. I can't think of anybody who has ever concerned him, except perhaps the man who killed his sister, of course."

Mark listened, but said nothing.

"I'm not sure I could say the same," Anna admitted.

"You're still troubled by what happened on the island?"

She nodded, looking away briefly. She felt that she could tell Mark her woes; he had known her since she was a young girl with scuffed knees and fading bruises. He had shown her kindness and what it meant to be a friend. He had seen her progression, from the girl with the dysfunctional family, to the woman seated before him. Not without scars, not without hurts, but stronger for them.

"Maybe I just need more time."

"I'm sure that's it," he said. "Unless…would it be a stretch to assume there are similar overtones in Ryan's present case? Young girls being killed, in a site of historic importance…" He trailed off.

She sighed.

"Not to mention the dates," he observed. "You'd have to be blind not to notice the significance, after recent events."

Anna felt her chest tighten. She had hoped that Ryan was right, that it was just somebody using the date as a snub to the Holy Island murders, but what if they were wrong?

What if her secret fears had a real foundation and the Circle still existed?

Mark saw the fear crossing her expressive face and reached across to pat her hand. He wished he could have done more. Instead, he simply said, "I'm sure that Ryan has things well in hand."

Anna smiled weakly. It would be disloyal to say otherwise, to express her worries for Ryan's health and the toll that the investigation was taking on him even after only a few days. Last night had been the worst so far. After visiting Keir Edwards, he had clawed at the bedclothes like a maniac, fighting Edwards all over again in his sleep.

She had tried to wake him to break the awful cycle of memories, but when his eyes opened, Ryan had looked straight through her. Then, he had been angry and irritable. Instead of finding comfort in each other, he had pulled away from her to roam downstairs for the remaining hours of the night.

She said nothing of that to Mark.

"I don't understand the mentality," she said, picking up the thread of their conversation. "I don't understand why people would chant and commit unspeakable acts of violence in the name of—what? Satan?"

Mark watched the confusion, the yearning to understand, and wished that he could help her. "People have committed all kinds of unspeakable acts over the centuries, in the name of one religion or another."

Anna frowned. "You think the Circle considered their cult to be a religion of some kind?"

"The press seem to think they're pagans, without a religion," was all he said.

"You and I both know that's a generalisation." As a historian specialising in pagan history, she knew better than most that it was misleading to apply such a vague label, especially in relation to contemporary practices.

Mark shrugged. "I suppose it's true, in a technical sense. If by 'pagan', they mean anyone who does not follow the orthodox, usually Christian viewpoint, then you could say that the Circle on Holy Island was pagan."

"You're saying they were 'unorthodox'?" Anna laughed. "Surely, that's an understatement. There are perfectly harmless groups of neo-pagans all around the country who dance and sing to the solstice, hoping for a good yield. The men and women who comprised the Circle were mentally unstable."

"Lucky, then, that it's been disbanded."

"I'm not sure that it has been." She spoke seriously again.

Mark raised his eyebrows. "What makes you say that?"

Anna locked her warm brown eyes onto his and he felt the usual pull in return.

"You said yourself, the dates are significant." She avoided answering the question fully, once again conscious that she was not at liberty to discuss the ritual markings found on Claire Burns' body.

"That could easily be a question of chance," he said reasonably.

She tucked her feet up beside her on the sofa opposite him, unconsciously returning to the foetal position as she thought of her misgivings yesterday.

"I know you're right," she said, trying to project an air of confidence. "I think I'm getting paranoid in my old age."

She offered a weak smile, but he was unconvinced.

"Anna, you know how much I care about you," he said earnestly, thinking that she had no conception of how much he cared. "If there's anything I can do to help you, I will."

She shook her head.

"No, really. I'm being silly. I'm probably tired, after one or two late nights."

They began to talk of other things; of history, of the places they had visited around the world, and the countries they had yet to see. All the time, Mark remained painfully aware of the subordinate position he occupied in her life and, try as he might, he could not help resenting it.

Keir Edwards completed a new personal best in abdominal crunches and was pleased with the results when he surveyed himself critically in the short panel of reflective Perspex, which passed for a window. The six-pack he had been so proud of was developing into a ridge of eight now. That was one of the few good things about spending long hours with

only himself for company: he could devote himself to…
himself.

Chuckling, he angled himself to check the time on the
white clock hanging at the end of the corridor. It was nearly
time for his regular eleven-fifteen telephone call.

He checked and re-checked the corridors for signs of
life, but heard only the usual ranting and shouting from the
solitary cells around him.

When he was satisfied that he would not be disturbed
by a wayward guard, he tugged the metal bed away from
the wall and with extreme care, removed a corner of
one of the breeze-blocks which lined the walls. Inside
the cavity, there was a grey sock, inside of which rested a
pay-as-you-go mobile phone with the ringer muted.

He tugged it free and waited for the call to come.

He spent a few minutes discussing recent developments
and then replaced the phone inside the hollowed space,
happy with the day's entertainment so far. He considered
topping it off with a phone call to one or other of the
pathetic women who wrote to him almost daily, vowing
undying love and affection, but the thought of having to
feign interest bored him before he had even begun.

Perhaps, on a slow day, he'd get around to it.

At the same time Mark Bowers left Anna's cottage, Ryan
found MacKenzie at her desk in CID Headquarters.

"Mac?"

Denise looked up from where she had been poring over the statements received from Claire Burns' family, for the tenth time. "Where's the rest of the team?"

"I left Phillips in charge of operations at Colin Hart's house. Faulkner is still going over things there and he's likely to be a few hours, yet."

"I heard about Geraldine Hart," MacKenzie said. "It's pointing dead centre at Colin, isn't it?"

Ryan pulled over a chair from a neighbouring desk, the metal legs scraping tracks across the thin carpet. He straddled the chair and rested his arms along the back of the seat, fixing her with his sphinx-like stare.

"Did you find any CCTV footage?"

MacKenzie sighed. "No. I've referred it to the tech team, but they'll be hours if not days…"

Ryan nodded. It was just as he had suspected.

"It's looking like Colin fled the house through the back garden," he said simply. "The DCs who had him under observation obviously didn't account for the trellising along the back wall, which enabled him to climb over into next door's garden. You can see where the ivy has been damaged and his footprints are all over the soil beneath."

MacKenzie felt a twinge of fear.

"There's an APW out—has been for hours." Ryan was quick to snuff out any panic. "His car is still on the drive, so we know he didn't have transportation of his own. There are no records of him having used his cards in the last six hours and certainly no car rentals from any of the agencies across the city."

"The helicopter couldn't find him?"

"We asked the traffic helicopter to have a sweep," Ryan replied. "They couldn't find him. No sightings, nothing. He's vanished, Denise."

"How?"

"Precisely my question." Ryan smiled, the light of battle turning his eyes from dark grey to pale silver. "I think someone picked him up."

MacKenzie frowned.

"How is it possible that the DCs missed that?"

"They were stationed outside Colin's house," he said. *And happened to be two of the most hapless blokes he'd ever met.* "The direction of his escape seems to end at the house three doors down. He climbed over the garden walls to get there and I'm betting he tried the back doors until he found one that was left open. In this case, the kitchen window at Number 28 was wide open to visitors. The DCs wouldn't have seen him coming out of the front door of a house which lies much further down the street, outside their eyeline."

"He's like a poor man's *Pink Panther*," she said, with a hint of her former flair. "What makes you think he had help?"

"Telephone records," Ryan replied without pause. "Colin made two phone calls from his home line yesterday—one was to his solicitor."

"And the other one?"

"Well, that's the interesting thing, Denise. I know exactly who the other number belongs to. In fact, so do you."

MacKenzie turned fully around in her chair, all ears.

"I'm wondering if you wouldn't mind undertaking some reconnaissance?"

MacKenzie crossed her excellent legs and raised one finely-arched eyebrow. She may have been spooked, but it would be a cold day in hell before Detective Inspector Denise MacKenzie wasn't up to a challenge.

"Talk to me."

Ryan walked across to the double doors of the Incident Room and with a sharp glance in both directions, locked them from the inside.

"This needs to be done properly." He wanted to make that clear, from the outset.

"Naturally." She paused. "Does Frank know?"

Ryan had thought about not telling Phillips for about a nanosecond before laying out the entire plan, in full. It was about knowing whom you could trust.

"He knows," Ryan said evenly.

He couldn't say that Phillips was entirely happy about it. In fact, when he had first aired the idea to his sergeant, he had nearly found himself in a headlock. He had coaxed and cajoled but eventually Ryan had played his trump card.

"Phillips," he had said. *"Do you respect MacKenzie, as a good police officer? Do you think she can handle herself?"*

"Course I bloody do! What the hell do you take me for?"

"Then, let her do her job. She can do this."

"Ryan, I love that woman. Do you hear me? If anything happens to her, I'll break your scrawny neck and I don't care how much we've been through."

They had shaken hands on it, because that was fair enough. If anything *did* happen to MacKenzie, Ryan would be ready to break his own scrawny neck.

DC Jack Lowerson looked up from his bored position playing solitaire at the sound of Ryan's purposeful stride down the centre aisle of the ward.

"Sir?"

Ryan nearly smiled at the eagerness. He conducted a quick assessment and thought that Jack's colour looked good. He also noticed that the same pretty young nurse bustled straight over to check that Lowerson had all he needed.

"I'm fi—"

"Actually, we could do with some fresh water over here." Ryan overrode Lowerson, all charm. The nurse hurried off to fill the jug on the table, which lay untouched.

"Fancy a walk?" Ryan asked cheerfully.

Jack gave him a bewildered look.

"I thought you wanted water?"

"Changed my mind. Let's go for a wander."

He led Lowerson out of the ward, one hand under his arm, checking the nurse's station as he went.

"Where are we going?"

"I'm busting you out of here."

Lowerson started to panic. While he was in the hospital, unwell, he was also safe from the world that awaited him outside. He still had no idea what he was going to do about it, but he wasn't ready to leave.

He began to dig in his heels, but Ryan practically shoved him inside one of the large hospital lifts before rounding on him.

"You ready to get back to work?"

Lowerson stopped fidgeting, in sheer surprise. "I—yes, I suppose so—"

"Yes or no?"

Lowerson followed instinct, to hell with the rest. "Yes."

"I need your absolute discretion, Jack. This goes no further."

The Adam's apple in Lowerson's throat bobbed up and down as he swallowed. If there was one thing that Jack understood, it was how to keep his mouth shut.

"What do you need?"

"I need you to be my eyes and ears, and to be a shield for MacKenzie."

"MacKenzie? What's going on?"

"I can't do it myself, Jack—I'm too recognisable, too visible. MacKenzie is working on a special project..."

He laid out the plan in summary and watched Lowerson's young mouth turn from eager to angry.

"I don't believe it," he hissed. "The bastard—"

"Cool, calm, collected," Ryan reminded him. "I need you to think with this." He tapped a finger to Jack's temple.

"I need forensic evidence," Ryan said simply. "I want to draw him out of hiding. I want him to be tempted to kill again—but this time, we'll be waiting for him."

"It's risky."

"I know," Ryan agreed. "That's why I need people around me that I can trust."

"You can rely on me."

Elsewhere, the streets were mobbed with a lunchtime crowd. Families looked for somewhere to sit and eat sandwiches while young children flicked yoghurt; office workers and shop assistants sought a quiet corner to themselves without needing to think about KPIs or the customer always being right. Pigeons circled above Grey's Monument, the stone needle jutting from the ground at the apex of Newcastle's historic centre. At its foot, teenagers lounged on the steps of the monument, chattering loudly. All around was activity; along the grand, nineteenth century streets, which led from there down to the cathedral and eventually to the River Tyne.

Two men walked along Grey Street, past the theatre with its Doric columns and signs advertising the Moscow State Ballet.

"He paid a visit to Lowerson this afternoon," Gregson began without any pleasantries. There was no time for them.

The High Priest continued to stroll along the busy street, confident that they would not be noticed amongst the crowds. "This is exactly what I anticipated," he said, without a trace of complacency or censure. Somehow, that made it all the more menacing. "Where is Lowerson now?"

"He left the hospital. I presume he's still with Ryan."

"What did they discuss?"

"Since Ryan hasn't come storming into my office, my best guess is that they discussed the current investigation, rather than the last one."

"Then you still have time."

Gregson did not miss the distinction. This was not to be viewed as a shared responsibility but as *his* responsibility. The sword of Damocles hung over his head, a constant reminder of the jeopardy of his position.

"I'll see to it."

"See to it personally, Arthur," came the tranquil response. "I'm well aware that you'd rather not sully your hands, but I would say the situation calls for it."

Gregson thought of the young detective constable and remembered a time, long ago, when he had been so young.

CHAPTER 19

An hour later, when Geraldine Hart's body had been transported to the mortuary and into Pinter's careful hands, Ryan yielded to the proper chain of command. He paid his next visit to the Detective Chief Superintendent, which he recognised was long overdue.

"Well, well." Gregson wasted no time on small talk. "I'm honoured."

Ryan's heard the sarcasm but stood firm.

"I apologise if I have not been as communicative as I should have been, sir."

"On the basis that you did, in fact, attend the scheduled session with Doctor Donovan and that you have, by all accounts, made progress on Operation Hadrian, I'm willing to let it slide."

"Thank you, sir."

Gregson grunted and, with a cheerful two-fingers to the ample signage declaring the building a 'NO SMOKING' zone, he lit a fat cigar. The thick smoke oozed, filling the air with its pungent aroma. Ryan presumed that the Chief had disabled the standard smoke detector fixed on the ceiling above his desk.

"Report," came the order.

"Sir, pathology and forensics reports are now very near completion as regards the bodies of Amy Llewellyn and Claire Burns."

"Give me the main bullet points," Gregson said.

"Three DNA samples were found on Amy Llewellyn's bracelet, but there were none remaining on her skeleton. Sampling of the fibres of her clothes is taking much longer and is nearly done, but in the meantime, we've only been able to look at those on the bracelet. One sample belongs to Amy herself, another has now been confirmed as belonging to Colin Hart, and a third remains unidentified."

"That looks damning," Gregson commented. "Doesn't it?"

"The samples are LCN DNA, sir. They're subject to argument, given the tiny sample sizes. There have been unsuccessful prosecutions on the basis of that evidence alone."

Gregson grunted a second time, signalling for him to continue.

"The bracelet was purchased from a shop we have identified in Newcastle, which is the only shop to stock that particular bracelet given the fact that the owner's son is the silversmith who produces them. The owner states categorically that Keir Edwards purchased ten such bracelets in cash, around the time Amy went missing."

"Intriguing. But Edwards' DNA doesn't account for the third sample on the bracelet?"

"No, sir—it doesn't."

"Even more intriguing," Gregson mused. "Could be any number of people, though. Maybe a friend tried it on, before the girl died."

"Yes, sir," Ryan replied, but he wasn't convinced.

"Carry on."

Ryan shifted his feet but didn't take the chair Gregson offered him. He preferred to remain standing for the next part.

"Following an interview conducted with Keir Edwards yesterday—"

"Come again?" Gregson spoke through a cloud of smoke. "I thought I heard you say that you had compromised the integrity of your investigation by conducting an interview with a man against whom you have clear personal bias, without seeking prior authorisation from me."

Ryan looked at his Chief with growing animosity. "I made clear from the start that my intention was to arrange an interview with Edwards, through appropriate channels. Phillips duly arranged this, giving Edwards ample time to seek legal representation. Phillips conducted the first stages of the interview, until Edwards made it abundantly clear that he would speak to nobody but me. Everything was recorded and above board."

"You actually believed that it was worthwhile to put yourself in that situation? You think the man gave you any truthful answers?"

"I was willing to put myself in an uncomfortable situation"—Ryan nearly laughed at the understatement—

"because I felt it would be for the greater good. If we are able to find anything useful in the answers he gave us, my time was well spent."

Gregson studied Ryan and thought, not for the first time, that it was a crying shame they couldn't see eye-to-eye in more areas than simple police work. The man was gutsy, he had conviction, and he was like an immoveable rock when the situation called for it. It was a bolt from the blue to realise that he would have liked him for a son.

He shook himself and focussed instead on the here and now. The answer to the next question he posed could be a game-changer for them all.

"Was there anything useful in what he said?"

"Edwards confirmed that he had a sexual relationship with Amy Llewellyn in the months before she died but he seemed to suggest that he 'gave her up'—in his own words—somehow bowing to another man he claimed to respect. I inferred from that a mentor of some kind—a man he looked up to."

Gregson said nothing, only listened while his stomach turned slow somersaults.

"He denied purchasing the bracelets, but admitted to having been in communication with Colin Hart."

"Clearly, he's trying to throw you off the scent," Gregson scoffed. "He refuses to admit to having killed Amy Llewellyn because he doesn't want to add to his list of convictions, or he likes feeling in control, bugger only knows. What about this Colin character?"

"There is a growing weight of evidence against Colin Hart. Copies of prison correspondence bear out Edwards' claim that the two have been in fairly regular contact and the letters record what can only be described as abnormal hero-worshipping. We believe that Edwards may have directed Colin up to Sycamore Gap, potentially to uncover Amy Llewellyn, and perhaps intending to bring Colin into the fold."

"Some kind of initiation, you mean?"

"Possibly. The fact is that Colin was one of few individuals aware of the exact spot where Amy Llewellyn was found. Our second victim, Claire Burns, was found in exactly the same spot only a few hours later."

"The second girl lived on his street, I understand?"

"That's correct, sir. She lived a few doors down and we have statements from various parties to suggest that Colin had an unhealthy obsession with her. Added to which, following the discovery of Colin's mother at his house this morning, we found files on his computer tracking his obsession with Claire, amongst other women."

Ryan thought of the names of the other women he had seen in Colin's file and was gripped with real fear.

"So, he's gone on the run," Gregson said, straightforwardly.

"Yes, sir. The surveillance team missed him, I regret to say. The mother died between six and nine yesterday evening, which covers the time Colin would have been at home, as well as a short timescale when he was at the station awaiting questioning.

"Sir, we have to assume that Colin is our main suspect in the murders of both Claire Burns and Geraldine Hart, given the facts I've already laid out. Additionally, his were the only prints confirmed on the syringe used to kill Geraldine, and there is a lot of circumstantial evidence which relates to items found on Claire's remains."

"Seems like a cut-and-dried case, if you ask me." Gregson stubbed his cigar out with a firm hand. "Colin thinks Edwards is a hero, because he's a bit of a nobody and wouldn't mind a bit of crazy-fame himself. Edwards decides to play along and lets him uncover one of his secret victims, one we've never been able to prove. Colin feels strong and special, so he looks at his own mediocre life and decides to shake it up a bit. Claire rejected him, so he pays her back, simultaneously drawing mega attention to himself, emulating the skill of the killers he has previously admired. He offs his mother, for good measure, since he's on a roll, then panics.

"Sound about right?"

Ryan considered the explanation and found it highly plausible. In fact, it would explain almost every aspect of the behaviour and certainly fit most of the forensic and circumstantial evidence in their possession.

Yet, it didn't explain the phone call that Colin had made, yesterday. It didn't account for the mentor Edwards had spoken of, with what Ryan believed was genuine conviction.

He remained silent, outwardly accepting of his commander's synopsis.

"What efforts have been made to recover him?" Gregson asked.

"We're going through all the usual channels to find him," Ryan answered truthfully. "We're keeping tabs on his bank accounts, looking into CCTV from the local area, and there's been an APW out on him all day."

"Let me know when you find him—and I'd appreciate being the first, rather than the last to know, this time."

"Yes, sir."

In the corridor outside, MacKenzie stood beside the vending machine with two bars of chocolate in hand. Ryan took one and, after the first nourishing bite, glanced across at his co-conspirator.

"Stage one is complete."

MacKenzie smiled and licked chocolate off her fingers.

"Edwards! You've got a visitor."

The hoarse voice of Terry, the prison guard, filtered underneath the door to his cell before it opened. With unhurried movements, Edwards rose from where he had been meditating on the bed, deep in thought.

"Anytime this year," the guard added, sullenly.

Edwards didn't alter his gait or his demeanour. They both knew that he topped up Terry's income with the monthly hand-outs that kept his kid in the latest trainers, in return for which Edwards' stash of mobile phones and cash was never uncovered during any of the spot-checks.

"I didn't realise your wife missed me so much," Edwards purred and enjoyed the sight of Terry battling against his natural inclination to pummel him to the ground.

"Shut up and turn around," the man said instead, snapping the handcuffs to his wrists with added force.

They followed the usual route through the long corridors until they reached a small conference room. He was never allowed into the main visitor's area. Much too chancy.

"Can you give me a clue?"

"You'll see, soon enough. Don't know how you manage it."

Edwards entered the small room and directed his gaze to the woman who sat at the table. Then, he let out a short, low whistle of appreciation.

"This is a delight," he said, quite candidly.

"I'm so happy that you had time to see me," came the breathless response.

My, but she has a voice like melted butter.

"I always like to make time for a beautiful woman." He smiled, but his eyes were calculating. "To what do I owe this pleasure?"

"We've been corresponding for a while now," she said coyly. "I finally had the nerve to come and visit you. I hope you're not disappointed."

"Not at all," he crooned. "I'm thrilled."

He thought of all the women who wrote to him and tried to recall her face. He came up blank, which was a red flag. For some things, he possessed a photographic memory.

"May I ask your name? You'll forgive my rudeness, but I'm sure you understand that I receive rather a lot of mail."

She waved a feminine hand but looked slightly put out, not to be the only one.

"I'm Ruth," she supplied. "Ruth Grant."

He flicked through his internal filing system and found her name. Ruth Grant, aged forty-one, resident of Newcastle upon Tyne for the past ten years. Widowed, mother of two. He didn't have a picture of her, which is why he hadn't recognised her.

"Of course!" he exclaimed. "I remember now. How nice to meet you, *Ruth*."

As the minutes ticked by, they talked of many things— of the world outside and of the man he used to be. She marvelled at his exploits and commiserated with his current situation, agreeing to help him wherever she could. Then, the talk turned to Ryan.

"I presume you've heard of the most recent news?" he asked.

Eyes like saucers, she shook her head. "Since they stopped reporting your story, I haven't bothered much with the news."

"Ah, well, let me enlighten you," he said, with his signature smile. "I seem to have been in the press again, and this time they're accusing me of murdering a girl ten years ago. Some student I've never even heard of."

"That's terrible," she gasped. "You're always being victimised."

"I know," he said sadly. "My lawyers keep trying to appeal the convictions, but how can I win against the corruption which is rife amongst the police? Just take that man—DCI Ryan."

"You mean, the one who found those cult killers up on Holy Island around Christmas?"

"That's the one," he said encouragingly, hating her more by the second. "He wanted to find someone to pin the murders on, so he picked me. He's fanatical."

Ruth clapped her hands to her mouth, shocked.

"You don't think…he let you go to prison, knowing you were *innocent*?"

It took real effort not to laugh, but somehow Edwards managed it.

"Yes." He nodded. "And he's trying to do it again. This time, he can't find any evidence against me, except the fact that I worked in the same hospital. It's a travesty."

"I thought—I mean to say, aren't they looking for a man called Colin? The guys at work were talking about some man who'd killed two girls and his own mother, then gone on the run. Everyone's a bit worried about it. Maybe the police aren't interested in you, after all?"

She regarded him with large, guileless green eyes.

"That idiot wouldn't have the brains," he spat.

"You mean Colin? Do you know him? My goodness, you're so famous!"

Edwards shrugged. "He's written to me several times, looking for inspiration in his humdrum life."

"Do you think he might have killed those girls?"

"How would I know?" he countered, layering on the charm by leaning in as much as he was able, pinning her with his chocolate-brown eyes.

It usually worked and, sure enough, she began to blush daintily. She really was quite lovely. He wondered what she would look like roped and bound, her eyes glazed with pain and fear.

"I just thought, since he's been writing to you, you'd be able to tell if he had killed anybody. You seem so intelligent."

He had always been a sucker for flattery.

"Colin's nothing more than a pawn."

Ruth hurried out of the electronic prison gates and, with a quick glance around her, made directly for the plain black Fiat, which was parked across the way.

Inside, she began to shed. First, the long, dark-haired wig, which masked the fall of molten red she had been born with. Second, the electronic wire, which lay plastered against her chest. When she felt that her breathing had returned to normal, she turned to the man seated behind the wheel.

"Well? Did you get it?"

"Clear as a bell," Lowerson replied, tugging the headphones from his ears. "He seemed to fall for it, hook, line and sinker."

"It looks that way," MacKenzie replied. "But he's a devious, unscrupulous man. He might have made me as soon as he walked into the room; we have no way to know for sure. He might have been playing along for his own amusement."

Lowerson's ready smile turned down at the edges.

"If we work on the basis that he believes you're one of his fans who can't resist him—"

"He's got the ego for it." MacKenzie snorted.

"If he truly believes that's who you were, then he could have been telling the truth about Colin. The chances of him recognising you from the newspapers or TV coverage are slim to none."

"I avoid the media like I would a fungal infection," she agreed roundly, running her fingers through her hair to shake off the feeling of having been in such close quarters.

"He seems to think Colin isn't our man," Lowerson said dubiously.

"Let's get back to Ryan and talk it over."

CHAPTER 20

Anna could see a car parked across the street. It had been sitting there for over three hours with a driver behind the wheel, though she couldn't see whether it was anyone she recognised. She stepped back from where she had been snooping behind the curtain in her bedroom and unconsciously clutched at her throat.

Was this another case of paranoia?

She tried to think rationally. The little row of mews cottages on the street where she lived in Durham had long back gardens leading down to the river. At the front, they were approached by a narrow road, which forked off from the main road. The spot was idyllic, with wonderful views, but it was also isolated, even though the city sprawled all around.

It certainly wasn't the usual haunt of visitors looking for overflow parking while they took a turn around the city centre. There were six cottages and she knew the cars belonging to each one, as well as their owners. Her own dark green Mini was parked directly in front of her cottage.

This car was out of place.

She worried at her lip for a minute, before reaching for her phone. She didn't like to disturb Ryan, not when he was so busy, but there was nothing else for it.

The phone rang three times before he picked it up.

"Anna?" His strong, direct voice came down the line. Already, she felt better, which was a troubling thought for her feminine principles. "Is everything alright?"

"I…look, I'm sorry to bother you at work—"

"Hearing from you is never unwelcome." His tone softened, wrapping itself around her like velvet.

"It's probably nothing."

"You wouldn't have called if it were nothing," he urged.

"There's a car parked outside the house … well, a few doors down, but it's been sitting there for over three hours. It might have been there even longer, but I was working in the study and then Mark visited—"

"Bowers?"

"Yes, he called in earlier," she said distractedly. "But I came upstairs to change, and I noticed the same car was sitting there. I first noticed it hours ago, when I opened the front door to Mark."

Busted. Sticky wicket. Rumbled. All of these words entered Ryan's mind and he realised the time had come to own up.

"Now don't get upset—"

"That's never a good way to begin a sentence." Her voice had cooled by several degrees.

"The car is probably one of ours," he said. "I felt it was best to keep you under surveillance, just for the moment."

There was a taut silence at the other end of the line and he rubbed the palm of his hand over his face, already anticipating the fallout.

"I see."

That was it?

"You do?"

"I see that, once again, you thought that you could control my movements, in a *high-handed* manner. You seem to have developed a unique talent for it."

Ryan was taken aback. "I was concerned for your welfare. I wanted to be sure that you would come to no harm. Is that so wrong?"

Anna sighed. "You don't *get* it, do you? It would have been so much more meaningful if you had taken the trouble to have a five-minute conversation with me about it first, before taking any unilateral decisions."

"It was my decision to make." The words were out of his mouth before he could snatch them back.

"I see."

Those two little words again. A dull throb started behind his eyes, so he closed them and tried to hear only her voice.

"I didn't mean that to sound so…"

"Domineering?" she offered.

He clenched his teeth. "Listen, all I meant to say is that I had to take a decision in the heat of the moment. The evidence is pointing towards someone with an obsession around me, or cases I've worked on. That includes you. I won't take any chances, Anna. You're too important."

She heard the worry and the burden he carried, but this was a question of trust.

"You probably don't realise this," she said, "but your boys aren't quite as good as they think they are. I was aware of someone following me yesterday lunchtime. I've been paranoid and scared ever since, which rather defeats the object, doesn't it?"

There was a lengthy pause at the end of the line. "Yesterday lunchtime? You're sure?"

"Yes, of course I'm sure. I ran all the way back to the university, like an idiot."

"The surveillance team didn't start until 3pm."

Anna felt an icy chill, like an insect crawling over her back.

"The car sitting outside—what make is it?"

"Ah, a dark blue BMW, I think." She headed back over to the window.

That settled it, he thought. The department didn't spring for luxury vehicles and he happened to know that the two-man surveillance team attached to Anna were supposed to be driving a Ford.

"Stay where you are and lock the doors, if you haven't already." He hesitated and then continued. "Arm yourself with something hard or sharp. I'm on my way."

Anna swallowed. "Ryan, the car outside. It's gone."

"Stay put, I'll be there in thirty minutes," he said urgently.

"Bollocks to that." She stopped him dead in his tracks. "I'll drive over to CID and meet you there. That way, you don't have to abandon your investigation at a crucial moment, but you still get to play Mother Goose. Win-win."

Ryan wanted to argue, but actually it made damn good sense.

"See you in half an hour. Oh, and Anna?"

"Yep?"

"I'm sorry."

"Do it again and you will be," she said smartly.

"Understood."

As Anna tugged on a pair of jeans and threw some basic necessities into a canvas bag, the two policemen tasked with keeping her under observation were carb-loading in the nearest greasy spoon at the end of a double shift. The order to stand down had come from a well-spoken man quoting Ryan's pass-code. In fact, with a subtle alteration of dialect, the disembodied voice had sounded just like him.

After speaking with the two men, Ryan ran a standard vehicle check.

And, wouldn't you know it, a dark blue BMW 3-series was registered to the same person who had taken a call from Colin Hart the previous day.

A few minutes before five, Anna butted through the doors marked with a grubby sign reading, 'Operation Hadrian'. Her nose was assaulted by the stale fumes of old sandwiches left forgotten on desktops and body odour, which hadn't quite been disguised by the liberal spraying of air freshener. Outside, the clouds had cleared overhead to make way for temperate summer skies. It was somehow harder to believe that people could kill when the sun was shining.

She saw Ryan gesticulating towards a large map of the region, which bore several bright red pins to indicate points of interest. He looked up as the doors opened, instantly alert. She wondered how he managed to walk through life without having some kind of major coronary incident, because she couldn't remember a time when he *hadn't* been alert. Each morning, he woke and was instantly on the ball. There was no languorous, lazy awakening with a yawn and a rub of his eyes. Whereas she needed to be coaxed from her bed, Ryan's rise into consciousness was immediate and he remained watchful and ready for action throughout the course of the day.

He smiled across at her and the muscles of his face relaxed slightly, so that he appeared less intimidating and more like the man she had come to know.

Then, he looked at what she held in her hands and struggled between conflicting feelings of gratitude and irritation. He had, after all, instructed her to come straight here and certainly had not sanctioned a pit-stop at the Pie Van to buy bulk provisions.

The rest of his team were not so proud and, spotting her in the doorway, abandoned him to fall upon the steaming food like a pack of ravenous lions.

She caught his eye and shrugged.

"I see that no further introductions are necessary," he mocked. "You're a disgrace, every last one of you."

"Always said I liked this one," Phillips mumbled, waving at her with a slice of corned beef pasty. He flipped the end of his tie over one shoulder, to prevent spillages.

Talk turned back to the investigation and she noticed that MacKenzie was missing from the gathering. The room was full of police staff. She saw Faulkner sitting at a hot-desk with a couple of CSIs leaning over his shoulder, while he analysed data on his computer. At another workstation, there was a bunch of other people she didn't recognise but presumed to be analysts of some kind. Behind her, standing along the back wall of the room like a trio of unruly teenagers, was DCS Gregson, flanked by Jeff Pinter on one side and a man she vaguely recognised as being Paddy Donovan on the other. It was a full house.

"Where's Denise?" she whispered across to Frank, who couldn't quite meet her eyes.

"Ah, she's just checking out a couple of things with Claire Burns' family," he said, for the benefit of their wider audience.

Anna was puzzled. Why the shifty looks?

"The word from Traffic is that our suspect has not been sighted from the air," Ryan was saying. "No stolen vehicles in the area; no car, van or other rentals. There's been no card or ATM activity whatsoever on any of Colin's known accounts in the last twelve hours.

"He could have had some cash in the house," somebody suggested.

"Might have," Ryan agreed. "More likely, he's managed to hole up somewhere, or somebody helped to shelter him."

There were mutters around the room at the prospect of an accomplice.

"Faulkner? Give us a forensic summary, please."

The Senior CSI shuffled to the front of the room.

"We have confirmed one of the DNA samples found on Amy Llewellyn's bracelet as belonging to Colin Hart. A number of suspect items have also been found in Hart's house, of the same type used to murder Claire Burns, such as a quantity of Lorazepam—which also ties in with the witness evidence that Hart had been stalking her for some time before she died. We spent the entire morning and early afternoon working over the crime scene at Number 32. Some of my team are still there, but I can tell you that the only prints found on the syringe used to kill Geraldine Hart belonged to her son, Colin."

"That syringe matches the size and shape of the puncture wound I found on Geraldine's neck," Pinter chucked in, from the back.

"Thanks, Jeff." Faulkner nodded, trying to pick up the flow of his speech again. "As I say, with the exception of one unidentified DNA sample on Amy's bracelet and one unidentified print found inside Colin's car, all other suspect prints and samples have been accounted for."

"Unidentified print?" This, from Gregson.

"Yes, sir." Faulkner sought out Gregson's bland stare and nodded. "It could be nothing. We wouldn't think anything of it, except for the fact that the rest of the house had only two sets of prints: Colin's and his mother's. They were obviously a very private family, without visitors, so the existence of a third set was unusual."

"Nothing flagged on the database?"

Faulkner gave a quick shake of his head.

"Then, it was probably the mechanic who gave the car its MOT," Gregson jeered.

"How about fibres?" Ryan pointedly ignored the last remark from his commanding officer.

"Well, the results have now come in from the clothing samples found around Amy's skeleton, but they had deteriorated so much that we haven't been able to recover any distinct evidence."

Everyone in the room felt disappointment, with the exception of two people, whose faces betrayed nothing of their relief.

"How about Claire?"

"Interestingly, there was no clothing found on Claire's body, as you know. There were very few fibres to test, other than the medical tape left around the body, which we've already identified as Micropore. In the case of Claire, her killer was a careful person." Faulkner scratched at his head while he remembered the things he needed to cover.

"Micropore was found inside Number 32, in addition to Lorazepam, syringes and so forth. Throw in the fact of

Geraldine's death and it's looking very much like Colin is our man."

As Faulkner stepped away from the front, Ryan gave him a bolstering slap on the arm. He cast his eye to the back row of his makeshift theatre.

"Jeff? Would you mind giving us a low-down on where we're at with pathology?"

Pinter straightened and loped towards the front, in that long-legged, sure-footed way of his. The sun shone through the dingy window along the sidewall, picking up the silver streaks running through his hair, and lending him a rakish air.

"Got the technicians going over Geraldine Hart now," he said, plunging straight in. "But I'd put money on her having died of cardiac arrest, following a massive dose of Lorazepam. There was a spent syringe on the floor beside the bed—the only one around—and its contents are confirmed as a match. Went in straight through the artery." He made a jabbing motion towards the side of his own neck, causing widespread discomfort around the room.

"No defensive wounds?"

"None that showed any obvious signs of a struggle." He shrugged. "There were some skin cells under a couple of her nails, so we'll test those and see."

"What about any other medication?"

"She was on a cocktail of drugs." Pinter tugged at the lapels of his navy blazer. His attire resembled that of an off-duty sea captain, Phillips thought resentfully, eyeing the beige chinos and smart navy jacket.

"That's the interesting thing, I suppose—"

"What's that?" Phillips snapped back to attention.

"Thing is, she was on so many drugs, in larger doses. She even had oral morphine, for special occasions. I suppose I can't understand why he—Colin—would choose to administer an overdose of Lorazepam, when he could easily have chosen something stronger and quicker."

There was a brief lull.

"Remember that this amateur likes to think he's better than The Hacker, or at least as good. He wants the fame and the glory of the Holy Island killers, without the hassle." Ryan said, in bored tones.

Pinter gave him a hard look. "There could be an intelligent reason behind his choice," he said.

"Nah," Phillips said, dismissing the idea with the back of his hand. "He's a coward, if you ask me. Look at how he's scuttled away to hide. He's probably snivelling behind some bins, somewhere. Not exactly the actions of an artist. Unless—"

"What?" Ryan asked.

"Well, it's a mad thought…" Phillips held both hands out, in mock embarrassment. "But maybe—I mean, are we sure Colin is even our man? Faulkner, you said yourself, you found other prints. Could be that there's an even bigger coward out there, hiding behind that poor bastard who's on the run."

"It's possible, you know," Ryan mused.

"We've been through this," Gregson boomed, from the back. "The facts point to Colin, so *find him.*"

"Well, that's the trouble, sir. He hasn't left much of a trail to follow," Ryan pointed out. "I've asked Doctor Donovan to give us some insights on his mentality. Doctor?"

Paddy weaved his way through the assembled staff, carrying his heavy bulk with grace.

"I haven't had much time to look at the case files, or to complete anywhere near a full report. I want you all to understand that what I say will be initial observations only. They shouldn't be taken as gospel."

"Understood," Ryan answered for the room.

"Alright, then. First thing to think about is an oldie, but a goodie. He lives with his mother and, as far as we can tell, always has done. No evidence of former relationships or significant women in his life. Lack of father figure— in fact, rather than becoming the 'man of the house' there's some potential for Colin to have been significantly emasculated, over the years. Bit of a Norman Bates figure, if you like."

"Okay, but how does that help us?"

"Well, the thing to remember is that he will have looked to his mother as both friend and foe. He will have been immensely protective of her, whilst also hating her at times. Fear of disappointing her, or bringing another woman into the house, will have prevented him from forming new and meaningful attachments, even if he wanted to."

"But we found the files on his computer," Ryan interposed. "He had files on several women, including Claire Burns. He's obviously interested in women."

Paddy nodded sagely. "Deep down, he will have known that these women were unattainable. It would have been 'safe' for him to develop imaginary worlds around them, to fashion himself as a great lothario, in order to cope with his ultimate reality. Because, in reality, he is likely impotent or able to become excited only by the thought of exerting control over women, perhaps violent control."

"If his fantasy women were unattainable, how come they've turned up dead?" Phillips slurped Irn-Bru, as he thought aloud.

"It's possible that the pressure of living an unwanted life eventually became too much to bear. His mother's behaviour may have become intolerable, combined with the incessant feelings of rejection from women whom he has placed on a pedestal. It may have broken something inside him."

"Aye, well, that's all fine and dandy," Phillips muttered, "and I'm sure we all feel *very* sorry for him. But we've got three dead women on our hands, Doc."

Donovan raised a hand, in understanding. "I'll come to the point. I think that it's possible Colin Hart experiences fugue states; episodes of time where he is more like his alter-ego, or the most confident side of himself."

"Like, when he's pretending to be DoctorKeir79?"

"Exactly," Donovan agreed. "While experiencing one of these 'states', it's possible that he behaved in a manner entirely inconsistent with his usual timid self. Turning fantasy into reality, if you will."

LJ ROSS

"Sounds textbook," Ryan commented. "Now, if I had multiple personality—"

"We don't call it that, nowadays…" Donovan started to correct him and then thought better of it. Now wasn't the time for semantics.

"If I had different alter-egos hopping around inside my head," Ryan started afresh. "Where would I go?"

Paddy scratched at the fluffy hair at the top of his head. "This area, Sycamore Gap, seems to have significance for him," he offered.

"Yes, but we're leaning towards thinking that Keir Edwards killed Amy Llewellyn, so maybe Colin only *adopted* the area as his own."

"*If* Edwards killed Amy Llewellyn and led Colin to her resting place, that would be consistent with his adoption of DoctorKeir79," Donovan agreed. "*If* Edwards sent him up there, he may feel it is incumbent on him to continue the pattern and deposit a body in the same place."

"You think he might be up there now?"

With incomparable timing, the DC responsible for reader-receiving pushed away from his desk at that very moment.

"Sir?"

"Yes?"

"Yes?"

Both Ryan and Gregson turned, leaving the detective constable in an awkward quandary. Sidestepping it, he spoke to nobody in particular.

"That was one of the uniforms. Three people rang in to report a man acting strangely beside the train station in Bardon Mill. Physical description matches Colin. Apparently, he stole a bike."

"How the hell did he manage to get up there?" Ryan burst out.

The bus and train stations were heavily manned by police on foot patrols, and the local news channels had the story of the manhunt on permanent loop, yet the man had somehow made his way to the station closest to Housesteads Fort.

"I want a team up there, right now." Gregson cut across whatever Ryan had been about to say. "The man is to be considered dangerous—approach with extreme caution."

"He's disturbed," Donovan felt bound to point out. Where he saw illness, others saw evil.

"Whatever," Gregson snapped. "Ryan, I want you to call in armed support."

Ryan frowned heavily, both at the tone of command and at the prospect of the firearms unit being deployed.

"Sir, we have no reason to believe he will be armed with anything we would not be able to neutralise with proportionate force. Given the man's previous crimes— if proven—the methodology does not suggest he will be armed with anything more than a manual tool."

"Objection noted and overridden," Gregson retorted. "Ryan, I want you leading a team out there within thirty minutes. Get it sorted."

The room was suddenly galvanised. Pinter melted away, back to his friends in cold storage. Donovan returned to his patients and his books, worrying about the man wandering the hills and fells. Gregson remained long enough to ensure that his orders were obeyed, watching and listening while Ryan put together a team to find Colin with minimal fuss, and then retreated to his office to handle some other pressing matters. Faulkner returned to his forensic taskforce, co-ordinating the ongoing effort there.

"Would it be best for me to go home?" Anna asked Ryan, at the first opportunity.

He did not answer immediately, weighing up the safest options.

"No, it's best for you to stay here. I'm sorry." He held her face in his hands, uncaring of the nudges and winks from his team.

"Ryan, for heaven's sake," she muttered, "I don't need babysitting. I'm perfectly happy to go back. We've just heard that Colin's miles away from here, which means he's not scoping out my little cottage, is he?"

"Please, stay here."

It was on the tip of her tongue to argue and then he gave her *that* look. The one conveying just the right amount of vulnerability and just the right amount of pleading, to prey upon her soft heart.

"Stop that!" She jabbed a finger into his chest.

He just looked.

"Oh, for the love of—" She blew out a long breath, striving for patience. "Fine. Fine! I'll hang around here like a lemming while you go off and play the hero, shall I?"

"That would be great."

With a quiet word to Faulkner, Ryan turned to make the necessary arrangements.

CHAPTER 21

The wind whipped across the wide, open space, and Colin shivered. His body was in shock and beginning to react to the cold. Where were his backpack and his jacket? He looked around with vacant eyes, trying to remember where they might be. His mind didn't choose to recall that they were tucked in the hallway cupboard of Number 32, because that would mean remembering what else lay hidden in that house.

As far as he was concerned, his mother was alive and eagerly awaiting his return.

He clutched Claire's uniform to his chest, drawing comfort from it, imagining that the clothes were more than inanimate material. He could still smell Claire's scent amongst them, which helped him to envisage that, perhaps, she was still with him.

His eyes were troubled as he scanned the fields.

Which way?

White-tipped fingers clutched at the folds of Claire's skirt as he tried to think which way to turn. Just a little further, he thought, just around the next bend.

He wandered into the wilderness.

Sirens screamed along the Military Road as a team of police officers made their way towards Sycamore Gap in off-road vehicles complete with reinforced glass. Outside, the air was thick and muggy. The fine weather that the people of Northumberland had enjoyed of late was near breaking point, the heavens ready to let loose the rain which waited to fall over the hills and vales.

Ryan held a car radio to his lips. "Sirens off," he said.

There followed an unnerving silence as, one by one, the vehicles obeyed. An army of blue and white crept closer to Sycamore Gap, with only the purr of well-tended engines and the crackle of rubber on tarmac to signal their approach.

"Team A to approach from the east," he continued. "If suspect is sighted, do not approach. I repeat. Do not approach."

There was a fizz of incoming messages to confirm that his order was understood.

"Team B to approach from the west," he continued. "Same rules apply. If suspect sighted, report, but do not approach."

The turning for Housesteads came into view and three cars peeled away from the convoy, while another three continued onwards to make their approach from the west.

"Last sighting of Colin Hart was an hour ago outside Bardon Mill," Ryan's firm voice sounded down through the radio. "Assume that the suspect is now within a three-mile radius."

The fort and visitor centre had already been evacuated and the car park stood empty when the cars turned into the gate. There was no sign of any human presence, only the stone ruins and abandoned buildings to prove that, once, people had reigned here. To the men and women who exited their vehicles, it was as if the land had overtaken once again. Where Hadrian had sought to tame it and to separate it, the country had emerged triumphant. They were reverent; a hushed crowd of people who acknowledged that it was they who trespassed.

While Colin stumbled over rocks and water, Doctor Jeffrey Pinter looked down at the bloated body of Geraldine Hart, lying rigid on the gurney before him. He turned the music in the mortuary to something jolly, dancing along to the beat in his head. He had dismissed the rest of his team, telling them that the prime suspect would soon be apprehended and therefore they could afford to take a few hours' break, after a taxing few days.

"Just you and me, old gal," he said gaily, snapping his mask into place.

He began to hum as he selected a small rotary saw and enjoyed the familiar thrum of power as it trembled along the tendons in his arm. He looked at it for a moment, detached and fascinated while the engine whirred, then drove it through flesh and bone with unflappable precision.

He spoke clearly into the microphone on his lapel as he went and, after the job was done, he made his own handwritten record, which he added to a bright blue plastic wallet. Afterwards, he scrubbed his hands with antimicrobial soap and hung up his lab coat. In the privacy of his office, he thought of the evening ahead and of the woman who awaited him.

He had worried, for a while, that he was too old for her. The mirror didn't lie, nor did the date on his driver's licence, which told him he was no longer a spring chicken.

Drawing himself tall, he brushed self-doubt aside. Doctor Jeffrey M. Pinter had a lot to recommend him, and she was sure to realise that. Women appreciated a man of experience, or so the women's magazines told him.

'Is your man a dish, or a dud?' That was how one such rag had posed the question.

Jeffrey regarded himself in the mirrors of the elevator as it transported him from the basement mortuary of the hospital and out into the world once more.

Dish, he decided.

Emerging from the automatic doors at the entrance to the imposing building, oblivious to the people who swarmed around him, he felt like a butterfly. A big, beautiful creature, ready to capture the attention of the world and one person in particular.

Anna watched Ryan leave with a gaggle of police staff in tow. He had another cloak on now, she thought. He was not only seeking out a man, he was seeking to avenge—which was something far greater. Watching him from the side line, she could not help but feel like a spare part, although she did not envy him his job, nor the faces of the dead who haunted him.

Thinking herself alone, she huffed out a breath and plonked down into Ryan's desk chair, jiggling her knees and wondering whether it would be worth trying to do some work. The soft 'tap' of a keyboard sounded from across the room and with a start of surprise, she realised that Faulkner was still seated at his desk on the far side of the Incident Room. She wasn't the only one who remained on the outskirts, while the cool kids went to play cops and robbers.

"Tom? Sorry, I didn't realise you were still here," she said in friendly tones. "Is there anything I can do to help?"

Faulkner looked up slowly, his unremarkable brown eyes squinting at her from behind thick glasses. His fingers halted on the keyboard and he rubbed at them to clear his vision.

"Hi, Anna," he said. "No, I don't think there's anything I can let you do without proper authorisation, much as I'd appreciate the help."

Anna nodded her understanding and swung the desk chair from side to side. "You look a bit worse for wear, hope you don't mind me saying."

Faulkner had to laugh. "Believe me, I feel it."

"It's been a strenuous few days."

"It's been a strenuous few years," he corrected her, giving up on the computer to rest his head in his hands for a moment.

Anna frowned and rose to walk across to him. "At the risk of sounding like a broken record ... anything I can do?"

Faulkner knew that she wasn't talking about paperwork now. Still, he shook his head. It was too late, he thought. Much too late for anything to be done.

Keir Edwards couldn't shake the feeling that something was wrong. It ate away at him, roaming in obsessive circles through his conscious mind until he could do nothing but try to understand what had escaped him.

The feeling had begun after Ruth's departure, he knew that much. That narrowed the window quite a bit. Initially, he put the wild, compulsive fantasies down to the fact that he had not seen a live woman in far too long. Even longer yet since he had seen a dead one, and Ruth had been very much to his taste, with her pale skin, rosy cheeks, bright green eyes and dark hair that rippled over one shoulder to tease him. She might have been a little older than his usual, but hey, he couldn't afford to be picky. As soon as he had seen her, sitting there in the poky conference room, he had begun to calculate the ways in which he could tempt her to visit again. After that, how he could begin to use her as a contraband mule, bringing him all those little extra luxuries he missed in his daily life. All the while, he had allowed himself the freedom to imagine all the ways he could kill her.

Freedom of thought was a marvellous thing.

Yet, these thoughts did not cheer him. *Why*? What was different?

Rising, he moved to the single drawer in the small wooden wardrobe and retrieved a stack of envelopes. He leafed through them until he found the one he was looking for.

Ruth Grant.

He re-read the letters he had received from her, the last one having arrived over three months ago. That was unusual. Normally, his adoring fans contacted him on a more regular basis. As he read the untidy, child-like writing, he couldn't help but notice the sloppy grammar and poor sentence structure.

It didn't fit the woman he had met earlier that day. She had been polished and seemingly well-educated.

A feeling slowly began to spread in his gut and his lips trembled. Roused, he grabbed at the papers and began to tear through them, searching for the newspaper cuttings he kept in a large brown envelope.

His breathing was harsh in the quiet cell as he scanned the black and white images, his dark eyes passing over Ryan's image more than once, often set against his own on a full page spread with the faces of the women he had killed lined up below, in chronological order.

He wished he could have it framed.

But that was for another time, he thought. He knew what he was looking for and he would not stop until he found it.

Eventually, his fingers stilled their frantic search and he held a thin scrap of newspaper loosely before him. On it was an image of Ryan in the foreground, standing alongside DCS Gregson after the final press conference on Holy Island. In the background, a line of police officers stood proudly, their arrogant chests puffed out at their own self-importance.

And there, amongst their number, stood Ruth Grant. Only, her hair was lighter. He couldn't be sure of the colour on the grainy picture, but it certainly wasn't dark brown.

He looked at the tiny print at the bottom of the image and traced a fingertip along the list of names until he found the one that matched.

Detective Inspector Denise MacKenzie.

With infinite self-control, he replaced the papers, re-stacking the envelopes neatly inside their drawer. Then, he turned and stared into the silent space, drowning out the distant sounds of prison guards walking the length of the corridor outside, and the constant thudding of his neighbour's boot against the cell wall.

For, like Ryan, his anger was cold and his memory long.

Arthur Gregson stood in front of the square mirror he had fixed on the inside door of one of the cupboards in his office. Appearances must be kept up and never once had he been caught with his laces undone, or his tie askew.

He had changed from his classic dark navy suit and white shirt, into a more casual outfit of black trousers and a dark polo shirt. He wore trainers, rather than his usual choice of highly-polished black brogues.

"Ought to do it," he murmured at his reflection.

He met his own eyes in the mirror and tried to see what lay behind them. Was there a soul to find there, after all these years? When he had made his decision to convert, he had always known that there would be hard times, to temper the good. Yet he was finding the edict concerning DC Jack Lowerson a particularly difficult one to bear.

He thought of the man he knew as the High Priest with a combination of fear and respect. Outwardly, he was a mild-mannered intellectual, someone who blended in with the crowd, which was exactly why he had risen to his present position so easily. After a spate of disappointing, ostentatious leaders, the Circle had chosen a High Priest who would not draw attention to their select group.

Yet the position was a poisoned chalice. No man who had worn the long animal pelt, the Master's representative on Earth, had been able to resist the beguiling lure of *power*. There had been some who enjoyed the money, some who preferred the glamour and the prestige, and others whose violent tendencies could thrive whilst cocooned by the Circle's unquestioning protection.

Arthur had seen all of them. He had served under all of them. In the early days, when he had been a man of Jack Lowerson's age, he had struggled to gain recognition. Nobody had seen his great potential, nor given him the chance to shine, until the Circle had invited him into their fold.

It had been an awakening, when he had been included as a part of something greater than himself. The cause was a true one, so he had thought, and in exchange for loyalty he had been rewarded.

Oh, how he had reaped the rewards.

Once a skinny young man with few credentials and little charm, he had flowered. Under careful tutelage, he had changed outwardly and bloomed inwardly. Gone was the stuttering teenager he had been. The promotions had come in steadily. The women had started to notice him too. His wife was amongst them; the most beautiful woman he had ever seen, standing pretty as a picture next to her father, a prominent businessman who had guided him towards several lucrative investments over the years.

Arthur combed the hair back from his face, thinking that he had aged better than his wife. There had been other women, too many to count, but he would always remember how she had been that day so many years ago, before life and everyday stresses preyed upon them both.

It might have helped if they had been able to have children.

He thought again of Jack Lowerson.

CHAPTER 22

The quiet of the Incident Room was broken by the loud ringing of Faulkner's desk phone, which echoed around the walls with a tinny, old-fashioned *brrrrriiiiiiing!*

"Sorry," he mumbled, trying to locate the receiver underneath the mountain of paperwork on the temporary desk space.

Anna just smiled, as she thumbed through a copy of *The Northern Historian* magazine she had found in the university archives, searching for an old article written by the now Professor Jane Freeman.

"God! Are you sure?"

She looked up again, at the unexpectedly harsh tone from Faulkner, who spoke urgently into the grimy beige receiver.

"Yes. Yes, of course. I'll head up there now." His voice lowered and his eyes skittered over to Anna, who remained seated at Ryan's desk a few feet away. "Are you sure it's *alright*?"

Another pause.

"Right-oh. I'm on my way." He replaced the receiver and looked at it for a couple of seconds while he pursed his lips.

Anna glanced over at Faulkner with a question in her eyes. He began shrugging into his jacket, noting that dusk was falling outside the smudged windows and would soon bring with it a cold evening breeze.

"They've found him," he explained. "Colin, that is. They've found his body, up at Sycamore Gap."

Anna put a hand to her mouth, in reflex.

"His body? You mean he's *dead*?"

It was funny, she thought, how human compassion worked. The man might have killed several women, but she could still find it in her heart to mourn the loss of another life.

"Yes." Tom rooted around for his glasses, then realised they were already tucked into the pocket of his trousers. He always kept a field kit in the boot of his car, containing all the materials and tools he would need for an initial walk-through of a crime scene.

"How? I mean, was he killed?"

"Don't know yet," Faulkner replied. "Ryan just said to get up there and make a start on the forensics. Might be that Colin killed himself."

Faulkner hesitated, despite the orders from his SIO. He fiddled with his car keys uncertainly.

"Are you—ah—are you going to be okay here, on your own?"

Anna looked around the empty space and felt a small wave of unease, but nodded cheerfully, batting him away with her hand.

"Of course! Your suspect is dead and I'm in a building filled with police officers. Couldn't be safer, could I?"

"It's not that…I, um."

He trailed off, feeling stumped.

"Tom, give me some credit." Anna smiled. "It's obvious that Ryan left you here to watch over me. Now, there's no need for you to bother."

Faulkner nodded, feeling much better about it. She was right, after all. Surrounded by police, she couldn't be safer.

But, as he left her in the quiet space, he wondered why the conversation with Ryan replayed in his mind; why he checked, then double-checked the instructions he had been given. He peered into the passing offices along the corridors of CID as he headed for the exit and was encouraged by the sounds of activity: phones ringing, men and women swearing at each other in jest, the tap-tap sound of fingertips hitting keyboards.

With a final glance over his shoulder, he headed out into the twilight and prepared to journey out into the hills.

Colin stood west of Sycamore Gap, beside the ruined mini-fortress labelled, 'Milecastle 39'. His thin shirt buffeted in the breeze, his hair repeatedly dashed against his face. Lost and lonely, he surveyed the world around him but with eyes only half tuned into the present. Beside him, he saw Claire as she had been in life. He could hear her voice on the air and he could feel her soft hand taking his. The brush of the wind was a caress and the broken stones a towering castle, rising nobly at his back and filled with people.

Not alone, after all.

"See, Mother," he murmured. "Everything's alright."

The present jarred for a moment when the tiny figures of real men and women intruded. They stole over the brow of a hill to the west, like black ants.

Colin tried to focus on them, but the ground shifted and moved. Voices of the women he had known droned on, an endless cycle of repeated rejection until another voice he recognised spoke loudly enough to drown them out.

"Colin?"

He turned, seeking its source. "Yes?"

"Colin, do you remember me?"

He squinted as the sun fell further into the horizon, up into the face of the tall man who stood a careful distance away from him.

"Of course, I remember you. You're DCI Ryan, aged thirty-five, six-feet three inches, dark hair, grey eyes. Mother and father living, sister deceased. Joined the Metropolitan Police aged twenty-three, moved to the North-East in 2008." He reeled off the facts robotically, in a funny, detached voice.

Ryan saw that the man's hands were almost white, and the fingers clawed at a bundle of shiny, pale pink fabric of the same type worn by waitresses at the Diner.

"That's right, Colin. I'm DCI Ryan, but you can call me 'Ryan', if you prefer."

"Thank you," the other replied politely.

"Pretty up here, isn't it?" Ryan remarked, taking stock of the immediate terrain. A few more steps and Colin would be over the side of a steep hill.

"Yes, very."

Ryan licked dry lips and fell back on training. Develop rapport; use the subject's first name.

"Colin, it's getting pretty cold out here, why don't we head somewhere warmer? We could grab a cuppa and talk things over. What do you say?"

The man's chin wobbled. He couldn't leave, not until his friend came for him. Besides, Claire was here. He could smell her, he thought, lifting the material to his nose.

"Colin?"

"*No!*"

Ryan held both hands out. "Okay, Colin, just relax." He tried another line. "Why are you here?"

Colin butted out his chin. "Can't tell you," he said, childishly, as his mind began to regress.

"How about I take a guess?"

Colin glanced over at him. The rules only said that you couldn't tell tales on your friends, but it was different if somebody happened to *guess*.

Ryan took the silence as an invitation to try.

"I think your friend, Doctor Edwards, sent you a postcard. Am I right?"

Again, no answer, but Colin continued to watch him, waiting for the next guess.

"I think he told you all about how real men break free, all about how to get a woman. Isn't that right?"

"He's got swarms of them," Colin mumbled, enviously.

"He told you that you could be just like him," Ryan continued, edging a little closer while he spoke in smooth, rounded tones.

Colin nodded.

"He told you there was something to find up here, didn't he?"

Colin remembered the gaping jaw of Amy's skeleton and he shuddered visibly, bile rising to his throat as he tried to block the images.

"I found her," he cried, clawing at the pink material like a comfort blanket. "I found her."

"That's right, Colin, you found Amy Llewellyn's body hidden inside the wall." Ryan spoke very, very gently. "Did you kill her, Colin? Do you know who did?"

The other man was rocking on the spot, back and forth, back and forth.

"No-o," he wailed. "No, I didn't. I'm sure I didn't."

"All right, Colin." Ryan was closer now, within touching distance. "What have you got there?"

He gestured towards Claire's uniform and Colin looked down at what he held in his hands with disconnected fascination before he wrapped his arms tightly around the material, fearful that it would be taken from him.

"It's Claire's. I'm looking after it for her."

Ryan sought to make eye contact with him, but Colin's eyes were aloof and spaced out, as if he had been doped.

"Where is Claire?"

Colin's chin wobbled again, and he shook his head, a spasm of movement while his mind tried to rid itself of the awful truth.

His jaw worked, struggling to form the words. "She's... she's dead," he managed, voice breaking and tears blurring his vision.

Ryan's voice remained soft. "Did you kill her, Colin?"

The other man shook his head vehemently.

"I loved her. I didn't. I swear I didn't kill her." But the tears started to fall as he remembered how angry he had been, how he had considered the possibility of ending her and then ending himself. Soft, encouraging words spoken over the telephone from a man who understood that terrible need.

"Maybe I did," he burst out, his voice carrying over the tranquil air, out into the night.

Behind him, Ryan made a brief gesture to Phillips, who stepped forward. Together, they each took an arm in a gentle but firm grip.

"Come on, mate," Phillips urged the tearful man who was around the same age. "Let's go and get a digestive to dunk in a sweet cup o' tea. I'm freezing my bollocks off, out here."

Colin looked between them and allowed himself to be led over the padded earth, back towards reality.

DC Lowerson's black Fiat pulled into an empty space on a wide, leafy avenue on the western edge of Jesmond, not far from the Town Moor. He pulled the hand brake and turned to his passenger with a nervous air.

"You sure you don't want company?"

"No." Denise MacKenzie took a moment to check her appearance in the side mirror. "You know I have to go in there alone, if this is going to work."

"The others aren't here yet," Lowerson argued, glancing again at the digital clock on the dashboard, which now read 20:14.

"They'll be along soon. Ryan said eight-thirty," MacKenzie replied, with a calmness she didn't feel.

"Phillips will lynch me, if anything happens," Lowerson mumbled, and MacKenzie turned to him with a laugh.

"Bless you," she said, tugging his ears towards her and placing a kiss on his freckled forehead. Then, her face fell back into serious lines.

"This is important to me, Jack. I think it's important to you, too. Both of us have something to prove."

Jack nodded, turning away to stare out of the windscreen. "Be careful," he muttered.

"Got all the bases covered," she returned, with a wink.

MacKenzie stepped out of the car and into the darkening night, looking up and down the upmarket street of Georgian townhouses. The air was heavy around her;

dampness clung to her skin and filmed her clothes, though the rain hadn't properly started yet. She crossed the road and walked further down the street until she reached a house with a dark navy BMW parked on the street outside.

The doctor was in residence.

CHAPTER 23

Detective Sergeant Frank Phillips considered himself an ordinary, reasonable man. A patient man, even. Well, after today, he would proclaim to all and sundry that he had the patience of a *saint*.

He cast a disgruntled eye over at his SIO, who was driving with the precision of an eagle and the speed of a flying bullet. Phillips' fingers gripped his knees in reaction. With Colin Hart safely strapped into the back of a squad car, under the supervision of two DCs and a medic, they raced back towards the bright lights of Newcastle.

"You said Lowerson was already in position?"

"Yep."

Always the conversationalist, Phillips thought, peevishly, before picking up the car radio.

"No radio. Use the mobile."

Phillips let the radio fall back into its holder. Anybody could tune into a police radio and you never knew who might be listening.

"He's not answering," Phillips said, after a few failed attempts to contact the young detective constable.

Ryan's lips hardened, as did his hands on the wheel.

"He knows we're on our way."

Ahead of them, the long stretch of road turned black as rain began to bounce off the tarmac.

"If anything happens to her—"

"I know, Frank."

Indiana Jones rang out, interrupting them. Phillips answered.

There followed a short, tense conversation, which correlated with the mounting speed of the car.

"What's going on?"

"Just keep your eyes on the road and try not to blow a gasket," Phillips said, feeling his stomach heave as fields and trees whipped past them. "That was Faulkner."

"Faulkner?" Ryan was surprised. "Has something happened to Anna?"

Phillips held up a hand, indicating that Ryan needed to shut up before he could answer.

"Faulkner rang to say he's on his way up to Sycamore Gap, but he's been delayed by traffic on his way out of the city. He's sorry to be later than expected."

Ryan frowned in confusion. "What the hell is he talking about?"

"I asked him the same question," Phillips paused while he waited for his entrails to settle back into position after the latest bump in the road. "He was totally blindsided.

Said you called him half an hour ago to say Colin was dead and you needed him up there, pronto, to work the scene."

"I never called him."

Phillips raised his eyes heavenwards. "I know that, guv. Anyway, I've told him to turn around and head back to CID."

"Anna?"

"She's still at CID, as far as he knows, and the place is filled with uniforms. Keep your hair on."

"We were right, Frank. Who would know she had been left with Faulkner? Who would know how to draw him away?"

"Aye, lad. Thank God my girl intercepted him first." He thought of Denise, beautiful and brave.

Ryan spared Phillips a brief glance and a muscle ticked in his jaw. The speedometer crept upwards, past eighty, dropping only when he made the sharp bends through the small villages and hamlets peppering the landscape as they edged closer to the city limits.

"Screw this," he snarled, and flicked on the siren for the single flashing blue light, which he had stuck on the driver's side of the roof.

They raced through traffic lights, along bus lanes and against one-way traffic with the kind of contempt for the Highway Code that impressed the local taxi drivers left in their wake. Lights began to appear in the windows of the houses and street-lamps flickered. The last of the sun's rays bathed the city of Newcastle and the night came to life. Beneath the moon and stars, men and women looked to the heavens. Some hoped for salvation; others for redemption. A chosen few waged war upon whomever resided there, turning their back on conscience. One man closed his eyes to the beauty of the sky and offered himself up to the hedonistic pleasure he had fought against for too long.

Anna finished reading an article written by Jane Freeman entitled, 'Myths and Magic of Northumberland's Greatest Historic Sites'. It had proven to be an interesting yarn; short on historical sources but long on unsupported but entertaining arguments about the real reasons behind the deaths of prominent historical figures in the region.

She flung it on the desk beside her and yawned, once more feeling small and insignificant in the open conference space. Though Anna knew there was a hive of police activity going on around her, she heard nothing outside the soundproofed walls of the Incident Room.

She spent another few unproductive minutes propelling the foam-stuffed desk chair from one wall to another, before giving up on that too.

Her eyes fell on Ryan's desktop computer, then on the small CCTV camera in the corner of the room. Nope, she thought. Better not to snoop.

Presently, the doors whooshed open with a small gust, to reveal a figure in the doorway.

"Jeff?" She raised her eyebrows and hastily wheeled herself back towards Ryan's desk with the heels of her shoes, feeling slightly flushed. "Nobody's here, I'm afraid. They've all gone up to Sycamore Gap."

Her brow puckered. "Shouldn't you be up there with them? I thought they needed a pathologist to confirm death or something like that?"

Pinter closed the door behind him with a gentle *click* and moved further into the room. He had discarded his navy blazer and stood in comfortable shirtsleeves. He placed his bag on the floor beside him.

"Good news! Colin isn't dead," he said.

"What? Why would Ryan say that he was? Faulkner's on his way—"

"Now, now," Pinter shushed her, moving further towards the desk where she sat. "Nothing to worry yourself about. Everything's taken care of."

"What do you mean?"

Pinter held up a single, bony index finger and retrieved a small vial of liquid from his inner pocket. Anna squinted at the label, which read, 'FLUMAZENIL', in plain black lettering. With dawning horror, she watched him place it on the desk between them, the wrinkles beside his eyes creasing into a broad smile.

Doctor Paddy Donovan clicked off the lights in the hallway and checked his pockets. *Keys, phone, wallet, bag,* he rattled off his mental checklist and reached for the front door. He was already running behind schedule and couldn't wait any longer.

When the door swung open, an unexpected visitor awaited him, walking slowly up the flagstone pathway to his front door.

"Denise?" His voice was laced with genuine surprise.

"Paddy," she began, apologetically. "I'm sorry to disturb you at home. It's just that you said I could stop by anytime, if I needed to talk things over. I can come back on Monday ..." she trailed off.

Donovan looked beyond her to the quiet street and made a split-second decision. Stepping back into the hallway, he flicked the switch on again and gestured her inside.

"You're always welcome, Denise. Come inside, and we'll talk." He took another glance over her shoulder as she brushed past him. "Did you come alone, or would Phillips like to come inside for a dram?"

"Oh, no—I'm on my own tonight. Frank's up at Sycamore Gap with Ryan. They found Colin dead, you know."

"Good heavens," Donovan replied, with a sympathetic tut. "Poor, troubled soul. God rest him."

He hesitated in the hallway, wondering where to lead her, but decided upon the study towards the back of the house. It was quieter there and less likely that they would be disturbed.

When she had settled herself comfortably into one of the expensive chairs, her copper hair fanning out against the mulberry leather headrest, he spoke again.

"Can I offer you a drink? Something warm? Better yet, something alcoholic—or are you on duty?" He winked, charmingly.

MacKenzie offered a cheeky half-smile in return. "We-ell, you know I probably shouldn't, but…go on then. If you've got a glass of something red and fruity, I won't say no."

"Don't move a muscle," he ordered, leaving her to survey the room while he nipped along to the kitchen.

This was clearly Donovan's personal retreat, MacKenzie thought, taking in the mementos encased in glass cabinets and the expensive sound system tucked away discreetly on a shelf to the side of an original Victorian fireplace. The colours were muted, every surface clean of dust. Above the fireplace was a large, framed pen-and-ink drawing of Satan's war against God, as told by Milton. It was a contorted, disturbed image and she was forced to look away. The French-style carriage clock on the mantle chimed eight-thirty in one loud strike.

There was only one exit; back through the doorway she had entered.

As he watched his quarry from the interior of an unmarked police vehicle, Arthur Gregson replayed the last conversation held with his High Priest. In the glove compartment rested a small, double-edged knife with an ornate ivory handle, reserved for occasions such as these.

"*Do it now,*" the man had urged. "*He will be alone. The area is secluded.*"

Gregson reached towards the glove compartment with reluctant hands. He unsheathed the blade, admiring its craftsmanship whilst at the same time thinking of how many lives it had taken.

"*It's not necessary,*" he had argued, once again.

The High Priest had looked upon his servant with mild, unyielding eyes.

"*Arthur, I've noticed a certain insubordination from you, recently, which I consider a mark of disloyalty.*"

Gregson held the blade in his fleshy hands, testing the weight.

"*I've supported you from the start—*"

"*You ought to be supporting the Master. I am merely his representative on Earth.*"

Gregson looked away, out of the window. What did he care for some ridiculous notion of satanic witchcraft? The man had gone mad, if he genuinely believed there was any substance to it. Perhaps Jane Freeman was right, he thought. It might be time for the Circle's first High Priestess.

"*You're wondering whether Freeman might make a good substitute,*" he had continued blandly, reading Gregson's thoughts with ease.

"*No, I—*"

"*You're thinking of how I might be ousted, aren't you? Perhaps your ego has grown sufficiently to consider yourself as a potential leader, hmm?*"

"Of course not."

"Perhaps you're even wondering if you have the balls to use that blade on me."

Gregson looked again at the knife resting loosely in his cupped hands and gripped the handle tighter as he imagined plunging it into the belly of his tormentor, watching him double over and wither to nothing.

Then, he thought wistfully, he would be free of him.

"You will never leave the Circle, Arthur. You have pledged your life to its work, to the work of the Master. If you abandon us, you abandon him. Who would accept your soul then, Arthur? God?" The High Priest had laughed, at the thought of it.

"You think he's a saviour, Arthur? Remember the cause, remember why we fight."

Gregson looked ahead, peering through the gloom to pick out the back of Jack Lowerson's head inside the black Fiat. Gregson had chosen his position with care and had parked in his present spot, engine and headlights off, long before Lowerson had rounded the corner. He had observed MacKenzie making her way to Donovan's front door and wondered how that would end.

The clock read eight-thirty and there was still no sign of Ryan or Phillips. He knew they would be coming; there was no question of this being an unplanned visit. There had been no discussion on the police radio, no planning in the Incident Room, but Gregson had known. Of course, he had known that Ryan would eventually put the jigsaw pieces together and be led here—so Gregson made sure he arrived first, waiting and watching. Still, time was marching on and if he was going to make a move, he needed to make it now.

Above him, the sky wept. Raindrops fell like warm tears, pattering against the bonnet of the car.

CHAPTER 24

Jack Lowerson watched the entranceway to the stone villa on the outskirts of the Town Moor, his thin fingers flexing on the steering wheel while he listened to MacKenzie's voice flowing through the headphones at his ears. He found himself enthralled by both the smooth tone and the direction of the conversation.

"You've been under a lot of stress," Paddy was saying.

"I have," Denise agreed. *"I really have. You'll laugh at the next part…"*

"What's that?"

"I was starting to think that the mastermind behind it all really was one of us."

There was a short pause and a tap, the sound of Paddy replacing his glass of port on the coffee table.

"That's getting a little far-fetched, don't you think? Let's try to think clearly, Denise. Look at the facts."

"I know that everything points to Colin and now he's dead. Doesn't that seem awfully convenient, though? Now he can't defend himself."

Paddy sighed and eased out of his chair.

"Perhaps you're feeling a sense of loss, now that a man has died. You found him unnerving, didn't you? Now that he's gone, perhaps you're feeling a sense of relief, which in turn makes you feel guilty."

Denise huffed out a sigh. *"The style doesn't fit Edwards or Colin Hart."*

"Why not?"

"It's like I said, earlier," Denise replied. *"The man we're looking for is better than both of them. Maybe he's too smart. I don't know if we'll ever catch him."*

"Maybe he doesn't want to be caught but he wants to be acknowledged for his work?"

"Yes!" Denise exclaimed. *"I think that's it, exactly."*

There was another pause before she continued, in a whisper.

"I don't know if I should tell you this, Paddy. I don't even understand it myself, but…I wish I could meet him. Just once. I wish I could meet the man who could beat us all."

Jack was so captivated that he missed the sound of his mobile phone the first few times.

He checked the time again. Ryan and Phillips would be on their way by now. Everything was going to plan, he assured himself.

Gregson stepped out into the rain. Yellow light from the streetlamps cast shadows along the handsome avenue.

The car door clicked shut behind him and he felt suddenly alone; no longer Arthur Gregson but a poor, hollowed-out shell of a man he might once have been.

His feet felt heavy as he stalked his prey. He was no natural hunter, but a carnivore who preferred to find his meat ready-packed on the shelves.

The black Fiat came into view and he was careful to remain in the shadows, tracing the path of the walls, which delineated where one house's front garden ended and another began.

He watched Jack for a several moments and found that he couldn't bring himself to take another step. He thought of the consequences of betrayal, of what had happened to Mike and Jennifer Ingles, up on the island. Panicked, he reached for the knife in his pocket and the edge of the blade grazed his palm, drawing blood.

Arthur sucked in a breath and tried to muster up some strength. It was a dispiriting thought, to realise that he was still the coward he had always been—time, money and a decent wardrobe hadn't changed that. His pulse pounded, and his hand trembled against the hunk of metal. Rain washed over his ageing face, stripping it of pretence, and soothing the sweat on his brow so that he could think clearly again.

He looked up, up, up into the sky. With childlike wonder, he watched the raindrops falling from above and traced the clouds plastering the night sky, moving and transforming before his eyes. He tried to read a message in their swirling folds, but could find none.

The clock was ticking.

Ryan made the turn along Eskdale Terrace and performed a hasty parallel park with a few jerky turns in the road. The surrounding area was manned by uniformed support and the side roads cordoned off. Residents had been contacted and told to remain inside their homes until further notice. There had been some loud-mouthing, some grumbles, but the mention of 'serial killer' in the same sentence as 'Jesmond' had been sufficient to quell their complaints.

Now the large houses were shuttered up for the evening, their lights blazing as if to ward off unwanted guests.

The road where they parked ran perpendicular to Donovan's street, where Lowerson had positioned himself—thereby allowing them to intercept a fleeing suspect from the front or the side. The back road was blocked by an unmarked police vehicle occupied by the same two handpicked DCs who had watched over Anna, and a couple of other constables for good measure.

Trusted men and women, every one.

Ryan fired up a mobile radio unit rather than the car radio and fiddled with the dials to find the right frequency.

"Lowerson? Come in."

Nothing.

"Lowerson? *Come in.*"

Hastily, he tried the man's mobile number, which rang out.

Ryan and Phillips exchanged a look and, without further ado, sprung out of the car.

"You take Lowerson, I'll get over to the house," Ryan shouted, on the run. Rain fell steadily, but the air was mild rather than cold. They passed the tall, silent walls of a well-known private school, which sang with the chirping voices of teenage girls during the weekdays but was now silent while they were at home, no doubt discussing the latest sensational gossip to come from the boys' school, which was conveniently located on the opposite side of the road.

"Bugger that," Phillips puffed. "I'm for Denise."

Ryan nodded his understanding. He would have expected nothing less.

"Don't enter until I tell you, Frank. We need him to attack or confess, otherwise we've got nothing."

Phillips' lips flattened at the thought, but he didn't argue.

Turning into Donovan's street, their steps slowed, so as not to make a commotion along the quiet pavement. Scanning the road, they spotted the black Fiat and Ryan gave Phillips a supportive slap on the shoulder before jogging across to it with a light-footed stride.

Reaching the car, he flung himself inside the passenger door and snapped the headset against Lowerson's ears.

The younger man yelped, rubbing at his ears. "Hey!"

"Try answering your phone, dipshit." Ryan snatched up the mobile, which had fallen to the floor on the passenger side.

Lowerson reddened. "Sorry guv. I got carried away."

"At least you're paying attention," Ryan muttered, before connecting his own headphones to the mobile radio unit. "How's the doc, this evening? Let's hope he's feeling chatty."

Seated inside Donovan's study, MacKenzie took another tiny sip of red wine, surveying him over the rim of the crystal glass.

"If you *could* meet this man, what would you say to him, Denise?"

MacKenzie recognised the change in Paddy Donovan. His eyes were no longer calm and faintly paternal, but feral—their pupils dilated in sheer anticipation of the kill. She imagined that she felt much the same as a deer in the wild, sensing that a lion waited to pounce from somewhere out of sight.

She fought to remain at ease, even while he moved around, somewhere behind her head.

"I don't know what I would say, really. He'd probably think I was beneath him," she said, coyly. "I would love to hear how he did it."

"Come, come." Paddy tutted. "You're a bright, lovely woman. What man wouldn't be flattered?"

MacKenzie looked away, modestly.

"I'm not his usual type," she continued with a trace of disappointment. "I'm older, for a start, with the wrong hair…"

She shook out her hair, so that it fell around her in soft folds. He watched the action and began to tremble.

"Nonsense, Denise," he said softly, moving towards a tall mahogany cabinet he kept in the corner of the room. Quietly, he retrieved the key, but didn't open it yet. First, he locked the door to the study, which turned smoothly. "Exceptions can always be made. But what about Phillips?"

MacKenzie trod carefully, now.

"He's a wonderful man," she said, honestly. "I care about him very much, but I can't help wondering …"

"What? What do you wonder?" He was eager now.

"I can't help wondering if the real killer has been searching for someone who might understand him. Someone worthy."

Donovan paused in his selection of a syringe and looked across to where Denise was seated with her back to him. Was she genuine?

"You believe you understand him?"

MacKenzie laughed and folded her arms, bracing herself. She judged that he was two or three paces behind her right shoulder.

"Oh, don't misunderstand me," she said. "I could hardly hope to understand him, not straight away, but I could *try*. All the other women, maybe they didn't appreciate him."

"It's possible, of course," Donovan agreed, sucking a massive dose of Lorazepam into the syringe. "Where are the others now, Denise?"

"Who? Ryan?"

"Yes."

She lifted a slim shoulder. "Still up at Sycamore Gap, I imagine," she lied.

"Did you tell them you were coming for...a debriefing session?"

Looking guilty, she shook her head. "I needed to see you, Paddy. I really did." She turned and looked up at him with large, green eyes. It was difficult, but she hoped that she looked submissive enough to tempt him. "I know I should have told Ryan, or Phillips, but I suppose I didn't want them to know. It's embarrassing, having to admit that I needed help."

He smiled slowly, moving across to place a hand on her shoulder. She felt the weight of it pinning her down.

"I've got a surprise for you, Denise."

"Oh? You're not going to tell me *you* killed those women, are you?" she asked innocently, clenching her jaw against what she knew was coming.

His arm swept downwards in an arc and she snapped her own arm out to brace against it, diverting the needle from connecting with the artery in her neck. Unfortunately, with some added force, Paddy rammed the point into the soft tissue of her upper arm and she felt the sharp sting penetrate through her shirt. MacKenzie clutched at it while her body began to slump, the neural pathways in her brain clogged by the sedative, no longer allowing her to control her limbs. He took the glass from her nerveless fingers, murmuring that there was no sense in causing a spillage.

While he replaced the syringe inside the cabinet, dunking the needle into a cup of strong medical disinfectant, her body slid gracefully off the chair. Her legs twisted beneath her and the back of her head thudded against the side of the coffee table, hard enough that she saw stars.

"There now," he said, breathing a bit heavier than normal as he fought to regain control. "Believe me, Denise, when I tell you that I will make sure you are my greatest masterpiece."

Face lax, her eyes watched him bend over with a middle-aged wheeze to retrieve his bag, which he placed on the coffee table beside her.

He crouched down to look into her face, pinching her skin to gauge the level of reaction. She didn't respond.

"Good," he muttered, resting his chin on his hands. She smelled the port on his breath, could see the tiny lines of broken veins across his cheeks, which were ruddy from years of eating rich food and indulging in one too many glasses of dessert wine.

She fixed her gaze straight ahead.

"I must say, Denise, that this isn't the way I planned my evening at all." He chuckled his booming laugh and she understood then how unthreatening he had appeared to those young women he had killed; they would have seen a man very much like their father and would have trusted him.

"You were right, of course, when you said that you're not quite my usual type." He bobbed his head, self-deprecatingly. "I've always been a creature of habit, I'm afraid. Never could stop myself falling for those pretty brunettes."

He sighed and stretched his arms out. "Getting creaky, in my old age," he explained, as if chatting over the dinner table. "I'm more than willing to make an exception for you, Denise. I've admired you very much over the years. A few times, I've considered ..." He shrugged off the rest of the sentence. "Well, isn't it amazing, how our wishes are eventually fulfilled? There was I, preparing to meet another lady, when you turned up on my doorstep like a gift horse. I never look one in the mouth, you know."

He boomed another laugh, delighted with himself, his eyes shining darkly in his excited face.

"Do you still want to *understand*, Denise? Even knowing that you'll suffer the same end?" He picked up a lock of her hair and brushed it out of her eyes with a gentle, if slightly trembling hand.

MacKenzie continued to stare fixedly ahead, spittle pooling at the side of her mouth and dribbling down the side of her chin. With the back of his cuff, he swiped it away.

"Up you go," he murmured, hoisting her body upwards until she was propped against the chair, her back bent and her arms limp. Then, he moved back to his chair and seated himself, picking up his glass of port once again.

"How shall we begin?" he mused. " 'Tell me what's on your mind'. Isn't that what I usually say?"

CHAPTER 25

Gregson could feel the sweat trickling from his forehead and into his eyes. He swiped a hand across them to clear his vision as he took the junction for the A1 northbound with dangerous speed. He knew where he was headed; it was the only place he could turn.

He couldn't explain what had happened to him, as he had neared the black Fiat where Lowerson sat absorbed by his surveillance task. How easy it would have been to ambush him or even to lure him away from the vehicle under some pretext or another. Unaccountably, he, who had never prayed, had begun to pray. Long forgotten words from Sunday school had streamed from his lips:

The Lord is my shepherd; I shall not want.
He maketh me to lie down in green pastures: he leadeth me beside the still waters.
He restoreth my soul: he leadeth me in the paths of righteousness for his name's sake.

Yea, I walk through the valley of the shadow of death: I will fear no evil; for thou art with me …

Before he knew it, he was running back to his own car, crying like a baby against the steering wheel before reality had set in. Not long after, he had seen Ryan jogging across the road to slip inside the black Fiat with Lowerson, his window of opportunity gone.

Gregson had botched the job and he knew that if his High Priest heard of his failure, there would be no forgiving slap on the shoulder. No, "Never mind, do it another time", or "Forget the whole crazy idea." Now, it was a question of damage limitation and, for that, there was only one place left to turn.

With the city behind him, everywhere was in darkness. The car he kept for his outings into the country smelled dank and stuffy with a combination of petrol and old boots, unlike the polished leather interior of the saloon he used for work. His mobile phone flashed on the seat beside him and he knew that he didn't have long.

Eventually, he turned off the motorway and headed deep into the heart of the countryside, past signs indicating villages with names straight out of folklore. For miles, he saw only the lonely beam of his car's headlights, until the flicker of lights appeared to indicate a secluded house.

It was time to bargain for his life.

Denise watched Donovan with the same fixed expression in her green eyes. If he had been less intent on regaling her with his brilliance and more focused on his task, he might have noticed that her pupils had returned to near-normal size. If he pinched her skin again, he might have observed a reaction this time.

Instead, Donovan sprawled in his leather chair and drank steadily as he described his childhood, where he had witnessed casual violence between his mother and father with more fascination than was normal for a six-year-old child. He had killed his first pet, aged seven, and went into nauseating detail about that turning point in his young existence. He spoke eloquently of childhood traumas and sexual fantasies and it took every ounce of professionalism for her to remain completely impassive.

Every now and then, she made sure to dribble a bit. It risked his return to wipe it from her chin, but it looked authentic.

"Everything changed with Amy," he reflected, gesturing with the port glass. "She was so bright. So *young*."

MacKenzie stared.

"Now, don't go getting jealous," he said, blowing a kiss at her mute body, lying propped against the chair opposite. The clock chimed the quarter hour and he was dimly aware that he should move things along.

Just another minute, or two, he thought.

"Amy came to me as a private client," he began. "She walked into my office one day and I was smitten." He thought back to that moment, ten years ago or more. She had worn tight blue jeans and a snug top, her dark hair poking out beneath a floppy hat—the uniform of a student in the early years of the new millennium.

"She'd been seeing a young man, who worked at the hospital where she was a third-year medic."

Paddy's face completely changed from middle-aged affability, to something hard and grotesque.

"That man is now a well-known personality," he continued, silkily. "Though, back then, he was nothing. Do you understand? *Nothing.*"

Swallowing the last of his port, he leaned down to grasp MacKenzie's jaw, forcing her head upwards to look at him.

"Pay attention, while I'm talking to you, Denise."

He rubbed the pad of his thumb over her mouth, forcing her lips apart and for a hideous moment she thought he might kiss her.

Instead, he thrust her away in disgust. She slumped back against the chair.

"I made it my business to find him and to get to know the man who had sullied Amy. Edwards needed to know that she was *my* property." They had fought, he remembered with a degree of fondness, but eventually he had overpowered the younger man. "I don't mind telling you, Denise, I've let myself go a bit over the years. Used to be much fitter."

He sighed, tapping his belly.

"But, then, what's middle age for? It's about time I enjoyed myself a bit. Life can't all be work, work, work, can it?"

He considered another glass of port, but with an eye for the time, stretched himself and prepared to hoist MacKenzie from the floor and into his waiting car. With any luck, the street would still be empty and anybody happening to notice would see a well-respected neighbour escorting a fine-looking lady out to dinner.

He'd put in enough hours knobbing about with the locals, listening to their silly chatter about Neighbourhood Watch and charity coffee mornings. Times like these, it paid off.

"What was I saying?" He scratched at his ear. "Of course, I was telling you about Amy. She was a very special, very *stupid* girl. I was prepared to give her everything, you know. I was a romantic, back then. We began a relationship, and over time she came to realise that Edwards was no good for her. He didn't accept that, at first. He tried to take her back. I couldn't allow that to happen."

He held the tips of his fingers against his lips, to still their quiver.

"I didn't intend to kill her, at least not *then*," he picked up the story again. "Like I say, I was younger, more at the mercy of my emotions. I had a few bad moments just afterwards. I would think that the police were onto me. Every time there was a knock at the door, I wondered if they'd found her. Then, before I knew it, a year and then two years had passed. I realised I'd done a better job than even I had imagined. Without some bumbling nobody happening to find her after all these years, she would have remained there, in our special place, for all time."

MacKenzie's legs were cramping badly. Her left knee lay at an awkward right-angle, but in her supposedly comatose state, she was unable to move it to a more comfortable position. Besides, he was almost finished. It wouldn't be too much longer before he would tell her about Claire Burns.

He stood up and she felt her heart stutter in her chest, her chest rising and falling too rapidly. She made a conscious effort to slow its rhythm, back to the slow, inconspicuous rise and falls of earlier.

As it happened, she was not his objective.

He moved back to the small mahogany cabinet and, this time, he brought out a silver bangle. It was the last one in his possession.

Moving back towards Denise, he lifted her slim wrist and clasped it around the limp bone, taking a moment to check her pulse. Slow and steady. He approved—that was good.

"Just a little present, my dear," He admired the way the silver serpent glinted against the pale skin and then let her arm fall back into place.

"The serpent is, of course, very symbolic. Originally, I bought ten of those bracelets, for another purpose entirely." He sniggered, like a naughty schoolboy having disobeyed his headmaster. "Instead, I gave one to Amy and decided to keep the other nine, just in case. Well…"

His eyes snaked away, to rest on the unseen photographs hidden inside his mahogany cabinet. Briefly, their images flashed in his mind, replaying the sensations, the power and the pleasure of it all. Desire made his voice thicker, when he spoke again.

"The one on your wrist is the only one I have left. You should feel very special, Denise. I don't hand them out to just anybody, you know."

MacKenzie thought of eight other young women, probably dark-haired, who were missing presumed dead. She wondered where he had killed them, where he had hidden them.

"I think it's perhaps best if we continue our little discussion on the road," he said, almost sadly. "Much as I'm enjoying myself, I can see that you're looking a lot more wide-eyed than you were a few minutes ago. Quite apart from that, I'm not in the habit of shitting in my own back yard." He boomed out his laugh.

MacKenzie watched him check and double check the contents of his bag, then roll his shoulders as he moved around the coffee table.

"Get out of my way!" Phillips squared up to Ryan, his short, muscled physique tensed for battle. It took every ounce of strength and training to hold him off.

"Listen to me, Frank. *Listen!*" The pummelling stalled, briefly, and the small collection of firearms officers and detective constables in position around the house raised their eyebrows in collective amazement. "The minute he admits to anything, we'll be in there like a shot, but he's prattling on about his childhood. We need him to talk about Amy or Claire or even one of the others he might have done. Hopefully, he'll squeal about Geraldine Hart, too."

Phillips battled against his instincts, which were strongly urging him to ram his SIO to one side and barge through the front door.

But he was a policeman first and foremost.

"The minute—the *minute,* he breathes anything useful, I'm going in."

Ryan nodded and relaxed his vice-like grip.

In his ear, MacKenzie's breathing rose and fell in comforting waves.

The car engine slowed, and Gregson held his breath when the engine stopped altogether. Ahead, light streamed onto the driveway from a powerful spotlight and a large dog bounded towards him from the direction of the front door. Slowly, Gregson stepped out of the car and allowed himself to be sniffed.

"What the *hell* are you doing here?"

The dog was called off, eventually.

"I didn't know where else to come," Gregson stammered.

"Your present troubles have nothing to do with me."

"It's Circle business!" Gregson shouted, no longer calm, nor reasonable.

"Let me take an educated guess and say that the reason you've arrived on my doorstep, sweating like a pig and stinking of desperation, is that you've failed to silence Lowerson. Correct?"

Gregson looked on with hatred. It was true, he had failed, but some small part of him rejoiced in the knowledge that, when his back was against the wall, he wasn't a pure-born killer. But now he needed help. If word got around that he'd bottled it, he would be the one found with a knife in his belly.

"Look, I said I would support you, that I would give you my loyalty if you run against him."

"And?"

"I need something in return!"

A pause, followed by a long-suffering sigh.

"This is a one-time deal, Arthur. I don't want you darkening my door again, understand? When the time is right, I want you backing me."

"You have my word." Gratitude made his voice wobble.

Jane Freeman led the way back into the sprawling stone barn she had converted into a luxurious home over the years. One of the many perks of loyalty, she thought, but nothing could beat writing your own ticket.

CHAPTER 26

Paddy moved around the coffee table and hunkered down until he was eye to eye with MacKenzie.

"Let's go, Denise," he said brightly, before reaching out to grasp underneath her arms. In doing so, he brushed the material of her shirt, tugging it out of place to reveal a slim, flesh-coloured wire taped to the skin between her breasts. His face twisted as he struggled to compute the meaning.

He looked up from the wire into eyes that were wildly green and very lucid.

"I've got a little surprise for you, Paddy," Denise ground out. Wasting no time, she slammed the heel of her hand up into the bridge of his nose, with a satisfying crunch.

He fell backwards, crashing onto the coffee table. Glasses shattered onto the polished wooden floor beneath and blood streamed from his face, splattering down the front of his shirt.

MacKenzie rose to her feet on slightly shaky legs, glad to be in charge of her body and mind. She circled around the back of the chair, reaching for the heavy, glass ashtray, which had fallen to the floor. She held it like a club, ready to use as a weapon if necessary.

When Donovan reared upwards, he was all animal. Howling, he leapt towards her, the bulk of his body scattering the chairs aside.

"Bitch!"

She prepared to fight.

The moment Donovan signalled his intention to move, Ryan had given the order: "ATTACK, ATTACK!" Three teams stationed in a triangle around the house prepared to intercept Donovan if he managed to escape. Stationed directly outside the front door, two constables battered through the oak door, which gave way after three good rams.

Phillips was first through the door, calling out "ARMED POLICE!" and Ryan followed closely behind with the firearms specialists. In a few short strides, they followed the sound of a loud crash towards the rear of the house.

"Denise!"

Phillips didn't wait for the battering ram but kicked open the door to Donovan's study with the strength of an angry carthorse.

He skidded to a halt, his face drooping into disbelieving lines when he saw the bloodied body lying still on the floor at the foot of the coffee table.

"You took your time, Frank Phillips!"

Dazed, they looked up from the unconscious body of Paddy Donovan and across to where MacKenzie stood, dabbing at a graze to her cheekbone with the edge of her shirtsleeve. Her other hand kneaded the aches which seemed to have leaked into her body, spreading in waves of pain from her neck. Now that the adrenaline was starting to drain from her system, the competing effects of Lorazepam and its antidote, Flumazenil, made her feel fuzzy. A headache throbbed, along with her right bicep—which sang with pain and victory but felt like a dead weight.

"Denise." Phillips crossed the room to take her face in his hands.

"Frank," she protested, a bit embarrassed, a bit moved. "I'm fine. Really."

Phillips cleared his throat and rubbed his hands up and down her arms before hugging her to him.

"Course you're fine," he said gruffly, stepping away deliberately. "Take more than some lunatic to knock you off your stride."

"Good job, Mac," Ryan added, with some admiration, then turned to issue instructions for Donovan to be properly tended by medics and transferred to a holding cell. "You pack a mighty decent punch."

MacKenzie grinned. "You think I do Pilates just to keep my ass pert?" she joked. "Knew that defence training would come in useful some day."

"You might want to take a look inside that cabinet," she added, with a nod towards the corner unit. "He keeps the key somewhere on him."

Ryan checked Donovan's pockets and found nothing. He ran light fingers over his shirt and the waistband of his trousers until he found what he was looking for.

"Bingo."

Grey eyes turned stormy as they surveyed the trove of evidence inside that cabinet; there were ten coloured folders, clearly labelled with the names of ten women, organised into what he presumed was date order. In the first folder, a single picture of Amy Llewellyn smiling brightly for the camera was pinned to a stack of medical notes on her psychological health and, above them, a sheaf of handwritten notes in the form of a personal journal. That would make for interesting reading, he was sure.

Eight other files listed the names of women he knew were missing, some of whom he recognised from Phillips' list of like crimes.

In the tenth folder, there were several grainy, long-range images of Anna, pinned to a stack of newspaper cuttings and handwritten notes.

Yet there were no notes on Claire Burns or on Geraldine Hart.

Ryan looked back down towards the man who was starting to come around. He groaned and shifted on the floor while a police medic checked his vitals. Once the medic was satisfied that he wasn't about to keel over, his wrists were quickly restrained.

Paddy struggled against the metal but eventually allowed himself to be lifted to his knees, then to his feet. Ryan stood apart, eyeing him with flat, emotionless eyes.

"This time, Paddy, it'll be me asking the questions."

———

When Ryan returned to the Incident Room, Anna was sitting back with a cup of lukewarm sludge and a Jaffa Cake, laughing along with Jeff Pinter and Tom Faulkner like they were old friends. On his arrival, all three came to attention.

"Ryan? What happened?"

Knowing what Donovan had intended, or at least having his suspicions proved correct, did not give Ryan any pleasure. It made his face hard and his voice harder.

"Exactly as we planned. Donovan confessed to Amy's murder and there's a truckload of evidence at his house. Faulkner? I need you to get over there and start going over it. We still don't know where he killed them. See if your UV lamps can help uncover a kill site."

Back to work, Faulkner thought, but with a degree of optimism he hadn't felt in a long while. He murmured his thanks to Anna and made ready to round up his team.

"Jeff? Babysitting duty's over. You had a date tonight. Why don't you see if she's still available?"

Pinter thought wistfully of the attractive blonde woman he'd met through an online dating service. He'd been as nervous as a schoolboy, but strangely relieved to receive Ryan's call for help. It meant he was still one of the team.

"Maybe we can have a late bite to eat," he agreed, smiling fondly at Anna in farewell.

Anna hadn't seen Ryan in this particular mood before. He was prowling around, but instead of facing her with that direct, merciless stare that was so much a part of his personality, his eyes were evasive. In fact, they were avoiding her.

"Ryan? What's the matter?" She stood up and moved across to face him.

He didn't answer directly but jerked a thumb in the direction of the door. "What's the beef with Faulkner?"

Anna crossed her arms, not appreciating the tone. "Perhaps you should ask him—"

"I have," Ryan bit out.

"In that case, you should be aware that Tom's been having some financial troubles lately. We had a bit of a chat about how he could try to manage, juggle things around a bit, that sort of thing."

Ryan listened with half an ear. He might have known it would be something completely prosaic that was troubling Faulkner. He'd have to have a word with him, talk about how the department could help. Hell, if the man was that hard up, he'd give him a loan. Thanks to various wealthy ancestors, money was one thing he didn't need to worry about.

He watched Anna and felt again the burning guilt of having so nearly been the reason for her coming to harm. If he'd been too late, if he'd missed a clue, she might have been the next victim to be found inside a wall cavity up on a miserable, windy hill somewhere.

"Why don't you tell me what's on your mind?" she tried again.

"Nothing's the matter," he snapped. "Jesus! Why does it always have to be *talk, talk, talk*? It's been a long day, chasing down a killer. How do you expect me to behave?"

Her eyes narrowed into angry slits. "You could start by at least being civil," she snapped.

"Sorry, *princess,* my manners fly out of the window when I'm trying to deal with homicidal maniacs," he flung back.

Anna wouldn't humiliate herself by becoming emotional. He didn't deserve such consideration. Instead, she walked back to the desk to retrieve her bag and coat.

"I'll be at *my* home," she said quietly. "You know where to find me, when you're in a better mood."

He could have stopped her, called her back. Instead, he watched her leave the Incident Room with her back straight and her head high. He knew he had behaved like a prize tosser. He knew the reason for it, as well. He couldn't stand being faced with her, alive and well, so soon after reading Donovan's detailed notes on how he had planned to mutilate her.

"Ryan has a prize, but it will bring him down a few pegs once I claim her," the man had written. *"What then, for his fragile psyche? Will he try to avenge, or crumble?"*

It wouldn't have been about Anna, he realised. Her death would have been a means to hurt him; a means for Donovan to prove his superiority, once again—just as he had killed Amy Llewellyn to cheat another man out of the pleasure.

Like a revolving door, Phillips entered as Anna left. Instead of her usual friendly 'Hello, Frank!' she offered him a murmured farewell. Her eyes looked suspiciously damp.

"'Bye, pet," he said in return, and then faced Ryan with a look of parental disappointment.

"Don't start!" Ryan pointed a finger at his sergeant and hoped it would be enough to stave off the lecture.

"None of my business, of course," Phillips mused. "But seems to me you've sent your lady packing after she waited here, patiently, not knowing what was going to happen. She trusted you to do right by her, Ryan."

"D'you think I don't know that? It's because of me that she needed to be here at all!"

Phillips scratched at the side of his chin, the fingernail rasping against the stubble on his chin. "Fancy yourself a bit, don't you?"

Ryan was shocked. Never, in thirty-five years, had anybody suggested he was arrogant. That didn't make it untrue.

"Look, lad, Donovan might have got his jollies at the thought of getting one over on you but, on the other hand, he might have targeted her anyway. Either way, no sense in beating yourself up about something you can't change."

"Thanks for the pep talk," Ryan retorted.

Phillips sighed. There was only so much he could say on affairs of the heart before he started to sound like an agony aunt. He changed the subject.

"Donovan's been checked into his cell for the night," he confirmed. "He's ranting and raving like a lunatic. We'll get no sense from him this evening."

Ryan nodded.

"And, Colin?"

"Fast asleep and dreaming." Phillips yawned himself, imagining the feel of his own memory-foam mattress with MacKenzie snuggled beside him. "So, what do you reckon has gone down?"

Ryan hitched a hip on the side of his desk and caught sight of the little framed picture of Anna. He snatched his gaze away.

"Edwards admitted to a relationship with Amy Llewellyn, which she called off, apparently because she didn't like the direction it was taking. We've got the university GP records showing sex-related injuries around the time she would have been seeing him."

Phillips grunted his agreement.

"For obvious reasons, she didn't feel she could run and tell Mummy and Daddy. She became depressed, so she took herself off to Donovan for private counselling. Maybe she thought nobody would find out. Turns out she was right."

"Poor lass," Frank said. "Probably had no idea what she was getting herself into."

"She stumbled into a spider's web," Ryan agreed. "One who hadn't made his first proper kill and was desperate to start."

"How does Edwards connect to Donovan?"

"From what Donovan told MacKenzie, it seems that Amy might have still harboured some feelings for Edwards. That would have made Donovan jealous; he can't stand competition and wanted her for himself."

"Aye, so he went to lay the smack down?"

That brought the ghost of a smile to Ryan's lips. "Seems like he and Edwards had a man-to-man chat, with Donovan coming out on top. I can't imagine that happening with Edwards today, but ten years ago? He was a younger, more impressionable man. He said himself that he respected his mentor. Perhaps they exchanged notes, learned from each other—he became a kind of protégé."

"Christ almighty, it's like a 'members only' club," Phillips said, with distaste.

"Yeah, but Edwards wasn't that good of a student. Obviously, he still made a play for Amy and that's what flipped the switch for Donovan. He says he didn't intend to kill her? Bullshit. He took her all the way out there, to Sycamore Gap, knowing that he would be coming back alone."

Phillips settled himself in one of the hard, plastic tub chairs, wiggling his hips to try to find comfort.

"He was stamping out his superiority," Phillips agreed. "Which means that Edwards knew it was Donovan all along."

"Edwards sent Colin that postcard of Sycamore Gap as a message, directing him up there, knowing all along there would be something to find. It's his form of revenge. It's a sinister thought, imagining him waiting for his moment to strike against Donovan; waiting until he had been lulled into a sense of false security. Don't forget, he's got a memory like an elephant."

"His loyalty has limits, though," Phillips observed.

"What do they say about 'loyalty amongst thieves'? Maybe there's a similar saying for whacked out murderers."

"So, Edwards used Colin to lead us to Donovan," Phillips summarised. "We could charge him with perverting the course of justice."

Ryan huffed out a laugh.

"Yeah, right. I can see the CPS spending their money and resources prosecuting a man who's already in prison for life."

Fair point, Phillips had to admit, then had a worrying thought.

"What if Edwards coached Colin into killing Claire Burns?"

"I would have said it was possible, but the skill needed to dissect her body in that way took some degree of medical training. Added to which, her torso was marked to replicate the Holy Island victims. That took inside knowledge, which Donovan had. More likely, when Donovan heard who had found Amy's body, he did a bit of digging and realised that Colin was connected to Edwards. He couldn't punish

Edwards, since he's already behind bars, but he could punish Colin." Ryan shrugged. "What's the best way? Killing the two people Colin Hart valued most in the world—Claire Burns and his mother, Geraldine. He had the opportunity to do both."

"Cold-blooded," Phillips said.

"Vengeful," Ryan added. "With the added bonus that the police would turn their sights on poor old Colin, the weirdo who has an obsession with true crime and lived across the street from Claire."

"Completely stitched him up." Phillips tugged at his lip while he thought about it. "It'll be an interesting chat with Donovan tomorrow morning."

"You're telling me," Ryan murmured. There were so many things he wanted to know. Chiefly, how Colin had come to call Donovan's home telephone number. Had Donovan ingratiated himself with the man in a psychiatric capacity?

Phillips yawned again. "Wonder what Faulkner will find in Donovan's house?"

"I dread to think."

With facts and statements crowding his mind, Ryan headed home to his empty apartment on the Quayside. Walking through the door, he no longer faced the ghostly image of his dead sister. Instead, the space felt devoid of any soul at all, and he wished Anna were with him. His body yearned for her and his mind sought the peace that she could bring.

The call from the Control Room came in the dead of night, jolting him awake from a light, fitful sleep. On a routine check of the occupants in the holding cells, the duty sergeant had made a grisly discovery. Doctor Paddy Donovan had committed suicide, his limp body found twisted at the end of a makeshift ligature tied to the tap on the little sink inside his cell.

The man had been nothing, if not resourceful.

CHAPTER 27

Thursday, 25ᵗʰ June 2015

"Phillips? What the hell is going on?"

Frank stood inside the foyer of CID Headquarters sipping sugary caffeine, awaiting Ryan's arrival. He, too, had been roused from his sleep and had left his foam mattress and his love to slumber peacefully while he returned to deal with the man who could have killed her.

"Short answer is that we haven't got a clue. Pinter's in there now, checking him over, but he says it looks like a classic case of suicide."

"Not good enough." Ryan jabbed a finger at his chest, causing Phillips to raise a mild eyebrow in warning. "I want to know who is the weak zebra, in all this. Donovan was transferred to Holding with a medic and two DCs, after being placed under arrest by yours truly. You took Denise home. Who failed to check him, through the night?"

Phillips took another silent sip of his drink before responding. "Logbook says that all personal items were removed before he was checked in. The duty sergeant swears blind that Donovan was checked and double-checked before he was put to bed. He seemed defiant, cursing like a sailor when he was booked in; nothing to suggest that he was a suicide risk."

Ryan's eyes narrowed. "This stinks, Frank."

"Aye, it does. There'll be an inquiry.".

"More than that." Ryan shook his head angrily. "Donovan, the world's most egotistical killer, decides to end himself before the glory of a high-profile trial? That's about as likely as icicles in hell. Have I stepped into the Twilight Zone, Frank?"

Phillips was lost for words, a state of affairs made worse by the arrival of their superior officer.

DCS Gregson strode through the main doors to CID, his face set into angry lines. He was groomed and dressed smartly in slacks and a work shirt, his white-grey hair once more brushed away from his strong-boned face. He glared at both men.

"Does somebody want to tell me what the bloody hell is going on?" His eyes blazed. "Ryan, the last orders I gave you were to find Colin Hart. I then hear that the man was apprehended and taken into custody under psychological supervision. Job done, I think to myself. Next thing I know, I get a call telling me a respected clinical psychiatrist has committed suicide whilst in police custody. Somebody give me a sodding report!"

Ryan surveyed him with interest. Gregson's eyes were awake and alert. He was dressed smartly but his hair was damp, despite the fact that the rain stopped hours earlier.

Either he had stopped for a shower before coming down, which was unlikely given the short timescales, or he had been up and about before the call came in. He glanced down at his watch, which read a little after four-thirty in the morning.

Ryan shook himself. He was starting to suspect everyone. "Sir, under my orders, a small team conducted a sting operation during which we were able to obtain recorded evidence of Donovan having killed Amy Llewellyn—"

"A sting operation? Have you gone mad?"

"No, sir." Ryan hoped not, at least. "DI MacKenzie conducted a successful 'honeytrap' scenario in which Donovan eventually attacked her, then proceeded to begin a confession of his crimes. In anticipation of this, DI MacKenzie was administered a dose of Flumazenil prior to entering the property, which offset the effects of the drug Lorazepam and enabled her to remain lucid. Officers including Phillips and myself were stationed nearby at all times. We had ears on her throughout."

Gregson continued to regard him with an empty-eyed stare. "You conducted all of this without my authorisation."

"Sir, the result was positive—"

"A man is dead, Ryan. A friend of mine is dead."

Ryan fought to remain patient. "I regret that you have lost a friend, sir, but that *friend* was a killer. Three women, probably more, are also dead at his hands."

"Donovan has committed suicide?"

This question was posed to Phillips. "Ah, yes, by all accounts. The duty sergeant checked him according to the usual guidelines, but it seems that Donovan took the first opportunity to hang himself. He used the material from his own shirt."

"I see," Gregson said flatly, turning back to Ryan. "You bring in a suspect using a highly risky entrapment scenario, endangering police staff—despite already having your prime suspect in custody. You then allow him access to the means by which to end his own life."

"I wouldn't say we 'allowed access'—"

"Shoddy job all round," Gregson ground out, quieting any defence from Phillips. "You," he said, pointing a finger at Ryan's mutinous face. "I hear young DC Lowerson is out of hospital, after you took it upon yourself to discharge him, without seeking medical advice. He certainly hasn't been cleared to return to duty. This all demonstrates to me that you have little or no concern for the welfare of the staff under your command."

"Sir—" Ryan shook his head, disbelievingly.

"You are suspended from duty, effective immediately, pending a full inquiry. I presume MacKenzie is recuperating after the stress of her experience; therefore, Phillips will take over your duties in closing this investigation down, reporting directly to me. You will turn over your warrant card, now."

Gregson held out his hand for the card.

For Ryan, the world seemed to have slowed to a standstill. His ears were ringing, the blood having rushed through his veins so loudly as to drown out all other noise. After a few seconds, the world filtered back in; the drone of early morning traffic, the murmured voices of police staff and the slurred ones of drunk and disorderly revellers from the previous evening. He watched one professional-looking man stumble into the building alongside two PCs with tired, fed-up faces. Two buttons had popped on his smart white shirt, now stained with alcohol and vomit.

With trembling fingers, Ryan drew out his warrant card and placed it into Gregson's hand. He didn't immediately withdraw it, but gripped Gregson's fingers tightly, forcing the man to face him. Ryan tugged him closer in an unexpectedly quick movement, and bore down upon him, silver eyes blazing into brown.

"I'm coming for you," he ground out, and watched Gregson pale under his tan. He let the hand drop away with disgust and then walked out of the building.

Phillips was torn. He wanted to follow his friend, to take his own warrant card and chuck it in Gregson's face, on principle alone. But this was the real world. He was now tasked with handling the fall-out with Donovan and Hart, something Ryan should rightly be overseeing. He watched the tall, retreating figure with regret.

Beside him, Gregson put a hand on his shoulder and sighed.

"We need men like you in this department, Frank. Steady, dependable men who don't take unnecessary risks."

"You need men like him too." Phillips shrugged off the hand and trudged away in the direction of the cells.

Gregson crossed his arms over his chest, feeling better than he had in a long while. He exchanged a meaningful glance with the duty sergeant at the desk, the man who had been responsible for booking Paddy Donovan into Holding and for logging any subsequent visitors.

Of course, the log would say that there had been no visitors at all, which was just as it should be.

Anna slept hardly a wink. Nightmarish effigies of men dressed in animal costumes had chased sleep away. Eventually, she had given up on the battle, tucked a blanket around herself and watched senseless television through the night and into the early hours of the morning. She remained alert, hoping that Ryan would come to his senses and walk through the door, tired but apologetic. When it became clear that wasn't going to happen, she had called her old friend Mark, just for somebody to talk to. Mark Bowers lived alone and usually enjoyed a discussion of Northumbrian history however early in the morning, but there had been no answer there either. It seemed that the small number of people who mattered in her life were dropping like flies, reminding her of just how isolated she had become.

She moved around the kitchen on autopilot, stirring tea and making toast she had no intention of eating. She was still dressed in the black leggings and oversized t-shirt emblazoned with a faded Bon Jovi slogan that she had worn the previous evening.

The toaster pinged at the same moment she heard the front door opening. Clutching her mug of tea, she moved into the hallway in time to see Ryan pushing the door closed behind him and falling back against the doorframe as if life had simply beaten him.

Snide, unworthy thoughts she had ruminated on throughout the lonely hours of the night simply melted away. He looked even worse than she felt; his eyes were glossy with fatigue and when they raised to meet her searching examination of him, she saw they were filled with melancholy.

"Gregson took my warrant card," he explained simply, the words slurred as if from drink, but he hadn't touched a drop.

"What? *Why?*"

They remained a short distance apart, neither of them ready to close the gap.

"Gregson thinks I was reckless; I went ahead with a sting without getting approval. Then Donovan killed himself."

Ryan's eyes closed briefly, as if the lids could no longer manage to support the weight.

"Donovan's killed himself? I don't believe it."

His eyes opened again, a crack of glistening silver. "Neither do I."

"Well, then, surely—"

"You don't understand." Ryan interrupted her righteous tirade on his behalf, though he was grateful for the sentiment. "They'll say it was an oversight, that Donovan wasn't properly supervised. Just, 'one of those things'. Gregson is angry because he doesn't believe Donovan killed those women."

"You've got evidence." Anna waved her free hand mutely.

"Yeah, for all the good it does me. Faulkner's found some forensics pointing at Donovan and we even have it from the horse's mouth that he killed Amy Llewellyn. He tried to disable MacKenzie with Lorazepam, just like Claire, and it was pretty obvious he was about to make a move on her, maybe take her to his kill site."

"Any idea where that is?"

Ryan dragged his fingers through his dark hair.

"Faulkner hasn't been able to find a site within the immediate proximity of Sycamore Gap. Expanding any wider would take weeks—months, even. I had hoped to ask Donovan outright but now it's possible we'll never know."

"What about Colin?"

"What about him?" Ryan spoke with anger, but it wasn't directed towards her. "I'm off the case, Anna. That means I can't interview him, can't access the files or investigate. Phillips and the rest of the team will have to handle it."

There was a short silence where she felt his heartache keenly. This was a man who had for years been defined by the work he did. It was his business to bring justice to the dead and their families, and now someone had robbed him of that purpose.

"Why would Gregson do it?"

Unconsciously, they had edged closer together, each within reach of the other. Anna could feel the warmth emanating from him, but it didn't match his cold demeanour. She stayed where she was.

"There's a good question," he muttered. She wished she didn't feel as much for him; wished she didn't understand how affected he was by the degradation, the injustice of it all. "He wants me out, on the grounds that my methods put officers at risk, particularly MacKenzie."

He digested the thought and, always a fair man, turned to Anna for an honest answer. "Do you think he's right?"

Anna considered the question, realising that he would not want platitudes or useless prevarication. Unlike Gregson, she understood that Ryan was a man who would rather cut off his own limbs than unnecessarily endanger life.

"Was there another way of outing Donovan?"

Ryan had thought of the ins and outs, in detail.

"I could have brought Donovan in for questioning, cards on the table, but we had no forensics to support a warrant or even take a DNA swab. He would have eliminated every scrap of incriminating evidence at the house and would likely have dropped back under the radar. He lasted for years between kills," Ryan reminded her. "Besides which, he had lined Colin up as the fall-guy. He had Gregson gunning for the man, based on the fact he's a prize turkey."

"How did Donovan know Colin?"

"That's another question I would have liked to ask both of them." Ryan nodded. "I assume that Donovan remains connected to Edwards, who connects to Colin. It's more than likely Donovan found a means to contact Edwards, who gave him some information on Colin Hart, enabling him to take advantage of his vulnerable character."

They gave in to the inevitable and settled into a comforting embrace, arms banded tightly.

"I'm sorry," he muttered against the top of her head, which was tucked under his chin. "I shouldn't have taken my anger out on you like that. I was angry at myself; if it weren't for your association with me, Donovan would never have set his sights on you."

He felt her body go still.

"Yes," he continued. "You were supposed to be the next on his list."

Anna said nothing for a moment, examining her own feelings.

"I understand that your natural inclination is to protect, and, in this case, I'm grateful for all the measures you took. Your instincts were obviously good. But"—she looked up into his eyes as she stepped away—"I'm more grateful that you choose to trust me now; enough to come to me when you're hurting, enough to tell me the truth about Donovan. It means more to me."

Ryan looked away, feeling foolishly happy.

"I want it to be this way between us," he agreed. "I can't hide who I am from you, Anna, just as you can't hide yourself from me. There may be other times that a lunatic delves into our private lives, other times you might be touched by danger. I hate thinking of it." He swallowed. "I hate imagining you being tainted by it, but—"

"Ryan," she said, as she put her hand into his, giving his fingers a reassuring squeeze. "I knew from the start the kind of work you do. Besides, I've already been 'tainted' by murder, if you recall."

She gave him a small, sardonic smile.

"That aside," she continued briskly, "what are we going to do about Gregson?"

Ryan grinned broadly for the first time in days.

"Now, you're talking."

At precisely three o'clock that afternoon, DCS Arthur Gregson stood atop a makeshift podium outside CID Headquarters. Behind him, young, ambitious men with an eye for promotion stood in a smart row of navy suits. In front of him, the local press were poised and ready.

Phillips, MacKenzie and Lowerson remained a good distance apart from the media throng, which was a statement in itself.

"Turns my stomach," MacKenzie said, fully recovered from the excitement of the day before. "Ryan should be standing up there, telling the press all about how a killer got his comeuppance."

The other two nodded their heads in unison.

"Far too bloody early to be talking about it," Phillips said. "Haven't had a chance to go over Pinter's conclusions, to discuss it all with the CSIs, *nothing*. How can Gregson stand there and say that Donovan killed himself when we don't know that for sure?"

MacKenzie's lip curled. "He's covering his arse."

"His and the department's," Phillips corrected. "But there's nothing to cover! Everything was done by the book, from start to finish."

MacKenzie gave him a quick squeeze.

"What are we going to do?" Lowerson spoke up, his eager voice laced with indignation on behalf of his SIO, the man he looked up to, modelled himself on and generally hoped to emulate one day. "Ryan shouldn't have been suspended."

"Aye, it's not right," Phillips agreed. He had tried to contact Ryan several times, but the number rang out. He told himself that Anna would look after him, but also knew that he would drive up to see him at the first opportunity.

"Ssh," MacKenzie hushed them all. "Let's hear what he has to say for himself."

"I can confirm that Doctor Patrick Donovan, an eminent clinical psychiatrist, was found dead in his cell early this morning," Gregson began, in sombre tones. "Although all measures were taken in accordance with the relevant guidelines, I am sorry to say that he apparently committed suicide."

A short pause, to convey regret.

"Doctor Donovan was arrested for the murder of three women: Amy Llewellyn, whose body was found at Sycamore Gap on Sunday morning; Claire Burns, whose body was found at the same location on Monday; and Geraldine Hart, a seventy-three-year-old woman who was found dead in her home on Tuesday."

"Did he kill himself to avoid being tried for his crimes?"

Gregson nodded wisely. "We can only assume that Donovan could no longer live with his actions."

There was a barrage of questions, until Gregson held up both hands to quieten the din.

"We are still piecing together the evidence in our possession," he qualified, "but we strongly believe that Donovan intended to frame another man for his crimes. To that man, who has suffered the indignity of police questioning, we offer an apology on behalf of Northumbria CID."

"*What?*" Phillips was about to blow a fuse. "Colin Hart connects to Donovan and Edwards! It was a legitimate line of enquiry!"

"We have since released that man without charge," Gregson was saying.

"Where's Ryan?" One observant journalist shouted out the question and Gregson smiled to himself, having anticipated it.

"Owing to certain...*regrettable* decisions made during the course of the investigation, Detective Chief Inspector Ryan has been suspended from his duties pending further enquiry. You may rest assured that all further matters relating to the deaths of those women will be handled under the unbiased, careful eyes of other highly competent members of Northumbria CID."

"Are you saying DCI Ryan couldn't handle the pressure? Did he harass Keir Edwards?"

"Did DCI Ryan overlook important evidence?"

"Where is DCI Ryan now?"

"Please, please." Gregson raised his hands again. "It would be inappropriate for me to discuss any further details relating to what remains an internal matter—"

In the shadows, Lowerson felt a burgeoning sense of disillusionment. Was this the reason he had joined the police force, to stab his fellow men in the back?

"Was the Circle involved?"

Gregson faltered, just for a second, seeking out the source of the question. His eyes came to rest on a sharp-eyed young woman, with a mic extended in her left hand.

"There is no Circle," he said stiffly.

"There are rumours that one of the women was ritually marked, as with some of the victims on Holy Island," the journalist persisted. "What if the dead doctor was part of the Circle? Is it still operating?"

Gregson felt a line of sweat trickle down his spine, beneath his dress suit.

"Any cult circle which previously operated on Holy Island has since been disbanded," he said quickly. "Next question."

"Amy Llewellyn went missing around 21st June 2005," the journalist hammered on, for all to hear. "There are at least eight other women on the Missing Persons Database who were reported missing on or around 21st June, for a period of over ten years. That looks like ritual, doesn't it? Will you be conducting a further search of the area around Sycamore Gap?"

Of all the questions he had anticipated, it was the one Gregson wanted to answer the least. To open the search would be tantamount to opening a can of worms.

"Once we have reviewed all of the evidence—"

"JUSTICE! JUSTICE FOR THE DEAD!" a man shouted from somewhere in the crowd. Following his lead, several reporters shouted out, calling for a thorough search. Gregson was starting to feel faint. He could already see the local and national news, plastered with the sorrowful faces of families whose loved ones had gone missing around the solstice.

Things were spiralling out of control.

From their position on the sidelines, Phillips and MacKenzie regarded Lowerson with a new level of respect. Out of nowhere, the man had dissolved into the crowd and shouted his plea, thereby ensuring that the case would not be brushed under the carpet with the kind of 'hush-hush' method Gregson had been angling for.

"Good lad," Phillips approved, with a hearty nudge in the ribs.

On the television monitor in the National Heritage visitor's centre on Holy Island, Doctor Mark Bowers watched Gregson's performance with a keen eye. The man looked nervous, he thought, and there had been no mention of them having lost any young detective constables during the course of the investigation.

In other words, Mark thought, his servant had ignored a direct order from his High Priest.

Interrupting his reverie, a young boy tugged at his sleeve, reminding him that he was due to give a tour to a group of primary school children. His face transformed into a welcoming smile as he led the boy towards the historic treasures dotted around the room in glass cases.

As he spoke of kings and queens, of warfare and Vikings, he thought of the future.

While friends worried for him and colleagues spoke sadly of his absence from the hallways of CID, Ryan flicked off the television screen and reached for the book resting on the cushion beside him.

Paradise Lost.

It had often been remarked that Ryan had eyes like a hawk. In reality, his eyesight was largely dependent on his level of sleep deprivation, but one thing he could lay claim to was having noted the appearance of Milton's seminal work one too many times for comfort over the past few days.

A copy on the bookcase in Donovan's office.

A quote from Edwards, in prison.

A pen-and-ink sketch above the mantle in Donovan's home.

No, Ryan thought, that wasn't coincidence.

He settled back to read.

EPILOGUE

One week later

Colin thanked the community mental health nurse for stopping by. In fact, her visits were part of a rigorous programme of care in his home environment. Every day, he and Mandy discussed his childhood, how he was feeling and then she administered an injection of a mild anti-psychotic into his rear end.

She had a cup of strong tea, a few biscuits and then left him with the harried air of one who was overworked and undervalued. That day alone, she probably had another ten appointments, not all of which she would be able to keep.

NHS cutbacks, he tutted sympathetically.

The house had been cleaned thoroughly by a specialist company who had gone over the rooms and in particular his mother's bedroom with a substantial volume of cleaning chemicals. The forensic team of CSIs, led by a methodical man in his late thirties and possessed of sharp eyes behind thick spectacles, had confiscated numerous personal articles from the house including his computer. That was no matter, Colin thought. Computers could be replaced.

Now, Colin felt truly free; even the air smelled sweeter, albeit laced with disinfectant.

He checked the time on his slick new watch. *Eleven o'clock.* Oops! Running later than usual this morning.

He selected a heavy volume from his bookshelf— *The Oxford Handbook of Criminology*—and settled himself on the sofa. Opening it, he took out the small pay-as-you-go mobile phone that lay nestled inside a crevice within its folds.

He dialled the number and did not have to wait long before Edwards answered.

"*My friend,*" came the beloved voice. "*I was beginning to think you'd forgotten.*"

"Hardly," Colin replied, crossing his legs as he reclined. He admired the smooth silk-cashmere blend of his trousers as they stretched over his thighs. He had treated himself to a few new things, modelling his style on Edwards' former days with a few select pieces from Ryan's outdoor ensemble.

"*I see that all has gone as planned,*" Edwards prodded.

"Better than expected, from your perspective," Colin said. "Ryan has been suspended from duty, I understand."

There was a quivering silence at the end of the line, while Edwards savoured the information.

"*How very unfortunate,*" Edwards cackled. "*In some ways, I wish my dear old friend, Doctor Donovan, had been able to see the mighty Ryan dethroned.*"

"Do you really think Donovan killed himself?" Colin was intrigued.

"*Of course not,*" Edwards laughed. "*The man was indomitable. I should have thought it would take a nuclear bomb to dispose of him, but apparently a bit of material and a couple of strong pairs of hands will do just as well.*"

"Who?"

"*Ah, now, all in good time. We all must have our little secrets, mustn't we?*"

Colin's lips trembled, just once. Keir Edwards was behind bars but still managed to exert power over him. What would he do without his friendship, his inspiration?

"I followed your advice, to the letter," Colin spoke again, seeking praise for his efforts.

"*Well done, Colin, well done indeed. Didn't I tell you, it would all come right in the end? Don't you feel better, having rid yourself of her cloying, hateful presence in your life?*"

Colin thought of his mother, with her flabby folds of wrinkled skin, her constant odour and her constant whining. Even thinking of her raised his blood pressure. Yes, he felt better. He felt like a man reborn.

"When the police came to take me in for questioning, I rang Donovan, just as you said. It seems Ryan followed the trail. It led him straight back to the psychiatrist."

"*Ha! And the vial?*"

"Yes," Colin said. "I told him I could hardly sleep, that I was at breaking point. He handed some Lorazepam to me from his own private store. Trusting fool."

"*Perhaps my old mentor had a heart, after all.*"

Both men laughed.

"I don't know what to do, now that she's gone," Colin found himself saying. "I'd grown so accustomed to her being there … and … and the flashbacks, they're quite bad." When he closed his eyes, he could see his mother's final shocked expression as he had stabbed the needle into her neck. He remembered, too, the woozy feeling of release as he had watched her body convulse and then die. He had cried a little, but the tears had been a mixture of regret and happiness.

At the end of the line, Edwards raised his eyes to the ceiling of his cell, fighting to remain composed in the face of such weakness. Why all the fuss about some old bitch who would probably have hung around for another thirty years, just to plague the man?

"*The flashbacks will pass,*" he snapped at Colin. "*Forget about your old life, forget about the old Colin. You are a new man.*"

When Edwards ended the call, with Terry the prison guard loitering outside to make sure none of the other guards should overhear his conversation, he could hear the distant sound of an old *A-Team* episode playing on the communal TV screen down the hall. He emerged from his cell and nodded towards Terry, whose family would be enjoying an unexpected holiday on the Costa del Sol. Edwards considered it money well spent.

He headed in the direction of the TV and thought about how much he loved it when a plan came together, especially one that had been years in the making.

ABOUT THE AUTHOR

LJ Ross is an international bestselling author, best known for creating atmospheric mystery and thriller novels, including the DCI Ryan series of Northumbrian murder mysteries which have sold over four million copies worldwide.

Her debut, *Holy Island*, was released in January 2015 and reached number one in the UK and Australian charts. Since then, she has released a further fourteen novels, all of which have been top three global bestsellers and twelve of which have been UK #1 bestsellers. Louise has garnered an army of loyal readers through her storytelling and, thanks to them, several of her books reached the coveted #1 spot whilst only available to pre-order ahead of release.

Louise was born in Northumberland, England. She studied undergraduate and postgraduate Law at King's College, University of London and then abroad in Paris and Florence. She spent much of her working life in London, where she was a lawyer for a number of years until taking the decision to change career and pursue her dream to write. Now, she writes full time and lives with her husband and son in Northumberland. She enjoys reading all manner of books, travelling and spending time with family and friends.

If you enjoyed reading *Sycamore Gap*, please consider leaving a review online.

The third book in the DCI Ryan series, *Heavenfield*, will be available from all good bookshops in May 2020—keep reading to the end of this book for a sneak preview!

ACKNOWLEDGMENTS

Following the publication of Holy Island, the first in the series of DCI Ryan mysteries, I was simply overwhelmed by the support of family, friends and the many thousands of readers who enjoyed a story set in beautiful Northumberland. As a first-time author, I had no preconceived ideas about how my debut novel would be received, but the warmth of its reception has blown me away. To all the readers who left reviews and sent messages, I offer my thanks and gratitude in helping it to reach the number one slot in the Amazon chart for the United Kingdom.

It is a truth universally acknowledged that a sequel is vastly more difficult to write, and I can wholeheartedly concur. Gallons of coffee went into the making of this book and multiple endings were considered. Throughout the process, my small army of confidantes, friends and consultants have helped me to steer the story along what I hope is the right path. As always, my husband James has been wonderful.

He has lived with the creative moods and subjected himself to multiple read-throughs and first-stage editing. He is the 'J' in 'LJ Ross' for very good reason: I might write the stories, but he keeps them afloat by helping me to focus on what I love best—the storytelling. My son, Ethan, is like a breath of fresh air on days when I can't seem to find the next scene and it is for him that I strive to write anything at all. My mother, father and sister have offered their constant love and support, not only in this venture as an author but in all the years before it. Rachael, thank you for loaning your fabulous hair to MacKenzie, along with your feisty spirit!

Special thanks go to James Moffa for the loan of his name and for allowing me to change his character completely for the purposes of fiction: I hope that he enjoys his gangster alter ego. Likewise, to Mary, Waleed and Kirsten for their medical and technical knowledge, and to Helen Greenhalgh for her insights into police procedure, which was much appreciated. As always, thanks to all of my friends who have encouraged me along the way and have helped to shape this book with their unfailing confidence. To Roger Clegg, I thank him for the use of his very special photograph in forming the cover of the book.

Extra special thanks go to Millie, a smart young cookie who inspired a new female character who is possessed of brains as well as beauty, just like her.

HEAVENFIELD

A DCI RYAN MYSTERY

LJ ROSS

CHAPTER 1

Sunday, 2nd August—St. Oswald's Tide

He expelled the damp air in short, panting breaths and the harsh sound of it echoed around the walls of the church. His eyes darted across the vaulted ceiling above him and he could smell his own sweat, sickly sweet and cloying.

How poetic that he, of all people, should find himself the victim.

The cold point of a gun prodded his right temple and the taste of fear was bitter and strong, like the bile which flooded his throat. His chest shuddered as he fought to stay calm, though he knew that the end must be near.

"I'm not afraid of you!" he shouted desperately, but there was no answering reply, only an angry shove from the metal aimed at his head.

He trained his gaze straight ahead and brought Anna's face to his mind, imagining her beside him.

How he loved her.

How he *wanted* her.

He heard the soft 'click' of a trigger being pulled back, ready to discharge.

"Just *do* it!" he burst out, tears leaking tracks over the lines of his face.

The sound of the gunshot was like a canon being fired in the confined space. Outside, resting birds squawked their disapproval and fluttered into the night, before settling once again into a silence that was almost religious.

The air was hushed and reverent as a line of men and women made their way up the gentle incline towards the place known as Heavenfield. A little stone church stood eerie and alone atop the hill, overlooking the rolling landscape of Northumberland. The sun made its final descent into the horizon at its back, casting deep amber rays over the fields while stars began to pop high in the darkening sky above. Nature was the master here and all around her handiwork bloomed; a patchwork blanket of lush green grass, gorse bushes and sprouting purple lavender.

The pilgrims held their lanterns aloft, moving like a fat glow-worm through the empty fields. Their feet made little sound as they moved across the mossy floor, trampling the ground where soldiers had fallen centuries earlier. Now, the only sign that a battle had once taken place lay in the simple wooden cross which marked the spot.

The pilgrim leader was surprised to find the heavy oak doors standing ajar. It was true that God's house was always open for business, but it was unusual for anybody to make the trip to this deserted spot unless they were part of the pilgrimage trail.

With slight misgivings, he led the crowd into the darkened interior. There was no access to electricity or running water here; only pungent gas lamps, which had not been lit. The glow from the pilgrims' lanterns filtered through the gloom and their excited chatter died abruptly. There was a loud shriek and the leader threw out his arms, urging them back.

A man lay sprawled over the altar at the rear of the church, blood and brains spattered across the floor and the wall at his back. In the sudden silence, they could hear the soft *tap tap* of his life force dripping onto the flagstones. Another man stood over the body, one bloodied hand held out in warning, his tall figure silhouetted against the stained glass window at his back by the last light of day.

"Keep your distance!" he barked.

"You've...you've killed him! Don't come any closer!" The pilgrim leader shouted, his voice wobbling. "I'm going to call the police!"

The man frowned, his dark brows pulling together. "You don't understand—" he said sharply.

"Keep back!" the pilgrim leader repeated, stumbling as the pilgrims fled the church, their lanterns swaying dangerously as they took the light with them.

Detective Chief Inspector Ryan watched them leave and wondered how long it would be before two of his colleagues turned up in a squad car. At least it saved him the job of calling it in. He mustered a detachment he didn't entirely feel and looked down at the shell of a man who had once been Doctor Mark Bowers, eminent local historian.

Ryan sighed, his breath clouding despite it being summer outside. The plain lime-washed walls were an effective barrier against the sun and, consequently, the room felt like a fridge.

Or a morgue, he amended, with an eye for the dead man.

He crouched to the floor and took a slow survey of his surroundings, eventually rising again dissatisfied. It was nearly impossible to see the details of the room now that the last of the sun had gone and the light from his mobile phone did little to help. He could still make out the lines of the body in front of him and the skin was warm to the touch; in fact, if he didn't know better, he would have said that Bowers had died only moments before. Blood oozed from the bullet-wound at his skull and was only just beginning to coagulate.

Yet, there was no gun and no other person for miles around.

The third book in the DCI Ryan series, Heavenfield, will be available from all good bookshops in May 2020!

LOVE READING?

JOIN THE CLUB...

Join the LJ Ross Book Club to connect with a thriving community of fellow book lovers! To receive a free monthly newsletter with exclusive author interviews and giveaways, sign up at www.ljrossauthor.com or follow the LJ Ross Book Club on social media:

 #LJBookClubTweet

 @LJRossAuthor

 @ljrossauthor